Kate Field lives in Lancashire with her husband, daughter and cat. Her debut novel, *The Magic of Ramblings*, won the Romantic Novelists' Association Joan Hessayon Award for new writers.

@Katehaswords
/KateFieldAuthor

A Dozen Second Chances

KATE FIELD

OneMoreChapter

One More Chapter
a division of HarperCollins*Publishers*
The News Building
1 London Bridge Street
London SE1 9GF

www.harpercollins.co.uk

This paperback edition 2020

First published in Great Britain in ebook format by
HarperCollins*Publishers* 2020

A catalogue record for this book
is available from the British Library

ISBN: 9780008317836

Set in Birka by Palimpsest Book Production Ltd,
Falkirk, Stirlingshire

Printed and bound in Great Britain by
CPI Group (UK) Ltd, Croydon CR0 4YY

To Catherine Bowdler, for being kind to herself

Chapter 1

Twenty minutes. The train would leave in twenty minutes, and time wouldn't stop however hard I wished for it.

I looked at Caitlyn, sitting across a table littered with half-drunk coffee cups; caught her surreptitiously sliding her sleeve back down to cover her watch – not for the first time.

'It will be fine,' Caitlyn said. 'No different than when I went on a school trip, only this one will last longer. I won't be that far away. Nearer than Nan. It hardly takes more than an hour to fly to Paris.'

She would be over five hundred miles away. I'd looked it up. She'd been further on school trips, but they had been finite – a matter of days. Now she was leaving for twelve months, but really, what were the chances of her coming back? Once she'd experienced the glamour of Paris, why would she want to return to rainy Lancashire? And while part of me wept at the thought of losing her, when I had already lost so much, another part cheered her on. I'd had plans to travel once. I knew what it felt like, that heady mix of trepidation and excitement, the belief that the world was storing up opportunities with your name on, waiting to be discovered. I wouldn't let anything get in the way of her discoveries.

'Of course it will be fine,' I said. I knew my allotted lines. We had played out a script all week: me trying to look pleased that Caitlyn was going, Caitlyn trying to look sorry. 'Freedom! At last!'

I managed a smile. I shouldn't have come. I should have dropped Caitlyn off at the local station to make her own way, not suggested driving down to Manchester and spending the night there before she caught her train. I had wanted to savour our last minutes together, not realising until now that sometimes a swift goodbye was a far less painful option after all.

'Freedom for you too,' Caitlyn said. 'You could let Rich stay the night, without fear that you'll corrupt my innocent young mind ...'

I made a non-committal noise, trying to disguise my instinctive aversion to that idea. Rich in my bed ... his face the first sight of my day ... He wouldn't expect that, would he? I thought we both had the measure of our relationship: it didn't include whole nights together. Physical intimacies, yes; emotional ones, no. Besides, I'd spent years enjoying my independence. I might now have an empty nest, but filling it with a man wasn't my idea of freedom.

Fifteen minutes. Caitlyn rummaged in her backpack and brought out a slim package wrapped in blue tissue paper. She held it out to me.

'I've got something for you. It's not much ...'

I unwrapped the paper with deliberate care, eking out the seconds. It fell open to reveal a tiny gift box, and inside that lay a stack of rectangular pieces of card. I studied the top one. It was beautifully illustrated around the border with a variety of my favourite flowers – Caitlyn had inherited Faye's artistic talent, as well as her looks. In the centre, a calligraphy message read:

BE KIND TO YOURSELF
VOUCHER ONE
I, Eve Roberts, have been kind to myself by
....

There were twelve numbered vouchers in total. I looked up at Caitlyn, bewildered.

'It's your challenge while I'm away,' she explained, with a grin that was achingly familiar. 'You've put me first forever. Now it's your turn. You have to treat yourself, do some things that are purely for you. It doesn't matter how small it is – even a soak in the bath with some fancy new bubble bath will count. But you have to fill in each voucher and send it to me, to prove you've done it. Promise?'

'Promise,' I replied, helpless to resist that grin, as I had always been. 'Thank you.' I forced myself to check the time. 'Do you think we should ...'

Caitlyn was out of her seat before the sentence was finished, wheeling her suitcase through the crowds to the platform for the London train.

'We'll still speak all the time, won't we?' she asked, hesitating at the platform barrier, ticket in hand. 'I mean, I know it's only Paris, we're not going to be a million miles apart, but ...'

'Of course we will. You'll get tired of hearing from me. Now enough of this. You can't miss your train. Gemma will be waiting. Give me a hug and get on your way. There are amazing times ahead of you!'

I wrapped my arms around her, feeling in our embrace the memory of a lifetime of hugs, from the tiny child around my knees, to the embarrassed teenager, to the young woman who now stood over me. Who knew when the next one would be? Caitlyn was the first to draw back.

'Thanks, Mum,' she said. 'For everything. I know I haven't said it, but I do appreciate how much you've done.'

I hadn't done enough. I could never do enough. I shook my head, dismissing such talk.

'Still Mum?' I said, though my heart tensed in dread at the possible answer. 'Would you prefer it to be Eve now?'

'No.' Caitlyn lunged forward for a last, desperate hug. 'You'll always be Mum. Love you!'

I waited on the concourse, my cheeks aching with a smile she couldn't see, watching until the last carriage of the train disappeared from sight, and wondered what the hell I was supposed to do with my life now.

It was late afternoon by the time I pulled on to the drive of my small, semi-detached house in the market town of Inglebridge in north Lancashire. The early March sun warmed the bricks on the front of the house as the light faded for the day, but I couldn't help thinking it a cruel illusion: with Caitlyn gone, the inside of the house was going to seem horribly cold and bare. I glanced across the road to my friend Tina's house, but there was no car on the drive, no sign of life – no chance of going through her front door for a while instead of my own.

The silence hit me as soon as I stepped into the hall. I was used to getting home from work before Caitlyn, and greeting an empty house, but this felt different; the silence was deeper, as if the bricks and mortar joined with me in mourning her absence. Before I'd even taken one step, I'd noticed the changes: her shoes were missing from the usual place by the front door; the peg where she hung her coat was empty; her house keys lay in the bowl on the table, because she had no use for them now. Would this ever feel normal?

The front doorbell rang, and I opened the door to see Tina. 'I saw you arrive home,' she said. Of course she did: Tina lived in the dormer bungalow immediately opposite my house, and missed nothing. She had brought over some sandwiches on the day we'd moved in, fourteen years ago, and we had been firm friends ever since. 'I came to offer tea and sympathy, assuming I can't tempt you to anything stronger. Forget the healthy living for today – your face says you need alcohol and plenty of it.'

'That bad?' I asked.

Tina nodded, without even a decent pause to consider her answer.

'At least two wine bottles' worth of bad. It's what I needed when Liam went off to university. I needed three bottles when he boomeranged back here!' She laughed. 'You look like you might burst into tears at any minute. You can't be on your own.'

'I was going to come over, but your car wasn't there.'

'Graham's gone to play golf. He'd better get back soon; the kitchen drawer has jammed, and I can't get it open. It had to be the one with the corkscrew in, didn't it? I've no screw tops left. It's at times like this I wish my neighbour wasn't teetotal ...' She grinned, and I laughed.

'But you do have a neighbour with some basic DIY skills. Let me get my toolbox and I'll have a look at the drawer.'

'I was hoping you'd say that. You're a lifesaver!'

And so was Tina; this was exactly the distraction I needed, as I suspected she well knew. I collected my toolbox from the garage and crossed the road to Tina's. As soon as she opened the door, I was assaulted by the deep thrum of rock music pervading the house from upstairs; another reminder of what

I was going to miss. Tina gave a wry grimace before bellowing up the stairs. 'Turn that racket down! Eve's here!'

The music faded by a barely perceptible notch.

'There! Twenty-four and almost house-trained.' Tina laughed and looked me up and down. 'I'll never get used to this. You look like a Boden model who wandered into the B&Q catalogue by mistake.' She opened the cupboard under the stairs and plucked a bottle from the pine wine rack tucked away there. 'I'll drink your share. No one counts on a Saturday, do they?'

While she was making me a cup of tea, I examined the drawer that was stuck. It was a disappointingly easy job to fix it; something was obviously catching when I tried to open it, but jiggling the drawer wasn't enough to move it. I'd brought over a metal coat hanger, and inserted this into the gap, manoeuvring it carefully until the contents shifted and I could open the drawer. I removed all the drawers and lubricated the runners while I was at it.

'You're better than a husband,' Tina said, snatching up the corkscrew. 'Graham would rather have a golf club in his hand than a spanner.'

I shrugged. 'I don't mind. I enjoy it.' More than I'd expected. I'd signed up to lots of basic DIY courses over the years, in a bid both to save money and be self-reliant, but had found a real sense of satisfaction in learning how to identify a problem and to solve it – in some aspects of life, at least.

I followed Tina into the conservatory, a recent addition to the bungalow and her pride and joy. South-facing, and with views across the small patch of garden to the fields beyond, it made the most of the advantage of this side of the street. My garden faced north, and looked out on to Winlow Hill, the highest peak in the area, and one that drew ramblers and tourists to Inglebridge throughout the year. It was a view that I loved; I wouldn't have switched sides of the street for any money.

'Did Caitlyn get off okay?'

'Yes. No delays, no cancellations. Where are leaves on the line when you need them?' I glanced at my watch. 'She'll be in London now. One night at Gemma's, and then they'll catch the Eurostar first thing in the morning. They'll be in Paris by lunchtime.'

'Lucky them! It makes me wish I'd tried harder at languages at school. I'd have given my eye teeth to have had the chance to drop everything and work in Paris when I was twenty, wouldn't you?'

'Yes.' I gazed out through the conservatory windows, seeing nothing. I remembered too clearly how, at twenty, the world had seemed there for the taking; remembered the plans built on excitement rather than practicality, to travel the globe, to take part in ground-breaking archaeological digs across the continents. It had all been so possible, so tangible. But at twenty-one, my world had shrunk; it had all become impossible.

Tina must have read something on my face, as she stretched across and rubbed my hand.

'Sorry. Me and my big gob. I didn't mean ...'

'I know, it's fine.' I clutched my mug between my hands. 'Sometimes life doesn't take you where you hoped it would. Better a different life than none at all. I'm the lucky one.' I sipped my tea, mentally pushing away the guilt that threatened to roll in like the mist over Winlow Hill.

'Are you meeting Rich tonight? Is he taking you out to cheer you up?'

Tina's attempt to lighten the mood wasn't a huge success.

'It's his access weekend. His children are staying so I won't see him.' Despite my best efforts, there was more relief in my voice than regret. 'Maybe we'll go out during the week.'

'You can do what you like now, can't you? Life begins at almost forty! You're lucky to have an empty nest while you still have the energy to take advantage of it. What plans do you have?'

'Nothing special ...' And then I remembered Caitlyn's parting gift, and I pulled the box of vouchers out of my bag to show Tina. 'Although Caitlyn has made me these, and I promised to do twelve things to be kind to myself ...'

'Ooh, aren't they pretty? She should sell these. I'd buy some.' Tina inspected the cards. 'Have you thought of anything yet?'

I shook my head.

'I know the perfect thing to set you off,' Tina said, reaching for her iPad. 'Are you free next Thursday night?'

'Maybe ...'

'I saw this advertised on my Facebook group for history teachers this morning. There's a talk on Thursday night at a private school in Yorkshire about the Romans in Britain.'

'A history talk? That sounds more like being kind to you,' I said, smiling.

Tina laughed. 'Hang on, I'm getting to your bit. The talk is a two-hander with a historian and an archaeologist speaking.'

I sipped my tea, feeling the first stirrings of disquiet. It was foolish – irrational. How many thousands of archaeologists must there be across the country? There was no reason to think it would be him ...

'Here we go,' Tina continued, tapping at the iPad screen. 'Jeremy Swann is the historian – you might not have heard of him, but he's written some interesting books about life in Roman Britain. That's your favourite time, isn't it?'

'Yes,' I said, when Tina paused for breath. It *had* been my favourite time. In the days when archaeology hadn't only been about the past, but my future. *Our* future.

'And they've done well to get this archaeologist,' Tina continued. 'He's been on the telly – did you see that programme, *Travels Through Time*? Paddy Friel's his name. Have you heard of him?'

Paddy Friel ... My head began to spin. I put down my mug.

'I'll find you a photo. That'll convince you to come with me.' Tina laughed and swiped the iPad screen. 'Here you go. Don't tell me it's not being kind to yourself to gaze at him for an hour ...'

Tina held the iPad up towards me. A man's profile filled the screen: a familiar face, if older than when I had last studied it in such detail, from the cleft in his chin, to the dark curls that tumbled around his face, still slightly too long for practicality. I thought I'd set aside my feelings many years ago, but as I stared at the picture, the emotions revived, flashing through my head like a spinning fairground ride: a dizzying blur of love, disappointment, hatred and anger.

'He's no expert on the Romans,' I said. I turned away from the photo. Those twinkling eyes stirred too many memories, the good memories, not the bad. I didn't want to remember those. 'He was always more interested in the Vikings.'

And in himself – no subject was closer to Paddy Friel's heart than Paddy Friel.

'You know him?' Tina looked more impressed than Paddy deserved. She smiled. 'You're a dark horse. How well do you know him? Academically or Biblically?'

'Both, once. It was all over a long time ago.'

'Blimey.' Tina goggled at me. 'I wasn't serious. But, really? You had a thing with Paddy Friel? How could you not have mentioned that before?'

'Because I'd rather forget all about him. I certainly don't want to meet him again.'

Tina hesitated, tapping her iPad screen with her nail.

'You won't meet him. We can sit at the back and sneak out as soon as it ends. There's coffee and biscuits afterwards, but we don't need to stay for that. Come on, I don't want to go on my own. And what about these?' Tina pointed at the pile of 'Be Kind to Yourself' vouchers. 'This is a perfect example of what Caitlyn had in mind. It's time to start thinking of yourself again, and what you want to do. Archaeology was once your passion. You've no excuse not to pursue it now. You definitely can't let some bloke put you off going to something that would interest you.'

Not just some bloke ... but still, as I looked down at Caitlyn's vouchers, a prickle of life stirred within me. I *had* loved archaeology once, had been fascinated by the opportunity to literally unearth traces of lives lived thousands of years ago. The Romans had been my favourite area of study. And why shouldn't I attend a talk on them, even if Paddy Friel would be there? He was nothing to me now, and he would have long forgotten me. The time when he, or any man, had any influence over my actions was long gone.

'You're right,' I said, picking up the vouchers. 'My first act of kindness. I'll go to the lecture, and no one will stop me.' I laughed. 'Paddy who?'

Chapter 2

Paddy Friel. Or Nigel Patrick Friel, to give him his full name, the name that only people who had known him in infant school days would know. And me – because once I had known him inside out, understood every shift and sigh of his body, comprehended every turn and contemplation of his mind. Until adversity hit, and I discovered that the man I thought I had known and loved was a sham in substance as well as in name.

We had met in our first year at university, both students of archaeology, but inhabiting very different social groups. He was part of the crowd of beautiful people, the sort of group my sister Faye would have naturally belonged to, but which was far out of my league. I'd noticed him at once – impossible not to, with those glossy dark curls, confident swagger, and the Irish accent that I only discovered much later was an exaggerated version of his real voice. Despite the small number of students on our course, I would have put money on him not knowing that I existed.

But then, in the third term of my first year, as I had wandered back to the halls of residence laden down with supermarket carrier bags that scored the flesh on my fingers, a shove in the back had knocked me to the ground, sending eggs smashing to the pavement and tins of baked beans rolling into the road. A hooded man had crouched over me, with a knife in his hand, and I had been too frozen with terror to react. And then, like a dark descending angel, Paddy Friel had appeared and knocked my assailant out of the way, making him run off. Paddy had picked up my shopping, escorted me back to my room and stayed with me until the police arrived. He had wiped away my tears, made me countless drinks, talked to me and, above all else, he had simply been there for me when I needed him.

Later that night, he had insisted that I join him at the local pub for a drink, determined that I had to leave my room again before the fear took hold and kept me prisoner. The next morning he had waited outside my halls to walk me to our lecture, and that had been the beginning of everything ...

The memories swept relentlessly through my head as I drove through Inglebridge on my way to pay my regular Sunday visit to my grandmother, Phyllis. She had moved into the local nursing home, The Chestnuts, eight years ago, after her first hip replacement, and had loved it so much that she never moved out again. It was a not-for-profit home, where fees were low, happiness levels high, and the staff were universally kind to the old people in their care. Gran thrived on living there, and at eighty-seven, showed no sign of leaving any time soon.

The Chestnuts occupied an old manor house, extended several times as funds allowed, and as usual I found Gran basking in the sun in the large conservatory, a pile of magazines at her side. She smiled as I approached, and I relaxed, all thoughts of Paddy Friel effectively banished. With Caitlyn's recent departure, and Mum having been settled on the Costa Brava for the last sixteen years, Gran was the only family I had left. I had never been so glad to see her.

'Hello, Gran,' I said, bending to kiss her soft cheek, and resting my head against hers for a moment too long. 'You're looking well.'

'You're looking thin,' she said, never one to mince words. 'Are you overdoing the exercise again? There'll be nowt left of you by Christmas at this rate. I'll be mistaking you for the turkey wishbone. You want plenty of best butter, chips cooked in dripping, and a good supply of gin. How else do you think I made it to my age?'

'Certainly not by flattering your nearest and dearest.' I laughed and pulled up a chair beside her. 'I don't know whether I should give you these biscuits now ...'

'All-butter shortbread?' I nodded. They were her favourites; I brought them every week. Woe betide if I produced anything else. 'I'll ring for tea.'

Gran pressed a button on the plastic emergency necklace she wore and shortly afterwards an exasperated carer bustled in. She took one look at me and rolled her eyes.

'You know the story of the boy who cried wolf, don't you?' she grumbled, but with a smile of undoubted affection. 'One of these days there'll be a real emergency and we won't come. I suppose you'll be wanting tea.'

'If it's not too much trouble,' Gran said.

'It beats some of the jobs I have to do round here ...'

'You shouldn't take advantage,' I said, when the carer had wandered off on her mission. 'This isn't a hotel.'

'Nonsense. I'm one of the least demanding ones in here. You should hear what Mr Jacobs asks them to do. No one wants to be on rota to give him a bed bath ...'

'Have you heard from Caitlyn yet?' Gran asked, when our tea had arrived and she had started on the biscuits. 'Is she in Paris now?'

'I don't know. She said she would text as soon as she could.' I touched the pocket where my phone lay, out of my handbag so I would feel the first vibration of a text arriving. 'I'm sure she's fine ...'

So I said; but that hadn't stopped me checking the news websites on a regular basis all morning, dreading reports of a fire in the Channel Tunnel, terrorist attacks in France, or a million and one other disasters that my imagination was all too happy to suggest. I was so perturbed by the ideas, that when Gran offered me her biscuits, I took one without thinking.

'Of course she'll be fine.' Gran patted my hand. 'She's a sensible girl. You've done a grand job.'

But it hadn't been a job – it had been love. Because Caitlyn wasn't actually mine. She was my sister Faye's child, the big sister I had adored with my whole being, until her sudden death when she was twenty-four, and Caitlyn just two. Faye had fallen pregnant around the time I started university, and she had never told us who the father was; it was all too easy to believe she didn't know, given her lifestyle. There had been lengthy debate about what should happen to Caitlyn after Faye's death, but it could only ever end one way. I had wanted her to live with me, whatever the personal cost – and it had been high, higher than I could have anticipated. But I had owed it to Faye. No price could ever have been too high.

'I can't help worrying,' I said now, drawing back from the past. 'Who knows what temptations she's going to face in Paris?'

'No more than I expect she's faced already.'

'Not on my watch!'

'So I suppose your mum knew everything you got up to, did she?' Gran laughed. 'I thought not. You've done your bit, love, and more besides. Time to let go. It'll do you both good to stretch your wings a bit. Here, have another biccie.'

I did, telling myself that it was my own small act of stretching. I usually tried to stick to a healthy diet, but already my worries about Caitlyn were eroding my good intentions. I didn't know how to stop, however old she was: I had a sudden vision of myself in Gran's position in fifty years' time, my phone clutched in my gnarled old hand, waiting for news of Caitlyn. Perhaps she was right, and I did need to learn to let go, but I didn't know how to do it.

'Here, you'll never guess who I saw t'other day,' Gran said later, when our teas were drunk, and I was getting ready to leave. She reached for a tatty magazine on the table at her side. 'I saved it for you. Have a look at the page folded over.'

Perhaps the unexpected sugar consumption had addled my wits, because I flicked to the marked page without a glimmer of suspicion. Oddly, it was the young woman in the photograph that I noticed first: luscious, thick blonde hair cascaded over bare shoulders and brushed against a large bust that could have earned her a place as a centrefold. I felt the familiar twinge of regret over my own boyish figure and chin-length brown hair, hastily wiped away when I turned my attention to the man attached to the woman's side.

'It's the fella you went out with, isn't it?' Gran asked, making it sound as if I had only had one boyfriend over my entire lifetime. It wasn't true: there had been several boys before Paddy. Not so many after, but that was hardly surprising, and not only because all my focus had been on Caitlyn. Paddy had taught me many things that I had been delighted to learn, and one thing that I hadn't. A broken heart can be broken a second time, and a third, until only the crushed fragments remain.

'And look who he's with!' Gran continued, oblivious to my discomfort. 'She was in *Emmerdale* until she ran off with someone's husband.'

I assumed she meant in the TV programme, rather than in real life, but who knew with these showbiz folk? Much against my will, my eyes strayed back to the man in the photograph. Here was Paddy Friel again, thrust to my attention for the second time in as many days, and no more welcome this time. It was a good photograph, I couldn't deny that: he was wearing black tie, which suited his colouring, and with his raffish curls and hint of five-o'clock shadow he looked like a pirate trying to infiltrate polite society. It was hard to believe that this confident, well-dressed man had once been the boy who left dirty underpants under my bed. Hard to believe, too, what weakness lay behind that charming smile.

I flicked the magazine closed and noticed the date on the front cover.

'This is six months old,' I said, dropping the magazine on the table as if it were soiling my fingers. 'He'll have moved on by now, probably several times. Doesn't he have a failed marriage behind him? Commitment was never his strong point.'

'He always was a handsome devil,' Gran said, with a wistful smile. She'd had a soft spot for Paddy, and he had given the appearance of being fond of her, but that was the trouble with Paddy: it was all style over substance, appearance over truth. 'You could forgive a man a lot who looked like that.'

I said nothing. Some things were impossible to forgive, however attractive the face. Not that I found him attractive any more: those feelings had died a long time ago, the least mourned of all my losses at that time. I picked up my bag and bent to give Gran a kiss.

'I thought I might have seen you as Mrs Friel.' Gran was on a roll; I wished she'd never seen the blasted magazine. 'I'd have liked a chance to get dressed up as grandmother of the bride. I'd have out-glitzed the lot of them. I still would. Where there's life, there's hope, eh?'

She looked at me with such pride and hope, that all I could do was smile back and kiss her again, too kind to tell her that life in my heart had been pronounced extinct many years ago.

I offered to drive Tina to the talk on Roman Britain the following Thursday night. As a longstanding teetotaller, I was used to being the designated driver, and I knew that Tina was hoping that to make up for missing tea and biscuits, we might find time for beer and crisps in a country pub on the way home.

'It's almost the weekend after all,' she said, as I turned off our street and headed towards the main road that carved through the countryside, leading to the southern Lake District in one direction and to the Yorkshire Dales in the other. I loved this patch of north Lancashire, hidden away from the hustle and bustle of city life; loved the fact that I could climb Winlow Hill behind my house and see no towns but Inglebridge, and beyond that, only fields, moors, and the occasional stone-built village.

I had moved here within six months of Caitlyn coming to live with me, desperate to escape our home county of Warwickshire, and all the familiar places where memories seemed to hang like cobwebs on every street lamp. I had known nothing of the area except that Gran lived within an hour's drive and that property prices were cheap. I had seen on the map that it was well away from any cities – any temptations – and that had been recommendation enough. Save for whisking Caitlyn away to a remote Scottish island – something I had briefly considered – it had appeared to be as safe a place as I could find to raise a child. And it was a fresh start for us, a place where we had no history. For someone who had spent her life wanting to uncover history, I had felt no compunction about covering ours up.

It had been a glorious spring day, and the setting sun was gilding the fields around us as we drove towards Yorkshire. Usually the view would have soothed away even the greatest anxiety. But tonight, not even the finest landscape could settle the nerves that jangled around my limbs. The talk sounded exactly the sort of thing I would have enjoyed many years ago, before my life twisted in a different direction. Was it wise to remind myself of that other possible life, when it might open up regrets that I had fought for years to keep at bay?

And then there was Paddy ... How would I feel to see him in the flesh, to hear his voice without the distance of a television set, for the first time in seventeen years? Why had I wasted one of Caitlyn's vouchers on this? This wasn't being kind to myself; it was more like voluntary torture.

The school we were visiting was a well-regarded grammar school, where the central building dated back centuries. It was a far cry from the 1960s comprehensive where Tina and I worked.

'Fancy working here!' Tina whispered, as we climbed an ornate wooden staircase towards the hall where the talk would be held. It seemed appropriate to whisper, as if nothing we could say would be erudite enough for this environment. 'Imagine teaching history in a place that has history of its own! I bet it's haunted.'

'I'd be happy to have a few ghosts helping me, as long as they could use the photocopier and knew how to fix printer jams.' I laughed. 'It would have been much easier to keep tabs on Caitlyn with a team of invisible spies at my beck and call.'

I hadn't worked at all for the first couple of years after Caitlyn came to live with me: it had been too new, too strange for both of us, and we had each needed time to adjust to the unexpected life we had been given, and time to get to know each other properly and cement our bond. When Caitlyn went to nursery, I had filled my days taking online courses to learn everything I could about computer software and office management until I was the most qualified PA I could be. I had then taken on part-time jobs until I saw the perfect role advertised: PA to the head teacher of the secondary school that Caitlyn would attend. The term time hours were convenient, and I could keep a discreet eye on Caitlyn and any trouble she might face: an ideal arrangement, as far as I was concerned, and I don't think she had minded it too much.

Tina and I took our seats at the back of the hall. It was a decent-sized crowd, and I was impressed by the local interest in Roman history until I realised that a large proportion of the audience were female, and particularly well-groomed ladies with shiny hair, smart clothes and full faces of make-up. Only a handful of parents would have made such an effort for our local comprehensive. Perhaps things were done differently in grammar school society. Or perhaps things were done differently in Paddy Friel's society, whispered a mischievous little voice in my head. I stamped it down, not before a pang of regret had flashed through me about my faded, knitted dress and barely there make-up. But I wasn't going to meet him. I didn't want to meet him. So what did it matter?

The historian, Jeremy Swann, spoke first and Tina was proved right: he was a witty, engaging speaker, skilled at throwing out titbits of information about how the Romans had lived, in the style of *Horrible Histories*, so his talk appealed to all ages. I leant to the side, so I could see him from between the assembled heads, hanging on his every word as my long-abandoned interest blossomed back to life. I had missed this, more than I wanted to admit.

I was still leaning, rapt, when Jeremy introduced the next speaker. I shot upright, not before seeing a familiar flash of dark curl. Tina gave me a nudge and a smile, but I stared at the ruddy, bald neck of the man in front of me and refused to look. I couldn't block my ears though. The first sound of that Irish lilt set my thoughts racing through the years, dredging up memories I had hoped never to revisit: the good memories, the tender memories of love, that made the bad memories so much more painful.

He was good, my objective self was forced to admit it. His enthusiasm covered the room like a silken net, gathering us all in, captive to the power of the story he was telling. Even I, who knew too well what a sham this was, what a false show concealing his true nature, felt the tug of excitement as he described the experience of working on an archaeological dig, of making a discovery that contributed to our knowledge of ancient times. But then he mentioned working at Vindolanda, a famous Roman site in Northumberland, and I couldn't listen any more. We had volunteered there together during the first summer we had been a couple, and the archaeological discoveries during the day took second place in my memories to the nights spent tangled together in a sleeping bag in a tiny tent for two.

'Wasn't he amazing?' Tina said, rousing me from the mental repetition of my shopping list – a surprisingly effective distraction, as it had reminded me that I was now shopping for one, and turned my thoughts to how much I was missing Caitlyn. 'He'll have inspired a few new archaeologists tonight. Inspired a few sweet dreams too for some of this audience. Phew! I think I'm having a hot flush. Can you hang on while I find a glass of water? There's sure to be a water fountain along the corridor somewhere. Back in a mo ...'

She scuttled off down the corridor, and I lurked at the back of the hall, safe in the knowledge that everyone else was leaving by the doors at the front, presumably in search of refreshment – a cup of tea with an extra splash of artificial Irish sweetener. I checked my phone for messages as the footsteps faded, the chatter died away, and the room fell silent. And then one voice carried the length of the hall, a voice I had heard more than enough of tonight.

'Eve?'

Chapter 3

Impossible not to turn, though my first instinct was to run out of the door. There he was, Paddy Friel, striding down the aisle formed between rows of chairs like a joyous bride dashing towards the groom; smiling in a way he had no business to, as if he was delighted to see me – as if it hadn't been his choice, oh so many years ago, to stop seeing me.

He paused, looked me up and down, and shook his head in apparent amazement. Curls bounced around his face, and he swept them back with a gesture that was so familiar it was as if he had swept the last seventeen years away too.

'I thought it was you. Eve Roberts. I can't believe it. How are you?'

He stepped forward, arms outstretched, as if to offer a kiss to my cheeks, the traditional greeting for long-lost acquaintances, I supposed. I folded my arms and moved away, wanting no contact with him. He could have stayed lost for all I cared.

'Hello, Paddy.'

His smile wavered. He could hardly misinterpret the coolness in my tone and action. Surely he couldn't have expected anything else?

'You're looking fantastic!' he carried on valiantly. 'Hardly changed at all. What are you doing here? Do you have a child at the school?'

'No.' I hadn't planned to say more, but when he continued to look at me, a growing question on his face, I was spurred into further speech. What if he thought I was there to see him? I couldn't allow that.

'I came with a friend.' Soon to be an ex-friend, I decided, glancing over my shoulder and seeing no sign of Tina. Where had she gone to find the water, the North Sea?

'I wish I'd known there was an expert in the audience.' He smiled. 'How did it sound? No glaring clangers?'

'It seemed okay.' He couldn't hold back a grimace at that faint praise; no doubt he was accustomed to gross adulation wherever he went as part of his celebrity lifestyle. I aimed a vague nod in his direction and edged towards the door, determined to wait in the car for Tina rather than endure this torture for a moment longer.

'Hey, wait. Don't rush off. What have you been up to? Did you carry on with the archaeology?'

'No. How would it have worked? It was impossible, wasn't it?' It was the word he had used in his parting note to me, seventeen years ago, but he didn't appear to make the connection.

'And how is everyone? Wendy? Douglas?'

'My dad's dead.'

The expression of shock and sadness on Paddy's face might have fooled anyone else. My dad had never for a second made me think he was disappointed with a second daughter – we were two of a kind, like Faye and Mum had been – but he had loved Paddy like a son, and the feeling had seemed mutual. But then I'd thought Paddy had loved me too, so what did I know?

'I'm sorry.' He reached out a hand, but I drew further back. 'When? How?'

'Another heart attack. Three months after Faye died.'

Briefly, his face crumpled with something like grief. My resolve to be indifferent shattered.

'You must know this! I wrote to you ... gave you all the details ... told you when the funeral was.'

He hadn't come. I had waited at the door of the crematorium, certain that despite everything, despite what he had already done, he wouldn't let me down on this; wouldn't let my dad down. He wouldn't leave me to face this on my own, when I had lost two of the people I loved most in the world within a few short months. Three, if I counted him. But I had learnt beyond doubt that day that Paddy Friel didn't think about anyone but himself; didn't care about anyone but himself, whatever lies he told to the contrary. I took a deep, juddering breath, and managed to control my emotions. I had wasted enough tears on this man.

'Ah, jeez, I wasn't at home. I didn't get the letter ...'

I shrugged; a convenient excuse if ever I'd heard one.

'It doesn't matter now. It's old news.'

I ignored his surprised expression at my apparent callousness. He had no right to judge me for being hard-hearted.

'And your mam?'

'Alive and well, and living in Spain. One of the advantages of my dad working in insurance. He left her a very comfortable widow.'

Paddy's puzzled gaze roamed over my face. Was he trying to work out where this bitter woman had come from, how she had grown out of the girl he had known? He didn't need to look far. I could hold up a mirror, let him see the answer for himself, but he would probably be too distracted by the view.

'And ...' He hesitated, scratched his cheek, pushed the curls back although they were hardly out of place. 'Caitlyn. How is she?'

'Fine.'

'How old is she now? Twenty?'

'Yes.' I was surprised he remembered.

'Is she here?' He started looking round. 'Is that who you're waiting for?'

'No, she's ...' I stopped short. Why was I wasting my breath? He'd made it plain enough when he left that he wasn't interested; that she was my niece, my problem. 'She's not with me.'

'Eve ...'

His hand landed on my arm and for a moment I was too stunned to shake it off.

'Hello! Sorry to be so long.' Tina returned at last, no sign of water, but a glass of wine in her hand. 'But I see you've managed perfectly well without me ...'

'And I see you've managed to turn water into wine,' I said, jerking my arm away from Paddy's hand.

'Sorry! I was looking for a water fountain, but then I ran into the teacher from my Facebook group and she dragged me away for something better.' She smiled and stepped around me, her eye on more interesting company. 'Hello. Pleased to meet you. What a fascinating talk! I could have listened for hours.'

'You should have been on the front row. I might have gone on longer if I hadn't faced a bored kid who seemed more interested in what he could excavate from his nose ...'

The sound of Paddy's laugh grated on my nerves. I didn't look, didn't want to see how that cleft in his chin deepened when he laughed, see how many more laughter lines he had earned around his eyes during our time apart. I studied a black and white school photograph that was hung on the wall, rows of young faces, of students who would probably now be grandparents; the prime of life behind them, whereas mine sometimes felt as if it had never started. Unlike the man I could sense was watching me. What a lot of living he had squeezed into the last seventeen years.

'Are you ready to go?' I asked Tina.

'There's no hurry …' She crumbled under the look I sent her and swiftly downed her wine. 'Of course, I can't miss my taxi.' She turned to Paddy. 'Do you do many school talks? I'd love it if you could come to ours.'

'There's no money in the budget for that,' I said. What on earth was Tina thinking?

'I don't charge for school talks. I'd be happy to come. Where is it?'

Before I could instruct Tina not to tell him – although I hadn't worked out how I could do that – she gave him what he wanted.

'Inglebridge High in north Lancashire. Would you travel so far?'

'Sure. I'd be happy to.' Paddy pulled out his wallet and took out a business card. 'Here. Get in touch when you've worked out some dates.' He held out another card to me. 'What do you teach?'

'I don't.'

The card dangled between us. I put my hands in my pockets, indicating as clearly as I could that I had no intention of taking it.

'Eve, can't we catch up sometime? There are things …'

'No.' I cut him off. 'I have nothing to say, and there's nothing I want to hear. Not every bit of the past deserves raking up, does it? You should know that better than most.'

* * *

Tina was unusually quiet as we returned to the car and set off home, and I was too busy concentrating on negotiating the country roads in the dark to break the silence. I was glad to have something to focus on other than the past few hours. The sight of Paddy had knocked me more than I had anticipated, stirring up all the old feelings for him. Feelings of hate, not love – that had died long ago.

'Pull over here,' Tina called, banging on the dashboard like an overenthusiastic driving instructor. 'This pub's nice. A bit gastropub with the menu, but fine for a couple of drinks.'

I turned into the car park obediently, and we wandered into the pub. It was an attractive place, tastefully decorated with a wooden floor, expensive wallpaper and cosy fabrics. A roaring fire and an abundance of lamps gave the place a romantic feeling – the sort of place where lovers might curl up in a corner, oblivious to the rest of the world. Or so I imagined. Romance played no part in my life. But that's what I'd chosen, so how could I complain?

I found a table within range of the fire, and Tina brought over a glass of wine, and a cranberry and lemonade for me. For the first time in many years I longed for a shot of alcohol to numb my feelings.

'I'm only having the one,' Tina said, conveniently forgetting the one she had already had at the school. 'I have 8B first period tomorrow. I need my wits about me. If I have to teach them in Year 9, I may stage a one-woman revolt. Hannah White never stops rubbing it in about how brilliant 8A are. Apparently, some of them can even spell medieval ...'

I laughed and began to relax, glad that we didn't appear to be heading towards a post-mortem of the earlier part of the evening. Although I wouldn't be sorry to hear of Paddy Friel laid out on the mortuary slab ... I sipped my drink, batting away the unworthy thought. I'd suffered too much loss to know that death wasn't something to be flippant about.

'Talking of Year 9,' I began, remembering a piece of school gossip I had overheard today. 'Did you know that the Biology lab ...'

Tina put down her glass with a decisive bang.

'Stop changing the subject,' she said. I had thought I was continuing the subject, but she gave me no time to protest. 'You and Paddy Friel. Come on, spill the beans. I've never met anyone who's dated a celebrity.'

'He's not a celebrity.'

'He's been on the telly.'

'So have thousands of other people. That means nothing, nowadays. You can't be impressed by him. His only talent is putting on an Irish accent and waving his hair around.'

'You mean he's not really Irish?'

'His name is Nigel, and he was born and bred in London.'

Tina looked crushed and I felt a fleeting twitch of guilt, but not enough to stop me continuing. 'It's an image he cultivated – calling himself Paddy, drinking Guinness, laying on the thick accent – all he needs now is to start talking about leprechauns. I bet he hasn't set foot in Ireland for years. The whole thing is a sham, to make him more popular and presumably richer. Cut open Paddy and you'll still find a weak and cowardly Nigel inside.'

'Don't hold back! Remind me never to get on the wrong side of you. You really don't like him, do you?'

'I hate him.'

When Tina flinched at the word, I sat back against the cushioned chair, swirling my cranberry juice. I had given the instinctive answer, but was it true? I had loved him once, but I didn't now. I had hated him once, but that had been seventeen years ago. I hadn't spent the intervening years sticking pins in a voodoo Paddy doll and cursing his name. There'd been no time for that, even if I'd felt inclined; I'd had Caitlyn to look after. My life had carried on, a satisfying one in many ways, especially where Caitlyn was concerned. Paddy Friel had rarely entered my thoughts, except when I'd been unfortunate and switched on the television at the wrong moment.

So no, perhaps I didn't hate him now. But if I was being forced to examine my feelings, I'd never managed to reach indifference either. As for forgiveness ... there weren't enough years in eternity for me to ever arrive at that point.

'How long did you go out with him for?' Tina asked.

'Almost three years, from near the end of our first year at university. We moved in together after we graduated.' A memory flashed up, of that tiny rented flat on the first floor of a semi even smaller than the one I owned now; of how ridiculously excited we'd been to have a place to ourselves; of how I'd felt safe there with Paddy, little knowing he would hurt me more than anyone outside that flat could have done.

'I'm guessing it ended badly. What did he do? Cheat? I don't suppose he's ever been short of offers.'

'He wasn't.' And yet I had never doubted his fidelity. He had told me whenever girls tried to chat him up; we had laughed together at some of the ridiculous things they had done to gain his attention. Perhaps it would have been easier if he had cheated. Perhaps I would have found it easier to forgive him if I was the only person he had hurt.

'He wasn't unfaithful,' I said. 'Or not in the sense you mean. But he did break my faith in him.'

I studied Tina, considered the confused expression on her face. I didn't talk about those days; everything was too closely bound together, the loss of Faye and of Dad, and Paddy's betrayal, all jumbling together into one twisted knot of pain, so I couldn't think of one of them without being reminded of the absence of them all. The acute feelings had faded, but they could never vanish. The encounter with Paddy had brought them closer to the surface than normal, and perhaps I needed to give them a moment's airspace before wrapping them up again. I took a long drink of my cranberry juice.

'When Faye died,' I began, my heart weeping as it always would at the sound of those words, 'Caitlyn went to stay with my parents. She'd had no contact with her father since she was born, and we didn't know who he was so couldn't get in touch. But anyway, she was ours: we couldn't have given her up to a stranger.'

She had been the most adorable child: thick white-blonde hair, huge blue eyes, and the ability to wrap us all round her finger. She was the image of Faye in every way.

'My dad wasn't strong after suffering a heart attack a few months before, and it soon became clear that the arrangement wouldn't work. The toll of his grief and the demands of a child were too much. I was living with Paddy at the time, and so the solution was obvious. Caitlyn would move in with us.'

How I had loved Paddy for agreeing to it! Despite the dramatic impact on our lives, the end to our plans to travel, he had backed me at once. We had begun by taking Caitlyn out with us for the odd day, so we could all get to know each other better, and my broken heart sputtered back to life when I saw my devastated niece take hold of Paddy's hand in the park one day, and whisper in his ear.

'So five or six weeks later, we packed up all her teddies and treasures and took her home to our flat, to begin our life as a family. And eight days later, just after we had celebrated her third birthday, just when Caitlyn had settled in and begun to trust us, to believe that we would always be there for her, Nigel Friel decided it wasn't the life he wanted, packed his bags and left.'

Chapter 4

I put down my pen and read back the note I had written to Caitlyn, hoping I had caught the right tone: cheerful, not wistful; entertaining, not embarrassing; missing her, but not too much. I was out of practice at this sort of thing. It was years since I had written a letter rather than sent a text or email. In fact, the last person I had probably written to was ... I sighed. He had proved he was good at leaving, so why couldn't he leave my thoughts alone?

'Shh!' Rich turned up the volume on the television. 'I'm trying to watch the football.'

The match looked no different to me than any other, but apparently it was crucial to the relegation positions and it was important enough to Rich that he had rushed through sex to be up in time to watch it. I hadn't minded that so much, but it had ruined the shape of our afternoon. We were normally able to kill a couple of hours in bed, followed by a cup of tea and a cursory chat before I headed home – a decent length for a visit. Today the bed part had barely taken twenty minutes, and there was something seedy about me leaving for home so soon. So I'd taken out the herbal tea bags I'd bought for Caitlyn, wrapped them into a parcel, and written her a note.

I reached in my bag and took out one of the 'Be Kind to

Yourself' vouchers. I needed to send her the first one, to show that I was keeping my promise, but what could I say? I had always been at pains to show no sign of regret at the direction my life had taken. I couldn't stop the 'what ifs' occasionally sneaking into my head: when contributing to the wedding or baby collections at work; when I'd inadvertently caught stories on the news about amazing archaeological discoveries. But I'd kept them to myself. I hadn't wanted Caitlyn ever to think I regretted giving it all up to be a mother to her. So how would it look that less than a week after she moved out, I had attended a talk on a subject that I had claimed not to miss? I decided to fudge it.

BE KIND TO YOURSELF
VOUCHER ONE
I, Eve Roberts, have been kind to myself by enjoying a night out with Tina!

That sounded suitably vague but fun, didn't it? Although 'enjoying' was stretching the truth thin. I taped up the parcel. Rich was still engrossed in the football, oblivious to my presence other than the occasional tut as I unrolled a length of sticky tape. A rectangle of sunlight illuminated the carpet, picking out the fluff and crumbs that were scattered like confetti. I suddenly felt stifled.

'I think I'll take this to the post office and go for a run,' I said. Rich pressed pause on the Sky remote control, and the football froze in mid-air. I was touched by this unexpected show of interest.

'Are you coming back here?' he asked.

'Yes, I'm leaving my car.'

'Great.' I smiled. How could I have thought he was oblivious? 'Can you pick me up some cans on the way back? This is my last one.' He waved a can of lager at me. 'And if you take at least an hour, the match will be over, and I can join you in the shower.'

Clinging on to my smile as he winked at me and restarted the football, I changed into my running clothes and headed towards the post office in the centre of Inglebridge. The spring sunshine was surprisingly warm on my face, and as I jogged through the residential streets towards town, and relaxed into the rhythm of the run, I stamped out my irritation with Rich as my feet slapped against the pavement.

Had it always been like this? Such a one-dimensional connection, an arrangement more than a love affair? We had been seeing each other for two years now, a series of snatched afternoons and evenings that could just about be strung together and called a relationship, but it was a hollow one. I hadn't met his children; he had only met Caitlyn because of an accidental encounter in the supermarket. We had never spent a whole night together or gone to social occasions as a couple. And I couldn't complain, because wasn't this exactly the type of casual relationship I had wanted, setting down the ground rules before we had even shared a kiss? He was a good-looking man, fit from playing football, and was single – quite a catch in a town that was popular with families. I'd done well to find him.

So why was I now feeling this creep of dissatisfaction with what we had? Because seeing Paddy again had reminded me what a real relationship could be like. The shared interests and mutual support. The conversation and the laughter. The excitement. And the pain. I should focus on remembering that.

Inglebridge town centre was bustling, as it always was on a

sunny Saturday afternoon. It was a charming, slightly old-fashioned market town, with a mixture of stone buildings from various periods clustering round the market square. An elaborately carved market cross took pride of place in the centre of the square, open to the sides but covered overhead so that tired shoppers could shelter inside for a while and watch the world go by. I had fallen in love with the place on my first visit, enchanted by the independent shops, the traditional twice-weekly market, and the cobbled lanes and alleyways that led off the shopping streets down to the river, where a medieval drover's bridge crossed the water. It had felt peaceful and safe, and exactly the sort of place where I wanted to bring up Caitlyn.

The quaintness of the town and the beauty of the surrounding countryside, not to mention the challenge of climbing Winlow Hill, drew a steady stream of tourists, particularly during the warmer months. As I jogged past The White Hart Hotel, a gorgeous Georgian building overlooking the market square, I came across the hotel's owner, Lexy, updating the posters in the smart glass frames on each side of the entrance.

'Tourist season begins!' she said, waving at the poster. I paused to read it: a special deal for dinner, bed and breakfast with a picnic and guides to local walks thrown in. 'At last! It felt like winter was never going to end this year. Let's hope this sunshine is here to stay. What do you think? Is it a tempting offer?'

'Sounds great.' I wondered about who would come: retired couples perhaps, able to enjoy a midweek break, or younger pairs escaping real life for a relaxing weekend in the countryside. It was something else I had never experienced with Rich; neither of us had shown any desire to go on holiday together. Was that normal? Normal for me. And the other sort of normal hadn't worked out well, had it?

'Now that the nights are getting longer,' Lexy continued, locking the glass display case, 'I've been thinking about ways to attract people in to the town centre again in the evening. You know the sort of thing – gin tastings, special menu nights – things I tried over winter but that weren't enough to tempt people out in the snow. We could do with some regular events too, so what do you think about setting up a community running group?'

'But you're not a runner.'

'Not yet, but I could do with getting more exercise. And you must know every possible route around here, so I thought that you were the ideal person to lead the group!'

I'd certainly run right into that trap. Lexy was smiling in what she no doubt hoped was a winsome way. It reminded me, fleetingly, of Faye. Even now, after so many years, the combination of grief and guilt felt like a fist thumped into my chest.

'What would it involve?'

'Not much! You would just lead everyone on a circular run – nothing too far, as we need to appeal to all abilities – or lack of ability. It won't be much trouble, will it, as you go running most days anyway. And now you can have company!'

It was tempting to point out that I didn't need company; that one of the benefits of running, apart from the physical exercise, was the freedom to switch off my thoughts and be truly alone.

'What's in it for you, if you're not going to run?' I asked instead.

'I'll join in sometimes, if it's not raining. And not too cold. I thought everyone could meet at The White Hart, so the run would start and end here. Then I could offer a discount on food and drink to anyone who had taken part. What do you think? It would be more fun for you than sitting at home on your own, now Caitlyn's gone. You're allowed to enjoy yourself! Although I still wish you'd enjoy yourself with a bottle of wine in my bar ...'

Something about Lexy's words made an unconscious echo of Caitlyn. Be kind to yourself, she had instructed me – and this would fall within the spirit of her rules, wouldn't it? Perhaps it would make a change to run with other people. What harm could it do? I had navigated the best part of seventeen years keeping a wary distance from people, with Tina being the only exception; making acquaintances but not engaging my emotions, so that I wouldn't have to face the pain of loss again. Lycra and sweat were unlikely to change that.

By the time I had run a couple of miles out of town, as far as the ugly 1960s secondary school where I worked and which was surrounded by a barricade of conifers to prevent it blotting the landscape, I was beginning to warm to the running group idea. My dad's premature death from a heart attack had galvanised me to change my diet and increase my exercise levels; I wasn't obsessed with keeping fit, but I tried to encourage healthy living where I could. This running group could be good for Inglebridge, and perhaps I could put posters up around the corridors and encourage some of the students to take part too. It was worth a try, wasn't it?

Mentally designing the poster, I didn't stop to check the driveway into school before crossing. It was Saturday afternoon – who would be there? A reckless idiot was the answer. I had taken two steps from the pavement when a racy, low-slung sports car tore down the drive at top speed, clipped me with the wing mirror, and roared off with an elongated hoot of aggression from the horn. As I tumbled to the ground, I caught sight of a scowling woman, a similar age to me, raising her hands in irritation and mouthing words that I was glad I couldn't hear.

I landed in doggy-style on my hands and knees, winded but otherwise unscathed, apart from some light grazes. My cheap leggings, on the other hand, had given in at the first hint of trouble and now sported a large hole in the knee; all the fashion in some quarters, but I guessed I was too old to pull off the ripped look. The perpetrator was long gone, having hit and run without so much as a backward glance.

I hauled myself up, brushed off the dirt, and hobbled a short way down the drive to check the school. The gates to the playground were shut and locked, as they should be, so it didn't look like the girl racer had been a burglar, unless she was casing the joint for a proper attempt. It was probably just someone misdirected by a sat nav, I decided, and didn't give the incident another thought as I ran back to Rich's house.

It was obvious that Gran had something on her mind within minutes of my arrival at The Chestnuts the following day. She didn't press her emergency button for tea with the same relish as normal and showed hardly a flicker of enthusiasm when I pulled out the all-butter shortbread.

'What's up with your hand?' she asked, as I tore open the packet.

'Oh, this?' I held out my palm. There was a red, grazed patch on the fleshy pad above my wrist, a legacy from my fall yesterday. 'It's nothing, only a scratch. I had a tumble yesterday while I was out running.'

I spared her the details; I didn't want her to worry, and it sounded unnecessarily dramatic to say that I had almost been run over. After a night's reflection I was ready to concede that I wasn't entirely blameless, by running off the footpath without checking first. It was a lesson I had spent years drumming into Caitlyn, so I had no excuse for ignoring it myself.

'Have you dabbed it with TCP?'

That made me smile. TCP had been Gran's answer to all our childhood complaints, from cuts and scrapes to sore throats. Even now the smell could take me back instantly to those carefree days, when we had stayed with Gran during school holidays; when we had run wild in the nearby park, and cycled around the streets with children we had never met before but who shared a common goal to have fun; when summers had always seemed long and sunny, and we had believed our whole lives would be the same.

'Yes, of course.' It was a lie. I couldn't bear to smell it now. 'It's nothing. But what's the matter with you? You don't seem your usual mischievous self. You haven't harassed the nurses yet or criticised the other residents.'

'It's the minibus,' Gran said, shaking her head. 'We've lost it.'

'It's been stolen?' I immediately thought of the woman in the sports car yesterday. Perhaps I should have been more concerned, if there was a crime wave sweeping town.

'No, it's conked out. It's been on its last legs for a long time, but last Wednesday it wouldn't budge. It was cinema night too, the most popular outing of the month. You can imagine the to-do.'

I could; I knew how important the monthly trip to the cinema was at The Chestnuts. It wasn't a real cinema – Inglebridge wasn't cosmopolitan enough for that – but the old playhouse held weekly screenings of classic films and the best seats in the house were reserved for The Chestnuts when it was their night out.

'Can it be mended?'

'No, it's knackered. Fit for nowt but the scrapheap, like the rest of us. On the up side, it's been a good week. The minibus is the only loss we've had.'

I hated it when Gran spoke like this, making light of mortality. Death held no fear for her; she was fond of telling me that she'd had a good innings, and wouldn't grumble when her chips were up. She wanted to go while she still had full control of her mind and her bladder, she would say, and I could understand that. But I wasn't ready to lose anyone else. I wouldn't ever be ready.

'So what will happen?' I asked. 'Will the minibus be replaced?'

'Aye, but only if someone snuffs it and leaves money to this place. There's nowt spare in the kitty at the moment.'

I didn't ask how Gran knew the financial situation of The Chestnuts. She knew everything.

'Could you use taxis for the time being?'

'We're banned since Mr Craig had an unfortunate accident in one a couple of months back.' Gran wrinkled her nose, and I didn't press for more details. 'We need to raise some money, but heaven knows how we'll do that. There's barely one fully functioning body between us.'

'There's the summer fair,' I reminded her. It was well supported by the town, as so many of the locals had sent relatives to The Chestnuts at one time or another. 'That will bring in some money.'

'That's earmarked for a new bathroom on the second floor. We need summat else. Come on, our Eve. You were always the clever one. Can you not come up with something?'

Like what? My gaze roved around the room, seeing all the dozing residents. A sponsored sleep? Then I paused at a painting of Winlow Hill over the fireplace. It wasn't one of the famous

Three Peaks in the area, but it was still a popular climb, and one that walkers liked to tick off the list.

'What about a sponsored climb of Winlow Hill?' I said.

'Aye, that's one solution. Kill us all off and then there'll be no need for a minibus ...'

I laughed. 'I didn't mean the residents. Relatives, people from the town, and perhaps tourists too ... We could sell drinks and cakes at the bottom. I wonder if we could try for a world record, for the most people to climb the hill in a day? If we could find an angle to interest the press, we might draw a good crowd. How much would we need, do you know?'

'Beats me. Do I look like a used bus salesman?'

I took out my phone, and quickly searched the internet for an idea of the cost of a relatively new minibus. My heart sank.

'It could be £20,000, depending on how many seats you need,' I said. 'I didn't realise it would be so much. We'd need hundreds of walkers to raise even a fraction of that sum.'

'We're not beaten yet,' Gran said. 'What we need is someone famous to head the campaign.'

'We don't know anyone famous,' I said, still flicking through minibus adverts on my phone. 'Old Fred Taylor from Fell Farm appeared on *Countryfile* last year, but I can't see him drawing a crowd ...'

I trailed off as a horrible suspicion crept into my head. I looked up. Gran was grinning at me and wagging her finger in my direction. How could I have missed where she was heading?

'No.'

'Why not? Your Paddy would be perfect. Send him up the hill and you'll have dozens of lasses running up after him.'

'No.'

'Don't be so stubborn. We need that minibus or we'll all go doolally cooped up here over the summer.'

'I'm not asking any favours from Paddy Friel.' I couldn't believe she had even suggested it. But Gran didn't know the full story behind his departure. She had been so fond of Paddy that I hadn't wanted to upset her. As far as she was concerned, we had mutually agreed to separate, a platonic break with no hard feelings. She knew nothing of his heartlessness, or my heartbreak.

'Why not? He's not shy of anything that brings him a bit of publicity, is he?' She reached over and patted my knee. 'Besides, I think he owes you, don't you?'

Chapter 5

The last thing I expected to see, when I pulled into the school car park the following morning, was a racy, low-slung sports car occupying a space. And not just any space; it was parked in mine. We didn't have official named spaces, but by convention we all had our regular spots and would stick to them, unless there was a torrential rainstorm in the morning, in which case it was every staff member for themselves in parking near the door.

'Look at that,' I said to Tina, who shared the journey in with me. I pointed at the offending vehicle.

'Graham would love one of those,' she said, referring to her mild-mannered husband. 'He fancies himself as James Bond in disguise.'

It was an excellent disguise: plump, quiet and kind, he suited his ancient Volvo estate more than a sports car.

'I wasn't admiring it,' I said, pulling in to the space next to it, and already dreading the backlash from the head of languages. 'It's in my space.'

'So it is. Who do you think it belongs to? Has someone been on a spending spree this weekend? My money's on that new maths teacher. I've caught him using my mug, and he definitely has an inflated notion of his own sex appeal.'

'I saw it here on Saturday, and it wasn't the maths teacher driving. It was a woman, but I didn't recognise her. We're not expecting a new teacher, are we?'

'Only the interim head, and I'm sure she wasn't due to start until next week.'

Tina promised to send me a text if she discovered a stranger in the staffroom, and I headed the opposite way to my desk in what was laughingly called my office, although it was no more than a cubbyhole outside the head's room, and the enormous multi-function printer took up more space than I did. This morning, I was surprised to see a scruffy cardboard box occupying the centre of the desk, in the one area that had been free of detritus when I had left on Friday night.

As I was staring at it, wondering where it could have come from, and what unpleasant task it must contain if someone had dumped it and run, the door to the head's office jerked open, giving me another surprise. Our head teacher, Mrs Armstrong, had gone off on long-term sick leave a couple of weeks ago, and we'd bobbed along in rudderless fashion since then as the deputy head had also moved on at Christmas and not yet been replaced; for some reason, our middle-ranking school buried in the Lancashire countryside wasn't attracting many applicants for the role.

A woman stood in the doorway, looking me up and down in a swift appraisal that immediately raised my hackles. Not that they needed to be raised much further – even without the scowl I recognised the driver who had knocked me over at the weekend. What was she doing here?

'Ms Roberts?' She buzzed the 'Ms' in an unnecessarily emphatic way, and glanced at her watch – another unnecessary affectation, when there was a perfectly good clock on the wall between us. 'Eve?'

'Yes?' I waited to see if she would remember me as her weekend victim, but there was no hint of recognition.

'Jo Blair.' She approached and stretched out her hand for me to shake, smiling in a way that seemed calculatedly hearty, putting me on edge rather than at ease. 'I'll be interim head for the next few months, until a permanent head is recruited. I'm glad you're early. I'm told that you're a wonder and will be my right hand. Come in and have a chat.'

Without waiting for my agreement – as my working hours hadn't technically started yet – she turned and walked back into Mrs Armstrong's office – or her office, as I supposed I would now have to think of it. I followed on behind, feeling uncomfortably like a naughty child about to learn my punishment. It was a pleasant room, with windows on two walls overlooking the playing fields, but as Jo took a seat behind the desk, I could sense that the atmosphere had changed already. Mrs Armstrong had made it warm and welcoming, so even the most wayward pupil or anxious parent had felt at ease. Now all that warmth seemed to have been sucked out through the open window. The room felt cold and impersonal; even the desk had been cleared, so all that remained on it were a computer and keyboard, telephone and a paper coffee cup from the petrol station on the Yorkshire side of town.

Jo waved at me to take a seat opposite her.

'I didn't think you were due to start until next week,' I said.

'I was due to go on holiday, but cancelled when this job came up. It was clear when I looked at the figures and statistics that I couldn't start a moment too soon. The exam results aren't impressive, are they? You must be aware of that.'

'We're low in the league tables, but ...'

'Exactly.' Jo interrupted before I could point out that the school excelled in so many other areas – in sport, in music and, most importantly, in sending confident, well-rounded young adults out into the world. 'That's going to have to change. There's been too much slack management. We need to see streamlining and efficiencies. I'm meeting the staff this morning to outline the vision for the way forward. Good teachers and good results will be at the heart of it.'

'We have some excellent teachers here. They couldn't be more dedicated ...'

'Some? That's not enough. We need all the teachers to be excellent.' Jo leant across the desk towards me. 'The governors assure me I can rely on you. You've been here a long time. You know all the staff – who isn't on their game any more, who has lost their motivation, who is letting standards fall. You'll hear things that I won't. I'm counting on you to help me, for the good of the school. I need you to be not only my right hand, but also my eyes and ears.'

It normally worked like a magic charm, someone asking for my help – I could rarely resist. But this? Spying on my colleagues, who I had worked alongside for years? Betraying the teachers who had taught Caitlyn, kept an eye on her for me, shaped her into who she was? I couldn't do it. I wouldn't.

'I'll help in any practical way I can,' I said, choosing my words carefully. 'But I won't spy on my friends, or tell tales about hardworking teachers who care passionately about this school and their students, and who are doing their best in difficult circumstances. That's not in my job description, and not in my nature either. But if there's anything else I can do, you need only ask.'

If I'd thought the atmosphere was cold before, it was nothing to how low the temperature dropped now. Jo sat back and crossed her arms, sending me a patronising smile.

'I think you misunderstand, Eve. I never suggested you should spy, only to work with me to identify areas of improvement. Of course, if you don't want the increased responsibility, I respect your decision. It is disappointing, when I had heard such good things about your commitment to this school.'

Jo tapped at her keyboard, and I took this as a sign that I was dismissed. I stood up, feeling bizarrely as if I had done something wrong. Had I? If nothing else, I'd clearly annoyed Jo, and that would make working in such close proximity awkward. But I couldn't regret my decision. I hesitated, wondering whether I ought to say something else, to try to smooth things between us.

'Oh, Eve?' Jo didn't look up. 'There's a box on your desk. It contains Mrs Armstrong's belongings. Please get rid of it. And on the subject of your desk ...' Now she looked at me, and it wasn't a friendly look. She clearly wasn't in the mood to smooth things out. 'I intend to introduce a clear desk policy. Have you any idea how much a data protection breach would cost, financially and reputationally? Everything confidential must be locked away. Your first job this morning is to clear your desk.'

She focused on her screen and started typing before I could tell her that I was fully aware of the rules and regulations concerning data protection, and that whilst my desk may look untidy, there was nothing confidential on there. I walked back out to my cubbyhole and glanced over at the desk. Perhaps untidy was an understatement. How long had it been since I last sorted through the piles of stationery catalogues, magazines and junk mail? Mrs Armstrong had kept me too busy. Well, I would soon show Jo Blair that a clear desk policy held no fear for me ...

It was lunchtime before I could catch up with Tina, and she did a double take when she saw me sitting behind my immaculate desk. I had reproduced Jo's minimalist look to perfection, with the exception of the photo of Caitlyn beside the computer monitor. No amount of arm-folding or disapproving looks would persuade me to part with that.

'Have you been fired?' Tina asked, goggling at the expanse of clear desk between us. Not even a paperclip besmirched the tidiness now. Of course, the desk drawers were bulging, but Jo couldn't take control of those too, could she? 'Have you managed to irritate our new boss already?'

'It wouldn't take much, would it? She's not fired me yet, but I'm wondering if it's only a matter of time. We've worked together for one morning, and so far, she's objected to the state of my desk, the smell of my peppermint tea, that I didn't divert my phone when I nipped away for two minutes to go to the loo, and that she doesn't like the way the computer files are labelled and arranged. She's also told me that I won't need to do any more typing for her, as she has a digital dictation system on her computer, which is more efficient. If I hear the word efficient one more time, I'll ...'

The door to the corridor was flung open and Jo strode in, abruptly cutting off my rant.

'The lunch system is inefficient,' she said. 'There's a queue halfway down the corridor, and staff members are wasting time having to police it. Make a note for the next staff meeting.'

I nodded but didn't move, and she continued to stare at me until I reluctantly opened a drawer a crack to try to remove a notebook and pen without her noticing the untidy state of the drawer.

'Can I help you? Mrs Wade, isn't it? History?' she said to Tina. Assuming Tina had only come around to gossip, I began to give a spurious excuse for her presence, but she waved at me to stop.

'I have some excellent news, Ms Blair,' she said, in a fawning manner that I thought unworthy of her. She held up a sheet of paper that I hadn't noticed before. 'The popular TV archaeologist Paddy Friel has agreed to come and give a talk one evening. It's excellent publicity for the school, and a great enrichment event for the students.'

'We won't be able to fit it in,' I said, glaring at Tina. How could she go ahead with this, after what I had told her about Paddy? 'Next term is too busy already, with the prize-giving and end-of-year musical evenings, and the hall will be set up for exams for most of the time.'

'I know all that, so I begged him nicely and he's agreed to come in the last week of this term. Isn't that great?'

The last week of term? There were only two weeks left until we broke up for the Easter holidays, which meant Paddy would be coming in next week. That was too short notice to arrange an event with anyone, let alone with someone I didn't want to see within twenty miles of here.

'That doesn't give us time to organise it,' I said. 'It's not just a question of advertising the event, but we need to make arrangements for school to be open late, and for staff members to stay behind ... Think of the costs for the small benefit it might have.'

I thought that pointing out potential financial implications would bring Jo over to my side, although it seemed incredible that we were battling over her. But Tina sent me a smile full of mischief.

'I've thought of all that. We could have it a week on Wednesday. There's a Year 10 Information Evening at six, so we could invite Paddy to start his talk at seven-thirty. As the school will be open late anyway, and staff present, it would be an efficient time to do it. You could include it in the newsletter tomorrow.'

I had to smile, and acknowledge her skill, even though my heart sank as Jo nodded in agreement.

'It's an excellent idea, Mrs Wade, well done. We can charge for tickets and drinks, to make a profit from the event. This is exactly what we need to see – initiative and positivity from the staff.'

I didn't know why she looked at me when she said that: I could be extremely positive when I chose. Just not where Paddy Friel was concerned. I was still smarting over the whole business at the end of the day when I met Tina at my car to share the drive home.

'You deserve to walk,' I said, unlocking the door and throwing my bag onto the back seat. 'How could you have arranged this with Paddy behind my back? You knew I didn't want him here.'

'But you heard how good he was at the other school. We hardly ever have events like that here. We're too out of the way to draw big names. Why should our students always miss out? If it inspires one of them it will be worth it.'

I shrugged and reversed out of my space with unnecessary speed. She was right, and I couldn't argue with her. I just wished it had been anyone but Paddy who was offering this golden opportunity.

'Besides, you don't need to come,' she added. 'He won't turn up until long after you've gone home. If you really don't want to see him, you don't have to. Forget you ever heard about the event.'

If only it were that easy.

Caitlyn telephoned at the weekend, brimming with excitement about her new life in Paris and her job as an au pair. Everything was fun and interesting; the family she was working for were lovely, and the children she was looking after were adorable. The weather, the food, the flowers, the improvement in her accent already ... she was enthusiastic about every detail.

My heart ached to hear her. She was so happy – happier than I ever remembered hearing her before. Was that my fault? Had I held her back, in our quiet Lancashire town, taping up wings that were twitching with the urge to fly? Had I held her close, when she wanted to be set free? Protected her, when she needed to test herself and learn from her own mistakes? I had done what I thought was best, for Faye's sake, but it was agonising to think that I might have promoted her safety above her happiness.

'How are you getting on with the Be Kind to Yourself vouchers?' Caitlyn asked at last, when even her enthusiasm for Parisian life was exhausted. 'You've only sent me one so far.'

'There will be another one on the way soon.' I laughed. 'You might not think it exciting enough. I had to buy some new running clothes, and I didn't go for the cheapest own brand this time.'

In a moment of mouse madness, I had clicked on a hi-tech outfit that apparently could breathe, sweat and possibly even do the running for me, or that's what I expected for the price. It was due to arrive on Monday, in time for the first running group meeting on Tuesday. After a sustained campaign of persuasion from Lexy, I'd given in and agreed to lead it for her. I was trying not to worry about what I had let myself in for.

'Is it going to make you look young, gorgeous and athletic – unlike the baggy things you've worn in the past?'

'I don't think it can perform miracles, even at that price.' Caitlyn's laughter floated down the line. I closed my eyes, and for a bewitching second it could have been Faye on the other end of the phone. 'I thought I ought to look the part, if I'm leading the group. That's if anyone turns up. Lexy has set up a Facebook event, but no one has signed up yet. No one has even said that they're interested.'

'But the middle-aged people who need exercise might not use Facebook.'

'That's a fair point. I'll tell Lexy that we need to write out flyers on parchment with our quill pens, and send them off attached to a pigeon ...'

'I didn't mean you. You're not middle-aged. Not yet.'

'Thanks!' Of course, I spoke too soon.

'Not until August, when you turn forty and officially go over the hill ...'

I clutched the phone more tightly to my ear, staggered by the overwhelming nature of how much I missed her, felt in every fibre and follicle of my being. Her absence was like a physical force, buffeting me from all angles.

'I can tell you're not missing me at all,' Caitlyn said. 'You're having too much fun with your running club and nights out with Tina. Where did you go? You didn't say. I hope it wasn't just cinema night with Gran Gran and the Chestnuts gang.'

'No, we went to Yorkshire.' I realised that probably didn't sound much of a treat to someone currently living in Paris. 'We attended an evening lecture.'

Caitlyn's silence confirmed that the extra detail hadn't helped elevate the outing in the excitement stakes.

'You did get the concept of the vouchers, didn't you?' she asked. 'You were supposed to be having fun.'

'It was fun!' Or it had been until a certain fake Irishman had barged into my personal space. 'It was all about Roman Britain and what the archaeological evidence tells us ...'

I trailed off. I had deliberately not given Caitlyn any details of the talk when I filled in the voucher. She knew my history, of course, and knew about my degree, but I had tended to play it down as a subject in which I had a passing interest, not one that I had intended to make my career. I had never told her about the plans Paddy and I had made before she came to live with us; the plans to take time out and join archaeological digs across the world. We had both been juggling a variety of part-time jobs to fund our travels; my share of the money had ultimately been used to fund time out with Caitlyn and our travels to Lancashire.

I had never mentioned Paddy to her at all, and as far as I knew she had no memory of him. I hoped not, anyway. But I certainly didn't want her to think that I'd been desperate for her to leave home all these years, so I could pick up my old life again.

'It was only ...' I began again, but Caitlyn interrupted.

'That's fantastic! I didn't realise you were still interested in all that old stuff. Are there any more talks you can go to?'

'No, I don't think so.' I conveniently forgot the fact that one was taking place at our school.

'That's a shame. What about going on a dig? Is that the sort of thing you used to do? You should definitely have another go. I bet you could volunteer for something over the holidays. Why not?'

'Well ...' Caitlyn was reminding me of someone again, but it wasn't Faye this time. It was me. Wasn't this exactly the same cajoling voice I'd used countless times to encourage her to join in with things she wasn't keen on? Since when had our roles reversed?

We said our goodbyes, and Caitlyn returned to her busy, delightful French life while I slumped on the sofa in front of the television in my empty house. I had no plans for the rest of the evening, or for Sunday either. Rich was busy with his children, Tina was away, and even Gran had told me to keep clear of The Chestnuts or face the consequences of a nasty gastric bug. I had no plans for the rest of the year. No plans for the rest of my life, whispered an impish voice in my head.

I thought about Caitlyn's suggestion of volunteering on a dig and the stir of excitement I had felt when she had mentioned it. Could I pick up where I had left off all those years ago? Could I volunteer on a dig over the summer? Why not, Caitlyn had asked. I thought about it all night, and couldn't think of an answer.

Chapter 6

Jo Blair didn't improve on further acquaintance.

'Is that business-related post?' she asked, when she caught me during morning break on Monday, with the parcel containing my new running clothes. I had just finished writing out a voucher to send to Caitlyn.

BE KIND TO YOURSELF
VOUCHER TWO
I, Eve Roberts, have been kind to myself by buying state-of-the-art new running clothes!

I would have denied it if I could, but the bag was covered with the name of the sports shop, making pretence futile.

'No,' I admitted. 'It's an urgent parcel I need for tomorrow.'

I chose not to elaborate; she looked wiry under her power suits, as if she worked out, and I didn't want to risk her turning up to join the run.

'It's not school policy to allow personal mail to be delivered here. I thought you would have been aware of that. Don't do it again.'

I was half inclined to think she was making it up – Mrs Armstrong had never mentioned the existence of such a policy, and her gin club parcel used to turn up here every month without anyone batting an eyelid. But I told myself it wasn't worth fighting over. I had my clothes and wasn't expecting any other deliveries, so there was no point falling out over it. We had to work together, and though our working relationship had been strained so far, never recovering from our initial chat, I didn't want to risk making it worse.

That was what I thought at break. My good intentions didn't last beyond lunchtime, when I returned to my desk and found a pile of posters dumped on it. I picked them up and marched into Jo's office without knocking.

'What are these doing here?' I asked, waving the stack of posters at her. A piece of dried Blu-Tack flew through the air and landed on her desk, in bold defiance of the clear desk policy.

'I found them scattered around the school, ruining the walls. Have you any idea how much it costs to paint the corridors in this place? Send an email to all staff telling them not to put posters up other than on the official display boards. Blu-Tack is banned with immediate effect.'

My blood, which had been lukewarm already, quickly escalated to boiling point.

'This has nothing to do with any staff member,' I said, thumping down the posters onto her clear desk. 'I put these posters up. Mrs Armstrong gave permission. They are all anti-drug posters. It's an important message.'

'Mrs Armstrong is no longer here and I'm withdrawing permission. It's sending out the wrong message to parents and visitors. We have an important event this week, with Paddy Friel's talk taking place, and the press will be here. We don't want to give the impression that we have a drugs problem in school.'

The reference to Paddy did nothing to calm me down.

'What does it matter what visitors think? Any decent parent would be pleased to know that the school was taking a stand – that we have a strong anti-drugs policy,' I said. She was usually a stickler for policy and procedure, so why not this one? 'Who cares about the cost of repainting the walls, if the posters make one student think twice before experimenting with drugs?'

Jo leant forward, and if I hadn't already concluded after a week's acquaintance that she was an efficient machine and incapable of human feeling, I would have sworn she was trying out a sympathetic expression.

'I understand, Eve, why you feel so strongly about this crusade, but you need to pursue it in your own time and not let your obsession ...'

I froze. She was giving me a pointed look – a look that suggested she knew things about me, about my background, that I certainly hadn't told her.

'My obsession?' I repeated. I couldn't believe what I was hearing. She clearly didn't understand at all. This wasn't an obsession. It wasn't a crusade. I wasn't charging into battle for my own glory, far from it. But what did this woman, with her own obsession for policies and efficiencies, know about the things that were really worth anything in life? 'Call it what you like. This is a million times more important than exam results and budgets. This is a chance to save lives. I can't think of any better way to spend my time.'

I was still shaking when I reached the staffroom, and Tina took one look at my face and shepherded me into the nearest empty classroom.

'What's up?' she asked, pushing me down onto a chair. 'Is it Phyllis? Caitlyn? Your mum?'

'No, everyone is fine. It's Jo ...'

'Oh crikey, what's she done now? The staffroom is still up in arms about her decree that we need permission to photocopy more than ten sheets of paper. What has she planned next? We can't cope with another of her bright ideas yet.'

'She's taken down all the anti-drugs posters.'

I didn't need to say more. Tina understood, more than Jo ever could, and immediately leant forward to give me a hug.

'Oh, love. What's she done that for?'

'Because posters might damage the school walls. And she doesn't want parents to think there might be a drugs problem here ...' I stopped. Jo's concerns were so trivial, when compared to what was at stake. How could she think any of that mattered?

'So what, we ignore the issue, and keep our fingers crossed that nothing like that happens here?' Tina said. 'She's more of an idiot than we realised.'

'She called it my crusade.' I looked at Tina. 'How does she know?'

Again, Tina needed no more explanation about what I was asking. She shrugged.

'I suppose it must be on your personnel record somewhere. Mrs Armstrong knew all about it, didn't she? About Faye, and how you came to have Caitlyn ...'

So Jo Blair had been snooping, grubbing round in our private lives – for what reason? Looking for the weak links, who she could then remove in a round of budget cuts? Perhaps I wouldn't have minded if it were my secrets she was raking over. But not Faye's. I didn't want her to know anything about Faye, didn't want someone like her to judge my sister. There had been enough judgement already. And what had Jo found out? The truth about

Faye, and how she had died, presumably. Because Faye had died unexpectedly, but not from an accident or a freak illness. She had died from taking a pill – a drug – that had turned out to be a bad one, and that had killed her.

But that wasn't the real truth about Faye. It wasn't how she deserved to be remembered. She had been so much more than the tawdry tale of her death that had featured in the local and national newspapers for days afterwards; sleazy journalists hadn't been able to resist front-page photographs and stories about the beautiful young woman who had thrown her life away because of drugs. She had been vibrant and funny, a wicked impressionist, a talented artist, and the most wonderful sister I could have wished for. Hardly a day went by without me regretting what I had lost, and even more, what Caitlyn had lost. I had done my best for Caitlyn, but it could only ever be second best to what she should have had.

I stared out of the window, nails digging into my palms as I forced my thoughts to stop there, not to prod at the memories of that time, at the bruise that would never heal. Tina took hold of my hands and uncurled my fingers.

'Sod Jo Blair,' she said. 'Print me out one of your posters and I'll put it up on the history display board. She doesn't have a key to open it, so it will be safe there. I'm sure I can convince some of the other teachers to do the same. A bit of rebellion will boost staff morale no end.'

By the time Tuesday evening arrived, I was in the mood for a fast and furious run, so it was disappointing to see a motley collection of people arrive for the inaugural running club event. Lexy's advertising on Facebook and in The White Hart had paid off in the end, and ten people turned up, ranging from a veteran of half-marathons to a lady who admitted with a cheerful grin that she hadn't run since her baby was born eighteen months ago, but she was keen to get back in shape.

One of the fitter runners, Winston, was vaguely familiar and after an extensive guessing game as we jogged along at an infuriatingly slow pace, we established that we had crossed paths at The Chestnuts, where his grandmother was also a resident.

'You're Phyllis's granddaughter?' he said, when we paused on the crest of the drover's bridge that spanned the river to the south of the town centre, to allow the others to catch up. I wouldn't have stopped if I'd been alone, but I couldn't deny the charm of the scene, or how peaceful it was to watch the water meander below us.

'Yes. Do you know her?'

Winston laughed. 'Everyone knows Phyllis. She's the Queen of The Chestnuts, isn't she? Nothing goes on there without her knowing, and no one comes and goes without her noticing.'

'Noticing or interfering?'

'Maybe both,' Winston acknowledged with a grin, as we set off again. 'I hear you're organising a sponsored walk to raise money for a new minibus.'

'Am I? I did suggest it, but I hadn't realised it was definitely going ahead.' I hadn't raised the subject again with Gran, in case she dropped any more hints about a celebrity endorsement. I wanted to help The Chestnuts, but there were limits.

'It's definitely happening. Phyllis has even decided on the date. The third Sunday in May. She had wanted it to be the Bank Holiday weekend, but then she decided that people might be going away for half-term, so she brought it forward.'

'But that's only seven weeks away! How am I supposed to sort it out in that time?'

'I did hear her mention that the Easter break was coming up, and you would have nothing else to do.' Winston laughed as he repeated what was undoubtedly one of Gran's bon mots. 'Tell you what, why don't I give you a hand? I'm on paternity leave for a couple of months. It will be good to keep my brain active. Only if you need the help,' he added, as I slowed to let him go first where the riverside path narrowed to single file. 'I don't want to butt in.'

Did I need the help? Probably, if I only had seven weeks. But I wasn't used to accepting it. I was the one who offered help, not took it. I had many acquaintances around Inglebridge, people who I would happily pass time chatting to, but in the seventeen years I had lived here, only Tina had slipped through my barriers and become a true friend. My Christmas card list was extensive, my Christmas present list short. It was the way I had chosen it to be. I prided myself on being independent, and on not relying on anyone else. My history had made me cautious; if I didn't get too close to people, I wouldn't go through the pain of losing them. But a sudden thought struck me, as I ran along the uneven path. I might be spared the pain – but was I losing out on happiness too? And why had a simple question about a sponsored walk turned the spotlight on my whole way of life?

The path widened again, and Winston slowed until I caught him up.

'Sorry,' he said, as we carried on running. 'I didn't mean to put you on the spot. Have a think about it. If you need some help, I'm here. Strictly speaking, me and a seven-month-old are here, but I'm probably better with a spreadsheet than she is.'

It could have been the embarrassed smile, or the reference to the spreadsheet that swung it – or perhaps I recognised in him the same urge to help that drove me. Before I could think better of it, I heard myself giving him an answer.

'I'd love some help,' I said.

I definitely seemed to have swapped roles with Caitlyn. Not so long ago, I had been encouraging her to stretch her wings and try new opportunities. She had taken childcare qualifications at a local college after A levels, and then found a job at a nursery in Inglebridge, but it had been obvious to me that she had been restless. She had always loved languages at school, and longed to travel, but I knew she hadn't looked for jobs abroad, and I knew why. She was worried about leaving me. So I had researched a huge variety of jobs in near and far-flung places that I thought she might enjoy, printed them off, and circled a few that she seemed most qualified for. She had chosen the au pair position in Paris, and I had polished my acting skills to feign delight when she won the job, comforting myself with the reminder that she might have ended up much further away.

Now she was playing me at my own game. I arrived home from work one day to find a large envelope postmarked from Paris. Inside, I discovered a sheaf of papers, listing a range of volunteering opportunities to work on archaeological digs over the summer, from Peru to Penzance. Caitlyn had circled one in the Cotswolds and added a message: 'Sounds perfect! Be kind to yourself!'

Flicking through the details she had sent, I couldn't deny it: it was perfect. The dig was taking place over two weeks on a site south of Cirencester, carrying on the excavation of a Roman villa. The photographs of what had been discovered so far were tantalising: tiles from a hypocaust system that would have been used to heat the villa, numerous coins and pottery pieces, and an amazing mosaic floor that I longed to see for myself. It was an area I knew relatively well, as I had been brought up in Warwickshire and had volunteered at another dig in the Cotswolds in the summer holiday before I started university.

And as my gaze roved over the details, soaking it all in, trying to keep a check on my growing excitement, I saw who was in charge of the dig: Christopher Porter, my former university tutor, the man who had taken my raw enthusiasm and polished it. I had learnt so much from him, and my heart fizzed at the prospect of working with him again, even as a humble volunteer. Some might call it a sign, but not me: I was no longer romantic enough to be superstitious or to set any store by fate. Even so, I moved the details to the top of the pile and left it on the kitchen table. I was curious, that was all. I already had a job, one that kept me quite busy enough. I wasn't going to do anything about it – was I?

Chapter 7

It was normally one of the most boring parts of my day – sorting through the post, allocating it into piles for each department, and filling the recycling bin with the junk mail the school inevitably received. I did it on autopilot. The last thing I expected to find was an envelope addressed to me, in the barely legible handwriting that I had once known so well, when I had eagerly pored over every loop and dot and cross of the letters that Paddy had sent me during those never-ending days of university holidays when we had been apart.

Now I looked at his scruffy scrawl and felt nothing but resentment that he had bothered me here, in a place where there ought to be no reminders of Paddy. Wasn't it bad enough that he was giving a talk at school tonight, against my wishes? Had I not made it perfectly clear that I wasn't interested in renewing our acquaintance?

The envelope sat on the edge of my desk throughout the morning, as I dithered over whether to open it or throw it straight in the recycling bin. In the end, and despite my better judgement, curiosity won. I opened the envelope and pulled out a postcard. The picture side showed Lindisfarne and my heart gave a few uncomfortable thumps, because we had visited there together during the glorious summer we had spent working at Vindolanda in Northumberland. He must remember, surely – so what was the significance of him choosing that card? I turned it over and read the message.

Dear Eve

Remember that summer? Happy times, weren't they?

I know I screwed up. I'm the biggest idiot going. But can we meet after the talk on Wednesday? There's something I need to explain – something I should have explained years ago.

Give me a chance.

Paddy

I read it three times, and it still made no sense. What good were explanations now? The moment was long gone, gone seventeen years ago, gone the moment Paddy had chosen not to attend my dad's funeral. A stubborn streak of love had lingered, to my shame, even after he had walked out on me and Caitlyn, but it couldn't survive a second rejection. And he really didn't need to explain his behaviour. I'd figured it out for myself. He cared about no one but Paddy Friel. What more was there to say?

'Personal mail again, Eve?'

Jo Blair lurked in the doorway of her office, staring pointedly at the postcard in my hand. My hand was trembling; I hoped she couldn't see that from where she stood.

'Junk mail,' I replied, and without a second's hesitation I crossed to the recycling bin and dropped in the postcard. 'Nothing important.'

'About the event tonight,' she said, with an unexpected degree of awkwardness. 'It would be helpful if you could be on hand for the Year 10 presentation, to set up the screen and the

PowerPoint slides. I haven't had a chance to familiarise myself with the system yet.'

'Why me?' I asked, my head still too full of Paddy's message to make a show of good grace. 'Can't one of the IT technicians do it?'

'They both have other plans. And I'm told that you are the expert on such things.'

That was true, but I wasn't going to be won over by a titbit of flattery, especially when she hadn't scrupled to let me know that I was her last choice.

'I have plans too,' I said.

'Really?'

Of course I didn't. That sceptical inflection in Jo's question was infuriatingly justified. Rich was working away, Tina would be at school drooling over Paddy ... My plans consisted of nothing more than a run and a night in front of the TV – an identical night to every other. Jo sniffed my weakness.

'It will all be over by seven o'clock. It will hardly eat into your night at all. I'm sure you will be keen to support school events. It's exactly the sort of thing I'll be looking at in the annual Performance Management at the end of the year. And I wouldn't be surprised to find that it's in your job description to help out.'

She smiled and retreated to her office, no doubt pleased with herself for that parting shot – because wasn't I the one who had relied on my job description when she had suggested I spy for her? How could I refuse now? Especially if our annual reviews were coming up. Reviews with Mrs Armstrong had been an opportunity to ignore the phone and have a natter for half an hour. I suspected Jo Blair would take it more seriously. And what if she appraised me and found me wanting? Did she have the power to sack me, as an interim head? What would I do without my job?

Determined to show my commitment, however much it pained me, I behaved as the model assistant at the Year 10 talk that evening, keeping my face neutral as Jo baffled the parents with talk of SPaG and cohorts as she tried to explain the exam system. Everything went so well that she even managed a 'thank you' as she wandered off to prepare for the next event of the night – Paddy's talk – leaving me to tidy up and make sure the hall was ready. I didn't mind. I glanced at my watch. One good thing about Jo's love of efficiency was that she had finished bang on time. I had forty-five minutes to make my escape before Paddy's arrival. He had never wasted time in the past by turning up a minute before he needed to, and I didn't expect he had changed. There was no danger of seeing him.

With thirty minutes to spare, I was about to grab my bag and leave when running footsteps echoed through the hall. I looked up, expecting to see a Paddy fan dashing for a seat on the front row – she or he would be disappointed to find they were already reserved for governors and members of staff. I was half right – it was Tina, and she was dashing my way wearing an anxious expression that immediately worried me.

'Have you finished?' she asked, grabbing the back of the nearest chair as she gasped for breath.

'Yes. He's not here already, is he? He's never usually early.' I pulled my bag from under my chair, assuming she had come to give me a warning, and touched by this evidence of Tina's friendship. I hadn't thought she understood my aversion to Paddy. 'Where have you put him? Is it safe to use the main doors?'

'Put who? Oh, Paddy. No, he's not here yet.' Tina glanced at the clock on the wall, and her anxious expression deepened.

'I asked him to be here for seven so we could chat through the arrangements. He's cutting it fine. Is he not good at punctuality?'

He wasn't good full stop – I thought I'd already made that clear. But I simply shrugged in response, accepting no responsibility for his faults.

'What did you want me for, if it wasn't about Paddy?' I asked.

'We have another crisis brewing – or more accurately, not brewing,' Tina said, with a rueful grin. 'Bev has had to go home because one of the kids is ill, so ...'

'No.' I knew where this was going, and I didn't like it. 'I'm not doing the teas. No way.'

'I wouldn't ask if there was anyone else. But you know what Jo Blair is like. She's expecting to make some money tonight, even if it's only a tenner. It will be on one of her spreadsheets. And she'll want to put on a good show as the press are supposed to be coming.'

That job had left a nasty taste in my mouth – having to ring up the local paper and invite them to the event, gushing about what a coup it was to have the renowned celebrity archaeologist Paddy Friel visiting our school. Part of me had hoped they would say, 'Who?' Unfortunately, I had spoken to a female journalist who had hardly let me finish my patter before she had begged to come.

'Surely there must be someone else ...'

Even I could hear the resignation in my voice. Tina pounced on it.

'You'd be in the canteen during the talk, so you wouldn't see or hear him,' she said. 'And I'd fetch him a cup of tea myself, so he wouldn't come anywhere near you.' She reached out and rubbed my arm. 'I know you didn't want to be here, but I have to make it work tonight. Jo has already been dropping hints about my Performance Management next term. Please help.'

I nodded. What else could I do? Tina had been a good friend to me over the years, and had saved my sanity on more occasions than I could remember. Friendship trumped personal inclination every time.

It wasn't a taxing job to set out the tea things; I'd done it countless times before. But when all the cups and saucers were set out, the biscuits displayed on plates and the '50p per cup' sign prominently displayed, I still had thirty minutes to kill before the first of the thirsty hordes were likely to descend. I messed around with my phone for a while, checked my emails, replied to a text from Rich and generally did everything I could to distract myself from what was going on in the hall.

I straightened a teacup and looked critically at the display. Were there enough cups? There were more in the cupboard that I had judged unnecessary – but what if my prejudice was underestimating the popularity of this event? What if I let Tina down?

It was a matter of seconds between the thought creeping into my head and my feet carrying me to the door of the hall. Standing to one side, I peered through the glass panel, focusing only on the rows of chairs stretching back down the length of the hall. It was far busier than I had expected, with the rows occupied to at least halfway; I would need more teacups after all.

I turned away and was about to return to the canteen when a familiar burst of laughter stopped me in my tracks, the sound slinking into my reluctant ears and pinning me to where I stood. I tried to ignore it, but his voice carried through the door as he spoke about the Viking occupation of Lancashire and the Cuerdale Hoard that had been found by workmen repairing the banks of the River Ribble near Preston in 1840; it was one of the largest Viking silver hoards ever found, and we had once been to see it at the British Museum. The Vikings had always been Paddy's favourite era, and his genuine enthusiasm was clear, to me at least; the Irish accent dimmed, and he sounded less like the TV star and more like the boy I had known. I closed my eyes and listened.

The scrape of a chair along the wooden floor brought me to my senses, and I dashed back downstairs, my heart pounding with renewed fascination about archaeology, and frustration that Paddy had helped inspire it. I set out more cups, filled the urns with tea and coffee, and prepared to lurk at the back of the room, out of sight.

It wasn't long before the audience arrived, laughing and smiling as if they'd had a good time – although the realisation that they had to pay for refreshments wiped a few of the smiles away. I sensed rather than saw Paddy's arrival; I was well hidden behind a group of parents, and a gaggle of Year 9s who thought they could pilfer biscuits without me noticing. But the sound in the room changed when he walked in: conversations dimmed; feet shuffled as people turned to get a better look. The air was thick with the consciousness of his presence, and with anticipation of who he might talk to.

It was sickening. All this, because he had appeared on television, and was objectively what some might consider handsome? I thrust a teacup into a waiting hand, sloshing the contents onto the saucer as I seethed at the shallowness of today's society. And then I smiled to myself for sounding more like someone of Gran's age than my own, and as I looked across the room, Paddy caught my eye and returned my smile.

Damn the man! He was as bad as the Year 9s, pilfering things that weren't meant for him. I focused on dispensing refreshments again, but the queue was drying up, and at 50p per cup, no one was coming back for seconds. I felt like a sitting duck behind my table as the crowd thinned around me. Spotting that Jo Blair was engaged in earnest conversation with a governor, I grabbed the almost-empty urn of tea and carried it into the kitchen, with the spurious intention of filling it up while hiding for as long as I could.

'Eve?'

My hand slipped, and scalding water splashed over it, making me yelp. Paddy was at my side at once, switching on the cold tap and holding my arm so that the cold water ran over the back of my hand. As soon as the pain was replaced by a heavy numbness, I shook my arm free.

'I can manage.'

'You should leave it under for fifteen minutes.'

'I am aware of that. I'm one of the school's designated first aiders.'

I didn't know why I added that. If we were going to trade achievements since our time together, it was hardly going to trump anything he could offer.

'Well done,' he said, and I glanced up, expecting sarcasm, but his smile appeared genuine. But then it always did. A line from Caitlyn's A-level Shakespeare text floated into my head: 'that one may smile, and smile, and be a villain.' It summed up Paddy perfectly.

'You're not supposed to be in here,' I said, turning off the tap and drying my hand on a paper towel. I had no intention of being trapped here for fifteen minutes. 'What do you want?'

'Did you come and hear the talk?' he asked.

'No.' I threw the paper towel in the bin. 'Don't you have enough adoring fans out there? Are you so desperate for praise that you have to follow people, hoping for a bit of flattery?'

'I don't give a stuff about adoring fans. None of that matters.'

'Really? Is it just the money you care about, then?' I said. 'Something must have motivated you to take the part in *Celebrity Speed Dating*, as it certainly can't have been for the critical acclaim.'

Caitlyn had been hooked on the show, and I'd been unlucky enough to catch a few minutes of it – fortunately not a segment featuring Paddy. It had been one of the worst things I'd ever seen on television, and had picked up scathing reviews – so of course, it had been a huge ratings hit.

'Sure I did it for the money. I'm not ashamed of that.'

The old Paddy would have been, the Paddy I thought I'd known: he was passionate about his subject – devoted to it, as I knew to my cost – and wouldn't have risked degrading it with tawdry TV shows. Briefly, I wondered what had happened to wreak the change, but I soon let the thought slip away. I had better things to do than waste a second of my time on Paddy Friel.

'Did you get my postcard?'

'Yes. It went straight in the recycling bin. We have nothing to talk about. I made that perfectly clear before. You were happy enough to leave me alone once, when it suited you. Why can't you leave me alone now, when it suits me?'

Paddy leant against the stainless steel work surfaces, his hands stuffed in his pockets.

'There are things we need to talk about,' he said. 'Important things. Don't be like this. I know this bitterness isn't you. What's happened to you?'

My mouth and my eyes gaped wide. Was he criticising me?

Who had made me bitter? Why had I ended up this way? He knew nothing about me, about who I was now.

'Life happened,' I said – no doubt in a bitter fashion. 'It doesn't always go the way you want it to.'

'No, it doesn't.' Something in his face, in his voice as he said that, caught my attention – something undoubtedly real. But before I could process that, my second least favourite voice cut through the kitchen.

'Eve? What are you doing? Why have you left the tea money unattended?'

Jo Blair stopped when she noticed Paddy, and her frown quickly changed to a smile.

'Mr Friel! Have you lost your way? Eve, couldn't you have shown him where to go?'

'I tried.'

Paddy's eyes glittered with amusement from behind Jo's back, and all at once, I remembered how different things had once been between us. How laughter had bound us together; how he had acted the clown, never satisfied until I collapsed, clutching the stitch in my side; how I had stored up stories from my day, exaggerating the absurdities in the hope of hearing his laughter; how our radar for comedy had been so finely attuned that it had often taken only one shared glance to set us both off. I had never experienced that with anyone else. It felt like I hadn't laughed like that in years. Seventeen years, if I was inclined to count.

'Hurry up with the tea,' Jo said, oblivious to the atmosphere in the kitchen. 'There's time to sell a few more cups.'

I nodded and picked up the urn, but before I could take a step, Paddy removed it from my grasp.

'Watch your hand,' he said.

He headed towards the kitchen door, and I hurried after him, with Jo Blair close on my heels. And as we made our procession into the canteen, I took a moment to analyse my feelings. Paddy's condemnation had been uncomfortable and unarguable. I did sound bitter, and it *wasn't* me. It had been my head talking, not my heart. When I looked there, I found no bitterness. I had hated Paddy once, but somewhere over the years it had gone, leaving mere indifference behind. Or not quite indifference. As I had been reminded so recently, there had been good times between us. The best, I had thought back then. Dig far enough down through the years, and there was a layer of our relationship where things had been perfect. Despite what had happened afterwards, I could never forget that. With my training, I should know better than to think that history could ever be irrelevant.

Paddy put the urn down on the table. I spotted Tina across the room, looking at me with concern. I shook my head at her. I didn't need rescuing. It was time to face up to this.

'What is it you want to talk about?' I called after Paddy, as he started to wander away. He turned back.

'Not here,' he said, gesturing round. The guests had started to leave, but too many remained, hovering in the hope of a moment with Paddy. 'Are you free later?'

'Not tonight.' It was too soon. I needed time to prepare for this.

'Tomorrow?'

'I'm working.'

'Friday? Term will have ended, won't it?'

I nodded. 'But you won't be here ...'

'I'm staying at The White Hart tonight. I can extend my stay.'

'There's no need to do that ...'

'There is. It's important. Meet me for lunch on Friday. Please, Eve.'

Was I a fool to agree? Maybe. Maybe I had always been a fool where Paddy was concerned. But when he looked at me with the same expression of wordless appeal that I had fallen for hundreds of times before, I couldn't resist now any more than I had then. I nodded again, unable to say the words, and Paddy smiled and walked away.

Chapter 8

Friday was the first day of the Easter holidays, but there was no chance of a lie-in. Before I had been daft enough to agree to meet Paddy for lunch, I had already arranged to call at Winston's house to have our first meeting about The Chestnuts fundraising campaign. With the sponsored walk only weeks away, there was no time to lose in starting the preparations.

It was a fine day, with a definite hint of spring in the air, and I walked through the centre of Inglebridge, enjoying seeing the morning sights I usually missed during term time: the shop-keepers setting out their signs on the pavements; the delivery drivers whistling as they dropped off their supplies; the volunteer litter-pickers scouring the streets as eagerly as treasure hunters. White vans stood abandoned on the double yellow lines outside the Pepperpot Café as the drivers queued for one of Merry's irresistible sausage butties; Mr Long, the oldest news-paper boy in town, cycled past on his way back to the newsagent's with his empty bag; old Mrs Davenport shuffled towards the kitchen gadget shop, where she and her Pekingese would sit and natter for a good hour.

I soaked up all the reminders of why I loved this little town, and they combined with the prospect of two weeks free of Jo

Blair to add a spring to my step, despite the looming audience with Paddy.

Winston lived in one of the new houses that had been built on a field on the far side of town a couple of years ago. The plans had caused outrage and sparked angry protests at the time – quite an uproar for such a peaceful town – but already the houses had been absorbed into the fabric of the place and no one batted an eyelid about them. I quite liked them – they had been clad in stone, with at least some thought as to what would fit in with the area – and Winston's was in one of the best spots, overlooking more fields – although it could never match my view of Winlow Hill.

Winston opened the door and we exchanged an awkward hello; it somehow seemed entirely different to meet as real people rather than as hot and sweaty runners wearing Lycra. He led me through to an open-plan living room, where a baby lay on a play mat in the centre of the room.

I stepped carefully around the plastic toys and bricks that littered the carpet.

'Sorry about the mess,' Winston said, waving his arm cheerfully to encompass the whole room, but making no effort to clear my path. 'You know what it's like with babies!'

I smiled and nodded, because I'd found over the years that it was the easiest way. No one wanted to hear the complicated truth: that I didn't know what it was like; I was a mother who had no experience of babies. People didn't tend to like hearing that my sister had died from taking drugs, as if the facts of her death tainted me too; as if our whole family were tarnished by our failure to stop her.

'Tea?' Winston asked, and as he headed to the kitchen area to make it, I moved aside a pile of children's books to make room to sit on the sofa. They were rather advanced books for the tiny bundle lying on the floor. I remembered reading some of them to Caitlyn. She had snuggled on my knee, sucking her thumb as I read to her, and I had battled with the feelings that still plagued me now; love and guilt made exquisitely uncomfortable bedfellows.

'Feel free to borrow it, if you're desperate to know how the story ends.' Winston grinned as he came back with two mugs of tea and caught me engrossed in *Where are you, Blue Kangaroo?*

'No need.' I laughed. 'I still remember every word. Caitlyn loved these books.'

'I don't think Mabel appreciates them yet.' Winston handed me a mug. 'We're convinced she's a genius all the same.'

Winston settled down in the chair opposite me and picked up the laptop that was lying on the coffee table at his side.

'How are you finding being on paternity leave?' I asked. 'It's wonderful that you're taking proper time off.'

'Isn't it? But you'd be surprised. Not everyone thinks so. Cheryl had some stick for rushing back to work, and I took some ribbing from my colleagues for wanting to stop at home with the baby.' He reached down and tickled Mabel's tummy, making her gurgle with laughter. 'But who wouldn't want to?'

Who indeed? Who would put their career above the precious gift of looking after a child? Only someone totally selfish. Only someone wholly self-absorbed. I thrust aside the mental image of Paddy. I would have to face the real one soon enough.

'Have you time to help with the fundraising?' I asked. 'I'd hate to take up time you could be spending with Mabel.'

'It's no problem. I've already made a start. Look.'

He swivelled his laptop round so that the screen faced me and any doubts I'd had about collaborating on this project were wiped away. He'd created an Excel spreadsheet, and though I couldn't see all the details, the colour-coding and highlighted boxes were enough to convince me that I'd found a soulmate. I shuffled forwards for a closer look.

'I've drawn up a timeline from now until the day of the walk, so we can keep on top of what needs doing when.' He had, and I couldn't have done a better job myself. 'Critical dates are in red, target dates in blue. My tasks will be orange, your tasks in green. What do you think?'

'It's perfect. You've obviously done this before. What did you say your job was?'

'Project manager.' Winston grinned. 'Does it show?'

'Just a little. Do you always deliver on time?'

'Of course.'

I laughed, and we spent the next half hour discussing the plans and populating the spreadsheet. I enjoyed myself so much that I wondered whether this would qualify for one of Caitlyn's 'Be Kind to Yourself' vouchers. Perhaps not, I decided. She wouldn't understand, and would probably storm back from France to set me straight. Then again, that might make it worth doing ...

Winston disappeared to change Mabel's nappy and I gathered up the notebook I had bought especially for this project. I flicked through the pages, ticking off items and admiring the progress we'd made, until I spotted something that we hadn't mentioned yet – my initial idea of attempting a world record.

'Did you have a chance to look into whether we can try for a world record?' I asked when Winston reappeared. I'd mentioned it to him on the run on Tuesday, but neither of us had known what it might involve. 'If not, you can add that to my list.'

'Already done. It didn't look promising. Can you hold Mabel a minute?' He deposited her on my knee before I'd answered, and pulled some papers out of the drawer. Mabel felt soft and wriggly in my hands; it was a largely unfamiliar sensation, as I'd been away at university when Caitlyn was this age, but it was not an unpleasant one. 'I don't think it can just be the largest number of people to climb Winlow Hill in one day, or something as local as that. Or that's how I interpreted the advice.' Winston waved the papers at me. 'It needs to be something that other people could try to beat – like the largest gathering of people dressed as pirates, or wearing top hats.'

'I suppose we could try to think of something like that ... people wearing flat caps?'

'Accompanied by whippets?' Winston grinned. 'Time's too tight anyway. It can take up to twelve weeks to get approval.'

I sighed in defeat and Mabel looked up at me with sympathetic eyes. I cuddled her closer and her eyelids began to droop.

'I suppose it's like riding a bike, is it? You never lose the knack. How old is your daughter?'

'Twenty.'

'Really?' I caught Winston's curious gaze on my face, as he clearly reassessed my age. 'So is she at university now?'

'She's living in Paris, working as an au pair. I have an empty nest.' I smiled, and reluctantly handed Mabel back to her father. 'Make the most of this little one while you can. You're lucky to have her.'

It took a great deal of willpower to walk through the doors of The White Hart at lunchtime, when every instinct urged me to scuttle on past and go home. The snug was empty, and I eventually found Paddy leaning against the bar in the dining room, chatting to Lexy, who was hanging on his every word. Another one bites the dust, I thought, wondering what other biting might have been going on during his extended stay here. Not that it was any of my business what – or who – he got up to, but I did feel a flicker of guilt that I hadn't thought to warn Lexy first.

About half the tables were occupied in the dining room, by locals and some unfamiliar faces, and I was pleased for Lexy that trade was picking up now the better weather was on the way.

'Not a bad lunchtime crowd,' I said, as I joined them at the bar. Lexy dragged her attention away from Paddy and switched her smile to one of friendship rather than flirtation.

'It's okay, isn't it, for a Friday anyway. We have a few trippers in. Although they don't seem big drinkers,' Lexy added, with an accusatory glance at me, as if I was responsible for a temperance revival sweeping through the town.

'Hello,' Paddy said, breaking into the conversation – ten seconds without attention must have been too much to bear. He moved towards me, as if he planned to kiss my cheek, but I neatly sidestepped out of his way. 'What can I get you? Gin and tonic?'

'I don't drink.'

'Still?'

That brief exchange almost floored me: the easy intimacy with which he offered my once favourite drink and remembered details that I would have expected him to have long forgotten.

'Where would you like to sit?' Paddy asked.

'Oh, we're not stopping.' I brushed away the shadows of the past. 'We're going for a walk.'

'A walk?' He glanced down at himself. He was smartly dressed

– I'd noticed that at once – proper trousers, not jeans, and a crisp blue shirt that looked good against his dark curls. He probably had a wardrobe full of identical ones. If I'd hoped to discompose him, I failed. He smiled, accepting the change without a murmur. 'I'd better grab my walking boots from the car. Back in a minute.'

He went through the rear door towards the car park, and I ignored the pointed look Lexy was giving me.

'So tell me,' she asked at last, when I refused to meet her gaze. 'There's no mistaking that atmosphere. What is he? The one that got away?'

'The lucky escape,' I responded sharply. I softened, seeing her surprise. 'Don't be sucked in by that charm, Lexy. It's skin deep. It doesn't reach his heart.'

'It's not his heart I'm interested in ...' she began, but stopped when the man himself walked in, clad in walking boots and an old fleece. This was closer to the Paddy I remembered than I had seen him so far, and an unwelcome pang of nostalgia threatened to breach my guard. I turned my attention back to Lexy.

'One picnic, as ordered,' she said, handing over a rucksack. It was part of the deal she was offering to hotel guests: a packed lunch and ideas for walks in the local areas. 'A map and walking routes are in there, although I doubt you'll need them. Have fun!'

I wasn't doing this for fun; it was necessity. I knew how persistent Paddy could be. If he had got it into his head that he needed to apologise, he was unlikely to leave me alone until he'd done it. Better to let him salve his conscience and disappear again. And perhaps it would do me good too, to blot out any bitterness that still lurked and finally put Paddy behind me.

Caitlyn had encouraged me to have a fresh start. Perhaps I could only do that when I had cleared away the emotional detritus of the first start.

I led the way out of The White Hart. Paddy plucked the rucksack from me and weighed it in his hand.

'Disappointingly light,' he said. 'I'm guessing there isn't a four-pack of Guinness in here. What sort of picnic is this?'

'A healthy one.' I had to look away, to resist the treacherous urge to smile at the horrified expression on his face. 'Are you going to do this for the whole walk?'

'Try to make you smile? Sure. Almost had you, didn't I?'

'I meant grumble. You're not going to make me smile.'

'Yeah, yeah. So you say. But you know I can't resist a challenge.'

I marched off, heading across the marketplace and towards the snicket that led behind the shops and towards the river. It wasn't the route I'd planned to take, but if he wanted a challenge, he could have one. We crossed the drover's bridge, allowing no time to admire the view, and after a few minutes of taking the relatively flat riverside path, I turned left up a stony trail that rose steeply up the side of the hill, not stopping until we reached the top, where a grassy ridge gave gorgeous views across Inglebridge in one direction and endless countryside in the other. It was one of my favourite views.

I watched as Paddy struggled up the last few metres, hands on his hips and sweat shimmering across his forehead.

'Jeez, Eve, this isn't a walk, it's a marathon hike. What's with the pace? Are you trying to kill me?'

'It was too good an opportunity to miss.'

He stared at me and then, unexpectedly, he roared with laughter. How I had loved that laugh – the way his eyes crinkled up, the way his whole face absorbed his amusement. How

I had once delighted in teasing it out of him. How times had changed.

'Take pity on me,' he said. 'Tell me you're at least a little bit out of breath.'

'Not in the slightest. Imagine what you could achieve without the Guinness.'

'Life without Guinness doesn't bear imagining.'

He hadn't found it so hard to embrace life without me. I didn't point that out. No bitterness, I reminded myself. No begrudging the life he'd made for himself. I sat down on one of the huge rocks that lay amongst the grass, and Paddy perched on the one next to me.

'It's lunchtime, surely to goodness?'

'Okay.' See? I could be reasonable. I could treat him kindly. It wasn't so impossible, was it? I picked up the rucksack from where he'd dropped it on the ground, took out a foil parcel and handed it to him.

'This had better be good ...'

Despite everything, I couldn't prevent a smile as he peeled off the foil and revealed a spinach and feta wrap. I passed over a bottle of water.

'Not quite the pie and pint I had in mind ...' He picked up the wrap and prepared to take a bite, but I put out my hand and stopped him.

'Actually, that one's mine. Here's yours.'

I gave him the other foil parcel and he eyed it with trepidation.

'I'm not sure I dare ... Just tell me it's not egg. You wouldn't do that to me, now would you?'

I didn't answer, and watched as he opened the package and gingerly lifted the top half of the soft white roll inside, to reveal two thick sausages smothered in brown sauce. It had always been his favourite, and when he paused, not speaking, I wondered if his tastes had changed. But then he smiled and looked across at me.

'My favourite. You're too kind to me.'

'Kinder than you deserve.'

'I wouldn't argue with that.'

I broke the gaze first, unsettled by the unexpected rawness of his answer, stripped of all the layers of charm. Was this the moment of apology? I turned away and bit into my wrap as I studied the view across town, feeling suddenly unready to hear whatever he had to say.

We ate our lunch in silence, which might have been comfortable if I weren't acutely conscious that this harmony couldn't last; that our time together was running on and sooner or later Paddy would spoil it by speaking. I had almost decided to force the issue, and demand to know what he wanted, when he stood up and wandered over to the other side of the ridge, looking down over the fields on the opposite side of the river to Inglebridge town centre. He moved backwards and forwards, scrambling around the side of the hill a short way to get a better look before he returned to where I was still sitting on the rock.

'Have you seen the land down there, to the left of the clump of trees?' He indicated in that direction. 'Do you see the area that looks like a small hill? Could that be a ditch round it?'

I didn't need to look where he was pointing. I had walked up here countless times in the past. I had studied the view in every direction. I knew exactly what he was talking about.

'It looks like a bowl barrow,' I said, referring to a type of Bronze Age burial mound that took its name from its resemblance to an upturned bowl. 'I know.'

'You knew it was here?' Paddy looked confused. 'And have you never investigated it?'

'No. I don't do that any more. I have a real job. I have Caitlyn and Gran to look after.'

'It can't have been completely impossible to keep up your interest, surely? Isn't there a local archaeological group? This could be important ...'

It was too much. My resolve to be calm, collected and not bitter collapsed. What did he know about what was important in life? He thought nothing of humiliating himself on television for money; he thought nothing of abandoning a child who had already lost the most important person in her world.

'How can you ask that?' I said. 'It *was* impossible to carry on with the plans we'd made. Isn't that exactly why you left us?'

I stood up and faced him, hands on hips, voice rising with every word, all sense of pride or self-preservation gone. I hadn't wanted this conversation, but how could I run away from it when it had been waiting for me for seventeen years? How could I not want to challenge him, get him to admit what he had been too cowardly to say to my face before?

But it turned out that Paddy still had the capacity to surprise me. He flopped down on his rock and ran his fingers through his thick curls.

'No,' he said. 'That wasn't why I left.' He stared at me, and I might have read pain in his eyes if I was prepared to believe him capable of any human feeling. 'It wasn't because I thought Caitlyn would be in the way. Jeez, Eve, how could you believe that was true? How could you think that of me?'

'What else was I supposed to think? Nothing else had changed. You didn't give me any proper reason for leaving.' He had waited until I had taken Caitlyn to nursery one morning, and then packed his bags and gone, leaving a note to say that he couldn't live like this. There had been no warning; the three of us had been growing more tightly knit by the day, and Caitlyn had been especially close to Paddy, even copying his accent when she said certain words. Nothing had prepared me for his sudden departure.

'I got that wrong. I'm sorry.' He stood up, scuffed his foot in the grass, and avoided looking at me. 'You deserved better than that crass note I left, but I took the coward's way out instead of explaining ...'

'No!' I jumped up, holding up my arms as if they could physically block his words from reaching me. Because it was all achingly clear now, and my blood ran hot with humiliation. Nothing else had changed, I had said it myself. So if he hadn't left because of Caitlyn, it could only have been because of me. Paddy must have no longer wanted to be with me. All these years, I had blamed him for his weakness, for not being willing to adapt his lifestyle to include Caitlyn. I thought her arrival had been the catalyst for his departure. But, in reality, it had been so much simpler than that. What a fool, what a self-satisfied fool I had been to never have considered it before.

He was watching me, frowning at my interruption. He was waiting to explain, but I couldn't bear to hear him spell it out. This man had been everything to me once: my past, my present and my future. It didn't matter how many years had passed. I had learnt to live with the fact that he hadn't loved me enough. I didn't want to hear that he hadn't loved me at all.

'You don't need to say any more,' I said. 'None of it matters now, does it?'

And I grabbed Lexy's rucksack and ran back down the hill, ignoring the sound of Paddy calling my name.

Chapter 9

Winston was leaving The Chestnuts when I arrived to visit Gran the following Sunday. We met in the car park and he introduced his wife, Cheryl.

'Good luck in there,' he said, raising his eyebrows. 'We seem to have an unelected committee of volunteers to help with the sponsored walk.'

'Don't tell me – my gran's the ringleader?' Winston nodded. 'Dare I ask what they have in mind?'

'They've come up with a wide-ranging list of ideas. For a start, they expect all the local businesses to offer sponsorship. They also want to know if we're organising Portaloos as they might not be able to manage otherwise.'

I groaned. The event might be on behalf of The Chestnuts, but I hadn't expected the residents to actually turn up. The last thing we needed was a bunch of incontinent, trouble-making pensioners.

'Some of the ideas weren't too bad,' Cheryl said. She was a smiley, petite blonde, and from first impressions seemed like one of those exhausting people who were unfailingly positive about everything. 'Like the refreshment stall and the event T-shirts. And they are all desperate to find a celebrity to start the event, although there's a lot of squabbling about who it should be. One of the BBC weather presenters is a popular choice.'

Cheryl laughed, but I wasn't in the mood for it. I could easily guess where this celebrity idea had originated, and Gran had better start behaving if she expected me to keep her in the all-butter shortbread to which she'd become accustomed.

'This is getting out of hand,' I grumbled. 'We're raising funds for an old folks' minibus, not Children in Need ...'

'Good luck going in there with that attitude.' Winston grinned and nodded towards the box in my hand. 'I'm not even sure that those biscuits will guarantee your safety if you repeat that.'

I was heading towards the doors when Cheryl called after me. 'Does your gran have a sweet tooth?' she asked. 'I'm events manager at the Fairlie House Hotel, and we're holding an Easter Afternoon Tea next Saturday. Are you free? Why don't you both come?'

'I don't know ...' It didn't sound appealing, if Gran was likely to use the occasion to nag me about celebrities.

'You'd be doing me a favour. It was my idea, and we're not fully booked yet, so I need to fill the tables. I'll give you a discount. And,' she continued, before I could reply, 'if it will help tempt you, I can offer you a staff discount at the spa too. How about a massage and a facial – shake off the winter pallor?'

How bad did she think I looked? I was about to refuse, when Cheryl smiled at me and carried on.

'Go on, treat yourself. We all need to be kinder to ourselves, don't you think?'

It was as if her words cast a spell over me, with the echo of

Caitlyn. Before I could give it another thought, my mouth opened, and I heard myself agreeing to it all.

Caitlyn took two days to return my latest call, during which time I'd convinced myself that she was lying at the bottom of the Seine – and that was the least disturbing scenario I'd come up with.

'Hello!' I bellowed when I heard her voice at last. She could probably hear my relief – if she could hear anything; the phone was practically vibrating with a deep thrumming sound at her end. 'Where are you? Are the children at band practice or something?'

Band practice! How old was I? I'd clearly been spending too much time at The Chestnuts. Caitlyn must have been distracted, as she wouldn't normally have let me get away with such a clanger.

'I'm off duty tonight,' she said. My imagination rapidly filled in the rest of the sentence in ways that I didn't want to dwell on.

'How have you been?' I asked. I meant, 'Are you okay and why did it take you so long to ring back?' and I should have known that with Caitlyn's language skills she wouldn't have any trouble with the translation.

'Everything's great. You don't need to worry about me.' She sounded great – there was none of the artificial brightness in her voice that I could hear in mine. Of course, that only strengthened my worries. What was she up to, now that she was away from my watchful eye?

'I'm behaving perfectly well,' she added, laughing, translating my silence as easily as she had my words. 'Good as gold. Squeaky clean. An absolute angel.'

'Okay, I get the picture.' I laughed, determined not to let my anxiety spoil these precious minutes. 'Tell me what you've been up to.'

She did – or what I suspected were the edited highlights, at least. Perhaps she would have told me more if I had merely been her aunt; perhaps then we would have had the sort of relationship where she would have confided in me about things she couldn't share with a parent. I felt a pang of regret about what we had missed – as if I needed anything else to mourn.

'How are you getting on with the vouchers?' she asked, sharply changing the subject when my questions must have veered too close to a sensitive subject. 'Are there any more on the way?'

'There will be soon. I'm taking Gran Gran out to a posh hotel next weekend for afternoon tea, and I'm booked into the spa while I'm there.'

'That sounds more like it. Is Gran Gran not joining you in the spa?'

'I asked if she wanted to. She said she used to enjoy a bit of man-handling, but those days have long gone.'

'Urgh, I'm not sure I wanted that image in my head ... But while you're talking about man-handling, has Rich moved in with you yet?'

Rich moving in? The notion had never occurred to me.

'No, and he won't be doing. Our house is a man-free zone. Anyway,' I continued, exercising my own sharp turn in the conversation, 'you know I told you about the sponsored walk to raise funds for The Chestnuts? Someone suggested selling T-shirts with a logo on to raise extra cash and I wondered if you'd have time to draw something for us? It doesn't have to be anything fancy.'

'No problem. Anything for you and Gran Gran. I'll email something over in the next couple of days.'

And then she was gone, back to her noisy, busy life, while I trundled on with my quiet, empty one.

'... and I'll show you the design she's come up with later,' I said to Tina. 'She's an artistic genius, like Faye. The T-shirts will probably sell so well that we needn't bother walking up the hill at all.'

Tina was proving herself a true friend, and had given up a day of her Easter holiday to help me paint my living room. It wasn't a massive room, and I could have easily managed it myself, but when she'd offered to lend a hand, I hadn't been able to resist accepting. It was the boring tasks like this that allowed the regret at living alone to creep in: I'd fought hard to become independent, but sometimes it was a treat to choose not to be.

'You're not seriously wasting one of your vouchers on this, are you?' Tina asked, as I poured paint into two roller trays. 'This is hard work. How is that being kind to yourself?'

'It's a fresh start. I haven't painted this room for years. There are still nail varnish marks on the wall from when Caitlyn had a sleepover for her sixteenth birthday.' I glanced around the room, taking in the scuffs and scratches that told the history of our time in this house: the marks that would look like blemishes to some, but represented precious memories to me. If I thought about it too long, I would never paint this room again. I shook off the maudlin thoughts as I grabbed a pile of old newspapers and taped a few sheets down around the edges of the room to protect the carpet.

We knuckled down to the painting, listening to the radio as

we worked. The local station was full of Easter adverts, encouraging us to spend our money at the sales or go on days out.

'What are your plans for the weekend?' Tina asked. I had hoped she wouldn't bring it up, and so far, had managed to skilfully change the subject whenever it appeared to be heading this way. It was another drawback of the single life; no one questioned a couple if they wanted to stay at home alone.

'No particular plans,' I said. 'I might spring-clean the kitchen cupboards.'

I probably deserved the disparaging look Tina gave me. All I needed was a cat to make my spinster status complete. It wasn't that I was a neat freak – far from it – but I hated to sit still and be idle. Idle thoughts had an unnerving habit of going where I didn't want them to go; such as back in time to last week's conversation with Paddy, and the painful revelation that our relationship had been a sham for longer than I'd realised.

'And I'm going to afternoon tea at Fairlie House and visiting the spa on Saturday,' I added, belatedly remembering that I was doing something exciting after all. 'Caitlyn was impressed. It was exactly the sort of thing she had in mind for the Be Kind to Yourself vouchers.'

'Yes, but you're supposed to be choosing things for yourself, not to please Caitlyn. You've spent the best part of twenty years arranging your life around her. Quite understandably,' Tina added, waving her roller at me when I started to object. 'But how is it freedom if the doors are open but you still walk round the edge of your cage?'

That was harsh – too harsh for me to want to hear it – and I turned my back on Tina and concentrated on my painting until every wall had been covered with the first coat and we escaped to the kitchen for a break.

'How are the plans coming along for the sponsored walk?' Tina asked, as we settled at the table with our cups of tea – ginger and lemon for me, builders for her. I wrote out the latest voucher for Caitlyn.

BE KIND TO YOURSELF
VOUCHER THREE
I, Eve Roberts, have been kind to myself by painting the living room!

'Amazingly well,' I replied, pushing the voucher to one side. Perhaps it didn't sound such a treat, when I saw it written down. 'Winston is an organisational whizz. Every tiny detail is on the spreadsheet, and if it's on the spreadsheet it gets done. I feel like a spare part most of the time.'

'Sounds like you've met your match.' She raised her eyebrows in a suggestive way. 'Shame he's married.'

'And totally besotted with his wife and daughter ... and far too young for me, even if I were looking, which I'm not ...'

'Blinded by lust for Rich?' We both laughed, although I wasn't sure why I joined in; it was hardly loyal. 'If you were looking, what would your type be? And don't say Rich. We all know you can do better than that. You've settled for him, not chosen him. I mean, physically I can see the appeal, but I thought you would have looked deeper than that. I'm not sure what else he has going for him.'

I recoiled in my chair as if Tina had slapped me. Had the paint fumes got to her? She'd never expressed an opinion on Rich before; not a good one either, now I came to think of it. Her invitations to dinner or Sunday lunch had never included Rich, but I hadn't minded. He wouldn't have fitted in. And what was that 'we' about? Who had Tina been discussing me and my so-called love life with? Anyway, she was wrong: this was exactly the relationship I had chosen. Another topic that I preferred to steer my idle thoughts away from. Introspection was rarely a good idea.

'We know what your type used to be,' Tina continued, taking her third digestive biscuit and dunking it in her tea. 'Tall, dark and Irish ...'

'Half Irish,' I corrected her, and could have kicked myself when she grinned; of course, I should have pretended not to know who she was talking about. 'If I had a type now, it wouldn't be based on physical things. It would be someone who was honest, kind and dependable.'

'You're telling me you're immune to twinkly eyes and a roguish smile?'

'If you're talking about Paddy Friel – and I'm not admitting he has either of those things – then yes, I'm fully immune and he administered the vaccination himself.'

'So there's no chance he's going to be the celebrity opening the sponsored walk?'

'None at all.' I rewound. 'Who said there's going to be a celebrity, anyway?'

'It's all round town. I heard it yesterday from Bob the butcher.'

Bob the butcher, whose father was a resident at The Chestnuts. I was going to kill Gran – unless she was the death of me first.

'We have no plans to invite a celebrity,' I said firmly. 'And if we did, it wouldn't be Paddy. He'd be the last person I'd ask. From what I've seen, he pimps himself around the country and would open a jam jar if there was money and a photograph in it. He hardly needs more publicity. He uses it quite shamelessly.'

'All the more reason to ask him.' Tina smiled. 'If he doesn't scruple to use his celebrity for his own ends, why should you scruple to use it for yours? It's for the good of The Chestnuts. You can swallow your pride, can't you?'

Could I? I hadn't come any closer to swallowing it by the time Saturday came round, and I could only hope it wouldn't ruin my ability to enjoy afternoon tea. I picked Gran up from The Chestnuts late in the morning, ready for the twenty-minute drive to the Fairlie House Hotel. She was waiting for me in what had been the reception hall of the manor house, wearing a bright pink dress that bordered on neon and a flowery hat. The look was only slightly marred by the thick white surgical stockings.

'Hello,' I said, kissing her cheek. My eyes smarted at her pungent perfume. 'You didn't need to wear a hat. It's not that posh a place.'

'I hope not, given as you've made precious little effort.' Gran pulled a face as she looked me up and down. 'Any road, it's not a hat, it's a fascinator. I've borrowed all this clobber from Mrs Pike. She wore it to her grandson's wedding four years ago.' I smiled, but Gran hadn't finished. She could have given the best comedians a masterclass in perfect timing. 'And then to the christening two years later.'

I didn't take the bait.

'Only just a great-grandma? Poor Mrs Pike. She's years behind you. The way you're going, you'll live long enough to become a great-great-grandma. I bet Mrs Pike can't hope for that, can she?'

Gran conceded the point and, trouble averted, allowed me to lead her to the passenger seat of my car.

'Pooh! What a pong!' she said, as I switched on the engine and a faint scent of floral air freshener began to waft around the car. I was amazed she could smell anything over her perfume.

'What do you need that for? Have you got a dicky tummy? I won't offer you a butty then.'

She reached into her shopping bag – I'd wondered why she had needed such a huge bag – and pulled out a foil parcel, which she unwrapped with as much care as if it were expensive wrapping paper, while I drove away from The Chestnuts and on towards the road that would take us to the Fairlie. I felt like borrowing the 'what a pong' line as a stench of egg invaded the car.

'Ham and egg,' Gran said with satisfaction. I caught her lifting up one side of the crust before giving a hearty sigh. 'Processed ham. Who's ever seen a square pig?'

'You haven't forgotten that we're going out for afternoon tea, have you?' I asked. 'You didn't need to bring food.'

'I can't miss my dinner. I might end up as scrawny as you. In my day, ladies had curves not angles, and we were all healthier for it.'

Conversation continued in this vein as I drove along the country lanes, with Gran and the sat nav seemingly vying to see which could nag me the most. I didn't mind – or not Gran, anyway. She could nag me, call me any names she wanted, because I adored her and because she was here. She was alive. The last seventeen years would have been impossible without her. When my mum had packed her bags and moved to Spain, Gran had packed hers and moved to Inglebridge to be near me and Caitlyn, selling the precious house she had occupied for almost half a century, and in which she'd enjoyed married life and raised my dad. A cut-price afternoon tea could never repay what she had done for us.

The Fairlie House Hotel was a gorgeous stone mansion with high, even windows revealing its roots in Georgian times. Sitting amid luscious parkland at the end of a long drive, it reeked of luxury and exclusivity and ... romance, whispered my heart, although it had been so long, I wasn't sure how my heart still remembered what that was. As I pulled up in the car park, even Gran was silent. It couldn't last.

'At least one of us is dressed for the occasion,' she said. She patted my knee – clad in a cord skirt and tights, because I had made some effort, even if it wasn't up to Gran's standards – and grinned. 'Don't worry, our Eve. They'll be so dazzled by my outfit, they'll barely notice yours. We can pull this off.'

Laughing, I took her arm and led her into the hotel. The silence in reception was overwhelming, our steps muffled by the thick carpet and our voices absorbed by the plush fabrics hanging at the windows and covering the chairs that formed a pleasant lounge area. Gran made a beeline for a sofa next to a table scattered with magazines.

'This'll do me,' she said, rifling through the magazines before sitting down.

'Are you sure?' I hovered. 'Perhaps I should skip the spa. It doesn't feel right abandoning you here.'

'I'll be right as rain,' Gran said, dismissing me with a wave of her hand. 'You go and enjoy the poking and prodding. It's a treat to read up-to-date magazines for a change, and I've got a flask of tea. I can keep an eye on all the comings and goings from here.'

She'd miss nothing, I was certain of that. Putting my misgivings to one side, I followed the directions to the spa and allowed myself to be whisked away to a scented, darkened room where I lay on a plinth in trepidation of what was coming next. It wasn't the thought of the poking and prodding that bothered me, rather the enforced idleness – the best part of an hour to be spent doing nothing, vulnerable to every stray thought that might choose to attack me. But they must have been potent essential oils they were spraying into that room, because the time rushed by, and far from having unpleasant thoughts, I couldn't remember having any thoughts at all. My mind was a total blank, and I felt more relaxed than I had done for months. I'd already filled in the next two vouchers, and decided this was definitely the best use of them so far.

BE KIND TO YOURSELF
VOUCHER FOUR
I, Eve Roberts, have been kind to myself by having a facial and massage!

BE KIND TO YOURSELF
VOUCHER FIVE
I, Eve Roberts, have been kind to myself by taking afternoon tea with Gran Gran!

I was soon brought back down to earth by Gran.

'Your face is shining like the moon,' she said, as I wandered back into the reception area to collect her. 'You should have brought some powder.' She stood up and patted my arm. 'You needed that. The frown line between your eyebrows isn't as obvious. I'm glad. Shall we go for tea now? I'm peckish.'

Afternoon tea was being served in a lavish dining room, decorated in rich creams and beiges and exuding the same air of quiet refinement as the rest of the hotel. It was a far cry from the package holiday hotels I had occasionally stayed in with Caitlyn, where the furniture had shown the scuffs of generations of rampaging children, and the dining room was more like the school canteen than a fine restaurant. I wondered who would choose to stay in a place like this – and who could afford it.

'Those with more money than sense,' Gran remarked, when I repeated the question out loud. 'All you need are clean sheets and a decent breakfast, not all this malarkey. White linen!' she said, scrunching the pristine tablecloth between her gnarled fingers. 'I wouldn't want to be responsible for the laundry bill round here.'

She had equally scathing remarks to make about the pale carpet and the silk fabric on the chairs, but she didn't fool me. She was loving every second of it – that was obvious from the sparkle in her eyes and the way her head twisted round in every direction so she could take in every detail. The story of this afternoon was going to keep her in conversation for weeks at The Chestnuts, and I was delighted that we'd decided to come.

My delight was short-lived. As Gran was exclaiming over the velouté – 'why can't they call it cup-a-soup instead of a fancy foreign name?' – my heart sank as some new guests were ushered to a table only a few metres away from ours. I recognised Jo Blair among them, and I could feel the relaxing effects of the spa swiftly dissipate.

She caught sight of me at much the same time and we exchanged a reluctant grimace.

'Don't you like it?' Gran asked. 'It's a bit thick but the flavour's not bad.'

'No, it's lovely,' I said, putting down my empty cup. 'I just spotted someone I didn't want to see.'

I should have known better.

'Who's that then?' Gran peered round, swivelling in her chair to stare at every table. 'Anyone I know? Have you had a falling-out with someone? That's not like you.'

'No.' I leant back as the waitress took my plate. 'It's the new head at school. The new interim head, Jo Blair.' I lowered my voice. 'She's at the table over there.'

I jerked my head to the left and Gran immediately stared that way.

'Which one is she? The po-faced one with the short hair? She looks like a ...'

'Gran!' I hushed her just in time; whatever she was about to say would neither have been polite nor quiet. She was temporarily distracted by the arrival of the main afternoon tea: tiers of neat rectangular sandwich portions and lamb Scotch eggs; tiny hot cross scones, chocolate egg nests, cupcakes decorated with rabbit faces, slivers of simnel cake and iced gingerbread chicks; and the one that was going to challenge my healthy diet the most – miniature chocolate éclairs, topped with a fondant carrot. It was an impressive display, and Gran was silent for the best part of ten minutes while she made inroads into the food.

'I've not seen her crack a smile yet,' she said at last, picking up the conversation where we had left it. Her memory could be disappointingly good for her age. 'Is she one of those who never smiles in case it gives her wrinkles? She's younger than I expected. Not much older than you. I can't say as I'd like to work for her, from all you've said.'

'I wasn't given a choice.'

'Make your own choice. I've always said you were wasted at that school. You've years of work left in you. Why do you want to spend them on a job you don't love? You get to my age and there's nowt to do but regret what you've done and not done. It's not much fun, let me tell you. If you don't like the path you're on, try another while you still can.'

And in those few minutes, Gran showed me again why she was so special. She could ramble for hours on inconsequential topics, and then cut you to the quick with such a sharp insight that it felt as if she'd seen through all your bluster.

'I'm not qualified to do anything else,' I said.

'You weren't qualified to do what you're doing, but you got qualified. You can do it again. Or why not use that degree you were once so keen on?'

Why not? Because that degree was now tainted by unhappy memories. Not just because of the obvious connection with Paddy and my heartbreak over him, but because it would always remind me of my dad, who had driven me around the country to visit various archaeological sites and museums and who had made me believe that I could do anything I chose. I had loved those road trips the two of us had undertaken together. What would he think of me now, clinging on to a job that no longer made me happy? Had my confidence dropped so far that I didn't dare try something different in case I failed? I had once been braver than this. Could I be brave again?

We were lingering over the dregs of our tea, probably both reluctant to exchange this rarefied place for real life, when Cheryl hurried over to our table. I started to thank her for arranging the tea, but she shook her head and interrupted.

'Have you finished?' she asked. 'There's something in reception that would be perfect for the sponsored walk.'

I stifled a groan, because Gran had been cross-examining me for the last twenty minutes about our progress, and I'd had more than enough for one day. But Cheryl was twinkling with enthusiasm about something, so I pushed my chair back reluctantly.

'Hang on,' Gran said. 'These aren't going to waste, not when we've paid for them.' She pulled out the silver foil from her handbag, that she'd so carefully salvaged from the ham and egg sandwiches, and wrapped up the leftover cakes. 'The Chestnuts gang will be glad of these. It's pork goulash tonight and that never goes down well.'

It was hard to imagine egg-scented éclairs going down well either, but I helped Gran pack away her goodies and we linked arms as we followed Cheryl from the dining room and back to reception. I was idly speculating on what could have made Cheryl so excited – something in a magazine? Branded water bottles? – when a familiar laugh assaulted my ears and my eyes gravitated to the sight of Paddy Friel sprawled on a sofa.

Chapter 10

I blinked several times, but it was no use. He was still there, still real, and still in the way of our direct route to the front door. And I thought Jo Blair had been an unwelcome sight! I would happily turn round and join her at her table if it meant avoiding Paddy. After our last meeting – after the humiliating realisation that he had rejected me, not Caitlyn, all those years ago – he was the last person I wanted to see.

My steps faltered and my grip on Gran's arm tightened.

'Ooh!' she said. 'Is that ...'

'Yes. Yes, it is.' I tried to draw her back, but the quietness of the hotel that I had admired on our arrival now proved an enemy as our voices carried over to Paddy and caused him to look up from his magazine. His smile was instant and appeared genuine.

'Eve!' He jumped up and made short work of the gap between us. 'This is great!'

'Is it?' That wasn't the word I would have chosen. How annoying was this? Seventeen years without him, and now he was turning up all over the place. 'You're like the bad penny, aren't you? What are you doing here?'

'The White Hart was full for Easter.' That didn't really answer my question, but he had already turned his attention to Gran.

'And would you look at you, Phyllis, not changed at all from when I last saw you.'

'Get on with you and your blarney. I bet you're surprised I'm still here, aren't you?' Gran said. 'You always were a smooth talker, Paddy Friel. It's no wonder you ended up on the telly.'

'You've watched the show?'

'I tried it once. It wasn't for me. I'll be under the earth soon enough without wanting a sneak preview of what's down there.'

Paddy laughed and leant forward to kiss Gran's cheek.

'You're invincible,' he said, and taking Gran's other arm, he gently pulled her away from me and towards a chair. 'Come and sit down and tell me what you've been up to. You're looking ravishing in that fascinator.'

'See?' Gran called, turning back to me. 'Even he knows it's not a hat.'

Paddy grinned at me, and I had to look away, because it appeared that my heart still retained the memory of loving that grin, whatever lessons my head had learnt since then.

'Do you all know each other?' Cheryl asked. I'd forgotten she was there. She smiled. 'Mr Friel is our guest for the weekend. I was going to see what you thought about asking him to open the sponsored walk, but if you're already friends that's even better!'

'I wouldn't say friends,' I muttered, but that grin flashed up and silenced me again.

'What's that about a sponsored walk?' Paddy asked. 'Don't tell me, Phyllis – you're trekking across the Sahara for Age Concern. I wouldn't put anything past you.'

'Perhaps next year.' Gran laughed, and settled down on a sofa. Paddy perched beside her on the sofa arm. I hoped Gran didn't think we were staying, now Paddy had turned up. 'Talk to our Eve. I think you're exactly what she needs.'

'Not what *I* need,' I corrected, not liking Paddy's speculative look. 'But a group of local pensioners might. We're holding a sponsored walk to raise money to buy a new minibus for Gran's nursing home. All donations are welcome. I have my sponsorship form here.'

I plucked it out of my handbag and passed it over to him. It wasn't an impressive total so far: I hadn't even reached £50 and Tina had donated £20 of that. I hadn't intended to involve Paddy at all, but if he could afford to stay at the Fairlie, I decided he could afford a decent sponsorship. He studied the form for longer than seemed necessary, tapping the pen against his leg, before scrawling something down and handing it back. He had matched Tina's donation.

'Thanks,' I said. 'Very generous.'

I hadn't actually meant to be sarcastic – although it was disappointing that a TV star could only contribute as much as a teacher – but perhaps Paddy took my response that way, because the look he gave me appeared, even to my biased mind, genuinely apologetic.

'I'm sorry, funds are tight this month ...'

'Yes, of course.' Hardly surprising that funds were tight if he had splashed out on a weekend at the Fairlie. What had Gran said? People stayed here who had more money than sense. Lucky Paddy to be in that position.

'Is there another way I can help? You said something about opening the walk?'

'We can't afford to pay. We're trying to raise money, not spend it.'

'I don't need to be paid. I'll do it gladly if it helps Phyllis.'

There was reproach in Paddy's voice as he reached out to take Gran's hand. She smiled at him with obvious pleasure. They always had got on well, and Paddy's affection for Gran was the one thing I had never doubted, even looking back through my bitter-tinted glasses. I softened – or perhaps I hardened, as the practical advantages of having Paddy on board took precedence over everything else. He would be a draw, I couldn't deny it, and raising money was the priority, by whatever means. I could put my own feelings aside, couldn't I?

'Are you free on the third Sunday of May?' I asked. I even managed what I hoped was a friendly smile. Cheryl gave me an encouraging thumbs-up from behind Paddy. I mentally gritted my teeth. 'The weekend before the Bank Holiday? If you are, you'd be welcome to come along and officially start the walk.'

'Would I be expected to finish this walk as well? How far are you going? You crack a mean pace ...' Paddy was tapping at his phone as he spoke but looked up at these words, smiling as if we had a shared joke. I didn't respond. Our days of shared jokes were in the past. I didn't want to start creating new ones. 'I can do that day. I'd be happy to help. We'll get you that minibus, Phyllis. What are you going to do with it? An epic road trip? I might be tempted to tag along.'

'I'm not sure you could keep up with our pace ...' Gran cackled with laughter and nudged Paddy's arm, although he needed no encouragement to join in. It was a joy to see her having fun. 'What are you doing up here, anyhow? And staying in this fancy place! Have all those parties in London got too much for you?' She shot a mischievous look my way and I braced myself. 'You're not after our Eve again, are you? Only, you'll have your work cut out to win her back after ...'

'Shall we get going?' I said, not letting Gran finish the statement, or letting Paddy give the inevitable denial. I hardly needed more humiliation from him. 'You won't want to be late for the pork goulash.'

Paddy jumped up and held out a hand to help Gran off the sofa.

'You are one of the reasons I'm here,' he said, glancing at me. 'I've come to have another look at that field near the river, where there was the possible bowl barrow. If we get the go-ahead for a new series of the TV show, it might make an interesting location.'

'Have you found anything?' The question slipped out before I could think better of it.

'We had a look through the local archives today. There don't seem to be any aerial photos of that field, or anything else that could help. We'll go on site tomorrow and have a proper look, see if it's worth doing more detailed investigations. I've got a good feeling about this one.'

I had missed this; not Paddy, although his enthusiasm was infectious, and was one of the things – beside the obvious – that had made him so attractive to me. No, it was the subject I had missed: the glory of the unknown that lay all around us; the excitement of the discoveries that were waiting to be made; the life of uncertainty, not routine. And as I stood idle, listening to Paddy's words, the regret flew in, soaring over the mental barricades I had tried to construct. This could have been my life. And remembering Gran's words from earlier on, I wondered: could this still be my life?

'Why don't you come along tomorrow?' Paddy said. 'You always had a better eye for detail than I did.'

Gran gave me an encouraging nudge. Paddy smiled. Despite

everything, despite Paddy's involvement, I was tempted – tempted so far that I had started to return his smile, on the brink of accepting. But then a stylish redhead sashayed across the reception from the direction of the stairs leading to the bedrooms, making an undoubted beeline for our group. Tall, slim, young and dressed for a night filled with cocktails and glamour, there was only one of us she could belong to.

'Hey, Paddy, sorry to keep you waiting. I felt like I had dust in places you wouldn't believe ...'

She smiled prettily at us all and my heart bled for her. She was barely older than Caitlyn; barely older than I had been when I had smiled at Paddy in the way she was doing now. I hoped he was going to be kinder to her.

'Eve, this is Posy, my research assistant.'

'Good to meet you.' I managed a smile, managed to resist the urge to pull her to one side and give her a warning. Research assistant, indeed! How stupid did he think I was? I'd never enjoyed weekends away in a luxury hotel when I'd acted as a research assistant. Gran was looking Posy up and down, and I dreaded to think what gem she might be about to utter. I took her arm and steered her towards the door.

'I hope you have a successful day tomorrow,' I said to Paddy. There was no way I would be joining them, playing gooseberry. My feelings for him might have faded long ago, but that didn't mean I would choose to see him with a new girlfriend, sharing the tasks we had once carried out together. 'I'll be in touch about the walk.'

The Easter holidays were over far too soon, and not only because I had to return to school and endure working with Jo Blair. It was also time for my mum's regular visit, not something I was looking forward to, especially without Caitlyn to keep conversation flowing this year. My mum ran a bar in Spain with her partner, Juan, and visited us twice a year: once in November, to deliver Christmas presents after the half-term break, and once in spring, when the Easter rush was over and before the summer season took off. Each year she arrived with enough luggage and duty-free to last a month, never mind a week, and her skin was browner, her skirts shorter and her bangles noisier than the previous visit.

She had arrived on Sunday and by Tuesday, as I let myself in after work, I barely recognised the house as my own. Magazines, nail files, flimsy cardigans ... there was clutter and paraphernalia over every surface. The kitchen bore the brunt of it, with dirty mugs and used teabags mounting up by the sink, and an army of pre-mixed cans of gin and tonic standing in line in my fridge. It felt more like living with a rebellious teenager than it ever had when Caitlyn was here.

'You're late,' Mum said, wandering into the kitchen wearing what looked suspiciously like pyjamas. She leant past me to grab a can of gin from the fridge, while I took out a carton of fruit juice. 'I thought the benefits of a school job were the short hours and the holidays.'

'Only people who don't work in a school believe that.' I smiled, trying to push aside reflections on a bad day at work; Jo Blair was hell-bent on trimming the budget for each department, and had hidden away in her office while furious department heads vented their anger on me. Thank goodness it was Tuesday – a vigorous run was exactly what I needed now.

'I thought we could have a Chinese tonight,' Mum said, flapping a piece of paper at me. 'I found this takeaway menu in the drawer.'

I felt a pang of loss; it was from Caitlyn's favourite takeaway.

'We'll have to eat late,' I said. 'I'm going running tonight.'

'But it's raining. Can't you give it a miss tonight? I'm only here for a week.'

'I can't. I lead the group.' I had considered – for the best part of thirty seconds – whether I should drop out this week, but had soon decided that it was too good an excuse to avoid another evening in with Mum. We had run out of things to say in the first couple of hours together, and our evenings passed making banal conversation on even more banal television shows. Mum had always been closer to Faye, and I had been closer to my dad. The wrong parent and the wrong child had been left to rub along together, making a strange imbalance in our family. The tragic events that should have pushed us together had somehow emphasised our differences and pulled us further apart.

'I'll make it a short run tonight,' I offered, my conscience prodding me to compromise. 'We run from The White Hart, so it will only take me a few minutes to get home.'

'The White Hart?' I should have known Mum would prick her ears up at that. 'The hotel on the market square? Do they serve food? I could wait for you there and we could eat afterwards. I'll put it on expenses at work. It's research, isn't it?'

It was a miracle that the bar in Spain was still trading if Mum spent all the profit on this type of 'research', but I agreed to the change of plan; Lexy would be grateful for the business, and it would make a change from another night in front of the television. It turned out even better than I'd anticipated: a few of the other runners had decided to take advantage of Lexy's discount on food for the running group and stayed for a meal, so we pushed a few tables together and all squashed up with each other. Mum was in her element – she loved a crowd – and she had enough tales of Spanish life to keep everyone entertained for weeks, never mind one night.

'Your mum's a hoot,' Lexy said, as I passed her on the way back from the ladies. 'I hope I'm like that at her age. You must miss her when she's in Spain.'

I smiled and nodded, because how could I explain? I missed the old mum, the one who had had a husband and two children. The woman at the table in front of me was an exaggerated version of her former self. Mum had always been loud and lively, in many ways the opposite of my quiet, studious father. Not many people would notice the difference now, but I did. I noticed the laughs that were too loud, too long; the smile that was artificially bright; the larger-than-life costume that shrouded the person she had once been. There was no universal guidebook for dealing with grief; she had chosen her way, and I had chosen mine. It was unfortunate that we had each chosen a way that sat uneasily with the other's.

Nevertheless, as the other members of the running group gradually wandered home, and it was only the two of us left, the atmosphere was less cautious than it usually was between us; perhaps we had both been reminded of who and how we used to be.

'They're a nice bunch,' Mum said, shifting from her seat across the table to sit on the bench next to me. 'It will do you good to mix more. Caitlyn said you were getting out and about at last.'

'Caitlyn?' I repeated, homing in on the most important part of this speech. 'When did you speak to her?'

'Last week. She looked so well ...' Mum stopped and swigged the dregs of her wine, not meeting my eye.

'You saw Caitlyn last week? Where? Did she visit you in Spain? She told me she couldn't have time off until August.'

'Don't blame Caitlyn. I made a surprise visit to Paris on my way here.' Mum shrugged. 'I miss her.'

I couldn't argue with that. I missed her too, but we had agreed that I wouldn't visit her in these first few months. She wanted to settle in and not risk feeling homesick, or so she had said.

'How was she?' I put aside my resentment at Mum's sneaky visit; there would be time for that later. 'Is she eating? Are her employers kind? Is she happy?'

'Very.' That brought me comfort, of sorts, but not much happiness. If she was happy, there was no chance of her returning home. But how could I not prefer her to be happy in Paris rather than unhappy at home with me? It was the conundrum of parents everywhere, I supposed.

'And Luc is gorgeous,' Mum continued. 'Have you seen him? And that accent ...' She fanned her face, laughing.

'Who's Luc?'

'Caitlyn's boyfriend.' Mum stopped the fanning and pulled a comedy grimace. 'She hasn't mentioned him, has she? That's children for you. Always needing their little secrets.'

And then her grimace faded, because there was so much subtext in those words, we couldn't fail to feel it. Caitlyn wasn't my child; and Faye had kept more than little secrets. I picked up my bag, deciding to leave further questioning about Caitlyn until I was less tired, and Mum was less drunk.

'Hang on,' Mum said, putting out her arm to stop me rising. 'There are things you've not told me either. I went to visit your gran today.'

I couldn't judge where this was leading from Mum's face. She'd had years of practice at holding her alcohol, and could down vast quantities of gin and still maintain an inscrutable poker face. What could Gran have told her? I didn't have secrets, and if I did, I would have trusted Gran not to share them with Mum; Gran had never entirely approved of her daughter-in-law, never believing that she was good enough for my dad. So what could Mum mean? Unless ... my heart sank. Gran wouldn't have mentioned Paddy, would she?

Careful not to fall into a trap, I pitched a casual question. 'What did Gran tell you?'

'That you weren't happy at work. That you were having problems with your new boss. You've not mentioned any of that to me. I thought you enjoyed working there.'

'I used to. But ...' I shrugged. The truth was, my motivation had been diminishing ever since Caitlyn left. One of the main reasons for taking the job had been to keep an eye on her. When she had gone on to college, there had still been the satisfaction of working with friends, and of knowing I was invaluable to Mrs Armstrong. There was no pleasure now in helping Jo Blair, and though she was only in the post as an interim measure, lately I had begun to feel stifled, not satisfied, and to dread the thought that this was all there was for another thirty years ... More worries to be put off for another day.

Mum drew her handbag onto her knee and took out a folded paper.

'Here,' she said, pushing the paper into my hand. 'It seems like a good time to give you this. Call it an early birthday present.'

Intrigued, I unfolded the paper. It was a cheque, made out to me, for £50,000.

'I'd have been happy with a new pair of trainers ...' I looked at Mum, too overwhelmed to take it in. Mystified too; she had always led me to believe that the bar turned a meagre profit. 'Where did this come from?'

'Your dad.' I must have looked even more mystified, because Mum hurried on. 'You know he was good with money. He started savings schemes as soon as I was pregnant, especially so you'd have a windfall when you were forty. He thought it would be a midlife treat.'

We were both silent while that sank in. Forty hadn't been the middle of Dad's life. Faye hadn't even made it close to that age. My hand shook, and I thrust the cheque back towards Mum.

'Is this mine?' I asked. 'Or ours?'

'Yours.' Mum clasped my hand, briefly. 'Faye's fund will go to Caitlyn.'

I nodded. That was right; that was what I would have wanted.

'Consider it your inheritance,' Mum carried on, 'because I can't promise there'll be much else. And it's better to have it now, while it can make a difference.'

'What am I supposed to do with it?' It was a question for myself as much as Mum. This was life-changing money. But did I want to change my life? And if so, in what way? I'd had no idea about Dad's savings schemes. I couldn't even begin to process this.

'Whatever you want,' Mum replied. 'Build a conservatory. Buy a fancy car. Go on a luxury holiday. Take a career break.' She took hold of my hand again, and squeezed it. 'Use it. Enjoy it. Just don't let it fester away in the bank, waiting for a rainy day that might never come. We know more than most that life's too short to waste a moment.'

* * *

Mum had been in bed for over an hour when I crept out to the garage in the dark. I couldn't sleep. Usually the evening run tired me out, so I had no trouble dropping off, but tonight too many thoughts were battering my head to permit any chance of rest.

I switched on the overhead light and went straight to the old wardrobe that had stood at the back of the garage since we had moved here. I pulled open the door for the first time in years and considered the contents. There was my spade, still with some dried topsoil clinging defiantly to the edge. Next to it stood a tower of assorted-sized buckets, used to carry away rubbish or any interesting finds on a dig.

A large rucksack lay on the wardrobe shelf. I plucked it down, the texture of the canvas between my fingers instantly evoking memories of the days when this bag had been my constant companion. I unfastened the buckles and reached inside, taking out the objects I found: a foam mat for kneeling on; pegs, twine, measuring tape and compass for laying out a site to form a grid of digging areas; paintbrushes and a four-inch trowel that made up my basic excavation tools. I held the trowel in my hand, reacquainting myself with its weight and feel, but it was hardly necessary; my hand reconnected with it as if it were a fifth finger or a second thumb. It was where it belonged.

In a side pocket of the rucksack, I found my old camera, so old that it took 35mm film rather than being digital; there was film in it, twenty-eight of the frames used. What would they show? Who might they show? I pulled out the notebook that accompanied it. I had recorded everything in here, every detail of a dig from first arrival onwards, noting the times and the weather conditions, sketching each find and listing each photograph I had taken.

I flicked through the book until I found the last page I'd

written on. It had been the dig in Kent, of course: a glorious two-week break we had taken late in the summer after graduating university, before we had knuckled down and filled our time with as many jobs as we could fit in, to raise the money we needed to travel. As I held the book in my hand, I could feel again the sun's warmth on the top of my head, smell the heat on our skin and see the wildflowers carpeting the woods that had adjoined the fields where the dig was taking place. And there was the list of the photographs I would find if I ever chose to develop the film, right down to number twenty-eight, which simply read, 'Paddy ▯'.

But next to my writing there was something else, something I hadn't written and hadn't seen before. A thick black asterisk marked the page, followed by the letters P.T.O. and, in case that wasn't clear enough, a wiggly arrow snaked its way to the edge of the page. I knew the writing, knew the style, knew only one person could have done this, but I was still unable to resist. I turned the page, and found what I was presumably supposed to find the next time I went on a dig: the time that had never come. Filling the next page was a sketch of a man in Viking costume and helmet but with Paddy's face, a man who was down on his knees and offering up a heart in his outstretched hands.

I leant against the wardrobe, absorbing every detail. He had always been a skilled cartoonist: a few quick strokes of the pen and he could create a wonderfully clear picture. And this picture was clear – but the message behind it wasn't. What had he meant? Was it just a quick sketch, dashed off as a surprise to make me smile next time I opened the book? Or had it been intended as something more? The man on bended knee, offering his heart – it could be interpreted in a particular way ...

This must have been drawn only a few months before Faye

had died, and before Paddy had left. Had I misunderstood him that day when we shared lunch on the hill? Had my assumption been wrong, that Paddy had gone because he didn't love me?

I snapped the book shut and a puff of dust and old earth blew into the air – an appropriate metaphor, I thought, because everything in that book was old and forgotten now. I wouldn't think about it; there was no point thinking about it. So Paddy had drawn a romantic picture – whatever he had felt in that moment was consigned to history when he walked out on me and Caitlyn. I had probably already given the sketch more thought than he had done at the time. I couldn't let my heart be stirred by this; one good gesture could never outweigh the bad.

I put everything back in the rucksack and returned it to the shelf, but I knew, without having to think about it, that my decision had been made. It wouldn't be another seventeen years before I looked at these things again. Maybe not even seventeen weeks. I switched off the garage light and returned to the house, to locate the details that Caitlyn had sent me about digs taking place over the summer holidays. Paddy's sketch wasn't the most important thing I had found tonight. I felt as if I had found myself.

Chapter 11

It was a perfect day for the sponsored walk up Winlow Hill: a light breeze propelled the occasional white cloud across a pale blue sky, and the temperature was predicted to be pleasant without being too hot for the climb. I rose early and gazed out of my bedroom window at the hill, peaceful now as it glistened in the early morning sun, and hoped that in a few hours it would be swarming with people. We had worked so hard on this event; it had to be a success.

There were several routes to the summit of the hill, some more of a challenge than others, and we had chosen the easiest one for today's event, to encourage as many families as possible to join in. A public footpath led from Inglebridge town centre and across a farmer's field, which gave access through a kissing gate to a wide track that meandered up the hill. The farmer had allowed us to use the field as the official starting point of the walk, and when I arrived Winston was already there, chatting with the St John Ambulance crew we had asked to attend, just in case, and supervising the positioning of tables around the field.

Our pleas for sponsorship had proved more successful than we could have imagined, especially – and I hated to admit it – since word had got out that a certain celebrity would be opening the event. The supermarket had provided bottles of water, and other local businesses had given a donation in exchange for a stand advertising their services. Even before the sponsorship money from the walkers was added, we had made a decent start towards our target.

By the time the walkers were beginning to arrive, the field had taken on the appearance of a village show. Stalls had sprung up in a circle starting at the kissing gate, advertising everything from insurance to range cookers to funeral plans – perhaps not in the best of taste, considering we were raising funds for old folk, but they had offered a decent donation that we couldn't refuse. Cheryl had persuaded the Fairlie House Hotel to contribute, and would be tempting walkers with samples of afternoon tea, and the local vet had a stall offering dog treats for the canine participants. I circled slowly, taking it all in. It was fantastic – well beyond anything I had imagined from the first moment of suggesting the sponsored walk – and I couldn't help feeling a flutter of pride that we had pulled this off, and that the Inglebridge community had rallied round with such enthusiasm.

'Hey, you didn't mention it was a big event. I'd have dressed up if I'd known.'

I turned round. Paddy was right behind me, wearing jeans, a fleece and scuffed walking boots, and a grin that was so distracting he could have been naked, and no one would have noticed. Not that it distracted me, of course.

'You're just in time,' I said. 'The local newspaper is here and would like an interview. Please mention The Chestnuts as many times as you can. They need a seventeen-seater minibus. If you can get that in, we may find a garage who'll do us a good deal for the publicity.'

He clicked his heels and gave a mock salute.

'Yes, ma'am. Any clues as to where the reporter is?'

'She's over there, handing out balloons, under the gazebo that says *North Lancashire Express*. And if that isn't enough of a clue, she's blonde and attractive. I'm sure your homing instincts will guide you to her.'

Grinning even more broadly, he ambled off towards the stand I pointed at and I headed off in the opposite direction, to find Winston and to make sure everything was in hand. It was a relief to see a steady stream of walkers beginning to approach from the direction of the town centre. We had timed the walk to officially start at 10.30 a.m. so that it would fit in with a picnic lunch along the way, and although we couldn't stop people setting off sooner or later than that, it looked like a good number were aiming for the official time. I tried not to think that it was the Paddy effect, but it was impossible not to notice that a small crowd was gathering round the newspaper stall where he was now chatting to the reporter.

I turned away and waved as I spotted the much more welcome sight of Gran being pushed across the field in a wheelchair by one of the carers from The Chestnuts. I hurried over.

'This is cheating,' I said, bending to kiss her cheek. 'You can't do a sponsored walk in that.'

'I don't know why they insisted I needed it at all,' Gran said, standing up and giving the wheelchair a disgusted poke with her finger. 'I told them I don't need wheels while I have two working feet, but would they listen? Would they heck. There was none of this health and safety nonsense in my day. The world's gone soft.'

Gran took a few steps forward and stumbled on the uneven ground. I grabbed her arm.

'Happen I should have chosen some better shoes,' she conceded. 'I've borrowed an outfit from Mrs Pike again and her feet aren't as dainty as mine. Perhaps I'd better not get them muddy.' She summoned the wheelchair with a wave of her hand and sank back down into it. The carer gave me a wink and I tried not to laugh.

'You are looking dolled up,' I said. She was wearing a lilac dress and matching floral jacket, which was certainly more understated than the neon pink outfit she'd chosen to wear to the Fairlie. 'You didn't need to make so much effort.'

'At my age, you make the most of every occasion you can. Who knows if there'll be another? Besides, I want to look my best for the photos.'

'What photos?' I asked, as we started heading towards the stalls. 'We haven't hired a photographer.'

'But the press are here, aren't they? It stands to reason that they'll want to meet me. I've been chosen to represent The Chestnuts.'

Chosen? I would have liked to have seen how that vote went: Gran putting herself forward and no one daring to disagree, at a guess.

'Is Paddy here yet?' Gran tried to see, but the increasing crowd was getting in her way. 'How am I meant to see anything from down here? I need a periscope. Don't they know who I am? This thing should come with a horn to shift people out of the way.'

I was still laughing when we reached the newspaper stand, and Paddy caught my smile and returned it at full strength.

'Never mind me,' he said to the journalist, who seemed to be hanging off his every word – practically drooling. It hadn't taken him long to reel her in with his fake charm. 'Here's the real star of today, our VIP visitor from The Chestnuts. Come on, Phyllis, I'm sure you'll have a thing or two to say.'

He bent down to kiss Gran's cheeks and, in one smooth move, took her hands and lifted her to her feet. I stepped forward, anxious in case she stumbled again, but there was no need; Paddy clamped his arm round her back and they posed for photographs like a pair of newlyweds, with Gran giving a running commentary between each smile as to exactly why The Chestnuts needed a minibus. She laid it on so thick, there wouldn't be a dry eye in the county if the newspaper reported her accurately.

'And let's have a couple in the chair,' she said, directing the photo shoot as she did everything else. 'If I try to look like a frail invalid, we might get a bit of sympathy cash.'

Paddy obligingly crouched at her side for more photos until the photographer and journalist pronounced themselves satisfied. Just in time: a quick glance at my watch showed me that it was almost 10.30 a.m., and a substantial crowd had gathered in the field, a greater number of participants than I could ever have hoped would turn up. There must have been several hundred people waiting to do the walk, some faces I recognised from school and around town, but many more who were total strangers, and I looked from Gran to Paddy, wondering whether charity or celebrity had been the greater draw.

'Speech time?' Paddy asked, and I simply nodded, too thankful that the day had turned out well to bother coming up with the sarcastic or bitter retort that I might otherwise have done. He made his way to the kissing gate where Winston was waiting, and proceeded to give what I had to concede was the perfect speech: short, warm, witty and with a charming reference to Gran as a representative of The Chestnuts. She rose from her chair to acknowledge the applause, and then Paddy strode through the kissing gate and started the walk.

'You missed a trick there,' Gran said, settling back down. 'Never mind sponsorship. You should have made him stand at the gate and charge for a kiss as folk went through. We could have made enough for a Mercedes minibus.'

'He's not that good,' I said, and could have bitten my tongue out when Gran gave me a saucy look. 'Not that I really remember ...' I added.

'It's no wonder you're living on your own, if a man like that's not good enough for you. I'm never going to be grandmother-of-the-bride if you're so fussy.'

'It's not fussy to want someone reliable. Someone who'll stick around. Besides,' I continued, although the point was coming too late, and I was conveniently ignoring Rich's existence. 'I don't need a man. I'm fine on my own.'

'If you say so.'

Gran stayed to watch the first tranche of walkers set off along the track to the hill, then returned to The Chestnuts to report back and no doubt to regale the other residents with tales of her impending newspaper fame. Winston was leading the way and I had planned to bring up the rear, although I'd definitely drawn the short straw, as it would be frustrating to amble along at such a slow pace behind the toddlers. I had assumed that Paddy would have doubled back and gone by now, only pretending to start the walk but not actually going through with it, so it was annoying as the crowd thinned to see a familiar mop of curly dark hair and to realise that not only was he still here, but he was coming towards me as well.

'I thought you'd gone,' I said, sounding very much like Gran with my grumbling tone.

'And duck out of the walk? Phyllis has sponsored me 50p if I can haul myself up and down the hill. I've been training specially. Look at the mud on these boots. That's real Yorkshire dirt, you know.'

'You could have bought them yesterday and stepped straight into a muddy puddle,' I said. But I couldn't resist a smile – his boots looked new but well enough broken in to suggest that they had seen some recent use. 'Don't let me hold you back if you're raring to go.'

'You're okay. I can't have you providing the rearguard on your own.'

'I'm not on my own. I'm waiting for someone.'

'Don't tell me Phyllis has just popped back to put on her Wonder Woman outfit before she launches an assault on this hill? Nothing would surprise me where she's concerned.'

The affection in his voice was obvious, and his smile was warm – dangerously warm. It was a relief to see Rich shuffling through the tail end of the crowd, and I waved at him with a degree of enthusiasm I'd probably rarely shown before.

'Here's Rich! You see, I'm not on my own. You can get off now.'

Paddy didn't budge. Rich shambled up to us, and as he bent down to kiss me, I struggled not to recoil at the stench of stale alcohol.

'Do you want some water before we start?' I asked. I didn't rate his chances of making it up the hill in this state. We'd be lucky to keep up with the toddlers. 'There are some bottles on the table over there.'

'Keep it down, Eve. My head's thumping.'

'Bad night?'

'Great night.' Rich grinned. 'The boys were on top form.'

Judging from the smell, the grey skin, the rasping voice and the fact he was wearing sunglasses, I guessed he used 'boys' to mean his friends rather than his children.

'Oh! Well, a blast of fresh air is exactly what you need to make you feel better. Shall we go?'

'Nah, I'm not going up there. I'm not up to it today. I shouldn't be out by rights, but I thought I ought to come along and give you some moral support.'

'Thanks. That was thoughtful.' I tried to turn my back on Paddy, who was still shamelessly hanging around, listening to this conversation. 'Are you going to be all right on your own?'

'Yeah, there's a match on at twelve so I'll put my feet up for a bit while that's on.' He was already drifting away. 'Come round later if you fancy it.' His cheek moved as he winked behind his sunglasses, and then he was gone.

After a few moments spent reining in my humiliation, I spun back to Paddy.

'Stop it,' I said.

'Stop what?'

'Disapproving. It's none of your business.'

'You're right, it's not.' I nodded and took a step away towards the kissing gate. 'Except ...'

I stopped. 'Except what?'

'Well now, he's a bit boorish for you, isn't he?'

'Boorish?' The word was so apt that it momentarily silenced me. Even after a few seconds to consider, my response was weak. 'He wasn't at his best today.'

'You're telling me. Seriously – you're in a relationship with him? What do you talk about? Does he live with you and Caitlyn?'

'No. And that is even less of your business, don't you think?'

I strode off across the field, hoping to put some distance between us, but it was no good. His strides were longer than mine and he soon caught up.

'Are you in love with him?'

'None of your business.' I wished I hadn't repeated that. It was tantamount to a 'no', wasn't it? Why couldn't I have said yes? It would have been the simple answer. It would have stopped this inquisition. But it wouldn't have been the truth. I knew what love was like, and it wasn't what I felt for Rich; I knew what it was like, because of the man now striding along at my side. He was the only man I had ever loved, until I had decided that I was better off without love; that love was too closely entwined with loss for me to want it again. I had chosen Rich precisely because while we had fun together, there was no chance of me falling in love with him.

'I didn't realise you had a significant other,' Paddy said.

'Thanks. Is it so unlikely?'

We had reached the kissing gate and Paddy waited, letting me go first. I turned round, holding the gate shut between us.

'No,' he said. 'Not at all.' He gestured to my left hand, resting on the top of the gate. 'But you don't wear a ring.'

'Don't be so conventional. Marriage isn't everything. You should know that. You disposed of yours easily enough, didn't you?'

He was better at this game than I was. He didn't spit out a hasty, ill-thought-out answer as I would have done. He didn't give an answer at all, or not a verbal one. But his face ... I couldn't miss the pain that flashed across it, or doubt that it was real. I pulled the gate towards me, and let him through.

It was wonderful to see so many people walking up the hill and enjoying the fresh air and exercise. The walkers covered the whole spectrum from serious hikers with their Gore-Tex boots and hiking poles, to enthusiastic but unfit young families in their trainers and wellies, who were puffing at the first hint of an incline. Children and dogs ran loose, enjoying their freedom, and chatter and laughter filled the air. I wished Caitlyn could have joined in, and that she could have been at my side instead of Paddy. But I had to admit, as we tramped up the hill, overtaking some of the worst dawdlers, his presence wasn't as irritating as I would have expected. He gathered a lot of attention – fingers pointed in his direction, greetings shouted his way as if everyone knew him, snatched photographs that I ducked to avoid when I could – but he didn't milk it as I thought he might. He accepted it with charm and good grace, smiling and waving back, but he never left my side. His attention was all mine – if I wanted it. It was only seventeen years too late.

As we neared the top of the hill, the grass was filled with groups who had stopped on the way up or down to enjoy a picnic with a view. I carried on to the peak and then paused to admire the panorama. There was much to admire. This was one of the highest summits in the area, and was one of my favourite places to stop and stare; one of the few places where I found contentment in being idle. Inglebridge town centre looked like a model village from up here, with the river snaking through like a piece of sparkling blue thread; over to the east were the Pennines and the Yorkshire peaks, and to the north-west the beautiful mountains of the Lake District rose up to meet the sky.

'This is quite something,' Paddy said. He turned round slowly, taking in the view in each direction. It was breezier here on the summit, and dark curls blew around his face. His cheeks were pink from the exertion and the sun, and his smile sparkled. He looked like a poster boy for the outdoor life, glowing with health and vitality. He could hardly have presented a starker contrast to Rich's appearance earlier.

'I can see why you chose to live here,' he continued. My smile dimmed; there had been so much more to the decision than the scenery. 'Have you been happy here? Was Caitlyn happy?'

'Yes.' There could be so much more to that answer too, but I chose not to go there. Happiness was like one of the shimmering bubbles that Caitlyn used to love to blow from soap; something to enjoy while it lasted, but too fragile to withstand a curious finger exploring it. Because if I thought too deeply, poked about in the past, how could I ever be sure that we had found the best possible happiness? Who knew if we might have been happier living somewhere else? What if we might have been happier living with Mum – or even with Paddy?

Looking away from the view and focusing on the hill again, on the here and now, I spotted Tina and her husband Graham, sitting with their backs against a rock, starting their picnic.

'I'm going to join Tina for lunch,' I said. I meant it as a goodbye, not an invitation, but Paddy trailed along behind me and within minutes was sitting next to Tina, laughing uproariously.

'Let's pool our resources,' Tina said. She started pulling Tupperware boxes and foil packages out of a large cool bag. 'I've got sandwiches, sausage rolls, pasta salad, Scotch eggs ...'

I added my contribution: chicken wraps, raw vegetables and a stash of fruit. We all looked at Paddy.

'Sorry!' He held up his hands and laughed. 'I have nothing to offer but wit, charm and conversation. Take pity on a starving man who matched Eve's pace up the hill, won't you?'

'That pace was hardly enough to break a sweat,' I said. 'But if you're so hungry, you can have Rich's share of the vegetables.' I pushed a tub of carrot and cucumber sticks towards him. He laughed.

'Have a Scotch egg,' Tina offered. 'I've catered for an army. I'll even give you one of my beers if you don't mind lager.'

'You're a marvellous woman, Tina.'

He glugged from his bottle of beer and Tina watched him with wide-eyed fascination that seemed wholly inappropriate in front of her husband. I nudged her knee.

'So what happened to Rich?' she asked, tearing her gaze from Paddy, but making me wish I hadn't distracted her. 'You said he was coming. Did he cry off?'

'He did come,' I said, avoiding Paddy's gaze. 'Only he decided he wasn't up for a walk after all.'

'Hungover, was he?' Tina laughed. 'You really are the odd couple. He must drink at least your share of booze. I'm surprised you haven't tried to convert him to your healthy ways.'

'I don't impose my lifestyle choices on others,' I replied primly. Unfortunately, my statement was ruined by a grinning Paddy, rattling the tub of vegetable strips in front of my face. 'He has sponsored me for the walk,' I added.

'I saw. I filled in the form after him. Two quid! Mean git. Not even the cost of a pint. I hope he's saving up to get you something special for your birthday.'

'Maybe.' Probably not. I didn't think Rich knew when my birthday was, let alone that it was a significant one this year.

'It's the big four-zero in August, isn't it?' Paddy said. 'What do you have planned?'

'Nothing much. I hope Mum and Caitlyn will come over. We could take Gran out for a meal.' I shrugged. It probably sounded pathetic in comparison to whatever adventure he had undertaken for his fortieth last December. But I couldn't imagine a better present than having my entire family under the same roof.

'I had a quiet one with Mam and Dad too,' he said, and when he smiled at me, for a strange moment it felt as if we had been stripped back to the people we had been in the past; back to those early, innocent days when our studies and our families and our relationship were all that mattered.

'Have a chicken wrap,' I said, and thrusting some food at him I turned to talk to Tina.

Lunch passed quickly and far more pleasantly than I would have predicted. Paddy had always been a social chameleon, able to fit in with any group – something I had once admired rather than taking it as a warning of his duplicitous character. He more than delivered on his promise to provide wit, charm and conversation, and even I couldn't resist laughing as he skilfully parodied the celebrity world he had found himself part of.

After lunch, we wandered back down the hill in pairs. I selfishly grabbed Tina's arm, so we could walk together, and though I felt a pang of guilt at leaving Graham to Paddy, from the snatches of conversation blown our way it sounded like they were getting on well. The kissing gate that would return us to our starting point was in sight when a small girl in front of us, probably about the same age as Caitlyn had been when she came to live with me, stumbled and let go of the balloon that she must have carried safely up and down the hill. Her anguished cry echoed across the hillside, so raw that it stopped us all in our tracks.

All except one. It happened so fast that it was hard to process what actually occurred. There was a blur of movement running past me, a figure leaping in the air to catch the balloon before it blew away, a cry of pain and then silence as Paddy fell to the ground, cracking his head on a rock.

Chapter 12

I reached him first.

'Paddy?' I shook his shoulder, probably more roughly than I should have done. His eyes were closed and he wasn't moving. 'Paddy?' I shook him again, and at last he lifted his head and regarded me, a dazed look in his eyes. Already a lump had formed on his forehead, and a thin trickle of blood ran down the side of his face. He tried to sit up, but clutched the back of his leg with a groan of pain.

'What's the matter?' I asked, as he lay back down, moaning. 'Have you hurt your leg?'

'Jeez, Eve, full marks for observation. When did you get your medical degree?'

I forgave him the sarcasm, seeing the agony etched across his face. Sarcasm was good; sarcasm meant he was alive, and had all his wits about him. For a second, when I had seen him lying motionless on the ground ... I shut down that line of thought and called out to Tina.

'Can you ring Dr Gould?' I handed her my phone. 'He should be down on the field somewhere. Ask him to come quickly.'

Turning back to Paddy, I began to gently feel along his left leg. He groaned when my fingers reached his calf, but didn't shout out again.

'There's no obvious sign of a break,' I said. 'Is it your calf that hurts?'

'The calf and behind the knee. There was a pop when I jumped ...' He struggled up on to his elbows. 'Where's the little girl? I've got her balloon.'

Despite the pain, he was still clutching the string of the balloon. I looked around and spotted the child standing nearby, clinging on to her mum's hand. I took the balloon from Paddy and handed it over.

'Idiot,' I said, kneeling at Paddy's side again. 'What did you do that for? There are plenty more balloons at the newspaper stand.'

'But she wanted that one.' Paddy closed his eyes. 'She reminded me of Caitlyn.'

The confession surprised me. It had been so long; I hadn't expected him to still remember her with the affection that I heard in his voice. There was no time to dwell on that, because Dr Gould came hurrying up.

'What have we here then?' he asked. 'Nothing too serious, I hope?'

He smiled, and I moved aside. Dr Gould examined Paddy's head and leg and took a history, demonstrating why he was such a favourite at The Chestnuts with his calm, unflappable approach despite the curious crowd that was peering curiously over his shoulder. I caught sight of a phone pointed in Paddy's direction and shooed people away before any more photographs could be taken. Paddy might not shy away from publicity, but even he deserved better than having pictures of his agonised, blood-streaked face splashed across the internet.

'There's nothing broken,' Dr Gould said, leaning back as he finished his examination. 'I think it's just a calf strain – tennis leg, they call it, as it's quite common in tennis players when they leap around. It's more common in men in our age bracket.' I had to smother a laugh at that: grey-haired Dr Gould must have been at least fifteen years older than Paddy. 'We need to get some ice on it as soon as possible.'

'Tina will have some.' I beckoned her over. 'Do you have an ice pack in your cool bag?'

'Of course I do. I can't stand warm Scotch eggs.'

Borrowing Tina's ice pack and a tea towel that she was also mysteriously carrying in her cool bag, Dr Gould applied ice to Paddy's leg.

'You'll probably need to do this every hour, at least for the first day or two,' he said, rummaging in his bag and bringing out a prescription pad. 'I'll give you some anti-inflammatories and painkillers. You should wear a compression bandage during the day. The chemist in town is open until five today and they should have everything you need. The important thing is to rest your leg and keep it elevated as much as possible. The first forty-eight hours will be the worst, but you'll probably be limited in what you can do for the next week or two.' Dr Gould closed his bag and stood up. 'The cut on your head doesn't need stitches, but it was a nasty bump. Someone needs to stay with you for a few days to watch out for any signs of concussion – behavioural changes, memory problems, clumsiness. Go to A&E if you have any concerns.'

Dr Gould waved and wandered off. I could already see one huge problem that nothing in his medical bag could fix.

'How are you going to get home?' I asked. 'Did you drive here?' Paddy nodded. 'Where do you live? Still in London?'

'No. Near Ripon.'

'Really?' That surprised me. He had been brought up in

London, and I had assumed he would be enjoying the celebrity life in the capital, not hiding away in North Yorkshire. But that was good news: it was only a couple of hours away, and presumably someone could fetch him. Unless someone was already here? I hadn't given any thought to whether he was on his own or not. Perhaps Posy was waiting for him at the Fairlie, beautifying herself in the spa in readiness for his return. She'd be disappointed to see him arrive back in this state. She'd probably had more exciting plans for the weekend than applying ice packs to Paddy's leg.

'So can Posy come and pick you up?' I asked. 'Or did she travel with you today?'

'Posy?' Even under the grimace of pain, I could make out Paddy's puzzled frown. I hoped it wasn't a sign of forgetfulness already.

'Wasn't that her name? The girl at the hotel? Or have you moved on to someone else now?'

'Posy is my research assistant,' Paddy replied with pointed emphasis. 'Not my girlfriend, if that's what you're suggesting. Posy has had more luck recently than I have in finding one of those.' He managed a half-hearted smile. 'I live on my own, so there's no one to collect me. Anyway, I'm booked in to The White Hart.'

'Great!' I smiled in relief. 'I'm sure we can figure out a way to get you there. The St John Ambulance probably have a stretcher ...'

Tina was staring at me. I pretended not to notice, but I should have known better than to think that would work on a woman who could terrify a room full of teenagers into obedience.

'You can't leave him at The White Hart,' Tina said. 'You heard the Doc. He needs looking after.'

'I'm sure Lexy could be persuaded to offer room service ...'

'Meals, maybe, but regular application of ice packs and help to the loo is going beyond the usual room service menu. And how can she watch out for concussion? Only someone who knows him would spot any change in his behaviour.'

She paused. She didn't need to say any more. This was my responsibility, wasn't it? I had asked Paddy to get involved with the walk, and I had to deal with the consequences. But it was more than a sense of obligation. I couldn't stand aside, watch someone suffering and do nothing, whoever it was. Even if it was Paddy. I watched him grimace with pain as he tried to get up. Especially if it was Paddy.

'Okay,' I said to him, though I couldn't believe I was saying the words. 'You'll have to come and stay with me.'

I unlocked my front door and stepped into the silent, empty house. My man-free house – or it had been, until now. I reckoned I had about fifteen minutes to race round tidying up and getting it ready for the arrival of the first man ever to spend a night here since I had purchased it. And not just any man – Paddy, the very last man I would ever have expected or invited to stay here. How on earth had this happened?

I hadn't taken my car out this morning, and Tina had offered to drive Paddy here and to call at The White Hart for his bags and at the pharmacy for his medication, so that I could have some time to make the house decent. Not that it needed much: it wasn't a large house, and I didn't make much mess on my own. I had cleared away the breakfast bowl and glass, removed anything personal from the bathroom cabinet and fitted the single bed in the spare room with clean sheets by the time I heard car doors slamming on my drive.

When I opened the front door, Paddy was standing on the drive, resting on a pair of crutches as he gazed up at the house. What was he thinking? Was he making a judgement – feeling relief that he hadn't ended up here too? There was still too much pain in his face to tell.

'I had a stroke of inspiration!' Tina called, as she and Graham retrieved a couple of bags from the car. 'I called at The Chestnuts to see if they had any spare crutches. It was the least they could do after Paddy was injured fighting for their cause. Come on, let him in, he needs to get that leg up.'

I moved out of the doorway and, with a weary smile, Paddy hobbled over the threshold, turning left into the living room.

'Bags are in the hall,' Tina called. 'We'll leave you to it. Ring if you need anything!'

Before I could beg them to stay, the front door slammed shut and I was alone with Paddy.

'You'd better sit down,' I said, following him into the living room and pointing at the sofa. 'I've brought some spare pillows to rest your leg on. Is that elevated enough? I didn't know how high it needed to be. Have you taken your painkillers yet? Do you need a glass of water? Have you felt any dizziness?'

Paddy lowered himself on to the sofa while I gabbled a million questions at him.

'I'm sorry,' he said, ignoring everything I had said. 'I know this is weird. You don't want me here, I get that. I'm the last person you want to look after. I'll be gone as soon as I can.'

This speech disarmed me. I had expected him to be irreverent, cracking jokes about the situation. This thoughtful, perceptive Paddy was a more welcome guest than the one I had envisaged. But I wasn't sure that was a good thing; did I really want to welcome him? Bitterness was so much more straightforward;

more in line with what my head told me I should feel about him.

'It's fine,' I said. What else could I say, when the vitality I had noticed this morning had been replaced by the gaunt face of pain? 'But I'll be back at work tomorrow, so you'll be on your own all day.' I glanced at my watch. 'If you would rather go home, there's still time for me to drive you, and you could collect your car when you're better. Your mum and dad could come and look after you, couldn't they?'

'No, they ...' He stopped, shook his head. 'They've a lot on at the moment.'

There was something in the way he said that – a story lurking behind his words – but he was plainly not willing to tell it and I wasn't inclined to ask. Providing practical assistance was one thing, but I didn't have to hang around making conversation too, did I? Surely he would have a telephone for that?

I pottered to the kitchen and came back with a bag of frozen peas which I helped position under his leg.

'I have salmon in the freezer,' I said, moving the TV remote control to the table next to him.

'Perhaps we should stick with the peas for now. The fish could get messy and begin to smell ...'

It was a lame joke, and I should have been able to resist. I tried my best to resist. But the Paddy smile was there – tinged with pain, but still so much like the smile I used to love seeing, that my own smile flashed up in response before I could stop it.

'I meant we could have it for dinner,' I said, retreating to the doorway, as if by moving away I could stretch this connection that had flared up between us until it snapped. 'It won't be anything like as fancy as you're probably used to.'

'Don't cook. The least I can do is pay for a takeaway.'

'No! I mean, it's no problem.' Far from it. It was the perfect excuse to hide away in the kitchen and avoid spending more time with Paddy. I'd already calculated that I could probably get away with a couple of hours by myself for preparing dinner and cleaning up afterwards, if I worked very slowly. I might even be tempted to bake a cake to spin out the time. 'Is there anything you need before I go and make a start?'

It was still too early to cook, so I busied myself for the next half hour in cleaning the oven – a job that even I, with my loathing for being idle, usually found an excuse to put off. But then, over the quiet burbling of the radio, I heard Paddy call my name.

I ran into the living room, expecting to find that he'd fallen to the floor at the very least; instead he was lying in state on the sofa, holding out my mobile phone and with a broad smile chasing away the extremes of pain that had marred his face.

'Your phone rang,' he said.

'And you answered it?'

'Hey, I'm not good for much else tonight, so the least I can do is be your secretary ...' He waved the phone at me. 'Aren't you going to take it?'

'There's still someone there? Why didn't you say?'

I snatched the phone off him and put it to my ear as I hurried to the kitchen again. I hoped it wasn't Rich, inviting me over to his house. How on earth was I going to explain that I was sharing my house with a man tonight, when I had never allowed him to stay? But my concern was blown away when I heard Caitlyn laughing.

'Who was that?' she asked, and I could picture the amusement on her face as clearly as if she'd been here. My heart sank under the weight of missing her. 'He has the sexiest accent – after Luc's, of course. And what was that about him not being good for much tonight? What have you been up to? Do I need to send you a few more vouchers so you can carry on?'

'Stop it!' I said, unable to resist joining her laughter. I closed the kitchen door, and sank onto a chair. 'It's the celebrity who came to start the walk. He's had an injury, so he needs to rest for a while. I have to look after him.'

My vagueness didn't fool her for a second.

'How long is a while? Until after dinner?'

'Yes ...'

'Or is he so bad that he needs to stay the night?'

'I don't know what you're implying,' I said, my attempt at primness undermined by laughter. 'But you're wrong. It's all perfectly innocent. I've made up the spare room for him.'

'Really?' Caitlyn's laughter abruptly faded. 'He is spending the night? Is that safe? I don't think you should be staying on your own with a stranger. Who did you say it was?'

'Paddy Friel.'

'Oh yeah, the archaeology man. I've seen some of his programmes. I thought his voice sounded familiar.'

My reply caught in my throat. I had never mentioned Paddy to Caitlyn, and had hidden away in the loft all the photographs and mementoes of our time together; the things that, despite what had happened, I hadn't been able to bring myself to throw away. But I had often wondered whether she would have any memory of him.

'I mean, he seemed nice enough on TV,' she continued, 'but you never know. That might all be an act. He might actually be a psychopath, who'll creep up and kill you in your sleep.'

'He's not steady enough on his crutches for that yet.' I tried to laugh it off, but there was no ignoring her concern. I would have felt exactly the same if the situation had been reversed, and she knew it; I had drummed safety into her too well. I wrestled, but I had no choice other than to come clean.

'He's not really a stranger,' I admitted. 'I used to know him, way back.'

'Mum!' she shrieked. 'You knew Paddy Friel? When? How come you've never mentioned that?'

'It was a long time ago. There's nothing to mention.'

I could tell by her silence that she understood. Paddy was part of the life-before-her, the time I never spoke about. I had always told her that it didn't matter – that nothing interesting had happened in those years, that there had been nothing to miss when my circumstances changed. My real life began when she came to live with me. It was an artifice we had chosen to maintain long after she was too old to believe it – the Father Christmas effect applied to my history. I couldn't bear that she should ever think she had been a burden.

'Text me in the morning to let me know you're alive,' she said, and I was happy to agree and change the subject. She had actually telephoned to find out how the walk had gone, and I took great delight in laughing over Gran's exploits and monopolisation of the newspaper photographer.

'I'll forward you the link when it's in the paper,' I offered. 'Send her a postcard to say how smart she looked. She'll love that.'

'Will do. Did she model one of the T-shirts?'

'No, but there were lots of people wearing them.' The T-shirts featuring Caitlyn's design had proved so popular that we had had to order a second batch. 'I wish you could have been here.'

My attempt not to sound wistful clearly failed.

'I'm definitely coming back in August for your birthday. We bought cheap flights yesterday and saved a packet.'

'We?' I repeated carefully.

'Me and Luc ... you don't mind, do you? I said he could stay with us. And you can hardly object now you've broken the no-men-in-the-house rule ...'

That was the trouble with children, I reflected, as I got on with preparing dinner after finishing the call with Caitlyn. You spent never-ending amounts of time and money encouraging them to be smart, bright, confident young people, and then they harnessed all that cleverness and used it against you.

I carried our dinner in on trays, ignoring Paddy's half-hearted protest that he could probably move to the table: he wouldn't be aggravating his injury on my watch. The sooner he made a good enough recovery to go home, the better. I switched on the TV – dinner in front of the TV! – another rule broken, but needs must – hoping it would deter conversation, but the painkillers must have kicked in as Paddy was looking far perkier.

'So that was Caitlyn on the phone earlier,' he said, spearing a cherry tomato. 'She sounds so ... grown up.'

'Because she is. Children have a habit of doing that.'

'So she's away at uni?'

'No. She's working in Paris.'

'When did she start calling you Mum?'

I swallowed a piece of salmon, not tasting it at all.

'After a few months. Everyone at nursery had at least a mum or a dad. She wanted one too.'

I would never have suggested it myself; the last thing I had wanted to do was take Faye's place. But then I had gone to Caitlyn's first sports day at the nursery she had attended before we moved here. It was a delight to see her running round and enjoying herself, unbroken by everything that had happened in the previous few months. But the playing field had been full of children scampering round, showing off, shouting, 'Look at me!' as they clamoured for their parents' attention. Cries of 'Mummy' and 'Daddy' had flown through the air like a colony of wasps, impossible to ignore. And then Caitlyn had won the giant egg and spoon race, and without a moment's hesitation, she had run up and clutched my hand, squealing, 'Did you see me, Mummy?' It had stuck ever since.

Tears filled my eyes. My feelings couldn't be reconciled: the love and pride I had felt for Caitlyn in that moment, and the guilt that it was a moment I should never have known. It should have been Faye on that playing field, not me. It should have been Faye for every subsequent moment – the first day at school, the sports achievements, the exam celebrations, the first period, the first boyfriend, the sleepovers, the holidays – even chatting to Caitlyn in Paris this afternoon. None of those moments should ever have belonged to me.

Paddy was watching me. I brushed my tears away roughly.

'As long as you're staying here,' I said, my voice sounding unsteadier than I would have liked, 'there's one rule. No talking about the past – any part of it. And that includes not talking about Caitlyn.'

'But, Eve, there are things ...'

'No.' I put down my knife and fork and looked at him. 'I don't want to hear your explanation. It was all a long time ago. I can't quite stretch to forgiveness, but I won't waste any more energy on being bitter. You're just flesh and blood, and you put yourself first, like everyone else. I can't blame you for that.'

'But ...'

'Don't. Stop pushing it. It still hurts, you know? Not your

part in it, so much now – but Faye, and Dad, and being reminded about what we have all lost. Just seeing you here brings it all closer to the surface than it has been for years. I really don't want to talk about it, or to rake over the rights and wrongs of what happened back then. It doesn't matter any more. You're happy with your life and I'm happy with mine. Let's leave it like that.'

He looked at me then and, from the expression on his face, it seemed as if an internal battle was going on. I wondered, briefly, why it bothered him so much; why he seemed to have this overwhelming need to dig around in our past, and to justify what he had done.

'If that's what you want,' he said at last. He reached out and gently rubbed the back of my hand. 'The last thing I ever wanted to do was hurt you.'

Chapter 13

It was all very well to have a rule that there would be no talking about the past; I couldn't control my thoughts as easily. Paddy was in the same house, sleeping under the same roof as me for the first time in over seventeen years. The smell of him lingered on the sofa where he had sat all afternoon. I could hear the bed creak in the spare room next to mine as he tossed and turned in the night. As I lay alone in bed, struggling to sleep, it was impossible not to remember the past and our time together.

We had worked well – been a good match, despite the awful circumstances in which our relationship had started. I had blossomed under his influence, finally lured out of the shadow cast by Faye, by having to go through life following in the footsteps of an older sister who dazzled everyone. Being the 'clever one' had sometimes seemed a small prize compared to what Faye had – the power to captivate all who met her, including me. But Paddy had made me feel the first choice at last. And for once I had led the way; I had settled down with Paddy, while Faye had flitted from one man to another, even after having Caitlyn. There were so many good memories from our time together; was it any wonder I had thought it would last forever?

Paddy managed to hobble to the kitchen table the next

morning, sitting in Caitlyn's place while I dashed about getting everything ready.

'You didn't need to get up so early,' I said. I'd been creeping round, hoping to sneak off to school before he woke up.

'It's fine. I couldn't sleep well.'

'You're not feeling sick, are you?' I'd read up on the signs of concussion. He shook his head. 'Is the leg any better?' I asked.

'Maybe.' I took that as a no. I had seen him trying to stifle a grimace as he walked in. 'Though I don't reckon I'll be able to drive home today.'

'I never expected you would. Dr Gould said it could be a week.'

'It can't be a week. I need to be somewhere on Saturday.'

I glanced at him, but he was looking out of the window, giving nothing away. It must be a date, I decided. He may not have a girlfriend, but he could still be going out on dates. Not that it was any of my business. The sooner he was out of my house, the better.

'What about work? Are you expected anywhere?' I asked.

'Not this week. I've a project design to work on for a proposed excavation in Yorkshire. I can be getting on with that on my laptop.'

It sounded more fun than a day spent with Jo Blair, even with the leg injury and the bruise adorning his head.

'I've made you a flask of coffee,' I said, gesturing at the large flask next to the sink. 'I'll put it on the table beside the sofa. Sandwiches for lunch are in the fridge. Is there anything else you need?'

'A working leg?' He smiled. 'Thanks. You didn't need to do that.'

I knew that, and I didn't need to pop home in my lunch break either, but of course I did. I'd tried to reduce his need to move as much as I could, but the upstairs bathroom was the one thing I couldn't fix to suit him. All morning at school I'd had visions of him misjudging the stairs with his crutches or having a dizzy spell and crashing to the bottom, sustaining even more serious injury, so as soon as lunchtime arrived, I abandoned my desk and drove home.

All was quiet when I let myself into the house, but I was relieved to find no body at the foot of the stairs. Peering in at the living room door, I spotted Paddy stretched out on the sofa, his leg raised on a pillow. A couple of magazines lay on the floor at his side, and his laptop hung precariously off his knee, as if unsure whether to follow. I stole across the room and looked down at him. He was asleep, and sleep had smoothed away the pain that had altered his face the day before. In rest, he looked more like the Paddy I had known; it was easy to imagine that the years hadn't passed, and that I was watching him sleep as I often had, struck with amazement that this man, whom I loved so much, was there in the bed beside me.

I shook away those haunting thoughts of the past. This man wasn't the boy I had loved. There was a small scar below the jawline on this man's chin that hadn't been there before, the record of an event I knew nothing about. A couple of grey hairs lurked amid the dark curls at his temples. The body, though covered by a shirt, was still visibly more muscular than the slim chest I had once held close to mine. I didn't know this man at all. And yet, as I walked away, the laptop safely removed to the floor, a sleep-soaked voice called out, 'Eve?' and my body turned, recognising and reacting to the sound with no input from my brain.

'What are you doing here?' Paddy's voice was husky with

tiredness. I knew that voice; it had whispered to me under the covers on too many late nights and early mornings to count.

'Checking you're still alive,' I said.

'Alive but not kicking yet.' A tired smile tugged at his lips. 'Are you glad or sorry?'

'I wouldn't wish death on anyone. Not even you.'

His smile vanished, and I wished I could have matched his light mood; but not on that subject. I couldn't joke about that.

'Sorry.' We both said the word at the same time. I shook my head. We were straying closer to the past than I wanted, in the atmosphere between us rather than in conversation. That was even more dangerous, and had to stop. 'Have you had lunch? Shall I get it for you?'

It was surprisingly easy to adapt to a new routine, I discovered over the course of the week. By Thursday, it had already become a habit that needed no thought: lunchtime arrived, and I picked up my car keys and headed home to check on Paddy. Even the evenings were transformed; whereas on my own I would fidget, desperate to keep busy, I discovered there was satisfaction to be found in sitting still and listening to the radio or watching television with Paddy. He was a quieter, more restful companion than I had expected, or than he used to be; perhaps because I had forbidden so many topics of conversation – but even when he didn't speak, something about his presence settled me enough to keep my rogue thoughts at bay.

But on Thursday night, when I slammed the front door shut behind me, after the worst day I had ever experienced at school, the last thing I wanted was company in the house. I was halfway up the stairs, craving the solitude of my bedroom, when Paddy appeared from the kitchen. He had abandoned the crutches, but walked gingerly, keeping his injured leg stiff and trying to put as little weight on it as possible.

'It's a modern miracle,' he was saying. 'The supermarket has delivered all manner of goodies so tonight you don't need to cook. To be fair, I can't claim to be cooking either, unless sticking something in the oven to heat up counts ... Eve?' He leant on the bannister and stared up at me. 'What the hell happened to you?'

'Nothing.' He pulled a sceptical face, as well he might. My skin felt unnaturally tight where the tears had dried and I had no intention of looking in a mirror any time soon. 'Bad day at work,' I added, as he continued to watch me, waiting for an explanation.

'Want to talk about it?'

'No.' It was an instinctive answer. I wasn't used to having anyone at home to discuss problems with. I dealt with things myself, with the occasional rant at Tina. But Tina was away on a school trip, and Paddy was here, and before I knew what was happening, I had descended the stairs and followed him into the living room where I sat down on the sofa and promptly burst into tears.

'Hey.' He sat down next to me and put his arm round my shoulders. He didn't say another word, but waited until I had cried myself out, then squeezed my shoulder and removed his arm.

'Want to tell me what happened?' he asked. 'Was there an accident? Has a child been hurt?'

His question helped calm me down. The situation could have been worse, much worse, although it had been hard to think like that at the time. I wiped my sticky cheeks.

'It was nothing like that,' I said. I took a deep breath, which shuddered through my chest. 'We had a call from the exam board today. Some A-level papers we sent them yesterday haven't arrived.'

'Right.' Paddy looked puzzled. 'Things are delayed in the post all the time. I bet you they'll turn up tomorrow.'

'No. They weren't sent by post. They were despatched securely by courier. Somewhere between school and the exam board, the courier has lost track of them. No one knows where the papers are.'

'Jeez, what a mess. So what happens now?'

I shrugged. 'I'm not sure. It's never happened before while I've been working at school. If the papers never turn up, I think the marks will have to be based on the other papers for that subject. Students who did well in the missing exam will be penalised.'

Paddy took my hand, and squeezed it.

'Sounds like you had one hell of a day.'

'That wasn't all.' I tried not to cry again, but I could feel the tears slipping down my cheeks. 'When Jo Blair found out, she went berserk. She went on and on about how she would have to explain this to parents, and the reputational damage it would do to the school. And then she blamed me, because I'd chosen and booked the courier company. It was a local company, one we've used for years without a problem, but she said that I should have used one of the big national couriers – that I'd jeopardised the future of the school and the students by my decision.'

I had never been spoken to like that in my life. Clearly, I'd been in the wrong place at the wrong time; Jo had hit out at the easy target, whoever was closest to hand. But the public dressing-down – in front of teachers and students – had been hard to take. I had spent years trying to help the school run smoothly, trying, in my own tiny way, to help the children of Inglebridge have the best future possible. Had I really damaged the prospects of these students? Ruined their chances of achieving the grades they needed for university, as Jo had suggested? I couldn't bear it if I had.

'Listen to me, Eve.' Paddy took both my hands and turned to look into my eyes. 'She's been a bitch and lashed out at the wrong person. None of this is your fault. You know it. Don't let the feckers grind you down.'

He said that in his broadest Irish accent, absolute earnestness on his face, and unexpectedly I laughed. He grinned back.

'You know what you need?' he asked, letting go of my hands. 'Go for a run. Pound the streets and imagine you're stamping on that head teacher of yours. Run until you're too exhausted to think any more.'

He was right: that was exactly what I needed, and exactly what I did, pelting through the streets and up into the hills until my chest burned, my thighs turned to jelly, and I gasped for air. By the time I arrived home, sneaking up the stairs for a shower before Paddy could see the state I was in, I was still thinking, but my thoughts were more rational. Paddy was right; I had done nothing wrong. The courier company I had booked had won awards for its service and had an unblemished record, as far as I was aware. Jo Blair had no grounds to blame me, and if she tried again tomorrow, she wouldn't find me such an easy victim. And as I rinsed the shampoo from my hair, I wondered how differently this night might have gone if I had been on my own as usual, without Paddy to talk this over with, without his sympathy and support. Without the comfort of his hug. I swiftly rinsed that thought away too.

When I came downstairs, hair still wet from the shower, Paddy was sitting at the kitchen table, reading a magazine. The oven was on and a delicious smell filled the kitchen. He looked up as I walked in and a strange expression passed over his face.

'You barely look a day older,' he said. I opened my mouth, but he held up his hand before I could speak. 'I know! No talking of the past. But you're almost persuading me that there's something to this healthy living.'

'There is. You should try it. Dare I ask what's cooking?' I peered in the oven and could only see an assortment of black plastic ready meal containers.

'Beef in black bean sauce.' He smiled as I glanced back at him. 'What's the problem? It has beans in it, so I figured it must be okay. And the Chinese are a healthy bunch, aren't they? Just look at how well they do in the Olympics. Right up there on the medals table. You can't argue with that.'

The meal was actually delicious, as Paddy was quick to point out after every mouthful until he'd wrung some reluctant laughter out of me. I sent him away to the living room while I washed up, and when I took him in a coffee, his leg was resting on a pillow again.

'Has it got worse?' I asked, gesturing at his leg.

'Maybe I overdid it today.'

'Do you think you'll be fit to drive tomorrow?'

'What's the matter? Need me out of the way for the weekend? Ah, don't tell me you've invited the boring man round to make up for missing him this week? I wouldn't want to get in the way of your love life.'

'You said he was boorish, not boring.'

'That too. Glad you remembered. Pining for you, is he? You

could have invited him round. I promise I'd have been on my best behaviour.'

I ignored the question. Rich had sent a text last night, letting me know he would be with the children at the weekend, so I wouldn't see him. There hadn't been much evidence of pining, either in his message or in my reply. We didn't have that sort of relationship. We were happy to be independent of each other in day-to-day life. It was a grown-up relationship of the type Paddy probably wouldn't understand. And talking of Paddy's relationships ...

'I thought you had a date on Saturday?' I asked. 'You said you needed to get away.'

'I do. Perhaps another night's rest will make all the difference. I get it, you must be desperate to see the back of me by now.'

If he'd said that at the start of the week, I'd have agreed. But now ... It hadn't been so bad having him to stay, although I could hardly believe I was thinking that. Tonight, when I had come home so upset, it had made a positive difference having him here, a difference I was still finding it hard to comprehend. I'd prided myself on my independence, but there were some things that independence couldn't provide; and now, as I relaxed over my decaffeinated coffee, listening to the music on the radio and the occasional rustle of Paddy's magazine as he turned the page, it did feel as if my problems with Jo Blair sat more lightly on my shoulders for having shared them. I didn't think it was Paddy himself that was the answer – although it was hard to imagine Rich having the same effect – but perhaps it was a lesson for me – that there were advantages to having a companion in the house that I'd forgotten about. And then I inwardly groaned. Companionship? Is that what I wanted? I might as well don my slippers and shuffle off to The Chestnuts now ...

'Here,' Paddy said, interrupting my thoughts. He held out his magazine. 'This will interest you. A haul of Roman coins has been found on a farm in Dorset. Some detectorists came across it.'

I didn't take the magazine from him. He waited, then leant across and placed it on my knee. I didn't need to look to know what it was. His archaeology journals had littered the house all week and I had studiously avoided them.

'I don't do this any more,' I said.

'Maybe not, but can you tell me you're not interested?'

I couldn't; I was itching to read it.

'I don't get it,' he said. 'You were the most passionate student in our year, and the brightest. That doesn't die. I know you had Caitlyn. I understand you not doing it then. But now? What's stopping you?'

'I have a house, a mortgage, a job, Gran ...' I reeled off the reasons. Reasons, not excuses, as I had assured myself many times. 'I can't disappear for weeks on end. I can't travel around the world like you, leaving everything behind.'

'I don't travel the world now.' He shook his head, as if to stop himself going further. 'You can narrow your dreams, without giving them up. Your job isn't making you happy. Archaeology did. And you'd be amazed at the developments since we studied at university. Airborne lidar can show up even the slightest earthwork remains. Drones are fantastic for taking aerial imagery, which can be used to generate 3D surface models. There's so much more data available now. The past is getting closer to us all the time. How can you not want to be part of it?'

I did want to be part of it. I couldn't resist. His words blew oxygen on the spark in my soul that had never truly died, fanning the flames of my interest – so high, that later that night, after Paddy had gone to bed, I took out my laptop and booked a place as a volunteer on the Roman dig in the Cotswolds that Caitlyn had found. Before I went to sleep, I took out my box of vouchers and filled in the next one:

BE KIND TO YOURSELF
VOUCHER SIX
I, Eve Roberts, have been kind to myself by signing up to volunteer on a dig!

'You're the talk of the school,' Tina said, as soon as she got in the car the next morning. 'Honestly, I go on one school trip and all hell breaks loose!'

She broke off to wave at Paddy, who was standing in the front window, watching us leave.

'He'd make a good house husband, wouldn't he?' She grinned. 'I bet he's been nice to come home to.'

'I can get a dog if I want a companion,' I said, reversing off the drive and conveniently forgetting that I'd had similar thoughts about Paddy the night before.

'A cat, surely?' Tina laughed. 'If you're determined to embrace the spinster's life, you need to adopt the full stereotype.'

'I'm not a spinster,' I protested. 'I'm an independent woman.'

'You do realise you can be an independent woman and part of a couple, don't you?' Tina shot me a speaking glance and when I didn't reply, carried on. 'Anyway, never mind that. For now. What happened yesterday?'

'Any particular part of yesterday?'

'Specifically the part when you had a run-in with Jo Blair, unless there was more excitement that I've not heard about.'

The memory of Paddy's hug drifted into my head. I let it drift back out. That had been support, not excitement. Tina didn't need to know about that.

'No other excitement,' I replied. 'That was more than enough for one day. How have you heard about it? School hasn't been open since then.'

'Phil Ward from Biology witnessed it, and he told Haf Patel, and she told ...'

'Okay, okay.' I turned onto Inglebridge High Street and passed The White Hart, waving at Lexy as she changed the day's menu outside. 'Is there anyone who doesn't know?'

'Probably Ned Tucker from Physics, as I don't think he has a phone, does he?'

That wasn't much comfort. By the sounds of it, news of my telling-off had spread round the whole of the teaching staff – staff I considered friends and colleagues, and who I would have preferred not to know about my humiliation. But I supposed that had always been too much to expect in a close-knit school in a close-knit town. I sighed. The prospect of facing Jo Blair had been bad enough, without knowing there would be gossips lurking on every corridor.

Tina patted my arm.

'You've nothing to worry about,' she said. 'Everyone knows you did nothing wrong. You should report her. She can't get away with speaking to you like that.'

'I'd rather just forget about the whole thing. There's only one more half-term to go, and then she'll move on, won't she?'

'Maybe not. She's told a couple of people that there hasn't been much interest in the post of permanent head, and that she might apply for it herself,' Tina said, and although I was concentrating on the road, I could hear the dismay in her voice. 'You can imagine how popular that news has been.'

I digested this information as I drove through town and on towards school. I'd convinced myself that I could grin and bear working with Jo for the rest of term, because then there would be a long holiday to recover and things would go back to normal with the arrival of a new head teacher in September. How would I feel about the prospect of working with Jo Blair for the foreseeable future? She was a similar age to me; she could conceivably stay in place until I retired. Almost thirty more years of this? I parked in my usual place and looked up at the school building where I had spent so many contented years. Contented wasn't as good as happy, a voice whispered in my ear – a voice with a distinctly Irish twang. Was this where I really wanted to spend the rest of my working days? A few weeks ago, it wouldn't have occurred to me to ask the question. What was going on?

Tina unfastened her seat belt and turned to me.

'And for the record,' she said. 'Don't think I didn't notice your reaction to Paddy Friel when I mentioned him.'

'I didn't react!'

'Exactly. You didn't start to spit or hiss, and smoke didn't emerge from your ears. What's been going on behind closed doors? You're warming to him, aren't you?'

'Only if by warm, you mean a couple of degrees above freezing point.' I laughed as Tina pulled a disappointed face. 'Okay. Perhaps not every bone in his body is evil.' I thought back to last night. 'He might not be the vain, self-centred celebrity I imagined. Not on weekdays, anyway. Now can we stop the interrogation and go into work? I don't want a telling-off for being late on top of everything else ...'

Chapter 14

The day passed more quietly than I had feared: Jo Blair was busy in her office and on the infrequent occasions that she passed by my desk, we managed to avoid any reference to the events of yesterday, by the simple expediency of not speaking at all. As far as I knew, the missing exam papers hadn't turned up, but apparently I wasn't trusted to be involved with that any more.

I was counting down the minutes until home time, and my last evening with Paddy, when my mobile phone vibrated and 'The Chestnuts' flashed up on the screen. My heart plummeting to my feet, I answered with a shaky 'hello?'

'Is that you, our Eve?' shouted Gran. 'Speak up, chuck. I can't hear you.'

'Yes, it's me,' I said, in a steadier but still quiet voice. The last thing I needed was for Jo Blair to catch me on a personal call. 'What's the matter? Is everything okay?'

I'd told Gran never to telephone me at work unless it was an emergency, and this was the first time she'd ever done it.

'What are you up to, more to the point?' Gran said. 'What's all this about your Paddy having an injury? You didn't do it to him, did you? And why is he at your house?'

'Of course I didn't do it! He had an accident on the walk. Didn't the source of your gossip tell you that?'

'Oh, I didn't look past the headline and the photo. Mrs Pike was too busy crowing that she knew something I didn't. You could ...'

'Hang on,' I interrupted. I glanced towards Jo's door and escaped to the corridor where I didn't need to whisper. 'What headline and photo?'

'The photo of Paddy in your front room. You should have tidied first. There were two dirty mugs and a plate on the coffee table. You don't want folk thinking you're a slattern.'

'But Gran,' I said, speaking slowly, as I was beginning to think there might be something wrong with her after all. She wasn't making any sense. 'I haven't taken any photos of Paddy at my house, so you can't have seen one.'

'I'm not doolally yet, thank you. Look on that computer of yours if you don't believe me. The whole world has seen it, not just me. I want the full story on Sunday!'

And with that she was gone, leaving me completely bewildered. I wandered back to my desk and typed Paddy's name into the internet search engine. The first result was for his Wikipedia entry – he was on Wikipedia! I tried not to be too impressed and instead clicked on the second result, for an article in today's online edition of a tabloid newspaper.

It was only a brief story, puffed out with regurgitated details of Paddy's previous TV appearances – more than I had realised, and a curious mix of serious shows and celebrity trash. The article mentioned that he had been injured in a 'heroic rescue' involving a small child – the balloon didn't get a look-in – while helping to raise money for a nursing home on behalf of an old family friend. And there was a picture of Paddy, lolling on my sofa with a brave smile on his bruised face and a huge bandage wrapped round his leg. I knew for a fact he hadn't worn that bandage in my presence this week, so it must have been an embellishment for the photograph. Talk about fake news! I couldn't believe he'd had the shame to go through with it, or that the newspaper had even published the story. Who was interested in this rubbish?

On closer inspection, I discovered that quite a few people were interested, judging by almost a hundred comments at the bottom of the page. They were mainly nauseating messages from adoring fans, commending his apparent bravery and offering some eye-watering remedies to help him recover, although one comment made me laugh: it told him to man up, cut his hair and stop being a 'big girl's blouse'.

I flicked back through the article, blood boiling. 'Old family friend' – I hoped that didn't mean me. Never mind the old, my feelings for Paddy were far from friendly. How dared he invite the press into my home and put my shabby furniture online for all the world to see? How vain must he be, how desperate for publicity, that he would use any misfortune to further his own career? While I had been rushing through my work, making time to check on him in my lunch break, had he been sneakily plotting and using my home for his own ends? What next – a full-page spread in *Hello*? I couldn't believe that I'd softened towards him this week, and even been glad of his company; he was clearly the same hollow man I had always thought him.

The usual Friday night happiness didn't even register as I stormed out of school at the end of the day and drove home at record speed. I said goodbye to Tina, slammed through my front door and marched into the kitchen, where I found Paddy busy cleaning the hob.

Far from being impressed, the sight increased my fury. Was *he* suggesting I was a slattern too?

'Are you sure you're well enough for that?' I asked, talking over his question about how my day had been. 'I see you've been able to take your bandage off now. Are you sure it's not too soon? I'm surprised you didn't go the whole hog and apply a plaster cast.'

'It's not as easy to buy one of those in the chemist.' Paddy laughed, but the smile faded quickly as he looked at me. 'What's wrong? Has that Blair woman had a go at you again? Do you want me to go in there and sort her out for you?'

'No! It's nothing to do with school. My day was going perfectly well until I saw a photograph of my living room on the internet!'

'Ah. It was the dirty plate, wasn't it? I should have spotted it. Sorry. But give me some brownie points, I've tried to make amends by tidying up and cleaning the kitchen since then, even in my poor injured state ...'

I glared at him. He really wasn't getting it. He really was so entirely self-absorbed that he couldn't think of anyone else at all. Did he expect me to be pleased with him?

'It has nothing to do with the plate! It's about you inviting strangers into my home without even having the courtesy to tell me, let alone ask. It's about the fact that you're using Gran and The Chestnuts to make yourself look good, and no doubt to try to get a role on some other shoddy TV show to earn more money that you probably don't even need ...'

'Not a shoddy TV show.' Paddy's voice was hard, and his eyes were flat, no hint of their usual twinkle. 'My agent phoned earlier. I've been offered a guest appearance on a BBC comedy panel show. And yes, it's decent money for cracking a few jokes and smiling into the cameras. Why would I turn that down?'

He was serious. What had happened to him? What had happened to that boy I had loved – the boy who had looked after me the day I had been attacked, who had tidied away my shopping and wiped away my tears? He hadn't cared about money or taken himself too seriously. He had been kind, passionate and had cared about others – at first, at least. And it suddenly occurred to me that I didn't know this man in front of me. I had accused Paddy of inviting strangers into my home, but I was the one who had allowed a stranger to stay.

'You really are a hollow figure of a man, aren't you?' I said. 'Every tear I shed over you was a waste. I should have celebrated my lucky escape.'

I walked out and went upstairs to get changed. I wasn't furious with him any longer – he wasn't worth the energy. But I was furious with myself. I'd known what he was like, how little substance there was to him. No one knew that better than I did. So what had I been doing these last few days, looking after him and treating him like a decent human being? Enjoying his company, whispered a mischievous voice in my head. How had I let him fool me again?

I had taken off my blouse and was looking for a T-shirt to wear for a run when I heard quick footsteps on the stairs.

Paddy's voice called out, 'Eve, let me explain ...' and then there was a cry of pain, a couple of thumps and silence. I rushed out of my room. Paddy was lying on the stairs, clutching his leg. I ran down to him.

'What have you done now? Has it popped again?'

'No, but jeez, it hurts like it did at the start.'

'What were you thinking, running up the stairs like that?'

'I was thinking that I didn't want to leave without trying to explain. Not this time. Believe it or not, I have grown up in the last seventeen years.'

I didn't have an answer to that. He was the one on the floor, but I was the one who felt wrong-footed.

'Wait there,' I said – needlessly, on reflection – and squeezed past him down the stairs. I returned with the crutches he had abandoned a couple of days ago. With some heaving on my part and some cursing on his, we managed to get him back on his feet.

'You've put on weight. You didn't used to be this heavy,' I said, catching my breath.

'I'd prefer to call it muscle. Not such a hollow figure, am I?'

'Not physically.'

He worked his way back downstairs and I followed until he was settled on the sofa again.

'You probably just overdid it,' I said. 'Rest now and it might be fine in the morning.'

'I hope so.' So did I. He might be desperate to go on his date, but I was equally desperate for him to leave so that life could go back to normal – the familiar life-without-Paddy that I had adapted to over the years.

He looked at me as I hovered by the door. I wondered whether I could still escape for a run if he was in pain again. 'Don't think I'm not enjoying the view, but feel free to put more clothes on before you tell me off for looking where I shouldn't.' He grinned. 'You didn't wear underwear like that in my day. Your man must be something special.'

I didn't bother covering myself up. What was the point? He had seen it all before, more times than I could count, although I was considerably more toned now – but then, I'd never had the joy of a child of my own, to sag and stretch everything out of shape. And the underwear wasn't for Rich, though he certainly appreciated it. It was for me – my one indulgence, a secret reminder that somewhere, deep down, I was still me: an independent woman, not a stand-in mother, forgotten aunt, ungrateful daughter or abandoned lover.

'I didn't let strangers in your house, for the record,' Paddy said, as I turned away. 'It was only Jamie.'

'Jamie?' I came back into the room.

'Tina's lad. From across the road.'

'Why was he here?'

'He came round for a chat while you were at work. He's interested in the media, and the newspapers and all that kind of thing.'

'So?'

'So I let him make up a story and take a photo, and gave him a contact name at the newspaper ...' Paddy shrugged. 'The bandage was his idea. I couldn't see any harm in it. I didn't think it would actually make it online. Must have been a quiet news day, you know?'

Was it true? Had he been doing a favour for Jamie, not grasping for publicity for himself? I didn't know. He could say one thing – look totally innocent – but behave in a different way entirely, as I well knew. How could I ever trust him again?

'I get why you don't want to talk about the past,' Paddy said, when I hesitated in the doorway. 'But don't judge me on it, okay? I'm not that boy any more.'

I nodded, but I still wasn't sure whether to believe him, or what to think if I did. So I took my usual course, and went for a run, climbing the hills around Inglebridge until I was too exhausted to think at all.

Chapter 15

Paddy hobbled into the kitchen the next morning, carrying his bag but wearing the grim face of a man who knew his hopes of a hot date were about to go pop as surely as his muscle had done a few days before.

'You're not fit to drive, are you?' I asked, flicking the kettle to make him a cup of tea.

'I can try.'

I watched him wince as he sat down at the table.

'Is your car an automatic?'

'No.' He winced again as he tried to move his leg, as if changing gears. He put his head in his hands. 'I've really screwed this up. I overdid it yesterday. I'm such an idiot.'

His reaction seemed extreme. It must have been quite some date he had lined up. But surely, if he was as attractive as people gave him credit for, the woman he was due to meet would be happy to wait? I didn't make the point. It could hardly have been less of my business. I concentrated on making his breakfast instead, wholemeal toast slathered with the butter he had included with the supermarket delivery. Gran would have been proud of him.

I carried his plate over to the table. He looked up.

'Eve, I don't suppose you would ...'

'Absolutely not! Seriously? You expect me to drive you home, so you can meet your date? I'm not your pimp, Paddy!'

He toyed with the toast on his plate and I backed away to the sink. He was unbelievable! Thinking only of himself again, albeit his carnal rather than financial desires this time. Why would he think ...

'It's not that sort of date.' I turned, because there was something in his voice, an odd reluctance that caught my attention. 'It's my mam. It's her birthday today.'

'Is it a special one?' I remembered as soon as he said it that Alison Friel's birthday had been sometime in spring, so perhaps he wasn't making this up. I couldn't remember how old she was. Could she be seventy? 'Is she having a party?'

'No. Not special and no party. But I told her I'd be there.'

'But she lives in London,' I said. 'You can't expect me to drive you all the way down there.'

'They're not in London. Mam and Dad have moved to Yorkshire. Near Ripon.'

Ripon? That's where he'd said that he lived too. They had always been a close-knit family, so it shouldn't surprise me that they all lived near to each other, but Ripon was an unexpected choice. Paddy's mum had been born in Yorkshire, but the family had seemed settled in London when I knew them, and Paddy's life was down there. Not just his celebrity life; according to Wikipedia, he owned an archaeology consultancy business in the south-east of the country.

Paddy was picking at his toast, not meeting my eye.

'Your mum will understand why you can't make it, when you explain the circumstances, won't she?' I asked. 'Won't a phone call do?'

'No. Ah, it's complicated, Eve.' He looked up at me, but I

almost wished he hadn't when I saw the bleakness in his eyes. 'She's not so good. I said I'd be there, and I don't want to let her down.'

Was I a fool? Maybe. Half an hour later we were in my car, following the road that wound through the valleys of north Lancashire and across to Yorkshire. It was a glorious late spring day, and the sun saturated the countryside with warmth, enhancing the rich green shades of the fields around us and making the new leaves sparkle on the trees. Paddy was silent, but I didn't mind. It wasn't a bad way to spend my Saturday, enjoying all this lush beauty; in fact, it was good to get out, invigorating to see somewhere different for a change. The sunshine felt like a foretaste of summer and seemed to offer hope, and the promise of good things ahead. Despite the company, I felt relaxed and happier than I would ever have imagined in Paddy's presence.

Eventually, Paddy directed me off the main road and towards a village on the outskirts of Ripon, until we pulled up outside a large, detached bungalow on a quiet country lane.

'When did your parents move here?' I asked, as I switched off the engine. I looked around: there were only two other properties in sight, and the views in every direction were tremendous. It was a far cry from the busy London street where Paddy's parents had lived when I had known them.

'A couple of years ago. Mam wanted to come back home to Yorkshire.'

He unfastened his seat belt and hesitated.

'Is there a café in the village?' I asked. 'I could wait there until you're ready.'

'No, you'd better come in. She'd never forgive me if I didn't offer you a cup of tea.'

He smiled, but there was an unexplained quality of sadness to it. I accompanied him up the drive, past a huge people-carrier parked under a car port, and along a covered path to the front door. A ramp led up to a double-width front door. I looked at Paddy for an explanation, but he didn't offer one. He rang the doorbell and pushed open the front door without waiting for a reply.

'Dad? Mam? It's Paddy!'

I followed him into a hallway with three wide arches leading off to other rooms, but no doors. A man emerged through one of the arches and it took me a moment to recognise Paddy's dad, Ray. His smile was as warm as ever, but in everything else he had shrunk and aged beyond what I would have expected.

'Hi, Dad.' Paddy bent and embraced his father. They had been of similar build, when Paddy was a teenager; now Paddy dwarfed him. He stepped back and gestured towards me. 'You remember Eve?'

'Of course. You don't look a day older.' Ray took my hand in both of his and squeezed it. 'Good of you to look after Paddy like this. How's the leg?'

'Yeah, getting better. Just a minor sprain.' Paddy glanced at me and I understood the silent appeal: no mentioning that he'd been in pain. 'How's Mam?'

'Having a good day. Come in, the pair of you.'

Ray led the way through the arch to the left and into a bright living room with huge picture windows overlooking the garden and fields beyond. But I couldn't concentrate on the view. Paddy's mum, Alison, sat in front of the window in a large wheelchair. If I'd thought Ray had shrunk, it was nothing compared to Alison. Her face was gaunt, and she looked the 'hollow figure' that I had accused Paddy of being. But her smile was as warm as it had ever been as she caught sight of Paddy.

'How are you, love?' she asked, holding out her right hand to Paddy. He took it and bent down to kiss her cheeks, resting his head briefly against hers. My heart ached at the gesture: he had always adored his mum. 'And don't think of trying to kid me. I saw the pain on your face when you walked in, though you tried to hide it.'

I'd noticed it too: he had been trying not to limp. He perched on the arm of the sofa at Alison's side.

'It's something and nothing,' he said. 'No need to worry. I'd be recovered by now if I hadn't overdone it yesterday.'

'Running around after the girls, like usual, I expect ...' Alison laughed but it turned into a cough and Paddy sprang up to help wipe her mouth. 'I hope you're not giving Eve the run-around again.'

I didn't think she'd noticed me, but I came forward and took her outstretched hand. Her grip was weak, but she held on to me.

'You've not changed a bit,' she said. 'Not like the rest of us.'

'But I'm older and wiser,' I replied, 'and no one gives me the run-around any more.'

'Well, I'm right glad to hear that.' She smiled and squeezed my hand, and her eyes twinkled in the way that Paddy's did. 'I'm glad to see you again, love. It's been too long. How's that little girl of yours?'

'Not so little. Look.' I took out my phone and showed Alison the picture of Caitlyn on my lock screen. 'She's working in Paris now, as an au pair. She loves it over there.'

'She's a beauty,' Alison said. Paddy was peering over her shoulder at my phone. 'Make yourself useful, Paddy, and put the kettle on. And there's cake in the tin on the counter. Your dad's soft, thinks I need a birthday cake at my age ...'

A couple of hours passed quickly and with more ease than I would have thought possible. Paddy's family had always been close, and the love that knit them so tightly together was obvious in every word and gesture between them. But after a while, Alison became visibly tired, her speech less frequent and more laboured, and Paddy stood up.

'We'll let you rest now, Mam,' he said. 'I'll just have a word with Dad about the conservatory. I've been offered a spot on a panel show so we can go ahead ...'

Paddy and his dad wandered out and moments later I saw them in the garden, gesticulating at the back of the house.

'You're having a conservatory?' I said, moving closer to Alison. 'That will be lovely, looking out over that view.'

'God's own country,' Alison said. Her words were starting to slur, and her breaths were shallow. 'Wanted to end my days at home.'

'I'm so sorry.' I perched on the sofa arm where Paddy had sat earlier and took Alison's right hand in mine. She hadn't moved her left hand at all since I had arrived. 'I don't know what to say.'

'Don't fret. Every curse and complaint has already been said. I went through the why me stage. Now I'm at the why not me. I wouldn't wish this on any other bugger.' She stopped and gestured at her water and I helped her to have a drink. 'Hate being such a burden. And so much not done.' Silent tears rolled down her cheeks. 'So much not done.'

I was wiping tears from both our faces when Paddy and Ray came back in. I said goodbye to Alison, hugged her frail body as best I could, and returned to my car so that Paddy could have a few minutes alone with his family. When he finally walked down the drive towards me, I wondered how I could have thought I'd seen pain on his face over the last week. That had been nothing in comparison to his expression now: true pain, from the heart, not the body. My own heart ached in sympathy.

We drove away and headed home in silence. Paddy looked too upset to talk and I couldn't think of anything to say that could possibly make him feel better. But when we were halfway home, I spotted the country pub where Tina and I had stopped on the night of the school talk when I had first seen Paddy again. I pulled into the car park.

'You need a drink,' I said, when Paddy looked at me. He smiled for the first time since leaving his parents' house.

'I can't argue with that.'

Paddy found a quiet table and I bought the drinks. I waited until he'd had a first, long swig of his Guinness before I reached out and took his hand.

'I'm sorry,' I said. I squeezed his hand and he gripped mine back, so tightly that it hurt.

I glanced around. There were a few other people in our section of the pub – couples, families, a large group celebrating a birthday – but no one was watching us, and no one was near enough to hear our conversation.

'What is it?' I asked.

'MND. Motor neurone disease.'

'And ...' I didn't know how to ask the question, or whether I should.

'There's no cure.' Paddy stared into his pint. 'No standard progression either. There's no way of knowing how or when she'll lose some function, or when ...' He stopped, took a breath. 'She slurred more words than usual today. That's not good.'

His forehead creased into well-established lines of concern that I hadn't seen before, marking him more clearly than ever as a man of his age rather than the boy I had known.

'When did it start?' I asked.

'About three years ago.' Paddy took a drink. 'She had some numbness in her foot, started to stumble and eventually the doctor ran some tests. It was the worst possible news. You just can't imagine ...' His drink was disappearing rapidly. 'Mentally, she's as alert as ever. It kinda makes it worse. She knows as every bit of power is taken from her. She knows exactly what's to come. How do you bear that?'

I had no answer. My experience of loss had been swift and unexpected. Painful though it had been, perhaps I had been lucky. What must it be like to go through this torture, seeing a loved one suffer and gradually fade? Day after day of grief, both longing for it to end and dreading that it would? I rubbed my thumb over Paddy's hand. Even when I thought I'd hated him, I couldn't have wished this on him. But I had never hated this heartbroken man in front of me.

He stood up, breaking the contact between our hands. 'Another drink?'

I had barely touched mine, and he headed to the bar for another pint, still walking stiffly on his injured leg. A few people looked at him as he passed, and frowned as if trying to place him, but he was lost in his own world and didn't seem to notice.

'Why didn't you tell me?' I asked, when he came back. 'You only needed to say, and I would have driven you anywhere.'

He shrugged. 'I don't talk about it. I choose to be in the public eye. Mam doesn't. She's a private person. You know that.'

'And so all the TV work,' I said, remembering the conversation about the conservatory. 'All the celebrity stuff ...'

'Yes. If it pays, I'll do it. The speed dating show paid for the garden to be landscaped so it was wheelchair-friendly. Then there's the car, the environmental control system, the top-up therapy, the extra holiday costs, the respite care for Dad ... She'll have the best of everything as long as I can earn the money for her.'

And this was the man I had accused of being hollow! I sipped my cranberry juice, wishing it was a glass of Merlot instead, to numb the shame that was eating away at me. I'd thought I was living with a stranger, far removed from the Paddy I had known, and now I knew it was true – but in the best, not the worst way. This man at my table was ten times the character the boy had been. Adversity had shaped him, made him stronger – made him someone that in another time, in other circumstances, I might have wanted to know better.

'So is this why you don't join digs abroad now?' I asked, as many of the things he had told me began to fall into place.

'I won't leave the country for more than a week, and I'll only go to places with regular and short flights home. We just can't know ...' He looked across the table at me. 'This is what I've been wanting to tell you. I get it now. About Caitlyn, about realising what's really important in life. I get why you would do anything, give up anything, for someone you love. I didn't understand it then. There was a lot I didn't understand back then.'

He reached out for my phone, which was lying on the table beside my car keys, and pressed the button to wake it up. Caitlyn's picture flashed up.

'I was a coward to walk out,' he said. 'I've had a long time to think about that. About what I missed.' He glanced at me, but I didn't stop him, even though he was well within forbidden territory. 'She's exactly like Faye. Have you looked after her entirely on your own? No partner? No contact with her father?'

'No.' I shrugged, and ignored the first question. Now wasn't the time to tell him how devastated Caitlyn had been when he left; how wary it had made me of hurting her again by introducing her to other boyfriends who might leave. 'We never found him. Faye must have fallen pregnant just after I started university. You didn't know what she was like back then. Let's just say that Faye didn't tend to stick with one boyfriend for long.'

I smiled, to try to take the sting out of my words. I hadn't meant them critically. Faye had never turned down an opportunity for fun or pleasure, whatever the consequences. *Live hard, die young,* she had once said to me. We couldn't have known how prophetic those words would be. I felt a quiet tug in my heart, as if the frayed edges of my well-worn grief were being pulled again.

'Has Caitlyn never wanted to find him? What would you have done if her father had shown up?' Paddy asked.

'I ...' The question floored me. I'd never seriously given it any thought. We'd always been honest with Caitlyn: that we didn't know who her father was, but that I, Mum and Gran would offer her as much love as she could ever need. What if someone had turned up and staked a claim on Caitlyn? How could we have given her up?

'I'd have been pleased for Caitlyn,' I said, clutching my glass between my hands. 'Assuming he was a good man who deserved her. But he couldn't have been a good man, could he? Faye's death was reported in all the national papers. All the stories mentioned that she had a child. A decent man would have turned up then, wouldn't he?' Thank goodness I'd never been put to the test, I added to myself. I wasn't sure I could have borne one more loss.

I held out my car keys to Paddy as we were leaving the pub. 'Let yourself in. I'm just popping to the ladies.'

I looked around and spotted the sign pointing past the bar. I started to head that way, but Paddy grabbed my arm.

'Couldn't you hang on? Only, the painkillers have worn off and I'm in sore need of a top-up ...'

'What?' I laughed. Was he seriously trying to stop me going to the toilet? But he wasn't joking; the frown had reappeared, and he was staring over my shoulder.

'Don't be silly. I'll only be a minute.'

'Listen to me, Eve. Don't go that way.'

I shook off his arm and took two steps towards the bar. The pub was divided into sections, creating cosy rooms for a more intimate atmosphere, so it was only now that I could see what Paddy had presumably seen over my shoulder. Tucked away in a corner, at a table for two that was spread with the remains of lunch, sat Rich and a young blonde woman scarcely older than Caitlyn. If I was in any doubt about the nature of their relationship, Rich clarified it when he leant over and kissed her, drawing her closer with his hand on the back of her head.

I recoiled. What a gullible fool I was. When Rich had told me he was spending the weekend with the children, I'd assumed he'd meant his own ...

Paddy put his hand on my shoulder, just as Rich disengaged his lips and looked up. He froze, then started to stand, knocking cutlery to the floor. While he bent to pick it up, Paddy grabbed my hand and dragged me out of the pub.

We drove home in silence. My head was too crammed with thoughts about the day to make conversation; all that I had learnt, all that had been revealed. All that had changed. Alison, Paddy, Rich ... But as I drove back along the country lanes, instead of Rich's betrayal, my uppermost thought was how, despite his own hard day, Paddy's instinctive reaction had still been to protect me, just as he had done when our relationship started all those years ago.

Chapter 16

It was inevitable that Paddy would come with me to The Chestnuts to visit Gran the next day. He followed me out of the house without us even discussing it, and I couldn't say no, even if I'd been tempted to. Not even a bumper tin of all-butter shortbread could beat an appearance from Paddy Friel in Gran's eyes.

We hadn't spoken about the events of Saturday, but it had been a comfortable silence; it felt like we were respecting each other's privacy rather than choosing to avoid awkward conversations. I didn't want to upset Paddy by pressing him to talk more about his mum, and although the situations hardly compared, I sensed that he was keeping silent about Rich for the same reason. Did he need to? Was I upset? Not enough. I knew what heartbreak felt like and it wasn't this. This felt more like a paper cut: a quick sting and then all but forgotten. What a sad reflection that was on a relationship I had hung on to for the last two years.

Gran's eyes lit up as soon as she saw Paddy walk into the conservatory. I was clearly relegated to third place behind him and the shortbread. Gran wasted no time in pressing her emergency button to call for attention. The carer did a double take when she rushed in and found Paddy sprawled in the chair at Gran's side.

'See!' Gran said, before the carer could utter a word. 'It's a real emergency. We have a celebrity here. We need proper china for our tea today, not those stained old mugs. And you should let everyone know there's someone here off the telly. They can sleep after he's gone.' She grinned. 'I can't wait to see Mrs Pike's face! This beats her nephew being on *Pointless*.'

I pulled up another chair and settled down on Gran's other side.

'So you're still here?' she said, passing the box of biscuits to Paddy to open. 'There's a turn-up for the books. There was a time when you made a habit of leaving, not sticking around.'

'Gran!' I tried to shut her up, but Paddy only smiled.

'Oh, he doesn't mind me,' Gran said. 'I mean no harm. Where are you living now, Paddy? Some swanky place in London, is it? One of those million-pound houses on celebrity row? You must have a bob or two to be able to afford to stay at the Fairlie.'

'The production company paid for that. No, I'm renting a flat in Ripon at the moment. Not a celebrity to be seen, thank heaven.'

'Renting?' Gran repeated, pulling a face. 'You should have put down roots by your age. I hope you're not eyeing up our Eve's assets ... not the financial ones, any road ...'

She nudged his arm and cackled with such glee that it was impossible not to join in, even when Paddy surprised me by looking my way and giving a lazy wink. Shortly afterwards, the room started to fill as the other residents of The Chestnuts shuffled in, and Paddy wandered round with infinite patience, chatting, listening and occasionally throwing his head back and roaring with laughter in exactly the same way he used to do. He focused his attention on the old people, milking his celebrity on this occasion, but for their benefit not his. He held hands, kissed cheeks, sat quietly and talked, with no one left out and nothing beneath his notice. Before Saturday, I might have assumed it was all a sham and condemned him. Now I knew it *was* a sham, to conceal his own terrible sorrow, and I admired him. It was a remarkable performance.

'Not lost any of his charm, has he?' Gran said, as we sipped our tea and watched him work the room.

'No.'

'Ooh, are you softening towards him again?'

'Maybe. But don't get carried away,' I said, when I could see from Gran's face that she was reading much more than I had intended into that one word. 'There's no need to be borrowing another of Mrs Pike's hats.'

'I wouldn't borrow.' Gran sounded outraged. 'The grandmother of the bride deserves a new hat. And if the day ever came when you were marrying Paddy Friel, I'd go the whole hog and have a new dress and new shoes too.'

'You're incorrigible!' I said, laughing.

'I do my best.'

Gabby, the manager of The Chestnuts, rushed out of her office as Paddy and I were leaving. I feared another complaint about Gran, but it was Paddy she wanted, not me.

'I wanted to thank you,' she said, blushing scarlet when Paddy smiled at her. 'Since that article appeared online last week, donations have poured in. A dealership has made us an offer on a minibus. We can afford a new one and still have cash to spare. You've worked wonders!'

'Ah, you're too kind,' Paddy said. 'Eve deserves all the credit. None of it would have happened without her.'

Now *he* was being too kind. I'd seen the state of the fundraising before Paddy's article had appeared in the paper. We'd done well, far better than I'd ever dreamt when I first came up with the sponsored walk idea, but had still been short for buying a second-hand minibus, let alone a new one.

'That's fantastic news!' I said to Gabby. 'If the public are so interested in the story, why don't we run a competition to find a name for the new minibus? Perhaps Paddy can come back to officially launch it.'

'Like the royal family do with ships?' she asked. 'Smashing the bottle of champagne?'

'Exactly. We could invite the press along to cover the event. It would be great publicity and might keep the donations coming in for a bit longer.'

Gabby agreed, delighted with the idea, but I hadn't done it for her, or even for The Chestnuts. It was for Paddy and maybe, if things worked out well, for Alison, and his quiet 'thanks' as we left the care home told me he'd understood.

There was an unfamiliar car parked outside my house when I arrived home on Tuesday morning. It was the first proper day of the half-term break, after the Bank Holiday, but I'd been up and about early with a visit to the dentist and a trip to the supermarket, leaving Paddy to fend for himself for a while. I let myself into the house, pausing in the hall to listen out for voices. But there were no voices – only the sound of music from the radio, drifting from the kitchen, and the sight of a bag at the foot of the stairs. Paddy's bag, so that could only mean one thing. He must be leaving. And wasn't I glad? Hadn't I been wanting to have the house to myself again? My answer to those questions wasn't quite as clear-cut as I would have expected.

I carried my shopping bags through to the kitchen. There

were more than usual: I had bought provisions for two. Paddy was in there, arranging some flowers in a vase.

'Caught red-handed,' he said, with a smile as I walked in. 'I ought to say green-fingered, but I suspect it's not an impressive display, is it?'

It impressed me: a dozen large-headed white roses mingled with vibrant lilac freesias, and the whole bouquet was surrounded by silvery eucalyptus leaves. It was a simple but elegant arrangement: the sort of thing that must have come from a proper florist, not the local garage forecourt.

'From one of your many admirers?' I asked Paddy.

'They're for you. Not from an admirer,' he added quickly. 'From me.' He laughed and brushed his hair back from his face. 'That didn't come out as I intended ... They're a thank you. For putting me up for the last week – or should that be for putting up with me?'

'Definitely the latter,' I said, going over to examine the flowers. I closed my eyes and inhaled the scent, taking the moment to let my feelings settle. No one had bought me flowers for years, not since ... Paddy. Paddy had been the last person to buy me flowers, but then it had been a token of love, not thanks. So many years had passed, layers of new memories building on top of each other all the time, but the foundation of them all was Paddy. Would it always be this way? I opened my eyes, saw him watching me, and smiled.

'They're gorgeous. Thank you.' I stepped back. 'You're going today? Are you fit to drive?'

'I drove the car here. There was a twinge or two, but nothing I can't bear.'

'So desperate to get away?' I could have kicked myself the moment the words slipped out. I didn't want it to sound as if

I'd miss him. I would rather not have felt that way, but tendrils of disappointment were wrapping round me, too tightly to ignore. I tried to lighten the remark. 'Is my cooking that bad?'

'Surprisingly good, considering how it was before.' He smiled. 'But I can't deny I'm worried I might get a taste for the healthy living malarkey if I stay much longer.'

'I had it covered.' I reached into one of the shopping bags and pulled out a four-pack of Guinness. 'This caused a stir in the supermarket. I've never set foot in the alcohol aisle, never mind bought any. It's a small town. News will spread that I'm having a midlife crisis or something.'

Perhaps I was. I'd had alcohol in the house before – I operated a 'bring your own bottle' system when friends came for dinner – but I didn't buy it. So why the exception for Paddy? Because there had always been an exception for Paddy, in everything. Something had drawn me into the unfamiliar section of the shop – a curiously attractive area with its wooden flooring, stylish bottles and feature lighting – and the Guinness had appeared in my trolley without me giving it a thought.

'I wish I could stay, and not just for the Guinness. It's been …' He shrugged. 'Unexpectedly restful. But I had a call this morning. I've been asked to take a look at a construction site in Essex. They've found some remains, and work's been halted until it's checked out, so it can't wait. And then I have to give a couple of lectures, and next week there's a TV awards ceremony in London …' He sighed. 'Time to return to real life. I think I might need this Guinness.'

'Take it.' Although I couldn't see why he sighed; it didn't sound too shabby a life to me. 'Are you up for an award?'

'The show is.' He laughed. 'You can say it – I don't deserve it. All I do is stand in front of a camera and talk about something I love. I don't save lives.' His smile faded, and he pushed back his hair. 'I need to win. If we win, we've been promised another series, and then there's more chance of other opportunities ... I need it for Mam. If there is a third series, I want to feature Inglebridge, and look more at that barrow, perhaps dig some test trenches. You may be seeing me again sooner than you think. Keep your fingers crossed.'

I followed him out to the hall, wondering whether I should keep my fingers crossed that he won or that he didn't. He reached into his bag and pulled out a padded envelope.

'At the risk of making you think I'm even more hollow, I've bought you this.'

He handed over the envelope and I pulled out a DVD of the first series of his TV show, *Travels Through Time*. Paddy's face stared out at me from the front cover, as if the appeal of the show lay solely in him, not the history they uncovered.

'Ignore the cover,' he said. 'I didn't have a say. Watch the show. I know you want to forget the past. I get that. But it wasn't all bad.' He tapped the DVD in my hand. 'The past can be inspirational and educational, and a blueprint for the future. You always understood that better than the rest of us. Watch this and remember how it felt. You deserve this, Eve.'

I hadn't intended to watch the DVD, and certainly not so soon. But after Paddy had gone, disappearing from my life with a soft kiss on the cheek and a wave of the hand – more than he had managed seventeen years ago – I stripped his bed, cleaned his room, cooked half the food I had bought for tonight and then ... Hours still stretched before me, the same as they had done before Paddy's visit – so why did those hours now feel so long, so empty? Paddy had taken the Guinness and my contentment too. He had made me think about the past in a way that I had chosen not to for years.

The DVD sat on the coffee table, winking at me, striving to capture my attention until in the end I snapped and shoved the disc into the DVD player. Three hours and three episodes later, having moved from my chair only once to fetch a cranberry and raspberry tea, I finally switched the television off, knowing that even halfway through the series, the damage was done. I was hooked. The show was a brilliant idea, contrasting the past with the present in order to highlight the similarities and differences. Over six episodes, the series followed archaeological investigations on three sites, discovering who had lived in the area and how the land had been used hundreds of years ago. At the same time, the programme showed what current life was like in the nearest town or village, featuring interviews with some real characters – and the locals were all encouraged to get involved with volunteering on the dig, and to connect with the history of their community.

The episodes had covered a variety of subjects: a medieval tithe barn in Herefordshire, a Roman villa in Essex and a Norman church in Kent, but there was one common factor. The passion, the enthusiasm and the curiosity of the whole team making the show was unmistakeable. And as for Paddy – whether talking about the dig, or drawing out hilarious anecdotes from villagers, he was a natural in front of the camera, and I chose that word deliberately. This wasn't a sham – it was a genuine performance from someone who knew and loved his subject and wanted to share his passion with others. He brought the show to life and, watching it, I could almost smell the earth and feel it beneath my fingers in the trenches. And a dormant piece of my heart started beating again.

The thoughts I had denied so long rushed in. I didn't want to be on my sofa, watching other people uncover history. I wanted to be in that trench myself, knee pads on and trowel in hand, scrabbling around in the dirt and dust, finding the clues about past civilisations and past lives. I wanted to discover the footprints of buildings and communities long buried – to help remap the world as it used to be in centuries gone by. And the more I thought about it, the more certain I became. I didn't just want to do it. I *had* to do it.

I would be forty in August: too young to stagnate in a job I increasingly disliked, and too old to let an opportunity pass by without grasping it. I was healthy and so was my bank balance – when would this chance ever come again? It was now or never. And as I watched the rest of the series, and took time over the half-term break to consider my future as I hadn't allowed myself to do before, I became increasingly certain about what my next step would be.

Jo Blair was surprised when I asked for a word on the first day back after half-term. I followed her into the office before she could refuse. She sat down behind her desk, assuming a position of power, but I remained standing: this wouldn't take long.

'Do you remember when you first arrived, and you asked me to spy on the members of staff?' I asked.

'Not spy,' Jo replied, clearly caught off guard by the question. 'I thought that as a long-serving member of staff you were well placed to give feedback.'

I nodded; it was semantics, we both knew that.

'I've reconsidered,' I said. 'I've given it a lot of thought over half-term, and I can't keep quiet. There's a member of staff who doesn't seem motivated to do their job. I'm concerned that you may consider their performance inefficient. Their commitment to the school isn't what it once was.'

Jo Blair leant across the desk. 'This is exactly the sort of information I was looking for. Well done, Eve. Who is it?'

'It's me.' I threw an envelope onto her desk, where it landed at a rakish angle in the middle, in delightful defiance of the clear desk policy. 'There's my resignation. I'll work to the end of term.'

I walked to the office door and then turned.

'Oh, and Jo? The way you spoke to me the other week was out of order. Harassment, bullying – I'd say it was gross misconduct of one sort or another, wouldn't you? All done in front of witnesses too. But I've decided not to report you, because you only have a few more weeks left at this school, don't you? You'll be starting your next interim post after summer. And I wouldn't want to harm your chances of moving on – or harm the chances of this school to be able to attract the sort of permanent head it deserves: one who appreciates its staff, and cares more about raising happy, confident children than about bottom lines, efficiencies and statistics.'

I walked out and returned to my desk, where I sank into my chair. I had no idea if it would work, and dissuade Jo from any thought of applying for the permanent role, but it was worth a shot. I reached into my handbag and took out one of the remaining Be Kind to Yourself vouchers. With hands shaking, and feeling a curious mix of exhilaration and terror, I wrote out the next card.

BE KIND TO YOURSELF
VOUCHER SEVEN
I, Eve Roberts, have been kind to myself by resigning from my job!

Tina was open-mouthed when I told her what I'd done.

'Resigned?' she repeated, as I drove along by the side of the river, heading back through the outskirts of Inglebridge and on towards home. 'Have you been drinking?'

'Of course not. In fact, this is the result of sober reflection that I should have indulged in months ago.' Maybe even years ago. 'The cheque from Mum has given me a chance I can't waste. I can afford to take some time off, try something different. It might be a disaster. It's undoubtedly rash to hand in my notice before I've even thought about what else I can do. But I have to give it a go.'

'So I'm going to have to drive myself to school from September? I'd better inherit your space or there'll be trouble.' Tina grimaced. 'I can't believe you're leaving me to face Jo Blair on my own, if she does apply for the head's post.'

'You never know, she might decide that Inglebridge isn't the place for her after all.' I smiled to myself. Jo Blair better had move on – if she returned in September, either in an interim or permanent position, my complaint would go in the next day.

We arrived home and as we left the car, Tina came round and gave me a hug, squeezing me so tightly I could hardly breathe.

'Good for you,' she said, drawing back. 'I don't know what's brought this on, but I hope it works out.'

'So do I.' I smiled. 'I need to try, while I can. I don't want to reach a point in life where I look back and see so many things not done.'

As Paddy's mum, Alison, did now. I had thought about her a lot since the day we had visited. Not only her, but Faye too, and even my dad. What opportunities might they have grasped if they had known what lay ahead? I felt as if I owed it to them to make the most of everything that came my way.

'It's been quite a momentous day, hasn't it?' Tina said, digging out her house keys. 'I think I'd better have a celebratory drink on your behalf. I don't suppose even this will knock you off the wagon, will it? Tell me you're doing something to mark the occasion.'

'I'll probably go for a run.' I grinned as Tina rolled her eyes. 'But I do have something special lined up for later. You'll have to wait until tomorrow to find out about that!'

I decided to walk to Rich's house after my run. It was a perfect early summer evening, and the sun still shone down from the pale denim sky, gilding the warm stone of the buildings in Inglebridge town centre. Even on a midweek night, the market square was half-filled with cars, and the restaurants and pubs buzzed with laughter and conversation as I passed by.

The French bistro, on the corner of the ginnel that led down to the river, looked particularly appealing with the dimmed lights, checked tablecloths and candles on the tables. Despite the tempting menu and brilliant reviews, I'd never been: it was phenomenally expensive, and I had usually felt obliged to support Lexy at The White Hart when I'd taken Caitlyn out for a meal. But with unexpected cash in the bank, and unused 'Be Kind to Yourself' vouchers in my bag, I vowed that would change. When Caitlyn and Mum came over for my birthday in August, we'd go to the bistro for a meal. We could even invite Gran, if we could persuade her to behave and not go on about frog's legs and garlic.

Rich had taken his children away over half-term, and so I hadn't seen or spoken to him since Paddy and I had caught him in the pub with his younger woman. The break had given me space to reassess our relationship, and what I wanted from it. The answer had been surprisingly clear.

I banged on the door. Rich opened it, nodded at me, and stepped back to let me in.

'You took your time,' he said, as he dropped down into his armchair, without offering me a drink. 'I thought you'd have been in touch to apologise before now.'

'Apologise?' I repeated, dumbfounded by Rich's attitude. I'd expected an apology from him, not an attack. 'What do I have to apologise for?'

'Don't play the innocent. I saw you in the pub the other weekend with that long-haired tosser off the telly.'

I leant back against the mantelpiece, needing to feel the solid marble beneath my fingers – to feel something real, unlike whatever accusations Rich was making.

'I'd taken him to visit his parents, because he'd injured his leg,' I said, and then immediately regretted the urge to explain myself, and the betrayal of any details of that day with Paddy. 'We stopped for a drink on the way home. It *was* innocent. *You* were kissing whoever you were with.'

'She's nothing.' He picked up his can of lager and took a swig. 'You don't need to worry about her.'

He thought I was jealous? How could he know me so little, after the two years we had been together? Paddy had been apart from me for seventeen years and he knew me better than this. And as Rich grinned at me, enjoying the moment and my perceived envy over his other woman, there was only one idea that sprang to mind. He *was* boorish. How had I missed it? Because I hadn't spent time getting to know him, hadn't chosen to look beyond the superficially attractive blond-haired and blue-eyed exterior. We had been compatible, both physically and in our limited requirements from a relationship, and I hadn't dug deeper – an irony, when all my training had been about looking below the surface before making a judgement. Who was the shallow one now?

But even before catching him in the pub, I'd begun to feel niggles of dissatisfaction. We had nothing in common, either in our interests or in our outlook. I didn't listen to him talk and admire his knowledge and his passion. When we sat in silence, it was awkward, not comfortable: our silence was independent, not shared. I would never weep myself to sleep over Rich, and I had thought that was what I wanted – but I'd been wrong. What was the point of being with someone who didn't stir your soul?

'I'm not worried about your other woman,' I said at last. 'I'm relieved you have someone else. It makes it so much easier to walk away. In fact, scrub that. I'm not walking. I'm running, as fast as I can go.'

'You'll regret it!' Rich called after me, as I headed for the front door, but he was wrong. I regretted many things, but I would never regret this one. I slammed the door shut on that episode of my life and headed home without looking back.

BE KIND TO YOURSELF
VOUCHER EIGHT
I, Eve Roberts, have been kind to myself by dumping Rich!

I'd wondered how long it would take Caitlyn to ring after receiving the latest vouchers. The answer was four days; she must have called as soon as my letter arrived.

'Mum? Are you okay?' she asked, cutting across my usual

battery of questions about how she was and what she had been doing.

'Never better.'

'But these Be Kind to Yourself vouchers you've sent ...'

'I'm doing well, aren't I? Two at once! This is so much fun.'

There was a brief silence at the other end and I could easily imagine that Caitlyn was rolling her eyes in the melodramatic way she did when I exasperated her. I tried not to laugh.

'It says you've quit your job.'

'I have.'

'And dumped Rich?'

'Yes. It's not before time, is it?'

Another silence. I was enjoying myself. Over the last few days, since cutting ties with work and Rich, I had felt a lightness and happiness that I hadn't known for a while – certainly not since Caitlyn had left. My future was empty – deliciously so. It was exhilarating, not terrifying as I might have expected. I almost felt as I had done when I had left university; as if the world was out there, waiting for me to make my mark on it. I didn't underestimate how lucky I was to have this chance.

'Have you started the menopause?' Caitlyn asked. 'Is this what it does? Makes you go a bit weird? Because, you know, the vouchers were only meant for fun things. Like having a facial or buying a new dress. I didn't mean to cause all this trouble.'

'A new dress? There's an idea ...' I laughed and took pity on her. 'I promise I'm not being weird. Weirder,' I added, in deference to Tina's frequent complaint about me and my temperate, healthy lifestyle. 'And you certainly haven't caused any trouble. You made me think more carefully about my life, that's all. Perhaps it is time to be kinder to myself, explore some of those opportunities.'

'Like going on the dig. I told you that was a good idea. But won't you miss Rich? I mean, you're not sounding exactly heart-broken, but you'll be even more on your own now. And it must be hard, at your age, finding someone who's in full working order.'

She giggled, and I sighed.

'You can't start the old age jokes yet. I'm still in my thirties.'

'Only for two and a half more months!' Oddly, that reminder actually made me even happier. Caitlyn would be back for my birthday; I'd be seeing her again in a few weeks' time. It was worth turning forty for that alone.

'Well, I'm glad you listened to me at last!' Caitlyn laughed. 'Remember what you've always told me. You're brave enough and talented enough and loved enough to achieve anything you want. It's your turn. Go for it, Mum. Love you!'

Chapter 17

Even on a day of relentless drizzle, the Inglebridge Saturday market was packed with shoppers. I visited every week, and there was always something new to see, as the stallholders displayed the best of the season's produce, and tried to catch the attention – and empty the pockets – of the tourists who visited town. I loved browsing among the stalls and chatting to the traders: selecting hunks of local cheese, cut from the truckle that had come straight from the dairy; choosing freshly caught fish from the assortment brought down from the Cumbrian coast; and filling my basket with vegetables still covered with soil.

But as I paid the greengrocer and moved on to the next stall, there was something new to see that I would never have expected: I glimpsed a mop of dark curls behind me. Just as I was convincing myself that it couldn't possibly be Paddy, a familiar laugh rang out, and the man turned and caught me staring.

'Eve!' Paddy smiled and stepped towards me. I wondered if he would try to kiss my cheek, but I was laden down with baskets, and he had a paper bag in his hand, so any closer contact was too tricky. 'I was about to call and see you. I even have gifts!' He waved the paper bag at me.

'From the bakery stall?'

'Ah, I know what you're thinking. I shouldn't tempt you with cream cakes when you're trying to stick to the healthy living malarkey.' That was close enough to what I'd been thinking. 'So I bought the flapjacks. Full of oaty goodness, aren't they? You can't object to that.'

He laughed, and I found myself smiling back.

'What are you doing in Inglebridge again?' I asked. It was almost a month since he had left my house, after his leg injury, and I hadn't heard from him since. Not that there had been any reason why I should.

'Haven't you heard? The third series of *Travels Through Time* has been confirmed. We've come to do some initial filming.'

I hadn't heard a thing; I'd been extra busy at school recently, working late some nights, trying to put everything in order before I left. It was hard to believe I was really going, and there had been the occasional pang of sadness when I had made arrangements for events that would take place in the next academic year, and which I wouldn't be around to see. Not enough pangs to make me regret my decision, though.

'You're definitely going to feature the barrow site?' I asked.

'It's definitely one of the ones we're considering. The investigations we carried out at Easter suggested there might be other barrows, less prominent than the main one we saw. We'll dig some test trenches, and if it looks interesting, draw up plans for a full excavation next year.'

An excavation on my doorstep! I couldn't believe that after staying away from archaeology for so long, it had now come to me.

'Well, good luck with that,' I said, starting to turn away.

'Hey! Hang on. Why don't you come round and have a look at what we've found out so far? I was on my way to your house to see if you'd be interested. And you might be able to help me with something, too. You don't know a local plumber, do you? There are three of us in a holiday let, and we've had to switch the water off because a tap was leaking everywhere. The owner seems to have gone away for the weekend. If we can't have a shower, it's going to get kinda smelly ...'

'Lucky it's raining then ...' I replied. Paddy laughed. 'I usually fix things like that myself. I can have a look, if you want?'

'If you're sure it's no bother. You're going to put us three men to shame ...'

'Let me take this shopping home, then I'll come round and have a look,' I said. 'What's the address?'

Half an hour later, I arrived at the semi-detached cottage where Paddy was staying. It was in a gorgeous spot, overlooking the river from the front, but it still seemed a come-down after the Fairlie, and even after The White Hart.

'Not quite the lifestyle you're used to, is it?' I said, as Paddy let me in. 'Was there no room at the Fairlie?'

'No money in the kitty for the Fairlie,' he replied. 'And I don't think they'd be so keen on us staying when we arrive back covered in mud from a day's digging.' He showed me into the kitchen, a pretty room with traditional Aga and large farmhouse table. 'You could say we're the lucky ones, having a house. The younger members of the team are camping.'

He hadn't always been against camping. We'd spent many happy hours wrapped in each other's arms under canvas as night had fallen, when the only sounds had been our own hearts beating and the screech of owls over our heads; hours spent exploring each other's bodies in total darkness, where the potency of every touch seemed magnified by the restriction in our vision.

'Although camping can be a pretty special experience,' he said, and when I glanced at him in surprise, I knew he was remembering those times too – I could see it in the warmth of his smile and the way his eyes lingered on mine. I broke eye contact first.

'Tell me where the leaking tap is and I'll get to work,' I said, and he grinned.

'Over there – the cold tap.'

I unscrewed the handle while Paddy told me about the barrow site, and what they had discovered so far from the local archives, an exploration of the field, and the lidar surveys. Their initial guess was that it was a Bronze Age barrow, not a later copy by the Vikings, which was probably disappointing news for Paddy. The good news was that there were no scars on the surface of the barrow, so it didn't look as if previous generations had already excavated and ruined the site, while hunting for the grave goods, such as pottery or jewellery, that might have been buried with a body.

It was fascinating, and I could have listened to him all morning. I removed a worn rubber washer from the tap and replaced it with a new one from my toolbox, and then when I'd switched the water back on and checked that the leak had stopped, I pored over the aerial photographs and plans that Paddy had spread across the kitchen table.

'Why don't you come to the site and have a look?' he asked, as we bent over the table, heads almost touching. 'The proper digging starts on Monday.'

'I can't. I'll be at school.'

'I could give you a preview tomorrow?'

'I'm visiting Gran.' I sensed Paddy turn his head and look at me. I stepped back, away from the table. Of course, I'd love to go – I wouldn't have hesitated if it had been anyone but Paddy who had asked. This was exactly what I wanted, to be back on a dig. But not to be back on a dig with *him*. Memories of the past were already circling round us. Why would I be fool enough to confront them head on like that? The good memories of Paddy brought as much pain as the bad ones; perhaps more.

'That's a shame,' Paddy said, shuffling the photos and documents back into a file. 'How is Phyllis? Still basking in her moment of fame?'

'It will keep her going for years,' I said, glad to be back on a safe topic. 'Or at least until the minibus arrives, and she can try and grasp a few more minutes of publicity at the official launch. She's got a taste for it now.'

Paddy laughed. 'She's an amazing woman. I can see where you get it from.' I had no response to that. His face gave no clue what he meant by it. 'So what are they doing without a minibus?' he asked. 'She mentioned how much they love the trips to the cinema. Are they still managing to go?'

'No. They haven't been since the minibus broke down.'

'When's the next film night?'

'Every Wednesday, but they only go to see the classic films. It's the first Wednesday of the month, so it should be on this week.'

'And how many from The Chestnuts want to go?'

'About a dozen, I suppose.' I shrugged. 'Why all the questions?'

'Because we could help. There are three of us staying here, plus you, and we all have cars. Between us, we could take a dozen to the cinema.'

Was he serious? He certainly looked and sounded serious. But why would he offer to do that?

'You don't need to ...' I said.

'I know. But I'd like to.' Paddy smiled. 'Don't write me off, okay? Whatever I was, whatever I did, I'm not that person any more. I can be pretty decent sometimes, you know.'

Gran obviously thought Paddy's offer was a personal favour to her. When we turned up in convoy at The Chestnuts on Wednesday night, ready to collect our passengers, she lorded it over the other residents, directing which car they should all go in, and generally getting in the way of the staff members who were trying to manage the excursion safely. I expected Gran would come in my car, but I should have known better.

'I'm travelling with Paddy,' she said, when I held open my passenger door for her. 'Mrs Pike is in with you. I spared you Mr Craig,' she added, with a grin. 'I thought he'd be better off in the car with leather seats, just in case. Easier to wipe down.'

It was a short drive into Inglebridge, where the film night was held in the old playhouse that faced onto the market square. It was one of the grandest buildings in town, built of pale stone, and with an imposing flight of steps leading up to an entrance that featured two huge columns on either side of double width doors. Plays were still performed there several times during the year – usually amateur dramatic performances, and always a pantomime at Christmas – but a community group had started the film screenings a couple of years ago, rotating between vintage favourites, cult classics, family choices and blockbusters. The nearest proper cinema was fifteen miles away, so this was a popular night out; I had often come along with Caitlyn, but had been reluctant to attend on my own since she went to Paris. Tonight was as busy as ever: as we pulled up outside the playhouse to unload The Chestnuts gang, a decent crowd was streaming up the steps and into the building.

The organisers always reserved a row of seats for The Chestnuts, but there was a problem tonight: they had reserved the usual number, not realising there were additional drivers, and if we all wanted to stay to watch the film, we were two seats short.

'Our Eve won't mind sitting somewhere else,' Gran said, dispatching me without a glance as I hovered in the aisle. She nudged Paddy, who she had initially allocated a seat in pride of place next to her. 'Look sharp. You'd better go and keep her company. She'll sneak off for a run, given half a chance, and she's scrawny enough as it is. Send that young cameraman of yours to sit with me. He's a bonny lad. He can share my toffees any day.'

'You don't need to stay,' I said, as Paddy vacated his seat in favour of the cameraman, and joined me in the aisle. 'If you'd rather go over to The White Hart, I can ring you when we're ready to leave.'

'Don't tell me you're rejecting me as well? I thought Phyllis was bad enough. Two knock-backs in one night will do terrible things to my ego.'

'I'm sure it's big enough to survive.' Nevertheless, I let him usher me towards two vacant seats, a couple of rows behind Gran.

'This takes me back,' Paddy said, as we settled in our seats, and the lights began to dim.

'To the last film you saw?' I replied, lowering my voice as conversations faded around us, in anticipation of the film starting. 'Surely that was a red carpet premiere? The Inglebridge playhouse must be a come-down after that.'

I had been joking, but I saw Paddy nod.

'It was a premiere. But who wants to watch a film, while

stuffed into a dinner jacket and sitting with people you don't know?' He leant towards me. 'I meant to the last film I saw with you.'

The opening titles of the film started to play, sparing me from answering. What had been the last film I'd seen with Paddy? I couldn't remember. That was the trouble with unexpected departures – not just his, but Faye's and my dad's too. Significant events weren't given the attention they deserved – the red carpet treatment they would have had, if we'd known what the future held. Memories that should have been savoured and preserved were allowed to fade. Last conversations, meals, jokes, kisses, could all be lost forever. And some last conversations could never be undone.

Tonight's film was a classic musical, *High Society*, which I couldn't remember seeing before. Many of the songs were familiar, even if the story wasn't, and they clearly went down well with the Chestnuts contingent. They were all singing along, and Gran and Mrs Pike seemed to be competing to see who could sing the loudest. I could feel Paddy shaking with laughter beside me.

'Who do you think is winning?' he whispered into my ear. 'I'd say Phyllis by a nose.'

'She won't be satisfied with such a narrow victory. She'll want clear ground between them.' As I spoke, Gran's voice rang out more loudly. I could hear giggles and murmuring from a group of teenagers nearby – an unlikely audience for this film, and I hoped they weren't going to spoil it for everyone else. But before I could turn and see if I recognised the culprits from school, Paddy sat up straighter in his seat and started singing as well. What on earth was he doing? He could just about carry the tune, but he wouldn't win any awards for his musical skills. He nudged me with his elbow, in much the same way as Gran might have done.

'Come on,' he whispered. 'Let's all join in.'

'I don't know the words!'

'Make something up. We can't let them be laughed at by a bunch of kids.'

I did, and soon a majority of the audience was joining in with the songs and belting out the choruses, and for once it felt like the community cinema was just that – uniting us all in appreciation of the movie and the music, transforming a simple film screening into a magical event that we would all remember long after tonight. And the Chestnuts gang was at the centre of it all, the first to launch into every song, holding the tunes through the less well-known sections, and one elderly gentleman was even waving his arms like a conductor. They were loving the experience – and I couldn't stop thinking that they had Paddy to thank for it. Far from being the shallow man I had believed him to be, he was revealing new depths every time I saw him.

'I hope I have half their spirit when I reach their age,' he murmured, leaning towards me again between songs. He was so close that his hair brushed across my cheek.

'I hope I reach their age,' I said. It was an instinctive response – I hadn't meant to bring the mood down – and I focused on the screen again, wishing I could recapture the light-hearted feelings of a few moments ago, wishing that the past didn't always lurk over me. And then, in the darkness, Paddy's hand reached out and held mine.

It was a merry group of pensioners that we returned to The Chestnuts after the film had finished. Gran was still humming songs from the film as she hobbled over to wish me goodnight.

'They don't make them like that any more,' she said. 'That Grace Kelly was quite something, wasn't she? You should take a leaf out of her book. Try to be more like her.'

'Blonde, elegant and about to marry a prince?' I laughed. 'You might be expecting too much of me.'

'Don't be daft. I meant like her in the film. Didn't it make you think, when she got back with her first love? Some folk are better off together. There's no point wasting time and being stubborn about these things.'

Why hadn't I seen this coming? Gran must have been delighted with the choice of film; it wouldn't surprise me if she had somehow arranged for this one to be shown. She never turned down an opportunity for mischief. I smiled, and shook my head.

'There's more chance of me marrying a prince than that happening,' I said. 'Don't start looking for a new dress any time soon.'

'Oh, I don't need to start. I've already got my eye on the perfect thing.'

She actually had her eye on something behind me, and with a creeping sense of inevitability, I turned and saw Paddy standing there. How long had he been with us? Not long enough to hear Gran's nonsense, I hoped.

'Goodnight, Phyllis,' he said, bending down to kiss Gran's cheek. 'Any time you want to go clothes shopping, just give me a call.'

Great! Now they were both talking nonsense. I frowned at them, but they smiled back with matching smiles of saucy innocence.

'Time for me to catch up on my beauty sleep,' Gran said. She nodded at me. 'Make sure you thank Paddy properly for going to all this trouble tonight. The least you can do is buy him a drink. Or take him back home for a mug of Ovaltine.'

Smiling at her persistence, I gave her a hug, and watched as the carers rounded up all the residents and herded them back inside The Chestnuts. Paddy waited with me.

'She's a marvel, isn't she?' he said. 'You're lucky to have her.'

'I know.' We hovered awkwardly by my car, and I wondered if he was thinking of his mum; probably twenty years younger than Gran, but in much poorer health. He smiled at me, but it didn't stretch to his eyes; sadness lingered there.

'I can't offer you Ovaltine, but you're welcome to a fruit tea,' I said, the invitation springing from my mouth before I'd had a chance to think it through. 'Unless you've got other plans ...'

'Bath, bed and book,' he said, his smile expanding. 'Nothing that can beat the offer of a fruit tea ...'

He followed me back to my house, and as I switched on the lamps and made our tea, the memories buffeted me again. How many times had we done this before? It felt so normal, to come home from a night out and share a drink with Paddy – although it had rarely been tea in those days; it hardly felt as if the years had passed at all. It was like being back in those initial few months after university, when we had shared our first flat and woven dreams about our future. They had been the happiest times I had ever known. And the day that Paddy had left had been one of the unhappiest times. How had it come about, that the man who had brought me so much happiness and so much pain, was sitting on my sofa now, telling me about the progress on the dig, making me smile with his stories, as if the past had been swept away and forgotten?

He caught me staring at him, as I studied his face, trying to reconcile the two versions of Paddy: the one who had hurt me and Caitlyn all those years ago, without any hint of remorse, and the man here now, who had given up his evening to take old people he didn't know to the cinema. Who was the real Paddy Friel? Could he really have changed so much? He broke off what he was saying.

'Is this weird?' he asked.

'Yes.' On so many levels. It was only a few weeks since he had been staying with me, after the sponsored walk, but this felt different; he was here because I'd asked him to be here – wanted him here? – not because there had been no other choice.

'Because of us? Or because you normally do this with your man, the boor? Am I in his place?'

I'd never done this with Rich. We'd never sat in my house together as the light faded, discussing our days and what our hopes were for tomorrow. We'd eaten together, watched television together, had sex ... greater intimacies than these quiet moments with Paddy, but my emotions had never been engaged as they were now.

'He's not my man.' I shrugged, not looking in Paddy's direction. 'We're not together any more.'

'Because of the woman in the pub?'

'Partly.' And partly because I had realised we weren't compatible; because spending time with Paddy had made me realise we weren't compatible. But I wasn't going to explain that to Paddy.

'Do you not think you might have been able to forgive him, in time? If it was a stupid mistake, and he could convince you he regretted it?'

Now I glanced at Paddy, because I wondered why he was persisting with this; what did it matter to him whether I could forgive Rich or not? He hadn't scrupled to share his poor opinion of him. He was leaning forward in his seat, mug clutched between his hands, watching me, a curious frown on his face.

'Life's too short to waste time on second chances,' I said. I thought about all the things I had to look forward to: leaving work, going on the Cotswolds dig, my birthday – and then what? Finding a new career? There was so much lying ahead of me; I wasn't going to take a step backward by getting involved with Rich again. 'Isn't that the point of a fortieth birthday?' I added, trying to lighten the mood. 'Isn't it the perfect time to start again?'

'You're right.' Paddy grinned, and the frown lifted. He leant forward, and clinked his mug against mine. 'Here's to starting again.'

Chapter 18

The last few weeks of the school year rushed by, and before I'd even come to terms with leaving, I was driving away for the last time, with a pot plant and a garden centre voucher as the only souvenirs of a thirteen-year career. Three days later, on a dank, drizzly Monday morning that didn't seem a particularly auspicious start to my glittering new future, I set off to the dig in south Gloucestershire – my first step towards exploring whether this might be my new career.

It wasn't the first time I'd taken part in a dig in the Cotswolds. My dad had first brought me to the area, on one of our weekend excursions while Mum and Faye were busy shopping. On our way home after a walk, we'd stumbled upon the site of a Roman villa, and called in to have a look. That accidental visit had changed my life. I'd hung on every word the tour guide had uttered, fascinated by the details about how it had been discovered and the archaeological work that was still going on, and marvelling at the intricate mosaics and the artefacts that were housed in a small museum – artefacts that had survived over hundreds of years.

My interest had been hooked from that day on, and when one summer I'd been able to spend a day volunteering there, I had known without a doubt that I wanted to carry on with this for the rest of my life. I'd even taken Paddy back to that Roman villa on one of his visits to our house, because it had been such a special place to me.

I'd avoided going back to the area until now, fearing what painful memories might be waiting for me there, especially of Dad and of Paddy. But now, as the weather brightened and I drove through honey-stoned villages and towns, and swathes of lush, rolling countryside, instead of sadness, I was filled with an unexpected sense of contentment. I had loved the days I had spent exploring this area with Dad; those memories would always be good and precious, despite the tinge of loss. As for Paddy, we had been happy when we'd visited here, I was sure of it; in the prime of our relationship, in those glorious months when the future still seemed ours for the taking, and I had believed that our love was strong enough to withstand anything. So I let the memories in, let them play out in my mind, but it was only sadness I felt, not anger. Seeing Paddy again, spending time with him, had done me good, and helped me gain some perspective at last. We'd loved well and parted badly, but I couldn't let the bad memories blind me to the good ones. It had all been so long ago. We were different people now. As we'd agreed that night of the cinema trip with Gran, it was time to start again.

The dig I was joining was taking place in a field a few miles south of Cirencester, and I'd researched it extensively online. It was an amazing story. Several years ago, the owner of the field had planned to build a garage block in the grounds of his manor house, and had uncovered the remains of an ancient wall when preparing for the foundations. He had done the right thing and called in a team of archaeologists. Their investigations and subsequent excavations had confirmed this as the site of a Roman villa, one of the largest ever found in the area. It was exactly the sort of excavation and the era that I'd loved the most at university. I couldn't wait to join in.

I had booked a room in a nearby village pub for the two weeks I was taking part in the dig, and it was only a short drive on the Tuesday morning to our meeting place. We weren't due to start work until nine, but I set off straight after breakfast, desperate to begin, and I soon found out that I wasn't the only one. Even though I arrived half an hour early, there were already a few people waiting by the Portakabin that was used as a finds office, including a familiar face – my old university tutor, Christopher Porter. He spotted me as I walked towards the group and met me halfway.

'Eve Roberts!' He put out his hand and shook mine with enthusiasm. 'I saw your name on the list and wondered if it could be the same one. How long has it been?'

'Nineteen years since graduation.' I grimaced, hearing it out loud. Where had the time gone? Back in my familiar uniform of old clothes and sturdy boots, I felt like an excited undergraduate again, not a middle-aged woman. 'Let's not dwell on that. How are you?'

I was trying not to be too shocked by his appearance: his once dark hair was now pure grey and he seemed a shrunken version of the dynamic man I remembered. A shadow lurked in his eyes, a sign of sorrow that I recognised. Impulsively I reached out and squeezed his arm, releasing him from answering the question.

'It's good to see you again,' I said. 'This dig looks amazing. Have you worked on it before?'

'Every year since it started. I've brought students down on field studies too. We both loved the Romans, didn't we? So what have you been up to, Eve? Still pursuing archaeology, I hope?'

'No, I haven't been able to. My plans changed. I had family commitments ...' I stopped. I didn't want to go into the whole history of Faye and Caitlyn here. I neither wanted nor deserved sympathy. And if this was a fresh start, I had to stop hiding behind my past. That was the whole point of coming on the dig, wasn't it: to discover more about the Romans' past and my future. Fortunately, Christopher was distracted by the arrival of more volunteers, and wandered away with the promise of more conversation later.

The dig was divided into sections, and the volunteers were split into teams to work each section. One team was assigned to digging further trenches, in order to follow the external wall of the villa to see how extensive it was; the current guess was that there must have been at least twenty rooms on the ground floor. Another team was working in an area where bones had been found in previous years: identifying the animals the bones came from gave an insight into the diet of the people who had lived there.

I wouldn't have minded that job – I loved the small details about day-to-day life – but I was placed with one of the teams who were exposing more of what promised to be an amazing mosaic-tiled floor, which would probably have been at the centre of the villa. A section about three metres square had been revealed so far, and almost all the tesserae – the small pieces of stone that made up the mosaic – were still in place and had held their colours well; predominantly white, black, yellow and brown, with some small patches of red and blue in more ornate decorative sections. It looked as if the mosaic featured scenes from mythology, and the level of detail was incredible. I couldn't wait to uncover more of it, and see if we could work out what stories were illustrated there.

My team consisted of a young couple in their mid-twenties, two male undergraduates who were Christopher's students, and Beverley, a single lady in her early fifties, who turned out to have come over from California to take part in this and several other digs over the summer. After brief introductions, one of the undergraduates volunteered to be in charge of drawing the plan, showing the precise locations of everything we discovered, and the rest of us entered the trench and set to work.

My trowel fitted in my hand as if it had never left. I knelt down in the trench, pads protecting my knees, and started scraping gently at the earth that covered the next part of the mosaic. The ground was hard and dry after a spell of warm weather and at first I worked gingerly, making cautious scrapes as I found my way again. But my confidence grew with every shift of the trowel, and soon my hands were moving over the soil as easily as they had done over a computer keyboard only a few days before. Muscle memory kicked in: this was what my hands had been trained for, not typing and filing and answering the phone.

I sat back and looked around at the various teams as they bent over their tasks with eager enthusiasm; I listened to the rhythmic clinks of trowel against stone, and I knew beyond doubt, before even half a day had passed, the answer I'd hoped attending this dig would provide. This was where I was supposed to be. This was what made me happy – what would make me happy in the future.

I sat with Beverley during our first morning tea break, and we chatted more about our backgrounds. She was an enthusiastic amateur, and although she had no formal qualifications in archaeology, she had years of experience in taking parts in digs all over the world. The list of sites she had worked on filled me with envy; it could have been a duplicate of the itinerary that Paddy and I had planned. I both dreaded and longed to hear more about her experiences over the next couple of weeks.

'You must have a remarkably understanding family,' I said, as she mentioned her plans for the rest of the year, including four weeks in Romania in late September, where she hoped to explore both the Roman and medieval history of the country, and fit in a visit to Transylvania. 'Don't they mind you spending so much time away?'

'Oh, I don't have family,' she said, smiling. 'The folks died long ago. I never married, never had children. I can do as I please. It's the best way to be!'

They were lines I could have said myself; they certainly described the life I had now. I could do as I pleased. So why was there a flicker of doubt in my mind about whether it really was the best way to be? I was spared from thinking of a reply by Christopher wandering over to join us.

'How are you finding it, Eve? Has it all come flooding back?' he asked.

'Yes!' I could hardly contain my smile. 'I'm loving it. It's like I've never been away.'

'Hey, do you two know each other?' Beverley said. She turned to me. 'I thought this was your first dig in years.'

'It is. Christopher was one of my tutors at university, more years ago than either of us would like to admit.'

'Eve was my star pupil,' Christopher said, sitting down on the grass beside us. 'She had a great eye for looking past the chaos of a site in progress and seeing the scale of what it had once been. And she was as happy working on the behind-the-scenes analysis as being on the front line of an excavation. She made the most thorough, incisive notes of anyone I've ever taught.'

'Good for you,' Beverley said, patting me on the shoulder. 'It sounds like it's a shame you gave it up. You need to get back at it! Wouldn't you welcome her back, if she's so great?' she asked Christopher.

'Of course I would.' I shrank with mortification at Beverley's less than subtle approach, but Christopher didn't seem to mind. 'We're always looking for keen postgraduate students. I'd love to see you back, Eve, if you're interested.'

Interested? I could think of nothing I'd like more, and for a moment my head swam with possibilities: of returning to university and working with Christopher again; of studying a Master's degree and perhaps going on to a PhD ... I had the money to allow me some time out from work, and what better way to spend it than by attaining qualifications that would allow me to carry out more interesting work in future?

But then the possibilities sank, weighted down with reality. I couldn't disappear off to a university at the opposite end of the country from home. I had a house – Caitlyn's home, if she ever chose to come back. I had Gran – it was all very well to miss visiting her for one weekend while I was on this dig, but not for weeks at a time. There weren't any other universities near enough to allow me to live in Inglebridge while I studied; the isolated location I had once sought was now a disadvantage. It was a tempting dream to return to university, but not an achievable one.

'Just say the word if I can help, Eve,' Christopher said. 'If I can't tempt you with academia, I have contacts with employers across the country. I'd be more than happy to give you an introduction.'

I thought about Christopher's offer frequently over the next few days. Perhaps it was an off-the-cuff remark – no more than politeness – but it niggled at me. As we worked together in the intense mid-summer heat, the various teams across the sections bonded together as one unit in a way I remembered well and had missed more than I realised. There was something special about a group of like-minded enthusiasts uniting in a common goal; success for one was success for all. When the bones team unexpectedly discovered a Roman coin, we all celebrated, poring over the tiny piece of metal with as much delight as if it were part of the Crown Jewels. And as the days went by, my conviction grew that this was what I needed to be doing, one way or another. I didn't know how I was going to take it forward and make it work, I only knew that I had to do it.

My evenings were spent in my room in the village pub, doing what I had resisted for years: researching developments in archaeology since I had studied it, and reading about discoveries that had been made in the last two decades. Some I hadn't been able to avoid, as they had been significant enough to make the news, such as the investigation into whether there were hidden chambers in Tutankhamen's tomb. But equally interesting were the smaller discoveries, often stumbled across by accident, such as the Watlington Hoard, a collection of coins, jewellery and bars of silver found by a metal-detectorist and dating back to the time of Alfred the Great. And it wasn't only new discoveries that fascinated me; technology had advanced so that old finds could be analysed in more detail than ever before.

I sat on my bed with my laptop on my knee, and pored over it all, feeling the past come alive in more ways than one, and longing to find out more; trying to hold back thoughts of the one person who could share my enthusiasm, and gladly tell me everything I wanted to know.

By Friday, muscles that I'd forgotten existed were aching, my knees were sore despite the cushioned pads, and my nose was pink even though I'd applied lavish amounts of sun cream. I was loving every second of the dig. The whole team had arranged to go out to the nearest pub for a drink in the evening, to celebrate a successful first week, and I had decided that I would try to get Christopher on his own, to discover whether he really did know any employers who would be willing to take on someone with more enthusiasm than experience. So it was concerning that by the time we stopped for our mid-morning tea break, Christopher still hadn't arrived on site.

'Do you think he's ill?' I asked Beverley, as we scrambled back down into the trench to carry on. It was a sign of how keen we all were: no one had thought to slack off in Christopher's absence. 'Should we try to find him?'

'Hey, you worry too much,' Beverley said, showing a remarkable insight into my character after only a short acquaintance. 'I heard you Brits don't like spending money. Perhaps he's hiding somewhere so he doesn't have to buy us all drinks tonight.'

I laughed, but that didn't sound like Christopher. I carried on with my work on the mosaic, stopping now and again to drink some water – it was another scorching day, and the sun was relentless on our heads. I glanced over at the young couple who were part of my team. They were working side by side as they had done all week, heads bent low together, talking and laughing as they worked.

'Sweet, aren't they?' Beverley said, catching where I was looking.

I nodded. I'd tried not to watch them too much. They were young, keen, in love and reminded me irresistibly of me and Paddy. We'd been like that once, in the glory days of our relationship: unable to bear being on the opposite side of a trench to each other, unable to survive more than a few minutes without sharing a smile, a touch, a moment to connect and to affirm everything we felt for each other. As I looked away across the dig site, I could picture Paddy exactly as he had been in those days – shorts, tight T-shirt, curls drooping in the heat ... Except the figure I thought I was seeing in my imagination looked remarkably solid, and it was moving towards me and waving a hand. What on earth was going on? Was Paddy actually here? I began to wonder if my brain had been addled by too much sun.

'Well, would you take a look at that!' Beverley murmured at my side. 'If that's lunch, I'm ready for it.'

So it was true! Paddy really was here on site. I wasn't ready for it. I was hot and sweaty, and my face was undoubtedly shiny from all the sun lotion. My hair was sticky and flattened by my hat – and oh, I was furious with myself for caring about any of that. Paddy walked up to the side of the trench nearest me.

'How're you doing, Eve?' he said, smiling broadly. 'Fancy seeing you here.'

'What are you doing here?' I asked. The information about the dig hadn't mentioned that Paddy was involved; I wouldn't have missed his name. 'Are you joining the dig?'

'I'm now leading it.' He leant forward and stretched out a hand to help me out of the trench. I took off my gloves, grasped his hand and climbed out, conscious of the other volunteers staring.

'What's happened?' I asked, immediately fearing the worst.

'Is Christopher okay? I knew I should have checked up on him this morning. He's normally the first to arrive.'

'It would have been too late. He left last night.' Paddy drew me away from the trench, so we wouldn't be overheard. 'He had a family crisis and needed to go home urgently.'

I hoped it wasn't anything too serious; a family crisis was never a good thing in my experience.

'But why are you taking over?' I asked. 'You're no expert on the Romans.'

'Do you think you could shout that any louder? Jeez, remind me never to ask you for an introduction.' He smiled, and I had to laugh at his expression. 'I'm free for the next week and could come down here at short notice. It was either that or cancel the dig.'

'I didn't realise you were still in touch with Christopher.' It was odd – Christopher hadn't mentioned Paddy at all over the last few days, although he'd known we'd been a couple at university. Now his silence made sense. He must have known we were no longer a couple.

'We've been in touch on and off since uni. My company has provided work experience for many of his students. We've become closer in the last few years.' Paddy's smile dimmed and he pushed back his hair. 'He has a daughter with chronic kidney disease,' he said, leaning towards me and lowering his voice. 'I've helped him out a couple of times before, covering events he was due to attend. When he phoned last night ...' He shrugged. 'Well, there was no question but that I'd come and take over.'

And so it went on – the gradual erosion of all my former prejudices against Paddy; the vain, selfish, shallow man, who proved that description wrong every time we met. Why did he have to keep showing me this decent, thoughtful side? I was glad I didn't hate him any more, but I could have settled for that – for tolerating him. Now I began to worry I was in danger of liking him – and look where that had got me before.

'Are you sure you're well enough?' I asked, stepping back. I wobbled on the edge of the trench and Paddy's hand shot out to steady me. His grip was strong and firm on my arm. 'Is your leg fully recovered? You wouldn't want to risk an injury again.'

'It's as good as new. But it's kind of you to care.' Paddy grinned. 'This is going to be like old times, isn't it?'

That was exactly what I was afraid of.

Much as I had enjoyed working with Christopher, I couldn't deny that Paddy brought a new dynamic to the dig. What he lacked in specialist knowledge – and if I was honest, there was less lacking there than I had expected – he more than made up for with his energy and passion. He was more hands-on than Christopher had been, spending time with each team, digging in the various sections of the trench, and uniting everyone at break and lunch in enthusiastic discussion about what we had found and what we were learning. He drew out opinions and ideas from everyone, and with a series of barely visible nudges and seemingly casual questions, stimulated theories and propositions that we might never have come up with on our own.

He was good at this; he stretched our minds, making us learn from each other, educating us without us even realising what he was doing. And all the time, as I watched him interact with the members of the dig – engaging the quietest members of our group, calming the cockiest, brushing off any mention of his television career – my opinion of him shifted, as the prejudices I had stood on for so many years wore away beneath my feet.

On Saturday afternoon, as I was making my way back from

the Portaloos – my least favourite part of any dig, but essential given the amount of tea we drank – I heard a whistle and then Paddy's voice calling my name.

'I'm not a sheepdog,' I grumbled, as I nevertheless stomped obediently over to where Paddy was working in the trench with the team looking for bones. My curiosity got the better of me. 'Have you found something?'

'A piece of pottery. Come and look.'

I scrambled into the trench and Paddy carefully handed me the pottery. From the shape, it looked like a section of a bowl or vase, as there was part of a flat base and a curved side. It was a good-sized piece, about fifteen centimetres high, and the glossy red colour was still so rich that it could have come straight from a shop that morning. It would be the job of our finds expert to clean it properly and analyse the details, but I gently brushed off some of the dirt, so I could have a closer look.

'What do you think?' Paddy asked.

'It's beautiful.' And it truly was – the curved section featured an exquisite pattern of trailing foliage and flowers, moulded in intricate detail. 'It looks like Samian ware, doesn't it?' I added, referring to one of the most common, high quality types of Roman pottery, which was distinguished by this vivid red colour.

'That's what I thought.' Paddy smiled at me. 'But do you reckon it's an original piece, imported from Gaul, or a British copy?'

'Hard to say. But based on the fine quality and the finish, my guess would be an import, probably from one of the better potteries. Is there a maker's mark?'

I carefully cleaned around the base, so I could see it properly. Decorated pots like this often carried a stamp or signature to show who had created the mould, and who had made the pottery piece. It helped to identify where a piece had been made, and also to date the pottery, as we knew that certain makers worked at certain times. There was a stamp on this fragment, but there were only two letters before it was cut off. 'L ... E ...' I read. 'That's not enough. We need the rest of it!'

'Yes, ma'am!' Paddy laughed. 'Come on, team. We have our orders.'

He grinned at me, and I smiled back, totally lost in the past; not in Roman times, but in our past – mine and Paddy's. I held out the fragment to him and he reached out to take it. His arm was tanned like the rest of him, from spending so much time outdoors. It was stronger and more muscled than it had been, and his hands were roughened from years of digging. This body was unfamiliar, and yet I knew it intimately. What would it be like now, to experience it on mine – the tender familiarity mixed with the exquisite pleasure of new discovery?

I caught my breath. What was I thinking? Paddy was still watching me, and I felt as if I'd been mesmerised. I rushed back to my own trench, horrified at the turn my thoughts had taken and hoping that the sudden warmth I felt was nothing more than an early hot flush.

Chapter 19

By the time Sunday evening arrived, I was ready for our day off on Monday. I was relatively fit from all the running, but the dig was physically demanding in other ways, using a different set of muscles, and I would be glad to spend a day on my feet rather than on my knees. The pub where I was staying didn't serve food on a Sunday night, so after a shorter run than usual – disappointing, because I loved pounding along the bridleways through the glorious Cotswold countryside – I went out for a meal in a neighbouring village.

It was still warm when I returned, and many people were soaking up the evening sunshine in the beer garden. By contrast, the interior of the pub was almost empty, and as I headed through the snug towards the stairs to the bedrooms, I almost missed the solitary figure sitting in a gloomy corner. It was Paddy, a full glass of whiskey in his hand and an empty one on the table in front of him. He seemed to be looking down at his phone. Of all the pubs, in all the villages ... I hesitated for only a moment, but it was long enough. He looked up and the distress on his face – so different from the laughing smile he had worn all day – made me ignore my better judgement and walk over to him.

'Hello,' I said, ignoring the bleakness, the hazy eyes, the fumes of alcohol and the overwhelming evidence of something being not right. 'You've not been staying here all week, have you? I'm sure I'd have spotted you over breakfast.'

'First night here,' he said, and there was less Irish, more drunk about his voice than usual. 'I've had to move around. Wherever there was a room.'

I immediately felt bad. Christopher had been staying with friends, but I hadn't considered how Paddy would manage to find accommodation in the peak holiday season, or given any thought to how he was spending his evenings. Should I have offered to meet up? I'd spent so many years avoiding all mention of him that it hadn't occurred to me to do anything else. Perhaps I needed to readjust my behaviour as well as my views. I pulled out a chair and sat down.

'I'll be crap company,' Paddy said, talking to his glass. 'No fascinating conversation. No witty banter. None of the blarney.'

'Fair enough,' I said. 'I didn't come over for any of that. You look terrible. What's the matter?'

In answer, Paddy tapped at his phone and slid it across the table towards me. It was open at a Facebook page for Amy Friel who, according to a recent status update from this afternoon, was ecstatic at the birth of her son. I studied the photo of a red-faced, crumpled baby, trying to work it out – trying to spot a resemblance.

'Is he yours?' I asked at last. Paddy met my gaze and the sadness on his face spoke for him.

'No.'

'But that's your wife?'

'Ex-wife.'

'She still uses the name?'

'Only useful thing about me, apparently.' He gave me a wry

smile. 'You were unlucky. You got all the grief and none of the benefits.'

My answer slipped out, unplanned. 'The only benefit I ever wanted was to be with you.'

'I know.' He glanced up briefly, and I saw a flash of deeper sadness cross his face before he looked away again. 'You were always too good for me, right from the start.'

That wasn't true. I hadn't always been good, far from it. But I was making the mistake I had warned Paddy against before – of talking about the past. Our part of it, at any rate – I couldn't help being curious about his.

'How long have you been divorced?' I asked.

'Two years.'

So she'd moved quite fast, to have found someone else and had a baby since they separated. She must have wanted to put Paddy comprehensively behind her. I knew the feeling.

'What did you do to cause the split?'

That made him look up again. 'Jeez, you really don't have much faith in me, do you? Can't you believe we just drifted apart? Had irreconcilable differences?' I waited, knowing him too well. There was more to this than he was saying. He sighed and took a swig of whiskey.

'The irony is,' he said at last, 'that this time, with Amy, it was the lack of kids that pulled us apart.' I flinched, wondering what I'd started, not sure I wanted to hear any more. 'We couldn't have them. Not for lack of trying – God, we tried until it felt like we hadn't done anything else – like talk, or laugh – for months. And then the tests showed nothing wrong with either of us, so we started IVF and that didn't work either, but it began to feel as if that was the only thing binding us together, you know ... Have you ever wanted something so desperately, but been terrified of what might happen if you get it?'

I shook my head. The only things I had ever wanted were beyond my reach. Faye. Dad. Paddy. All gone too soon. All impossible to get back.

'And then Mam was diagnosed,' Paddy said. He was talking to his glass again. 'We had money saved up for a third go at IVF. I wanted to use it for Mam instead – to go private, get a second opinion, get her anything she needed. Amy didn't agree. We were getting old, she said – our time was running out.'

'So what did you do?' None of this was my business, but I was engrossed. This story hadn't featured on Paddy's Wikipedia page. This was a part of his life after me that I knew nothing about. And I wanted to know, because these were the stories that had changed him; these were the things that had transformed the boy who had walked out on me into the man slumped in the seat opposite me now.

Paddy sighed. 'I took the money and spent it on Mam.'

'Without telling your wife?'

'I told her I was going to do it. She said she'd leave me if I did. I stuck to my word. She stuck to hers. But you tell me – how do you choose between the family you want and the family you already have? Sometimes there are no good decisions and you have to make the one that feels right at the time, you know? Was it wrong?'

I shook my head. Not because I was agreeing with his decision, but because it was impossible for anyone else to judge it. I wasn't surprised at the decision he'd made – it was the one I would have expected Paddy to make: based on gut instinct, how he felt in the moment, without reflecting on what the consequences might be. He'd always had an impulsive nature. But without being in his shoes, I couldn't say if he was right or wrong. And I couldn't judge his wife either, bizarre though it seemed to me that she should have left him over this. I had no idea what it must have been like for her, desperate to have a baby and not receiving the support she wanted from Paddy. How could I say whether I would have made the same decision in her position? Although it was hard to imagine being with Paddy, and choosing to give him up.

'I'm sorry, Paddy,' I said, and reached out and fleetingly brushed my thumb against his. He let go of his glass and grasped my hand.

'I loved her. Amy. Not like ...' He broke off, squeezed my hand. 'In a different way, but a good way, you know? We were happy. And when she left, and I realised she wasn't coming back ...' He looked at me and I couldn't tear my eyes away from the expression on his face. 'Jeez, it hurt like hell. And it made me realise what I'd done to you. What you must have felt back then – and Caitlyn too. I'm sorry, Eve. I got it all wrong. I made the wrong call. You deserved better than that. You both did.'

I pushed back my chair, breaking contact with Paddy. I didn't want to hear this. What was the point? I had spent years learning to live with my own regrets. How would it help to know that he had regrets too?

'Another drink?' I didn't wait for an answer, but headed to the bar and ordered another whiskey. I dithered over my own drink. I had never come so close to craving alcohol – or rather, the numbness, the oblivion it could bring. Why had I thought it a good idea to have this sort of conversation with Paddy tonight? I should have stuck to my decision not to rake over the past. It was easier to keep an emotional distance from him when I could focus on the bare facts of what he had done – leaving me and Caitlyn when we were both bowed down with grief, and counting on him to carry us into the future.

But now I could see the facets and nuances of another Paddy: the man at the table behind me, with tears in his eyes, aching over a child who could have been his; the man who prostituted himself on television to help his dying mother; the man whose enthusiasm for archaeology had revived my own interest and who I wanted to learn more from. He had grown up, become more introspective, more thoughtful and more sensitive. A new Paddy, with the looks that I had loved and the character I wished he could have shown before ... It was a dangerous mix. I could feel the emotional distance closing day by day, whether I wanted it to or not. Alcohol would be a terrible idea tonight. I resisted temptation and ordered myself an orange juice.

Paddy smiled when I put the drinks down on the table.

'You won't help me drown my sorrows?'

'You're more than capable of doing it on your own.'

'I hate being on my own.' He picked up his fresh glass. 'When I look at Mam and Dad ... still together, despite everything. Still strong. Stronger, if anything. Why can't I have that?'

'You're seriously asking me to answer that?' I said.

'Wouldn't I like the answer?'

'Probably not.' Because what other answer could I give, but that he'd had all that with me – or the potential for all that – and he had chosen to throw it away?

'And what about you? Still on your own? Or have you had a change of heart, and forgiven your man?'

I sipped my drink and gazed around the pub. It was beginning to fill up now as the night grew cooler. The landlord had switched the lights on, making it seem pleasantly warm and snug, even on a summer's evening. It struck me how much I'd missed this: nights out in cosy pubs, being part of society, being with someone else. I'd probably shared more conversation with Paddy this evening than I had over months with Rich. The appeal of the independent life seemed to have dulled tonight.

'Eve?' Paddy needled when I didn't say anything.

'There won't be a change of heart.' Should I be honest? I supposed Paddy deserved it, after some of the things he had told me tonight. 'I'm not going to forgive him. I don't care enough about him to try.'

He looked at me then with unexpected clarity for someone who had drunk several whiskeys.

'Will you ever forgive me?'

The question hung, suspended between us. At last, I gave the only answer I could.

'I don't know.' And the moment stretched, because that answer seemed too much, too bare, and we both knew it. Why couldn't I give the same answer as I had done about Rich? That I didn't care enough? Because it wouldn't have been true. How I wished it was.

I finished my orange juice and began to push back my chair.

'Wait,' Paddy said. 'What are you doing on your day off tomorrow? Have you made plans?'

'Yes,' I said, relieved to be back on safe ground. 'I'm going to Bath.'

Paddy laughed. 'Let me guess. The Roman Baths? I should have known. Haven't you had enough of the Romans this week?'

'As if I ever could.' I smiled. 'Anyway, I'm not just visiting the Roman Baths. I'm going to the thermal ones too. It's one of my Be Kind to Yourself treats.'

'Your what?'

'It was Caitlyn's idea.' I'd forgotten I hadn't mentioned them to him. I rummaged in my bag. 'She made some vouchers for me when she left home. She insisted I had to do some things to treat myself after she'd gone, and send her the vouchers to prove what I'd done. Look.' I held out one of the cards to him. I'd already filled it in.

BE KIND TO YOURSELF
VOUCHER NINE
I, Eve Roberts, have been kind to myself by going to the thermal baths!

'Caitlyn designed this? She's artistic?' He ran his finger over the floral pattern that filled the edge of the card. I wondered if he was thinking back, remembering the times he had spent colouring in with Caitlyn. It had been one of her favourite activities, and Paddy had always been first choice to help her with it. 'She's talented.'

'She takes after Faye.'

He nodded. Faye's paintings had been like her: full of life, colour and brilliance, extraordinary in their imagination and execution. It was the only career she had ever considered, and her paintings were beginning to sell well in the months before she died. 'No interest in archaeology?' he asked.

'None at all. She hated history.' I smiled. I'd done my best, but she had still dropped the subject at the first opportunity. 'She settles the nature not nurture debate. None of my influence has rubbed off.'

Paddy tapped the card in his hand. 'This is your influence. This is kindness. Faye wouldn't have done this. She never spared a thought for anyone but herself ...'

I stared at him, surprised. What was he talking about?

Everyone had loved Faye; she had dazzled and charmed wherever she went. But he only met her after Caitlyn was born; perhaps she had been wrapped up in herself and her baby then, but wasn't that normal? He didn't know her like I did. She had spared a thought for someone else: me. She had always looked out for me and protected me; he and Faye had been the two people I had counted on most.

'What do you mean?' I asked. 'Why would you say that?' But he looked at me, took a swig of his whiskey, and shook his head.

'Forget it. I didn't mean a thing. Too much whiskey and it starts doing the talking for me ...' He smiled. 'Let me come with you,' he said. 'It's years since I've been to the Roman Baths.'

I was about to say no, but even drunk he knew how to find my weak spots.

'Help me out, Eve. I could do with a distraction, you know? Take me with you or I'll only have the whiskey for company, and you wouldn't be wanting that now, would you?'

How could I say no when he put it like that? I couldn't in all conscience leave him to spend the day assaulting his liver, and weeping over a baby that in another life might have been his, could I? That was the only reason I agreed. It certainly had nothing to do with the brown eyes that twinkled at me in a way I had never managed to resist; nothing to do with the warm smile that wrapped around me like no one else's had ever done. This was a favour for him, not something I would have ever chosen. So I gave him a reluctant, 'fine', and headed off to bed.

I drove us down to Bath the next morning, not confident that the alcohol would have cleared from Paddy's bloodstream yet, although he looked perkier over breakfast than I did. I don't know how he managed it; no one would believe that I was the one who practised healthy living. There was no sign of a hang-over as he spent the whole journey talking. He told me about some of the most memorable digs he'd been on over the years; about how he had set up his own archaeology business and the sort of work he undertook with that; and he made me snort with laughter at the behind-the-scenes gossip from his TV show, and the celebrity programmes and events he had taken part in. He was indiscreet and irreverent, seeming wholly unimpressed and unswayed by the celebrity world other than as a means to an end. He didn't mention his mum or anything about his personal life, and I was glad; there had been enough soul-baring last night.

We found a space to park near the Royal Victoria Park, and strolled in the morning sunshine towards Hot Bath Street, where the thermal baths were located.

'Shall we meet up later?' I asked, when we arrived. 'I'll be a couple of hours.'

'No need for that,' he said. 'I'm coming too.'

'Coming where? In here?' I pointed at the entrance to the baths. Surely he wasn't serious?

'Yes. We agreed last night. And I thought I was the drunk one ...' He grinned.

'But I thought you meant you wanted to come to Bath. Capital B. Not actually in here.'

'What's the problem? It's not a ladies only session, is it?'

'No.' I despaired as soon as the word slipped out. Why had I admitted that? He'd thrown me the perfect excuse and I'd let it slip through my butter fingers. 'You don't have any swimming trunks,' I said, with a flash of inspiration.

'You mean I can't skinny dip?' He threw back his head and roared with laughter, presumably at the look of horror I could feel freezing my face. 'Ah, you're so easy to wind up. There must be somewhere I can buy a pair. Know anywhere that sells tight Speedos?'

He was having far too much fun at my expense. I rallied.

'Go straight down there to Stall Street,' I said. 'But don't go for the Speedos. They show every lump and bump – or lack of them. They're so unforgiving to the less well-endowed, aren't they?'

Paddy grinned and leant close to my ear. 'No worries there,' he murmured. 'Don't tell me you've forgotten.' And he headed off towards the shops, leaving my cheeks flaming and my head whirling with memories I'd tried hard to hold back, and that I definitely didn't want to be dwelling on when I was about to see Paddy in a state of undress.

He was a quick shopper and soon returned brandishing a carrier bag. We entered the baths and after a protracted argument, he insisted on paying the entrance fee in exchange for my having driven to Bath. I thought I'd be able to give him the slip in the changing room, but after being given our wristbands, towels and dressing gowns, we were directed to a unisex changing area.

'I like this place already,' Paddy said, and smiled in my direction. Ignoring him, I shut myself in a cubicle and changed into my bikini as quickly as I could, hoping to be safely hidden in the Minerva pool before he could see me, but my luck was out again. He was clearly as quick at changing as he was at shopping. When I peered from the door of the cubicle, Paddy was waiting for me. At least he was wrapped up in the waffle dressing gown he'd been given – no one ever looked sexy in one of those. And that was exactly how I wanted to think of him – as not sexy – not like in those memories that were fighting so hard to take root in my head. Why had I ever agreed to him coming here with me? I should have known it would lead to trouble. It wasn't emotional distance I was struggling with today, it was physical.

My heart sank when I realised we needed to shower before entering the pool. Paddy stripped off his dressing gown without hesitation and stepped under the water. I watched. I couldn't help myself. Not sexy? Who was I kidding? He didn't have a six-pack, but the years of digging had given him a solid, well-defined chest that the skinny young Paddy would have loved. And I had to be honest – the young Eve would have loved it too. The old Eve wasn't immune to it either.

'Had a good look?' Paddy called as he stepped out of the shower, brushing back his damp hair and smiling at me. If he was interested in upgrading from television to film, I would have cast him as a leading man on the spot. It was a mesmerising performance. I pulled myself together.

'Yes,' I said. 'They're not bad shorts for a quick purchase. Shame about the price tag, though. Ruins the look. Unless you're selling yourself? In which case, I don't think you're worth it.'

I shuffled over in my robe, grabbed the price tag that was hanging out of the back of his shorts, and yanked at it to remove it. Or that was the plan. The actual result of my yanking was that Paddy's shorts gaped away from his body, revealing a very shapely buttock. The label finally came off and the elastic waistband of the shorts snapped back in place.

'When you've finished playing with me, Eve, do you think you could get a move on?' Paddy grinned as I stood rooted to the spot in mortification. 'We've only paid for two hours. Much as I'm enjoying the foreplay, on this occasion I think we'd better skip to the main event.'

Sod him, I thought, as he continued to watch me, waiting. Why was I dithering? I wasn't normally so self-conscious. I didn't care about stripping off in front of a group of strangers. Paddy was just another one, wasn't he? There was no reason to think he might look and judge, noting the changes of almost twenty years, even though I had done exactly that with him. He mixed with celebrities now. My pale, athletic body would hold no interest for a man used to orange skin and surgical enhancements. I stripped off my robe and stepped under the shower.

I closed my eyes as the water ran over my face. When I opened them again, Paddy was standing in front of me, offering a towel.

'Looking good for forty,' he said.

'I'm not forty yet,' I pointed out – although I hoped I wasn't going to go to seed in the few weeks left before my birthday. 'And that's not even old. You should know.'

'You're right. There's still a lot of life left to enjoy.'

'We can only hope so,' I said. He reached out and rubbed my shoulder, his bare flesh touching mine for the first time in years, but it was the understanding behind the gesture that affected me more than the physical contact. I had lost Faye and Dad, and he would lose Alison. There was a new bond between us that had never been there before.

I could have filled out every remaining 'Be Kind to Yourself' voucher over the course of the morning and still have needed more. The spa was fantastic, and I would have enjoyed it on my own, but Paddy made it special in the way only he could. We swam, relaxed in the whirlpool, floated in the open-air rooftop pool, and all the time we shared conversation, laughs and an easy silence that made me feel twenty again and as if anything was possible. But it was all an illusion, as temporary as the steam rising from the pool and drifting away beyond sight. I wasn't twenty, and there were no possibilities here. I should know better than this.

When our time was nearly up, we stood at the edge of the roof terrace and looked out over the Bath skyline, seeing the Abbey, the Circle, the Royal Crescent in the distance, and the hundreds of people hurrying about their daily lives. It was time for a reality check.

'Don't do this, Paddy,' I said, as the sun dried our hair and his arm rested against mine.

'Do what?'

'This. Being charming. Reminiscing. Flirting,' I added, because there was no other word for what he'd been doing today, whether he had meant it or not. 'Trying to make me fall in love with you again.'

'Again?' He turned away from the view to look at me. A loose curl, drying in the sun, blew across his face. 'You mean you stopped?'

'Of course I did. It's been a long time. What did you expect, that I spent the years wearing black and pining for you?'

'Would have been nice ...'

I laughed. And this was exactly why it was so dangerous to spend time with him. Whatever I said, whatever I thought, my heart had a mind of its own where Paddy was concerned.

'Would it be such a bad thing to try again?' Paddy asked. His finger traced an entrancing loop around my wrist and across the back of my hand.

'Yes. Been there. Done that. Got the scars. Don't want to do it again.'

'You think you can stop yourself?'

And that was the question, because, despite everything, I really wasn't sure I could.

'I don't know,' I admitted. 'But *you* can stop it. If you ever cared about me in the past, do this for me now. Don't let me fall for you again. My heart's been broken too many times already. Leave it alone, won't you?'

'I won't break it again,' he said, and sealed his promise by pulling me into a damp hug and kissing the top of my head.

Chapter 20

'So have you invited him to your birthday party?' Tina asked. 'Now that you're on such close terms?'

'Not close,' I corrected, wondering if she had listened to a word I had told her about the time I'd spent with Paddy at the dig. She was definitely putting her own interpretation on what I had said. 'Not as distant.'

I was splitting hairs, we both knew that – luscious curly black ones. I deserved the withering look that Tina gave me as she pulled up a weed and threw it into the wheelbarrow. I began to wish I hadn't volunteered to help her renovate her back garden over the summer, but when she'd mentioned the plan and that her husband Graham would be at work, I hadn't been able to resist offering my assistance. I had plenty of time to kill now, as she was fond of pointing out, and plenty of experience at digging. And aside from the relentless inquisition, and although I still ached from the excavation the week before, I was enjoying it. If I couldn't find a future in archaeology, I could always fall back on labouring ...

'Anyway, it's not a party,' I said. 'Only some friends gathering for a meal. It would seem very tame after the sort of parties he's used to, with wall-to-wall celebrities, champagne by the bucketful and goodie bags worth more than we could earn in a month.'

It wasn't an exaggeration; he had told me about attending a party just like that. After our trip to Bath, we had taken to sharing dinner together in the pub each night, and he'd made me laugh until I cried with his description of some of the things that the more desperate minor celebrities had done to catch the attention of the press at one of those parties. Paddy had sold his free gifts afterwards to raise money for his mum.

Perhaps I had hoped that Tina would contradict me – insist that Paddy would want, even expect, me to invite him to join us on my birthday. But she missed her cue, and instead, she nodded in agreement.

'The French place is posh, but it can't compare to The Ivy, can it?' She straightened up from where she had been bending over a flower bed, and rubbed her lower back. 'Did you see him on the sidebar of shame yesterday? He was leaving a London club, with a busty blonde clinging on to his arm. It's a pity she didn't cling so tightly to her modesty. Her dress left nothing to the imagination.'

'I didn't see it.' I was deliberately not looking online. I didn't want to stalk his movements, or to keep thinking about him when my feelings had tiptoed so close to the edge of forbidden territory during our time in the Cotswolds. On the other hand, perhaps it would cure me of any softer sentiments if I watched him parade around with a stream of attractive women, and hang out with busty blondes only hours after sharing a farewell breakfast with me? But that would only work if I believed what I read in the newspapers. Paddy had already told me how contrived it was – how his agent would often pair him with someone on a night out, specifically to boost his career or hers. Blondes were the preferred choice because of the contrast with his dark hair, he had said. His personal taste had never been for blondes, as I well knew ...

I shoved my spade into the ground again, trying to push away such thoughts. Tina had decided to dig up a row of rose bushes to make way for a vegetable patch, and that was my job for the day. The bushes did look tired and straggly, and I should have approved of the interest in healthy living, but I couldn't help a pang of sadness as I levered the spade under a root to lift out the plant. I would miss seeing them when I visited Tina. Paddy had been the first person to buy me roses – the only person who ever had: six perfect red blooms, because it was the six-month anniversary of the day we had started going out. He had said that six was his lucky number, and that he would buy me six more for our six-year anniversary. Would he have remembered, if we had made it so far? One more thing that I would never know.

'Have you no plans to see him again?' Tina asked. She had the easier job, resting on her kneeler, genteelly weeding. I was beginning to wish she had a more physical job so that she would run out of breath for talking.

'No. Why would I?' I carried on quickly, in case she felt inclined to answer that. 'Although I suppose I will see him on Friday. Only because he's coming to officially name and launch the minibus at The Chestnuts,' I added, when Tina looked more interested than the comment deserved. 'Gran is insisting that I attend too, although I'm not sure why. I've done my bit with the fundraising.'

'But don't you want to see him?' she asked. 'I thought you said you got on well when you met in the Cotswolds. Did sparks not fly again?'

'Absolutely not.' There she went again, putting words in my

mouth. I was sure I hadn't told her that we had got on well; although if I was being honest, it was probably accurate. We *had* got on well, better than I could have expected – and definitely better than I could have wanted. It wasn't sparks flying that I was worried about. They could be stamped out. It was the slow-burning fires causing the sparks that were much more dangerous, quietly taking hold and spreading until it was too late, and you were consumed. That wasn't a position I wanted to be in again.

'I've managed without Paddy in my life perfectly happily for seventeen years,' I said. 'I don't need him in it now.'

'Don't you?' Tina smiled at me. 'I'm not sure you can claim perfect happiness unless you try the alternative, can you? What if there's more happiness on offer? You wouldn't want to miss out on that, would you?'

'I'm glad to see you've got your glad-rags on, our Eve,' Gran said, when I wandered into her room at The Chestnuts on Friday evening, to see if she was ready for the official naming ceremony of the minibus. She was exaggerating: I was wearing a floral tea dress, which matched the month rather than the weather; I hadn't made any special effort – or not much. 'Is this in honour of the bus or are you seeing a fella later? Do I need to start looking for a dress? Perhaps an emerald green one for the Emerald Isle ...'

'You already have a gorgeous dress,' I said, ignoring her insinuations and kissing her cheek. I pointed at the yellow frock she was wearing. 'Another of Mrs Pike's? That woman must have to pay for an extra room to house all her clothes.'

'I'll have you know this is brand new,' Gran said, smoothing the fabric over her knees. 'We've been having lessons on the internet. Who knew that all the catalogues were on the one screen now? Isn't that a grand idea? I picked this up in a summer sale. Seventy per cent off! You'd be hard pressed to better that.'

'It was a bargain,' I agreed. Probably because no one else wanted to buy that colour, but I refrained from making that observation to Gran. 'Stick to the online shopping, though, and don't browse elsewhere. There are things on the internet that would make your hair curl.'

'Really?' Gran grinned. 'Happen I could save a bob or two on that girl who comes in to do my perm ...'

I prowled round the room, picking up her bag and stick and all the other things she insisted she needed for the ceremony, as if she was going out for the day rather than into the car park for an hour. I didn't often come into her room, as she liked to hold court in the conservatory when I visited on Sundays. She had updated her photographs since I had last been in, and now a picture I had given her of Caitlyn in Paris sat between one of me and one of Faye when we had been of a similar age. I had never asked Gran to update my photo; I didn't think either of us wanted to be reminded that I was growing old and Faye wasn't.

I stared at the photos of Faye and Caitlyn side by side. Although I had pictures of Faye in my house, I rarely looked at them now, and it was possible to forget, sometimes, how similar they were. Over the years, as Caitlyn had grown older, she had stopped being an extension of Faye in my eyes and become herself. It hadn't always been that way. At first, I had seen Faye in every look and gesture of Caitlyn's, a comfort and a torment in equal measure.

'They're so alike,' I said, as Gran joined me in front of the pictures.

'Looks-wise, maybe,' she replied. 'Caitlyn's a proper bonny lass, like her mum. Takes after you in all other ways, though.'

I glanced at Gran, wondering if she meant that as a criticism, but she smiled at me. 'You did a grand job, love.' Her voice gave an unexpected wobble. 'You should be proud of yourself. I couldn't be prouder of the pair of you.'

That 'did' burrowed into my heart and left a hole. I wasn't ready for the past tense. My job wasn't done. I loved her too much to ever stop looking out for Caitlyn; I owed it to Faye to never stop looking out for her.

'Is it time to go?' I asked, unwilling to pursue this conversation and to accept praise I didn't deserve. Gran glanced at her watch – a gold Rotary given to her by my granddad on their wedding day, and brought out for special occasions along with her chunky sapphire engagement ring. I never met him; he had died after ten years of marriage, and Gran had never married again. 'I struck gold the first time,' she had always said, if anyone asked. 'You don't settle for brass after that.' I took her arm and squeezed it, touched once again by her devotion to him after so many years; her devotion to all of us.

'I reckon we've kept them waiting long enough, don't you?' Gran said, and grinned. 'Best foot forward. Time to make our entrance.'

It was a cloudy but dry evening, with the muggy warmth of early August, and this display of decent weather had helped to draw a small crowd to The Chestnuts for the naming ceremony. I looked around as I led Gran out of the front door. A minibus-sized object stood on the drive, covered in a blue cloth and gold ribbon – the corporate colours of the motor company who had provided it, I noticed, from the conspicuous sign next to it. Some of the dining-room chairs had been brought outside and set up in rows nearby. A couple of trestle tables on the lawn were laden with drinks and cakes donated by the families of the residents; I'd sent in a bottle of elderflower pressé and some of Gran's favourite shortbread, and I hoped there would be some left for her. And there was Paddy, standing in front of the cake table, a cupcake in his hand, which he couldn't seem to find time to eat because of the determined conversation of a young boy.

'Shall we rescue him?' Gran asked, nodding in Paddy's direction.

'I don't think he needs it,' I replied. Despite being hampered by the cake, Paddy looked wholly absorbed in the conversation, leaning down towards the boy, answering every question seriously and gesturing with his free hand. This was just how I had seen him with the volunteers and students on the dig: patient, enthusiastic, a natural teacher. The thought flashed into my head: is this what he might have been like with Caitlyn, if he had stayed? But I felt no bitterness on my account, only sadness on hers, that she had missed having this man in her life.

Without any intention on my part, we gravitated towards Paddy in time to hear him answer an earnest question about how he rehomed any worms he uncovered on a dig. Apparently satisfied that the worms were treated kindly, the little boy ran off. Paddy looked up and caught me watching. He smiled.

'Phew,' he said, pretending to wipe his brow. 'That was the toughest interview ever.' The joke didn't reach his eyes, and I felt a pang of sympathy for the man who had sat with me in the pub, regretting the missed opportunities in his life, and yearning for a child who would never be his. But perhaps it was empathy, not sympathy, because hadn't I spent much of my life doing something very similar? Maybe we both had the life we deserved.

Paddy bent down and kissed Gran's cheeks. 'Look at you, Phyllis. Bringing some much needed sunshine to the occasion.'

'What do you mean?' Gran said, pretending to object while she merrily soaked up the attention. 'This is grand weather for Lancashire. You're a soft southerner at heart, Paddy Friel, despite being half Yorkshire.'

Laughing, Paddy turned my way and kissed my cheeks too. The young Paddy had never kissed my cheeks – there were no memories attached to the gesture – and yet ... It was all one great mass of confusion. So much about him was familiar and so much alien. Was the essence of the man I had loved still there? Were the parts I had hated? Or – and perhaps this was the biggest danger – had he genuinely grown into someone else, someone I might fall for all over again? His brown eyes smiled right into mine. I mustn't fall. I had bolted the door of my heart long ago, so that no one else could reach in and touch it. But a little voice whispered inside me: *what if someone had never truly left?*

'Look sharp,' Gran said, giving me a nudge with her elbow, and drawing my attention away from Paddy. 'I think the action's about to start.' She looked at Paddy, who was still holding the cupcake. 'Could they not run to a bottle of champagne to christen the bus? What are you supposed to do with that? If it was made by Mr Craig's daughter, it could smash the windscreen if you're not careful.'

'Don't worry, they haven't got me doing anything more strenuous than cutting a ribbon. Even that has to be done under supervision.'

'In case you injure yourself?' I asked. 'Are you that valuable?'

'Not me.' Paddy laughed. 'They're more concerned about the bus's bodywork than mine. It does nothing for the old ego, I tell you ...'

'I suppose that's the way of fame,' I said. 'One day you're enjoying the champagne and red carpets, the next you're lucky to have a hard cupcake and a patch of muddy grass.'

Paddy roared with laughter, much more than my comment deserved. Gran nodded at us both.

'About time you two were friends again,' she said. 'No one's getting any younger. Shall we head on over? I don't want to miss anything.'

She linked her arm with Paddy's, gathered me in with her stick, and led us back to the drive where the chairs were beginning to fill up with residents and dignitaries. Ignoring the seats, Gran made a beeline for a man with a camera in his hand, and I sidestepped the stick and hung back, smiling as she posed for photographs with Paddy. Winston and Cheryl passed me, pushing a sleeping Mabel in her pram.

'You should be up there, taking some credit,' Cheryl said, pointing towards the photographer. 'Winston won't put himself forward either. This is all down to your hard work.'

'I wouldn't dare steal the limelight from Gran,' I said, laughing. 'This is her last chance to make the papers. She's been looking forward to it for weeks. The fundraising was originally her idea, as she keeps telling anyone who'll listen.'

'Do you know what the winning name is?' Winston asked.

'I haven't heard. I just hope it's not *The Phyllis Roberts* ...'

The launch ceremony passed off well, and the minibus was duly christened with the name that had won the public vote: *The Alfred Wainwright*, after the legendary Lancashire man who had produced famous walking guides to the nearby Lakeland fells. Gran would be disappointed: I knew that she'd suggested *Not Dunroamin'*. The manager of the motor dealership made a worthy speech about how pleased they were to support a good cause, and then it was Paddy's turn. He woke everyone up again with a hilarious account of the adventures a group of pensioners might have, travelling around the country on a road trip in the bus. It was one of those seemingly effortless performances that must have taken considerable preparation in advance, as he name-checked many of The Chestnuts residents and gave them roles on the grand tour – with Gran as conductor, of course. The delight on the residents' faces made tears clog in my throat.

'I think you made their day with your speech,' I said, finding myself beside Paddy after the press had finally finished taking photographs.

'Ah, I wouldn't have said that. But if I did, they deserve it, don't they? It was no bother.'

No bother, he said – but he must have contacted someone at The Chestnuts to find out the names and personalities of the residents, to give them all such accurate roles in his story. He must have spent time thinking about his speech, writing it and learning it – and all for a group of old people he didn't know and was unlikely to see again. How did that fit with the notion I had clung to all these years, that Paddy Friel was only interested in himself? It didn't – of course it didn't.

'How's your mum?' I asked, as we crossed the lawn to the table serving drinks. Only soft drinks were left now, including my rejected elderflower pressé, although a can of Guinness mysteriously appeared from under the table when Paddy approached. We wandered further down the garden, away from the other guests, and he took a long slug of beer before replying.

'She's not so good,' he said. He stared down at the can in his hand. 'It's taking her speech now. Her mind is still full of things, you know, but she's struggling to get it out. It's unbearable to see her frustration. Jeez, Eve, you wouldn't want to watch an animal suffer like this, never mind your mam ...'

I stepped forward and hugged him. What else could I do? I couldn't watch *him* suffer. He returned the embrace one-armed, minding his Guinness, his head resting against mine. And a memory came rushing back of us doing this before, but the other way round – of him wrapping me in his arms and comforting me when the news first came that Faye had died, as if he wanted to squeeze the pain out of me and protect me from further hurt; before we had realised the implications of her death for us and our planned life together. How had I forgotten that? Because I had let his one bad act of leaving Caitlyn – leaving me – wipe out years of good deeds. I tightened my hold, trying to offer the comfort he had once given me. But as I finally pulled away, he dipped his head and kissed me.

The forbidden taste of alcohol and Paddy ... Which was more intoxicating? I stepped back, and wiped the back of my hand across my mouth.

'What are you doing?' I asked, glancing round to see if anyone had noticed. 'I was offering you sympathy, nothing more. You promised not to do this!'

'I never promised not to kiss you.'

'You did! When we were on the rooftop in Bath ...' I tried to remember. What words had he used? 'You said you wouldn't break my heart again.'

'I won't.'

He wasn't smiling. He wasn't making a joke of this. I felt unsteady, wrong-footed. So what exactly had he meant by that kiss? Nothing I wanted to hear. And yet ... I wished I could wipe a hand across my mind, to stop it reliving the moment, stop it making a connection with all those other remembered kisses from before, as if a string of fairy lights were coming on one by one, connecting the past with the present until I couldn't help but see how perfectly our lips fitted together, and always had. Before and after, no kiss had ever affected me like Paddy's. That hadn't changed. So what was I to do now?

I glanced around, anywhere but at Paddy. The garden was emptying now, and I spotted Gran sitting by herself on one of the few chairs still outside. I hurried over, and crouched down in front of her.

'I'm sorry, I didn't mean to abandon you,' I said. 'I was just ...' What? Kissing Paddy? My mind went blank – of excuses, but sadly not of memories.

'No need to fret about me,' Gran said. 'I was having a nice little chat with the journalist. I'm sure you were having a nice time too.'

She said this with a twinkle that made me suspect she'd seen exactly what I'd been doing, until I noticed that Paddy had followed me over and the twinkle was directed at him. He was more persistent than a shadow, I thought, standing up again. What was the matter with the man? Missing when I needed him most, and now I didn't need him, I couldn't shake him off. He smiled at me and that train of thought fizzled away.

'Don't think you have to hang around here with me,' Gran said. 'They'll be dosing us with cocoa and shipping us off to bed soon enough. You can get off now if the pair of you have plans for the night.'

Paddy looked at me in enquiry. He could look all he liked. I wasn't falling for Gran's tricks.

'I do have plans,' I said. 'After I've helped clear up here, I've arranged to speak to Beverley on Skype. You remember Beverley,' I said to Paddy. 'She was with us on the dig in the Cotswolds. The Californian lady.'

'She was fun.' Paddy smiled. 'Where is she now?'

'In Spain. She's working her way across Europe, and doesn't go home until November.'

'It's a great way to spend the summer.'

I nodded. It probably was. He should know. I assumed that after he left me with Caitlyn, he'd picked up our plans to volunteer at digs across the world and fulfilled them by himself; it was one subject we hadn't discussed since we met up again. I could only imagine what it would be like to explore the world in that way. But he could only imagine what it was like to raise a child, to help them develop and grow and become their own person. Having witnessed his sadness in the Cotswolds, how could I envy his life over mine?

'Never mind helping here,' Gran said, prodding me with her stick. 'Take Paddy out somewhere. He put on a good show for us. The least you could do is buy him a drink.'

'Don't you have to get home?' I asked him.

'I'm staying at The White Hart for the weekend. I thought we could do something tomorrow.'

Do what, exactly? More kissing? He was smiling at me in a way that was dangerously familiar. Thank goodness I had a perfect excuse.

'I'm busy tomorrow. It's the Inglebridge agricultural show. I'm taking Gran.'

'Really?' Paddy turned his attention to Gran. 'I didn't know you had a secret interest in cattle, Phyllis.'

'I don't. Can't stand the pong. I only agreed to go so Eve

wouldn't be lonely on her own. She normally takes our Caitlyn. I'd rather stop here and take part in the dominoes rally.' That put me in my place – and it wasn't a particularly comfortable place to be. Shouldn't I be worried about *her* being lonely, rather than the other way round? What next? Would she be inviting me to join the dominoes game soon? It was beginning to feel like life was ending at forty, never mind beginning.

'So that's sorted,' Gran said, waving her stick from Paddy to me. 'I'll stop here and you two can go together.'

The Inglebridge agricultural show had been one of my favourite days of the year ever since we had moved to the town, and was one of the first events I marked in my new calendar each January. It was an important day for the local farmers, and competition was fierce to win the colourful rosettes for having the best sheep, pigs and cattle, but there was equally stiff rivalry amongst breeders to own a prize-winning budgie or rabbit. There was fun for the general public too, and the main arena in the centre of the showground held livestock parades and equestrian events such as show-jumping and carriage-driving, as well as special stunt displays that always drew a huge crowd. The arena was surrounded by tents full of local crafts and food, an astonishing variety of trade stands, and a funfair that seemed to grow bigger and better each year.

Caitlyn and I had attended every year, spending the whole day there whatever the weather, until we had staggered home, exhausted and happy and laden down with shopping bags. This year, after Caitlyn had accepted the job in Paris, I had wondered whether to go at all until I had come up with the brilliant plan to take Gran: I had even paid extra for seats in the arena grandstand, so she could sit down whenever she wanted. Never had I imagined, when I bought the tickets so many months ago, that I would end up going along with Paddy.

It wasn't what I'd planned; it wasn't what I'd wanted. But as the day rolled on, and the sun warmed our heads and made everything seem more cheerful, I couldn't regret being there with Paddy. His curiosity knew no bounds – it was what made him such an excellent archaeologist and TV presenter – and he started conversations with people I recognised from previous years but wouldn't have thought to approach myself. We learnt about the tips and tricks to prepare a bull for showing; heard fascinating stories about classic car rallies from the owner of a gorgeous Austin 7 saloon dating back to 1931; and learnt about the development of a new micro-brewery at a local farm, which even I found interesting – although not as much as Paddy, who sampled the beers with great delight. His enthusiasm for it all sparked mine; his curiosity sparked mine. I'd been visiting the show for sixteen years and felt as if I'd hardly noticed half of it before. And that was Paddy – that was what made him special, what had made me miss him so profoundly when he left. He didn't just share life. He enriched it. I wasn't sure it was helping me to be reminded of that.

We bought our lunch from the food stands – the inevitable sausage sandwich for him, and a bowl of steaming vegetable paella for me – and squeezed onto the benches in the grandstand while we ate it. This year, the stunt display featured horse riders who had appeared as body doubles on popular television dramas, and who stood on, dangled off and performed tricks on horses while cantering around the arena, jumping over obstacles and leaping through fire. It was an entrancing performance, and we laughed and gasped at the near misses and daring stunts, cheering loudly with the rest of the audience when it was over.

After the equestrian display, there was a sudden change in the mood, as the head teacher of Inglebridge primary school led a long crocodile of children into the arena. I'd seen this advertised in the show programme, and hadn't planned to watch, but we were wedged in high in the grandstand with no easy means of escape. One of the teachers at the primary school had died earlier in the year, after fighting breast cancer, and the children were going to release pink balloons in memory of her. The head gave a moving speech, as did the teacher's widower who was flanked by their two teenagers, and then the balloons soared into the air as cheers and applause rang out across the showground.

I couldn't help myself; a few stray tears rolled down my cheeks as I listened to the glowing tributes and watched the balloons drift away on the gentle breeze. The teacher who died had worked at the school for many years – she had taught Caitlyn – and she had been known to many of the children and parents attending the show today. It was a fitting goodbye from the Inglebridge community, but it was inevitable that my own personal goodbyes in my family would enter my mind too.

The crowd in the grandstand started to move, and Paddy grabbed my hand.

'Come on,' he said, pulling me up and leading me down the steps. 'It's time for the funfair.'

'No ...' I began to protest, but he put his finger up to my lips.

'Yes,' he said. 'We're going to have fun. We need it.'

He was right, of course. It proved exactly what we needed to lift the mood again. We had a go at the hook-a-duck stall – Paddy won a plastic sword, which he brandished at me in brutal Viking fashion before handing it over to a less successful little boy. We rode sedately on the painted carousel horses, and raced round on the dodgems, laughing as we chased and bumped into each other; enjoying ourselves as if we were still the young Paddy and Eve, lovers with a life of adventure ahead of us, rather than the middle-aged pair scarred by tragedy and loss.

Paddy caught my hand as I stumbled down the steps away from the dodgems, dizzy from the movement of the cars and the abundance of laughter. He led me away from the fair and towards the bank of trees that lined the side of the show-ground, until we were out of the crowd. He stopped and looked at me.

'What do you say to me kissing you now, Eve? I'll give you a fair chance this time. Would you pull away?'

Would I? His eyes were locked on mine. I reminded myself that this was Paddy – the man who had abandoned me with a grieving child. But it was also the Paddy I had loved more than I had thought it possible to love another person; and the Paddy who had shown me this year that he had become the decent, thoughtful man I had always believed him to be. The question chased around my head, searching for the right answer, but it was too late – my body was already leaning forwards, ready to meet his.

My mouth had almost reached his when the sound of my phone rang out from my bag.

'Ignore it,' Paddy said, the words blowing against my lips.

'I can't. It might be Gran.'

I drew away and took out my phone. It stopped ringing just as I tried to answer. There was a long list of missed calls on the screen, all from the same unfamiliar number. All from France, according to the display. The blood that had so recently roared around my body now seemed to freeze in my veins. Before I could call the number back, the phone started ringing again.

'Mum?' It was Caitlyn. There was no time for relief, as the word ended on a sob. 'Mum? I need you.'

Chapter 21

'What's the matter? What's happened?' Paddy had been pacing around me as I spoke, and he clutched my arm as soon as I ended the phone call. 'Was that Caitlyn?'

I nodded. 'She's been mugged. Her bag was snatched – her purse and phone have gone.'

'But nothing worse? She's not hurt?'

I shook my head. I'd had to be calm and soothing when talking to Caitlyn, but now the tears I had supressed ran down my cheeks, and I felt a complicated mix of horror that she had suffered this and rclicf that it hadn't been anything worse. And Paddy pulled me into his arms, because of course he understood, like no one else could. He knew that I wasn't only thinking of Caitlyn; I was remembering my younger self and reliving the assault I had experienced on the night we had properly met. As he rested his head on mine, it felt like we had come full circle; that once again he was the Paddy who had been there when I needed him, not the Paddy who had left. I clung to him, overwhelmed by how glad I was to have him with me now.

'I have to go to Paris,' I said, drawing back. 'She said she's fine. I believe her. But I need to see her for myself.'

'I'll come with you.'

'But you have your work, and your mum ...'

'They'll be okay for a couple of days. I want to come. If nothing else, my A-level French will be more useful than your Latin. Let me help.'

I stepped back and studied him. He was smiling, but it wasn't the usual, charming Paddy Friel smile. It wasn't the TV smile, designed to captivate the viewers and keep the ratings high. It was a smile for me, designed only to offer reassurance and support, friendship and maybe something more. And any last, lingering doubts I might have had were finally swept away. The Paddy I had hated for so many years wasn't actually real. The real Paddy was here in front of me, offering to stay at my side, not run away. I didn't hate this man. Far from it. I'd asked him not to make me fall in love with him again. Why hadn't I seen that it was already too late?

'Yes,' I said to him, and I walked back into his embrace. 'Please come.'

We were lucky. There were seats available on a flight from Manchester to Paris the next day. Paddy made all the arrangements and then went home to pick up his passport, leaving me time to go shopping for a new phone and handbag for Caitlyn and to visit Gran before Paddy and I met again at the airport for the flight.

I had fiercely guarded my independence for years, but found it oddly liberating to be able to let go and accept help from someone else now. I'd been lucky with Caitlyn over the last seventeen years. She had enjoyed excellent health – no broken bones, nothing more serious than chicken pox ever troubling her – and even the teenage years had been more peaceful than I had imagined after several years working in a secondary school.

I hadn't missed having someone to share my worries with, because there had been no proper worries to share.

But even though I had spoken to Caitlyn again, and she had convinced me that she really was fine, the scare of her initial phone call haunted me and made me question the value of my independence after all. As Paddy sent me texts through the day, telephoned to finalise our plans, and distracted me with conversation and laughter at the airport and through the flight, I realised that although I could have done this on my own, I didn't want to. And I realised something else. It wasn't weakness to lean on someone else; it took strength to trust someone enough to do that. And despite what had happened in the past, I trusted Paddy.

We travelled on an evening flight, and even with a private transfer from Charles de Gaulle airport to the city centre, it was after eleven o'clock by the time we pulled up outside the hotel that Paddy had booked in the Saint Germain district. In the twilight, I could see the pale stone façade of the building rising five floors high, with huge full-length windows decorated with black iron railings adorning the front face of the hotel. Two carriage lights glowed a welcome on either side of the double-width wooden door, where the name of the hotel was discreetly embossed on the stone surround. It looked an expensive place, a boutique hotel rather than the budget accommodation I had been expecting, but perhaps it had been difficult to find two rooms at short notice and he'd had no choice but to upgrade. I hesitated at the entrance. He would have booked *two* rooms, wouldn't he? I glanced across at him, and he smiled and squeezed my hand, which didn't help answer the question.

Paddy checked us in and we travelled upstairs in the lift to one of the highest floors. He led the way down a thickly carpeted corridor and opened the door to a room.

'Here you go,' he said, holding open the door for me. I went in and found myself in a gorgeous bedroom, beautifully decorated with white panelled walls and mirrored wardrobes, and lit by an ornate chandelier. Lush teal velvet fabric covered the bed and hung on either side of the tall balcony windows.

He followed me in and set my bag down at the foot of the king-sized bed. I glanced from it to Paddy.

'Are you ...' I stopped, undecided where to go with this. Question or invitation? What did I want?

'I'm in room 43. It must be down the corridor.' Paddy dropped a lingering kiss on the top of my head. 'You know where I am if you want me.'

I woke early the next morning, pushed back the voiles and opened the windows, revealing a charming view across the Saint Germain rooftops. The morning sun bathed my face and I felt an unexpected flash of exhilaration at being here. I'd already spoken to Caitlyn, and she had sounded well – so well it hardly seemed as if she needed the comfort I had come all this way to offer. She would be working through the day and so we had arranged to meet for dinner – the four of us, as she insisted on introducing me to her boyfriend, Luc, and I could hardly abandon Paddy, even if I'd wanted to, when he had done so much to bring me here. Until then, we had a whole day to spend in Paris, and with my worry over Caitlyn diminished by our conversation, I was keen to cram as much as I could into the few hours we had here before flying home tomorrow.

I'd never visited Paris before. Unsurprisingly Paddy had, although I chose not to ask for details of any romantic trysts he'd enjoyed there in the past. He swept us through the city like a local, combining some 'must see' moments with his favourite places. We enjoyed breakfast in a bustling café tucked away on a quiet street near the hotel, before we visited the Montparnasse Tower and ascended to the observation deck to admire the incredible views across the city and towards the Eiffel Tower. We marvelled over the stained glass at Sainte-Chapelle; strolled along the banks of the Seine; and enjoyed delicious fresh fish for lunch in a restaurant overlooking the river. Later, we visited the Luxembourg Gardens, which looked amazing with the perfect blue sky overhead and the flowers in full bloom.

We sat in a shaded spot in the gardens, exhausted by our whistle-stop tour – and by the wine, in Paddy's case, and all the food I had enjoyed, in mine. Although there were lots of other people strolling in the gardens, it felt incredibly peaceful, as if all this beauty had been laid on solely for us.

'What's the verdict?' Paddy asked, turning his head to look at me. The summer breeze had roughened his curls through the day, and the first signs of a five-o'clock shadow were darkening his chin. He looked like a laughing pirate, an enticing mixture of danger and fun. 'Have you fallen in love?'

Had I …? I stared at him, blinked, opened my mouth but couldn't speak.

'It captivated me the first time I came,' Paddy continued. 'I know you've only seen a fraction of it, but it's a great city, isn't it?'

'Oh! The city! Yes, absolutely. I do love it.'

Paddy grinned at me. I had always loved his smile, the way it encompassed his whole face, lighting it with joy.

'What did you think I meant?'

'Oh, the food, of course. Is that terrible? You were being

highbrow and cultural, and I was only thinking of my stomach …' I laughed. 'I'll need extra-long runs this week to make up for today. I've been very bad, and we haven't even had dinner yet.'

Paddy reached across and took hold of my hand.

'You could never be bad. In anything. You're an incredible woman, Eve Roberts. Jeez, when I think about what you've done, giving up everything to look after Caitlyn … and when I think about what I did … You're so good, I don't feel worthy to even be here beside you, sharing the same patch of grass.'

I wished I was as good as he believed. I wished I deserved these things he was saying. I moved towards him and put my free hand over his mouth.

'Don't,' I said. 'That's all in the past. Let's not think about that any more.'

There was something curiously vulnerable about him, when only his eyes were showing his feelings. I watched as the expression in them softened until I would have known he was smiling even if I hadn't felt the curve of his lips beneath my hand. And then his lips moved again and pressed a kiss against my palm.

I drew my hand back a couple of centimetres. He leant forward and kissed my palm again. We did this twice more and his eyes never left mine. And then, when he was close enough that I could feel his breath, warm against my cheeks, I withdrew my hand completely and he leant forward and pressed his lips to mine.

It was unexpected, and yet inevitable, because where else had the day been leading? And I kissed him back – because it was Paddy; he was in my bones, and always had been, an essential part of me. I didn't need any other reason. And if I did, I still had some 'Be Kind to Yourself' vouchers unused in my bag, and

I would have given up every last one, and reclaimed all the others, to pay for these moments in Paddy's arms. This wasn't for old times' sake – it wasn't a nostalgic embrace, or about rekindling the past. I wanted to kiss this Paddy – the man he was now. This was about the present – and maybe about the future too.

Eventually, he eased away.

'What time are we meeting Caitlyn?' he asked.

'About eight.'

He checked his watch. 'So there's time to visit one more place. I know you wanted to see everything you could. Or ...'

He let the sentence hang. He didn't need to speak the words. I knew what he meant. This is how we had always been: totally in tune with each other's needs and wishes. I had wanted to see everything; I might never come back to Paris. But everything was right here in front of me. I scrambled to my feet and held out my hand to him.

'Let's go back to the hotel.'

Paddy Friel. Paddy Friel was lying in bed beside me. Paddy Friel was lying in bed beside me, naked. His hand was curved round the small of my back; his toes were touching mine. I stared at his face on the pillow, and wondered if I would ever manage to stop smiling.

Paddy opened his eyes, and eased forward until his lips brushed across mine.

'Just so as you know,' he said, as his hand slid over my back, 'I've changed my mind. You're not good. You're bloody fantastic.'

'You're not so bad yourself,' I replied, laughing. 'For a man of forty, anyway.'

He didn't let me get away with that, and tightening his arm round me, he drew me on top of him. He sighed.

'I suppose we should be getting up, if you still want to walk to the restaurant.'

That should have been my line. I should have been thinking about Caitlyn. Already I had let this thing with Paddy, whatever it was, distract me from the most important person in my life. But I couldn't think of anything except the feel of his skin against mine, and the way my whole body tingled with pleasure.

'What if we get a taxi?' I asked.

He laughed. 'Then we would have time for this ...'

It was ten past eight when the taxi pulled up outside the restaurant that Caitlyn had chosen; I was amazed that we'd managed to be as punctual as that. I spotted her at a table near the back as soon as I walked in and quickened my pace, feeling all at once a mum again, with the first stirrings of guilt that I had spent hours in bed with Paddy this afternoon, when I had come over to Paris to offer her comfort, not to have fun. She waved and stood up as I approached, and we met in a hug that was probably embarrassingly desperate on my side. I didn't care. She was here, and she was safe. Nothing else mattered.

I stepped back to look at her properly. She looked well – incredibly well, considering the tears of two days before. Even on a cursory glance I could see the changes in her. There were the obvious physical ones: her long, blonde hair had been cut to her shoulders, her face glowed with a natural tan and I didn't recognise the stylish clothes she was wearing. But there were other changes too, perhaps only visible to someone who knew her as well as I did. She seemed taller, brighter, more confident – glittering like Faye had once done, just as, with the shorter hair, she became less like her in appearance.

It didn't take long to work out the cause of the changes. As soon as I had pulled away from Caitlyn, the man who had been sitting with her at the table rose and rested his hand on her waist and she immediately leant into him. This must be the infamous Luc. I'd been through 'meet-the-boyfriend' experiences before, with adolescent boys who made me feel achingly old. Luc was something else: no more than twenty-five, I guessed, but with the assurance of a man twice his age, and with gallons of charm that coated his every gesture like honey. My first impression was that he reminded me of Paddy. I had no idea whether that was a good thing or not.

'*Enchanté*,' Luc said, grasping my upper arms and kissing my cheeks. He smiled at Caitlyn. '*Tu ne m'avais pas dit que ta maman était aussi ravissante*.'

'Hello,' I said, floundering for the first time this trip with my ignorance of French. I hoped he could speak English, or my planned interrogation wouldn't go well. I turned to Paddy, who I distinctly remembered offering to be my translator on this trip, but he wasn't paying attention and was busy staring at Caitlyn. No wonder; she would catch anyone's eye, and as a mother or an aunt I couldn't have been prouder of her. I wished I knew what Paddy was making of her. Was he remembering the child he had known, and trying to find traces of her in the woman?

Caitlyn was returning Paddy's stare with interest until she transferred it to me.

'Good job we were given a table for four,' she said, with a mischievous grin. She leant forward on the pretext of giving me another hug and whispered in my ear. 'A vast improvement on Rich.'

'It's not ...' I began, but stopped when vivid memories of rolling in bed with Paddy less than an hour ago flashed through my mind. I hoped I wasn't blushing; thank goodness the bistro was dimly lit. Caitlyn laughed.

'I think Paris agrees with you,' she said. 'I can't wait to hear all about what you've been up to today.'

All of it? That wasn't going to happen. I glanced at Paddy, who was grinning as broadly as Caitlyn. Belatedly, I realised I should have made the introductions.

'This is Paddy,' I said, as he came forward and kissed Caitlyn's cheeks.

'Delighted to meet you,' Paddy said, and he looked it; he hadn't stopped smiling since we'd left the hotel. I looked round the table as we all sat down and marvelled at how normal – how right – it felt for the four of us to be together like this. Six months ago this would have been impossible; I would have done anything to avoid Paddy Friel. Now he was at my side, his arm brushing against mine, the very proximity of him making my blood warm with desire, and it felt as though, somehow, I'd passed through time and found myself in the life I should have had. And it felt wonderful.

'We should have champagne, do you think?' Luc asked, gesturing for the waiter.

'Not for me,' I said. 'I don't drink. Water will be fine ...' But the waiter was already here, pouring champagne into four glasses.

'Now you can't let that go to waste,' Paddy murmured to me. 'Be kind to yourself. We've lots to celebrate, haven't we? All of us here, together.'

Paddy was as intoxicating as anything in the glass he was holding out to me. My resistance wavered. I had given up alcohol many years ago, an instinctive reaction so that I would never get drunk or lose control again. But one glass wouldn't do any harm, would it? Paddy was right – there was a lot to celebrate, and it was a long time since I had felt like that, maybe too long. Caitlyn was here, Paddy was here; we were together as I had once thought we would always be. Perhaps this was meant to be. Perhaps this was our time. For the first time in as long as I could remember, I had some hope that the future would be better than the past. That was worth celebrating, wasn't it?

We clinked glasses, looking into each other's eyes as Luc insisted that was the French way, and I took my first sip of champagne. It was delicious – crisp and cold, and the bubbles tingled on my tongue. How had I forgotten this? My glass was half empty before I knew it. I delved under the table, gave Caitlyn her new phone and handbag, and took out the box of 'Be Kind to Yourself' vouchers from my bag. There was so much about today that would qualify: the sightseeing, the indulgent meals, the hours in bed with Paddy. I glanced at him, ready to exchange a secret smile, but he was listening to something Caitlyn was saying. I filled in one of the remaining cards:

BE KIND TO YOURSELF
VOUCHER TEN
I, Eve Roberts, have been kind to myself by drinking champagne!

'Only one glass,' I said, laughing and showing the card to Caitlyn and Paddy in turn. 'Don't tempt me to have another.'

'You're allowed to indulge yourself when you're in Paris,' Caitlyn said. 'They do amazing profiteroles with hot chocolate sauce here. You must try them.'

'You are still eating fruit and vegetables, aren't you?' I asked, trying not to imagine what else she indulged in when I wasn't around.

'Yes, Mum.' Caitlyn rolled her eyes, and she and Luc laughed – affectionately, I hoped, but it still jarred. What was Paddy making of this? I didn't want him to see me as a frumpy old nag, especially not after this afternoon; but when I looked towards him, he was lost in thought, so it seemed that I'd got away with it.

The food was amazing, and I loved seeing Caitlyn, but as the evening wore on, I couldn't help feeling that our relationship had shifted; that perhaps by coming to France she had passed over an emotional border as well as a geographical one, to a place where she no longer needed me in my role of mother. As she chatted to Paddy, responded to all his questions about her interests and talents, and what she hoped to do with her life, I saw her through his eyes and it struck me more forcibly than ever that she was adrift from me now; a beautiful, independent young woman, not the child I had cared for.

'This is so weird,' I heard her say to Paddy, as she finished her third glass of champagne. Her third! Of course I was counting; I hadn't imposed my teetotal life on her, but I'd never seen her drink more than the occasional glass of wine before. Although I couldn't object – somehow my one glass seemed to be mysteriously lasting all night. 'I feel as if I know you. The accent is so familiar. Do you get that all the time, from being on TV?'

'Sometimes.' Paddy looked at me. 'Eve?'

I nodded. He was nudging me, and I couldn't ignore him. How had I not thought this through? I had often wondered whether Caitlyn would remember Paddy, and perhaps here was my answer. She had only been young when she came to live with us, but they had been close; perhaps something about him was stirring her memories. It felt too much like deception not to explain.

'I told you before that I knew Paddy,' I said, fiddling with my napkin and trying to sound as neutral as I could. I had to tread a careful line; if Paddy was to be part of our future, I didn't want to say anything about him that would sound like a criticism. 'There was a bit more to it than that. We went out at university, and lived together for a while after that. You were only tiny, but I suppose it's possible you remember his voice from then.'

'Really?' Caitlyn grinned. 'It's a shame you split up. It would have been cool to have had a famous dad. Never too late, though, is it, if you're back together now!'

'We're not ...' I couldn't complete the denial, but I couldn't confirm Caitlyn's assumption either. Neither Paddy nor I had spoken of our feelings this afternoon; there had been no time to discuss whether it was the start of something or merely the impulse of the moment, another Paris indulgence. 'It's complicated,' I said, picking up my glass and suddenly glad of the miraculous refills, even though my head was starting to feel blurry, and my thoughts had slowed right down. I turned to Paddy, wondering how he was dealing with this conversation. It couldn't be easy for him, but rather than looking awkward or embarrassed, he was smiling at Caitlyn with undoubted pleasure.

'Paddy?' I said. I repeated his name, but he didn't appear to hear me, and carried on his conversation with Caitlyn, telling her about his TV experiences, making it sound a much more glamorous life than the one he had told me about. I watched them both, half-formed feelings of unease beginning to creep into my befuddled brain. I didn't know what I had expected, after the hours of pleasure I had shared with Paddy, but it wasn't this; it wasn't to feel as if he had showered away all trace of me and moved on already. I could understand him being curious about Caitlyn; it must be fascinating to see what she had become and to try to spot the traces of the child she had been. But was that his only interest in her?

Snippets of circumstantial evidence started to gather in my head. I remembered the young woman he had been staying with at the Fairlie House Hotel; I remembered the countless photographs of him in the press, with young blondes hanging off his arm; I thought of Rich, a man of a similar age to Paddy, abandoning me in favour of a younger woman. My stomach turned over. Was Paddy attracted to Caitlyn? I couldn't believe it – but how else did I explain his total absorption in her tonight?

The suspicion, once implanted and watered with alcohol, grew with every smile, every look that lasted too long, every laugh that seemed too loud. Instead of lingering as I would have wanted, soaking in every moment of Caitlyn's company, I found myself making an excuse to break up the party early: a convenient headache, due to the unaccustomed champagne. We said hurried goodbyes, and Luc offered to call a taxi, but I needed some fresh air to sober me up and blow the muddled thoughts out of my head. We started walking back towards our hotel.

'Ah Eve, this is my fault,' Paddy said, trying to take my hand. 'I shouldn't have filled your glass up. It must have hit you hard after so many years without alcohol.'

I brushed off his hand and folded my arms to resist any further attempt. Something had hit me hard tonight, and it wasn't just alcohol. It was a punch to the heart, bruising my confidence in Paddy and in myself. I was only two weeks short of my fortieth birthday. In Paddy's arms this afternoon, those years had felt weightless, insignificant. Now every week of those forty years felt like scars on my body, face and mind, marking me as someone old, someone past my prime. Had I really been stupid enough to think Paddy might have feelings for me, when he had the whole world to choose from?

'Caitlyn's fantastic, isn't she?' he said, and I could hear the warmth in his voice. As a mother, an aunt, I should have cherished those words; as a newly suspicious lover, they were the last ones I could wish to hear – a death knell to my hopes.

'Yes, she is. And Luc's lovely,' I said, with pointed emphasis. 'They make a perfect couple.'

'You think so? He's a charmer, I'll give him that. I'm not sure he's good enough for her, though.'

The hypocrisy of this, from a man who employed charm like his own personal currency, was the final straw. I stopped walking and turned to Paddy.

'Who would be good enough for her?' I asked. 'You?'

'What?' I could see from the street lamps the frown building on his face. 'What are you talking about?'

'You! The way you were with Caitlyn tonight. You couldn't take your eyes off her. Are you attracted to her, is that it?' I didn't wait for him to reply. I couldn't; the words were pouring out by themselves, as they had once before when I'd drunk too much, with such horrifying consequences. 'It's disgusting. You're old enough to be her father!'

I saw the shock hit his face; saw him stagger back as if I had struck him with my fists as well as my words.

'Jeez, Eve, you don't know what you're saying. I *might be* her father!'

Chapter 22

Paris by night was extraordinarily beautiful. The sun had set but the twilight sky was still deep velvet blue over our heads. Street lamps cast pools of light like giant stepping stones marking my way as I ran past the elegant couples strolling home, not caring where I was going, only trying to get as far away from Paddy as I could.

What had he meant, that he might be Caitlyn's father? How was that possible? I hadn't known him when Faye fell pregnant. Caitlyn was born only a few weeks after we had started going out; I remembered what agony it had felt, in those early days of our relationship, to leave him for a weekend when I travelled home to see my new niece. It made no sense.

I paused when I reached a bustling side street, busy even at this time of night with people sitting at tables outside bars and cafés. Smoke and noise drifted towards me and instead of running on, I sat down at an empty table, managing to order a brandy from a waiter, and to beg a cigarette from a man at the neighbouring table.

I had taken one sip and one puff, and was choking over one or the other, when Paddy sat down opposite me. He took the cigarette and stubbed it out, and directed a stream of French at the waiter, ordering something that I didn't understand. Shortly afterwards, the waiter set a black coffee and a glass of water in front of me.

'Is this decaf?' I asked.

'Unlikely,' Paddy said. 'It'll do you less harm than the cigarette.'

I shrugged, in what I imagined was a Gallic way; I could speak the body language, if nothing else. Paddy had never approved of me smoking. I had been a social smoker when we met, but he had weaned me off the habit – easy to do, when the rewards of quitting were so sweet.

'You must have made a mistake, surely?' I asked. 'About you being Caitlyn's father?'

He sighed, picked up the brandy glass and gulped it down. 'No mistake. I'm so sorry, Eve. I could be her father.'

'But how? The timing doesn't fit ...' I trailed off. I was fixating on the timing and ignoring the other obvious issue. If Paddy thought he could be Caitlyn's father, that meant he and Faye had ... How? When? I scalded my tongue on the coffee, determined not to ask. If I asked, I would know, and what would I do then? Memories of my afternoon with Paddy were already transforming, with Faye taking my place in the images in my head.

'I met her before you,' he said, and I shut my eyes, because I wanted to watch him say this even less than I wanted to hear it. 'She was a girl in a bar during Freshers' Week. Another student, so I thought. She bought me a drink, we chatted, we went outside. It was five minutes against the wall in the pub car park. I don't know where she went after that. I didn't see her around the campus again.'

I knew where she had gone. She had come back to my room in halls, high on life, reeking of alcohol and sex. Faye hadn't gone to university and had begged to visit me during Freshers'

Week, so she could see what it was all about. And it had been all about her, of course. She had floated round the campus, captivating everyone she met, and fitting in better than I ever could. I was sure the night I remembered must be the same one that Paddy was talking about. Faye and I had gone into town together, but had lost each other, and I had eventually returned to my room, frantic with worry about where she might be; mobile phones hadn't been a fact of life back then. But while I had been pacing the floor, wondering whether she was safe, she'd been ... I shuddered. My poor, darling Caitlyn. She deserved so much better than this tawdry start in life.

'I never betrayed you, Eve. I didn't know you then.'

I opened my eyes. Paddy was leaning towards me, his arms resting on the table. Shadows covered half his face – and how appropriate that was, because it felt like I'd only ever half known him.

'Not then,' I said. 'But after I'd introduced you to Faye – for the first time, I'd thought – you betrayed me every day by not telling me the truth.'

'I didn't even remember her at first,' Paddy said, flinging back in his chair. 'And then when I stayed at your house one holiday, she started messing with me, dropping little hints so I didn't know what to think: was Guinness still my favourite drink? Did I want a quick this or a quick that? Did I like Caitlyn's name? She'd chosen an Irish one especially ...'

'That's not true,' I replied quickly. 'She had a doll called Caitlyn as a child; she always loved the name. And Faye wouldn't have done any of that. She wasn't like that.'

'Sure she was. She was a selfish, manipulative bitch and everyone but you could see it.'

I pushed back my chair, threw a couple of notes on the table, and walked away. I had no idea where I was or where I was going, but anywhere had to be better than listening to more from Paddy. But halfway down the street, I stopped. I was overlooking the obvious, again. This wasn't about me, or Paddy, or Faye. It was about Caitlyn. I turned back. Paddy was following me, his hands in his pockets.

'After Faye died,' I said, 'when Caitlyn came to live with us, and you decided to leave ... You knew all this? You knew you might be her father – the only parent she had left – and you abandoned her anyway?'

The answer was there on his face, impossible to escape; impossible to forgive.

'Yes.'

And then I turned my back on him and walked away.

It was late when I finally made it back to the hotel, but it hardly mattered. There would be no sleep after tonight's revelations. Instead, I pored over my phone, scrolling through all the photos I had of Caitlyn, looking for any resemblance to Paddy – an expression, a feature, anything that might prove either way whether she was his daughter. There was nothing, or nothing that was obvious to me. Physically she resembled Faye and always had done. Were there any signs in her character? She was a talented artist, but Faye's artistic skills had been in a different league to Paddy's doodles. She was good at languages, but that didn't prove anything, did it? Even Mum had picked up decent Spanish in her years living abroad.

I stopped at a photograph of Faye. It had always been one of my favourites: I had taken it in Mum and Dad's garden, and Faye was holding a toddler Caitlyn and laughing as she looked at something over my shoulder. Something or someone? Sudden suspicion flashed into my mind. Had Paddy been there? It was quite possible; we had spent most holidays alternating between his house and mine. Could Faye have been smiling at him? There was a teasing air to the smile ... but if I thought that, I would believe Paddy and condemn Faye. How could I do that? Faye wouldn't have manipulated and tormented him like that. I couldn't believe it, couldn't believe that she could be so different to the sister I thought I had known. If I did, it would be like losing her all over again.

And yet ... as the night went by, and I sat in a chair by the window without catching any sleep, I couldn't ignore the truth. Through all the years I had been going out with Paddy, Faye had apparently known that he might be Caitlyn's father, and had said nothing to me. I had accused Paddy of betraying me by not telling me. Wasn't Faye equally guilty – more so, because of our bond of blood? Paddy's revelation had put a damaging filter over those memories of the last few years with Faye, years I had treasured after she died. Everything looked different now. All those times that Faye had encouraged Caitlyn to go to Uncle Paddy, said with a laughing smile that I hadn't thought twice about at the time; all the conversations I had shared with Faye, when I had told her of my growing feelings for Paddy, and she had joked what a brilliant father he would make ... Had she been mocking me, not teasing? I would never know; these doubts would stain my memories of her forever, because there could be no explanation, no apology. The purity, the innocence of our relationship and my feelings for her could never recover from this.

I must have fallen into an exhausted doze eventually, because I was woken by a persistent banging on the door of my room at just past six. I knew who it would be, but still staggered over and opened the door. Paddy's fist was raised, ready to knock again. He had showered and changed, and I felt acutely conscious that I was still wearing yesterday's crumpled clothes: the dress that he had helped me into when we were rushing out to the restaurant last night; the dress I had imagined him taking off me later. How much had changed in those few hours!

Before I could speak, he reached out and stroked the side of my cheek. My treacherous skin still blazed at his touch.

'You haven't slept. Are you okay?'

Okay? How could he think any of this was okay? I didn't reply.

'Stupid question,' he said, squeezing past me into the room, although I hadn't invited him in. 'This is a mess. We need to talk.'

'Do we?' I sat down on the crumpled bed, and flinched when Paddy sat down on the other side. Hardly twelve hours ago we had been entwined together in this bed, skin sliding over skin, so close that it had truly felt as if we were fused into one; the sheets still bore the scent of him, of us, which was why I had spent the night on the chair.

'You said more than enough last night,' I continued. My voice sounded flat, hoarse from lack of sleep. 'What else is there to say? I used to hate you for what you did – walking out on us when we needed you. But that was nothing compared to what I now know you did. You walked out on us, knowing that Caitlyn might be your own child. What sort of man would do that?'

'Not a man. A boy. A young, foolish and cowardly boy.' Paddy stood up and wandered over to the window, tugging a hand through his curls. 'Jeez, you can't have hated me as much as I've hated myself. You were everything, you know that, right?'

He was looking at me, I could tell, but I wouldn't meet his gaze.

'Faye dropped her hints for a while, but then it stopped. It was as if she'd never said anything. And it was easy to convince myself that she'd just been winding me up, because that's what I wanted to believe. I'd stopped even thinking about it. But then Caitlyn came to live with us, and one day she said something – in my words, my accent – and it freaked me out. Made me wonder all over again whether she really might be mine. You didn't notice that time, but what if it happened again? What if she started to look like me too – or if we had children who looked just the same? I couldn't live like that, with this huge secret ready to explode; every bit of happiness laced with fear that it might be the last. And I couldn't face telling you the truth, and hurting you even more than you were already hurting; couldn't risk damaging your feelings about Caitlyn when she was depending on you. So I had to leave. And leaving you was the single hardest thing I've ever done.'

The rawness in his voice was breaking my heart all over again. But Paddy hadn't finished yet.

'It was an impulsive decision, made when I was a stupid boy. I wouldn't make the same one now. I wouldn't even have made the same one a year later. I went around the world, and worked on some of the digs, as we'd planned, but it wasn't the same without you. Don't think I had an amazing time and never gave you another thought. That's not true. I grew up and I realised what I'd done. The regret was always with me.'

I couldn't help myself.

'So why stay away?' I asked. 'If you regretted it so much, why not come back?'

'I almost did in those first couple of years – more times than I can count.' Paddy sat down next to me again. 'And each time,

I stopped myself. I would have been coming back for me – to stop me blaming myself, to stop the guilt. When I thought about what was best for Caitlyn, I knew I couldn't come back. She would have been settled with you by then; and perhaps you would have found a new partner, though it killed me to think of it. I couldn't do anything to rock that. It didn't matter who I was to her. That was only DNA. You were her real parent. She needed you more than she needed me.'

He reached out and placed his hand over mine on the bed, twisting his fingers with mine. I studied his face. It was the same face that I had fallen in love with twice, and yet it could never be the same now. My eyes were roving, trying to read the truth in his features, looking for any resemblance to Caitlyn, just as I had studied photos of her through the night. Was this how it would always be now? Not able to see one without immediately thinking of the other? Scrutinising them both, whenever they were together? Suspicion placing a negative filter on love? How would I live like that? I couldn't. And if it meant saying goodbye to one of them, there was no choice about it. Paddy had made the decision for me in the past, leaving me with Caitlyn. Now I wouldn't hesitate to make the same decision for myself.

'Over the years, I convinced myself that it couldn't be true,' Paddy carried on. He seemed determined to make his confession, however much it was hurting us both. 'It had been a one-off, quick fumble. Hardly anything. What were the chances of a pregnancy from that? But years later, when Amy couldn't have a baby, I began to think about it again. When I had the tests, I thought it might have removed the doubt, if I'd been infertile. But I wasn't ... And then when I found out this year that Amy was pregnant with her new man, the niggle wouldn't go away that I might already have a child. And only a couple of weeks later, by some miracle, you turned up at that school when I was giving a talk and it seemed I'd been given a chance to find out ...'

'That's why you were so pleased to see me then?' I interrupted. 'When you said you wanted to explain, it was about this – about Caitlyn? All the visits to Inglebridge since then, all the questions about my life, all the time we've spent together, the offer to come to Paris,' I ended on a half-sob. 'It's only ever been about Caitlyn?'

I withdrew my hand, stood up and went into the bathroom to pour a glass of water. I looked at myself in the mirror. A tired face stared back, stained by lack of sleep and the remains of yesterday's make-up. An old face. I was twice as old as when I had first met Paddy and, as I now knew, twice as stupid. How could I have fallen for his charm again? It was a sham, just as surely as it had been last time. He had never been interested in me; I was nothing but the means for him to get close to Caitlyn. He had just confessed as much. Why had I let him fool me again? And why, out of everything, was it this confession that had caused me the most pain?

I wiped away the make-up, washed my face, and brushed my hair until I looked presentable again. I wasn't going to fall apart this time, any more than I had the last. Then, I'd had Caitlyn to force me to hold myself together. Now ... The sounds of the city waking drifted through the window, and I rallied. Life was going on outside these rooms, and mine would go on too. I had a future. I had a house, friends, and a new career in archaeology to explore. I was an independent woman, more so than ever, with Caitlyn settled and money in the bank. I had managed without Paddy Friel until this year. I would learn to manage without him again.

My resolve wavered when I returned to the bedroom and saw Paddy sitting on the bed, exactly as I had left him, one hand still lying on the covers where it had been joined with mine a few minutes ago. There were tears in his eyes, and he looked defeated – an expression I had never seen on his face before. He jumped up and came towards me.

'That came out wrong. It was about Caitlyn at first,' he said. He tried to take my hand, but I shook him off. 'I just wanted to see her for myself. I thought that if I saw her, spoke to her, I would somehow know the truth; I would know if she was mine. But soon it was all about you. I started to fall in love with you again when you strapped that bag of peas to my leg. I didn't stand a chance after that. You have to believe me, Eve.'

I didn't have to – but oh, how I wanted to! My body was still drawn to him, even as my head and my heart were pulling away. Yesterday I had given my whole self to him, as if we were half our age and nothing could tear us apart. But I should have known better. I should never have allowed myself to hope.

'Get out, Paddy,' I said.

'You don't mean that. Yesterday ...'

'What about yesterday?' I asked, fighting to keep the tremor out of my voice. 'That was just sex.'

'No, it bloody wasn't. Not on my side. And I don't believe it was for you either.' He stood up, facing me. 'You're really saying it meant nothing? Like with the boor?'

'Not like Rich. Don't flatter yourself it was that good.'

It was a cheap shot. I regretted it as soon as I saw the pain flash across his face; because even now, seeing his pain hurt me too.

'Yesterday I behaved like an idiot,' I said. An idiot who drank champagne and thought that Paddy Friel might love her. Idiot hardly covered half of that. 'Today I'm myself again. I have a flight to catch and I'm not going to miss it simply so that you can ease your conscience by confessing and making excuses. Leave me alone.'

He took a few steps towards the door, then stopped.

'I need to know if she's mine,' he said. 'I want to do a test.'

'No.' I opened the door and clutched the handle to steady myself; I needed to hold on for a few more seconds. 'You said it yourself. She's better off without you. We both are. If you don't leave now, I'll ring reception and ask for you to be removed. I mean it, Paddy. This is over.'

Finally, he left. I slammed the door behind him, and collapsed onto the bed in tears.

Chapter 23

'What the heck are these?' Gran asked, as I handed her the box of biscuits I had chosen for her at Charles de Gaulle airport. 'Are these shortbread?'

'Something similar. You probably won't notice the difference.'

Gran gave me the withering look that comment deserved.

'Very kind of you,' she said, putting the unopened box down on the table at her side. I expected it would find its way into the Christmas tombola – and knowing my luck, I would win it back. 'But you don't need to give me anything fancy. The regular shortbread will do on Sunday.'

It was Thursday – not my usual day to visit Gran, but forty-eight hours after my return from Paris, I needed some of her healing skills. Not that she had any medicine that could heal my wounds this time, but being with her, listening to her acerbic comments about her fellow inmates – as she liked to call them – would provide a distraction, at least. Or so I thought.

'Are you sure there's nothing up with Caitlyn?' Gran asked, breaking off from an eye-watering anecdote about Mr Craig and a cold flannel. 'You look peaky, and more your age than normal. How will anyone believe I'm only sixty-five now?'

'She's fine,' I said. 'More than fine. She loves it over there. She seems very happy with Luc. I can't imagine she'll ever come home.'

'Rattling around your empty nest, are you?' Gran patted my hand. 'It's early days. Mark my words, this time next year you'll see it as a blessing.'

'Is that how you felt when Dad moved out?'

'No. I never stopped missing him. I never will.' Gran adjusted the blanket over her knees; it was an unusually warm afternoon, even for August, and we were sitting in deckchairs in the garden. 'So if it's not Caitlyn that's given you the hangdog look, it must be Paddy. Did things not work out in Paris? I thought he'd have managed to put a bit of colour in your cheeks by now.'

Was that a euphemism? Judging by Gran's smile, I had a horrible feeling that it was.

'Don't tell me you've had words again?' Gran asked. 'What's he done this time?'

I didn't reply. Where would I ever begin? I was still trying to get my head round the whole sorry mess – veering from despair to disbelief and back again. I had no idea what I should do or how I should feel. I had changed my seat on the flight back to Manchester, so I wasn't next to Paddy, and had dashed out of the airport before him, but he was being more persistent than I had expected. He had tried to ring and left messages so often that in the end I had blocked and deleted his number, but had then immediately regretted it. It was all very well deciding that I should hate him again, but my heart wasn't receiving the instruction from my head. I missed him – or the man I had spent time with over the last few months, at least.

'Come on, you can tell your old gran. I've been around for long enough. Not much can shock me now.'

'Paddy might be Caitlyn's father.'

Clearly Gran hadn't been around quite long enough, as she stared at me slack-jawed. Perhaps I should have broken the news more gently, but what good would that have done? The facts were the facts, and they wouldn't change whatever words I used.

'You're having me on,' Gran said at last. 'Who told you that? They want their bumps feeling. Take no notice of claptrap like that.'

'Paddy told me.'

'He always was a joker,' Gran said, but I could see the doubt creeping across her face. 'He's pulling your leg. Too many pints of Guinness. I'm right, you'll see.'

I wished she was, but not even Paddy would joke about this. And I'd seen the desire in his face, heard the crack in his voice as he'd suggested that Caitlyn might be his daughter. He believed it was possible, and that meant I had no choice but to believe it too.

'He ran into Faye when she visited me at university,' I said, sparing Gran the sordid details of the fumble in the pub car park. The less I thought about that, the better. 'It was long before I met him. He says he'd forgotten about it until I took him home, and then Faye reminded him and wound him up about Caitlyn being his. But she wasn't like that, was she? She wouldn't have been deliberately cruel. And she wouldn't have risked hurting me, if I'd overheard something like that.'

It was the thing that had haunted me most over the last couple of days, eclipsing Paddy's part in all this. Why hadn't Faye told me that she had a history with Paddy? The only explanation I could come up with was that she had seen how much I loved him, and had kept her silence to protect me; so it made no sense that she would tease Paddy about it. Gran was silent for a long time, but eventually reached out and took my hand. She squeezed, and despite her frailty, her thick wedding band pressed into my fingers.

'You always did see the best in her,' Gran said. 'And you still do. Bless you for that.'

I stared – what did that mean?

'You mean you think it's true?'

'Eh, I can't answer that. But she was always jealous of you. I wouldn't put it past her to have made mischief.'

I laughed – I couldn't help it. Jealous of me? It was absurd. Faye had everything: she had been brilliant, beautiful, popular, a talented artist ... If anyone should have been jealous, it was me. But I hadn't been, because I had adored her. However much attention she received, it was never as much as I thought she deserved.

'Oh, she was a bonny lass and clever, right enough,' Gran said. 'But she didn't use it. We'd have called her flighty in my day. She couldn't settle down to her schoolwork, or get a proper job, or find a steady relationship. But off you went to university and found your Paddy ...' Gran sighed. 'It wouldn't surprise me one bit if she'd tried to stir things with him.'

Reaching past Gran, I picked up the box of biscuits, tore off the cellophane and picked out the biggest one I could find. I didn't want to believe anything Gran was saying, but her words had brushed off the dust on memories of Faye that I had chosen to bury with her: suspicions and feelings that I had ignored, such as the occasional overzealous flirting with my boyfriends, or the cutting jokes about being boring when I had stayed in to revise for exams rather than going out with her. I would never have relied on such selective evidence in my archaeology work, so why had I in my private life? Because I had loved her. It was as simple as that.

An aeroplane passed overhead, breaking up the perfect blue of the sky with a thick white trail.

'What do I do now?' I asked Gran. 'Paddy wants to know the truth. He wants to take a paternity test. I said no, but ...'

But. Something else that had haunted me since Paris, keeping me awake through the long hours of the night. Was it the right decision? There had been no thought behind my refusal; it had been an emotional response, not a considered one. Had I let my disappointment with Paddy, my feelings of betrayal by Faye, blind me to what was the right thing to do? I'd told him, on the day we had visited Alison, that I would have been glad if a decent man had come forward as Caitlyn's father. Why should it be different, because the man in question was him?

'You've done your best for Caitlyn over all these years,' Gran said, as if she was replying to the thoughts in my head. 'You won't let her down now.'

'You think I should tell her?' I asked. 'I should let the test go ahead?'

'She might have a father – and a good one, whatever you might reckon of him just now.' She patted my knee. 'You know what it's like to have a good father. You wouldn't want our Caitlyn to miss out on that.'

My fortieth birthday conveniently fell on a Saturday, and I had booked a meal at the French bistro in town to celebrate. Caitlyn, Luc and Mum were due to arrive the day before and would be staying for a week. I had looked forward to their visit for so long, but I couldn't wish for it now, when such a life-changing task lay ahead. Because after hours and days of soul-searching and deliberation, I knew there was only one way forward.

When Caitlyn arrived, I would tell her about Paddy, so she could choose whether to go ahead with the paternity test or not. Gran had been right: I couldn't let her miss out on the chance to have a father. It didn't matter how old she was: I had lost my dad at a similar age as she was now and had never stopped wishing he was around. When I thought about the life experiences Caitlyn might have ahead of her – buying her first home, getting married, having children – a father would make a difference to everything.

And I couldn't help going back to one particular thing that Paddy had said in the hotel room in Paris. He had told me that he had stayed away from us because Caitlyn had needed me more than him. Perhaps now the situation had reversed, and she needed a parent – a *real* one – more than she needed me. Perhaps it was time to fall back, become the aunt I should always have been – a friend rather than a mother. It was complicated – my feelings towards her weren't constrained by labels – but I had to do what was best for her.

As for my feelings towards Paddy ... Once the initial shock of Paris had worn off, and I had recovered from the effects of the alcohol and lack of sleep, I hadn't been able to hate him again. It was too late for that; the man I had got to know this year didn't deserve to be hated. But I couldn't let myself carry on loving him either, if he was Caitlyn's father. Watching them develop a relationship would be a constant reminder that I had been second in line with Paddy, as I had been with everything else where Faye was concerned; that the man I had hoped to have children with myself had instead formed that bond with my sister. And it would remind me of her betrayal; because the more I reflected on it, the more I thought that a good sister would have told me the history that first time I introduced Paddy to her as my boyfriend; would have let me decide for myself whether I wanted to be involved with someone who might have fathered her child.

And beyond all that, I couldn't risk coming between Paddy and Caitlyn. If they were to have a proper relationship, there couldn't ever be one between Paddy and me. I couldn't hand her a father, only to steal away some of the time and affection he should give to her.

Paddy was still being persistent in his efforts to contact me; I had to give him credit for that. He had started sending letters and postcards, and correspondence from him was piling up in the house like invitations to Hogwarts. I'd made the mistake of glancing at some of it, and my tears had smudged the ink until the words were illegible. It was like the early days of our relationship, when he had left notes and doodles for me everywhere, and though I tried to harden my heart against it, it affected me as much now as it had then. But I couldn't let it. I had to be neutral, neither loving him nor hating him, because neither option would be compatible with his being Caitlyn's father.

The correspondence hadn't mentioned Caitlyn, but I couldn't imagine he'd abandoned his wish to take a paternity test. I knew very well that he could contact Caitlyn direct and ask her himself, and I could only trust that he wouldn't do that; I wanted to break the news to Caitlyn, to give her any support she needed. But I'd forgotten, until the French bistro contacted me to confirm numbers for my birthday meal, that I had invited Paddy to join us when we were in Paris. Would he still come? I had no idea; but I couldn't take the risk that he would turn up and speak to Caitlyn before I was ready. Now I regretted my hasty decision to delete his number from my phone; but I remembered that

Tina might have it from when she had arranged his school visit all those months ago.

'I'm in the garden,' she yelled, when I wandered over one afternoon and knocked on the front door. I went through the side gate and found her sprawled on a sun lounger in the back garden, wearing a swimming costume with the straps off her shoulder.

'It's a good job it's only me,' I said, sitting down on the steps beside her. 'Are you trying to compete with Year 11 for the best tan? Even if the sun shines every day until the start of term I don't think you'll do it.'

'It's not for school,' Tina said, rolling over and narrowly avoiding taking our relationship to a whole new level by exposing more than either of us had bargained for. 'It's for Saturday night. The bistro is a bit fancy. I've bought a pale blouse, so I need a bit of colour to pull it off. I'm regretting going sleeveless, though – it's good for the hot flushes but does nothing for the bingo wings. All things for you to look forward to,' she added, grinning. 'Although you're so lean with all that running you'll probably never need to worry about wobbly bits.'

'I wouldn't have minded having some wobbly bits,' I replied, laughing and indicating my small chest. 'I've yet to find an exercise that can increase the bulk up here.'

'Did you never do this one when you were growing up? I must, I must, I must improve my bust,' she chanted, thrusting back her elbows in time with the words. She just managed to grab the top of her swimming costume before I could see for myself whether the exercise had worked for her. 'I'll go and throw some more clothes on. Are you stopping for a drink? Water, or can I tempt you with something stronger, like a cup of tea?'

'I'll have a glass of wine if you're opening a bottle.'

Tina laughed until she realised I was serious.

'I know I've been trying to persuade you for years, but alcohol isn't the answer,' she said, suddenly transforming into Tina the teacher. 'Are you sure?'

'Positive.'

Why not? Paris had changed everything. Returning home, I had taken great pleasure in roaming the once-forbidden section of the supermarket, picking out a selection of wine based on price and pretty labels. I had resisted the spirits, so far, although I felt it was only a matter of time before I succumbed to the temptation of some of the gin bottles.

Tina returned wearing a dazzling kaftan and carrying two glasses of wine.

'Cheers,' she said, clinking her glass against mine and settling back down on the sun lounger. 'This is weird. I hope you're not going to get pie-eyed after one glass and need carrying home. Graham is away tonight. I'll have to stick you in the wheelbarrow and trundle you over the road. Anyway,' she continued with an abrupt change of subject. 'Why are you looking so smart? Are you going on a date? Is this Dutch courage?'

'It's not a date,' I replied. I couldn't imagine ever going on one of those again. 'I had the job interview I told you about this afternoon.'

'Sorry, I completely forgot that was today.' Tina leant forward. 'How did it go? Is this why you're on wine? Are we celebrating?'

'Not yet. I think it went well. It's hard to tell, isn't it? It's so long since I had an interview that I've forgotten how to read the signs.'

The invitation to the interview had come out of the blue, the day after my return from Paris. My old tutor, Christopher Porter, had let me know that an archaeological consultancy set up by a former colleague was looking to take on a couple of graduate trainees. It sounded the perfect job: they were happy to take on trainees of any age, and however long ago they had graduated, and although the firm's offices were based in Yorkshire, they worked across the north of England, so I could mainly work west of the Pennines if I wanted. They offered a six-month trainee programme, at the end of which I would have an Archaeology Skills Passport, which would help me apply for another job. It was a dream role, and the people who had interviewed me had been lovely, but I was trying not to get my hopes up. Although I had spent weeks trying to catch up on all the developments in archaeology that I had missed, there was a seventeen-year gap in my CV that was hard to reconcile with my professed enthusiasm for the subject.

'When do you find out?' Tina asked.

'Next week. Today was the last round of interviews.' I sipped the wine, trying to suppress a grimace. The odd thing was, now I had given myself permission to drink wine, I wasn't sure I was actually enjoying it. Apart from the champagne in Paris, more often than not I'd rather have been having a cup of tea after all. Was this a symptom of impending middle age?

'I wish they would make us wait longer,' I added. 'I'd rather live with the hope than the disappointment.'

We chatted for a while longer, but I declined a second glass of wine. I stood up to go.

'While I'm here,' I said, trying to sound as casual as I could, 'you don't still have Paddy's contact details from when you organised his school visit, do you?'

'I probably have his card somewhere. Why do you need it? You've just been to Paris with him – I thought you'd have exchanged more than phone numbers. You've not fallen out, have you? I was looking forward to meeting him again at your birthday meal. To talk history,' Tina added, with an unconvincing grin.

'He's still coming, as far as I know. I just need to double check, to confirm numbers with the bistro. I seem to have mislaid his number.'

It was feeble, and I could see Tina was making a valiant effort not to interrogate me further, but she managed to find his number, and I sent a text to Paddy, suggesting we meet at The White Hart on Saturday afternoon, before the birthday meal. His reply was almost instant, agreeing to the plan. So now all I had to do was to break the news to Caitlyn that she might have a father ... How on earth was I supposed to do that?

Chapter 24

Mum, Caitlyn and Luc flew into Manchester airport on Friday morning, my last day as a thirty-something. I'd offered to pick them up, but Mum had declined the offer, no doubt glad of the chance to spend some time on her own with Caitlyn. Even though I had taken Caitlyn over to Spain every year, and welcomed Mum's visits to us whenever she wanted, it could never be enough, as I now understood. The last few months, with Caitlyn away in Paris, had made me realise as I hadn't before how difficult the separation must have been for Mum, when I had made the move north and out of daily reach.

It was early afternoon before I heard a taxi pull up outside the house, and I rushed to the door, eager to get a glimpse of Caitlyn. Despite a day of travelling, the Parisian gloss I had noticed before was still evident, in the chic clothes she wore and the confident way she paid the driver and wheeled her case up the drive, closely followed by Luc.

I pulled her into a hug as soon as she was within reach, pleasure at seeing her my overwhelming feeling. But as we pulled apart, and she started to complain about their delayed flight, I found myself studying her face more intently than I had ever needed to before. Every detail was familiar – but was there more to that familiarity than seventeen years of living with her? Were there traces of Paddy in the twist of her mouth or the shape of her eyes that I had failed to notice before? Was this Paddy's daughter stepping into my house? I didn't want to know; but I couldn't live with this uncertainty either.

'Are you okay, Mum?' Caitlyn stopped chattering and turned to look at me. 'You're looking flustered. Is it the thought of the big four-zero? If it's any consolation, you could still pass for late thirties.'

She laughed, and I couldn't help joining in.

'Less of your cheek. I am still late thirties – yes, very late,' I added, as she opened her mouth to point that out. 'At least let me enjoy my last few hours, before I wake up tomorrow with wrinkled skin and hair sprouting from my nose and ears ...'

'Don't worry about that,' Caitlyn said. She looked at Mum, who was still standing awkwardly on the wrong side of the threshold. 'Shall we tell her?' Without waiting for an answer, Caitlyn rushed on. 'It's part of your birthday present. We've booked you in to have your hair and nails done tomorrow afternoon. I'm sure you can sort out any unwanted hair while you're there.'

'Tomorrow afternoon?' I repeated. That was when I had arranged to meet Paddy. 'What time?'

'Three. You'll be finished in perfect time to get changed and go to the party. But don't worry, we have plans for the whole day, so you won't have a spare moment to feel sorry for yourself.'

'Thank you.' I hugged Caitlyn again, and Mum too, who had now moved as far as the hall. It was lovely of them to do this, but it ruled out any chance of a secret meeting with Paddy before the meal. 'I'll look forward to it.'

'You should have had your nails done before,' Caitlyn said, grabbing my hand and looking at my short nails. I had always kept them short – better for digging, and in more recent years, for typing. 'It would have been a perfect way to use your vouchers. Be kind to yourself, remember? How many have you got left?'

'None! You see, I've been exceptionally kind to myself. I'll give you the last two tomorrow. One of them involved buying a new dress for tomorrow night. You must approve of that.'

'Sounds good. You'll have to show me later.'

'Later?' I repeated, as Caitlyn pushed her bag and Luc's to the bottom of the stairs and walked back towards the door.

'I said I'd catch up with a few friends in town this afternoon. You don't mind, do you? They're dying to meet Luc! I'll let you know if we'll be back for tea. Love you!'

And with that they were gone, strolling away down the street towards town without a backward glance. Mum touched my arm.

'Shall I put the kettle on? You look like you could do with a drink.'

I followed Mum into the kitchen and let her bustle around making tea. Things had been easier between us since her last visit, and our telephone conversations were lasting longer than ever before, but some awkwardness still lingered now we were face to face. I thought Caitlyn would have stayed with us, to help smooth things along; I hadn't realised she would barely step foot through the door. But why should I mind? I was only an aunt, not a mother, even if my feelings didn't recognise the distinction.

'Caitlyn tells me you were with Paddy in Paris,' Mum said, when we were settled at the kitchen table with our tea. 'Paddy Friel.' As if there could be any doubt who she meant. 'I didn't know you were friendly with him again. Are you sure? After the way he treated you ...'

Glancing across the table, I saw a look in Mum's eye that I instinctively recognised, but hadn't expected. It was the wariness of a tiger, ready to guard her cub. It was how I had felt about every boyfriend Caitlyn had brought home, wondering if he might hurt her and what I could do to prevent it. It had never crossed my mind that Mum might feel the same way about me, even at my age.

'It's nothing,' I said. 'We met a few times over the summer, that's all. He helped out when I needed to go to Paris to see Caitlyn.'

I stared down at my tea. That wasn't all; not even a fraction of it, on my side at least. But how could I be sure what he had been feeling all summer and why he had come to Paris? I thought he'd been helping me; that it had been like that day when we had first met at university, and he had rushed to my rescue without a thought for himself. I'd taken it as evidence that he cared for me. But nothing was certain now. I couldn't shake off the suspicion that his offer to accompany me had simply been a way for him to see Caitlyn. I'd wanted to hurry to her side, to check for myself that she was safe. Had he felt the same – paternal instincts prompting his offer to accompany me, rather than romantic ones? And if he had, how could I criticise him for that? I sighed. This was all such a mess.

'What's the matter?' Mum said, and she reached across the table to squeeze my hand. 'Don't tell me nothing. I'm your mum. I know when something's not right.'

It was true – even though I'd had little obviously in common with Mum, she had always been able to read me, always known exactly how I was feeling. So how much more must she have known about Faye, when the two of them had been so close? I should have thought of this before; if anyone knew Faye's secrets, it would be Mum.

'Do you know who Caitlyn's father is?' I asked.

My attempt to surprise her didn't work. She took a moment before she looked up at me, but her face gave nothing away.

'No. You know that. We went through all this when Faye first told us she was pregnant, and again when Caitlyn was born. Faye told us nothing. If we'd had a name, we would have contacted him after she died.'

'So Faye never mentioned a name at any time? Never even made a hint or suggestion about anyone? Anyone at all?'

Mum sighed and sat back in her chair. 'I see. I suppose you mean Paddy.'

'You knew!' Tea splashed out of my mug and down my hand as I slammed my cup on the table. 'So it's true?'

It felt as though my world was shattering. Deep down, I hadn't wanted to believe it. But if Mum knew what I was asking, before I'd mentioned his name ...

'It's true that Faye suggested it,' Mum said. 'Not just suggested – she tormented him with it for a while.'

'But I never heard any of it!'

'No. I hoped you wouldn't.' Mum's bracelets jangled as she pushed her mug across the table from one hand to the other. 'She was careful not to say it in front of you. And I soon put a stop to it when I realised what she was doing.'

That fitted with what Paddy had said in Paris; that the comments from Faye had suddenly stopped. Was it because Mum had interfered?

'Why would she say it at all if it wasn't true?' I asked.

'That was Faye. I loved her to bits, but God knows she wasn't perfect.' Mum brushed away a tear from her cheek. 'She lived for attention, and most of the time she got it, especially from you. But then Paddy came along. You worshipped her until you met him, and then he was everything to you. It was clear to all of us that he wasn't just another boyfriend. Perhaps she thought that if she stirred up some trouble, she would frighten him off so you were all hers again. But of course it wasn't true about Caitlyn. How could it be? Faye hadn't met Paddy until you brought him home.'

So Mum hadn't known the truth about Faye and Paddy. That was some comfort at least; that not everyone was keeping secrets from me.

'She had met him. Paddy told me in Paris. They met during Freshers' Week – you remember that Faye came to stay with me? And they ...' I shook my head. I couldn't say the words. 'So it's true. Paddy might be Caitlyn's father. And he wants to take a test to find out.'

Mum covered her mouth with her hands, and a steady stream of tears rolled down her cheeks, carrying her mascara with them. 'And I told her to stop spreading lies ...'

I went round the table and hugged her. And it was a loaded hug, intended to offer her comfort, to share her grief, and also to acknowledge this reminder that although she'd had more in common with Faye, she had loved me just as much. She had argued with Faye to protect me, and that meant more than I could say in any words.

'Did she really never tell you who Caitlyn's father was?' I asked at last, when we had dried our eyes and I had returned to my seat.

'Never.' Mum shrugged. 'I always assumed she wasn't sure herself. We looked through her things after she died, but we didn't find any clues.'

Her things! Why hadn't I thought of that? Faye's personal belongings were in the loft, stored in case Caitlyn ever wanted them. She hadn't chosen to look at them yet, but perhaps I should. Mum might have searched for evidence of Caitlyn's father before, but it was possible she had missed something; equally possible that she might not have understood something that I would.

I stood up. 'I'm going to have a look.'

'I told you, there was nothing there ...'

'A fresh pair of eyes can't do any harm.'

'Can't they?' Mum stood too, and looked at me across the table. 'If you found something – something that proved Paddy was Caitlyn's father – what good would it do you?'

None. It wouldn't do me any good at all. But I'd already decided to tell Caitlyn the truth and let her decide whether to take part in a paternity test, and I wasn't going to change my mind; as Gran had reminded me, it might do Caitlyn some good, and what further motivation did I need? The sooner we found out the better, as far as I was concerned, so this torturous state of uncertainty would be over.

Mum followed me upstairs and climbed the ladder into the loft after me, her bracelets jangling all the way. Stacked in the corner, behind the Christmas decorations and boxes of Caitlyn's old schoolbooks, stood a couple of large plastic trunks filled with those possessions of Faye's that we had chosen to keep. There wasn't much; it upset me every time I came up here to see a life so extraordinary reduced to this meagre collection of mundane items. I lifted the lid off the first box and started taking out the contents: CDs, books, costume jewellery – all things kept to show Caitlyn who Faye had been, rather than because of intrinsic value. An old shoebox of assorted photographs came next, brim-full of memories of our childhood and teenage years.

I rummaged through the box and stopped short as I found one of me and Faye in my first-year room at university, during that fateful Freshers' Week – an old-fashioned selfie, taken with the timer function on a proper camera, the top of our hair missing as we'd posed in the wrong spot. Had this been taken before or after her encounter with Paddy? I'd never know if the smile on her face was a result of pleasure at being with me, or of having been with him. I threw the photo back in the box, and moved on to the next pile of belongings.

There was a stack of diaries, from the pre-smartphone days, but only appointment diaries, nothing personal. I flicked through the diary for the year Caitlyn must have been conceived, looking for I don't know what – names? Dates? A highlighted entry saying, 'Caitlyn was conceived today!'? But there was nothing significant: just the regular sort of dental and optician's appointments; the dates when Faye had visited me during Freshers' Week; and a mysterious number of asterisks against certain dates that could have meant something or nothing.

The diary for the following year was the same, save that antenatal checks and GP appointments filled the first few months and a sketch of a stalk carrying a baby was marked on a day in July.

Mum was hovering nearby, and despite the tan and the bright clothes, she seemed to have faded at the sight of these reminders of Faye.

'She drew a stork in July,' I said, holding out the diary. 'But that's not right. Caitlyn was born in June.'

'That must have been her due date. Caitlyn came three weeks early. Don't you remember?'

'No.' It had been the busy end-of-year time at university, and I would have been in the first flush of my relationship with

Paddy. I probably hadn't paid much attention to the details beyond the baby being a girl and everyone being well. But was it significant, that Caitlyn had been due in July? I picked up the diaries and flicked back nine months. October. After Freshers' Week. And then I noticed what I had missed on my first inspection of the diary: a red circle around the date, five days after Faye had visited me. Faye had always marked the start of her period that way. I flicked forwards. There were no more red circles until after Caitlyn was born.

'Look,' I said, showing Mum the page. 'Faye had a period in October. The diary might not tell us who the father is, but it tells us who it isn't. Paddy can't be Caitlyn's father, can he?'

I stared at the page, trying to take it in. After all the trauma, all the worry of the last couple of weeks, was it really as simple as all that? It looked it; but would one red circle be conclusive enough for Paddy? And what it did mean for me? I couldn't even think about that yet.

'Well, that's that, then,' Mum said. She squeezed my hand, and I squeezed back. 'I'm going back down. Seeing all her things ...'

I nodded. Opening this box had made grief a sharp pain again, rather than the dull ache that we had grown used to living with. All these possessions should have been in Faye's home, not stored in my loft; the dated CDs were a reminder of a life frozen in another time. As Mum disappeared through the loft access, I packed up the box again, pausing on one of the CDs. I'd bought it for Faye, but had probably listened to it more than she had done. I opened the case and pulled out the cover leaflet, intending to remind myself of the lyrics printed there, but as I opened it out, a photograph and a slip of paper fell out.

It was a photograph of Faye and Caitlyn, taken in her hospital bed judging by the background. Faye looked beautiful – even after giving birth, her luminosity shone out from the image. I bent down to pick up the paper. It was a sheet of good quality writing paper – a rare sight these days – and contained only a few scrawled words in handwriting I didn't recognise.

'Don't send any more photos. I told you I didn't want it. It was your decision to go ahead. You asked me to choose, and I chose my wife, so you can stop your games. Don't contact me again. M.'

Didn't want it? Was the 'it' Faye's baby? Had this note been written by Caitlyn's father? I tidied away the box and climbed back downstairs. Mum was sitting in the living room. She wiped her eyes quickly when I walked in.

'Did you find anything else?' she asked. Before I could reply, she pointed at the note in my hand. 'What's that?'

I sat down next to Mum and gave her the note. She read it in silence and her hand was trembling as she put the paper down on the coffee table.

'Poor Faye. A married man,' she said. 'I did wonder. I hope to God she didn't do it deliberately – get pregnant and try to pressure him to leave his wife. It sounds that way.'

'She wouldn't have done that!'

'She might have done, if she thought he was losing interest.' Mum took my hand, and rubbed it between hers. 'She had her flaws. It doesn't mean we loved her any less. But you were always the stronger and kinder one, taking after your dad. What you did for Caitlyn proves that. I can't think that Faye would have taken on your child, if the situation had been reversed. Your dad and I were so proud of what you did.'

She looked at me then, and I could see the love and pride in her face. And I couldn't bear it, not when thoughts of Faye filled my head, not when the loss of her felt so visceral again. For all these years, I had mentally accused Paddy of being a sham, of not being what he seemed – but I was far worse than him. I wasn't what I seemed. Because I hadn't been strong or kind, not to Faye. I had let her down when she needed me most, and I couldn't accept this display of love from Mum when it was the opposite of what I deserved.

'It's not true,' I said, and I withdrew my hand from Mum's because she wouldn't want to offer comfort when she heard what I had to say. 'I'm not kind. I wasn't kind to Faye.'

Mum tried to interrupt, but I wouldn't let her. I had to get this out at last. My guilt had haunted me for too many years, directing my thoughts and behaviour.

'Something happened on the night Faye died that I didn't mention to the police, or at the inquest,' I said. 'It was my fault that she took the pill that killed her.'

We'd been out to a club that night; a rare night away from Paddy for me, but Faye had nagged about how boring I had become until I agreed to go out with her. It had been fun at first, and I'd let my hair down, drinking more than I had done for a while. But then Faye had drifted off to hang about with a group of lads I didn't know and I'd grown tired of dancing on my own. So I'd gone to find her, to see if we could go home, and had caught her with a pill in her hand.

Even in my drunken state, I'd been horrified; Faye had always loved a good time, but I couldn't believe she would take drugs. I'd told her to get rid of it, reminded her that she had a daughter at home, shouted at her not to be so stupid, and finally knocked the tablet out of her hand. I'd left the party on my own, and after I'd gone, Faye must have bought another pill that had led to her death.

That was what I'd told everyone, when Faye's death had been investigated. That was the truth. But there was one detail I'd never shared with anyone else, even Paddy.

'You know we argued about the drugs,' I said to Mum now. She nodded. 'It was worse than I told you. We were drunk. We both said some vile things. She said that I thought I was better than her, because I had a degree, and she said that there was no way Paddy would stick around with someone as tedious as me. There was much more along the same lines. And I said ...'

I paused. Mum was watching me, her face pale, but I couldn't stop now – just as I hadn't been able to stop then.

'I took some money out of my purse and threw it at her, and I said that she could buy more drugs and kill herself for all I cared. And that's exactly what she did.'

Chapter 25

'The £20 on the mantelpiece,' Mum said.

I stared at her, not understanding.

'Did you throw £20 at her?' Mum asked. 'Two tens?'

'Yes. How do you know that?' Did it matter? Surely Mum should be angry with me for what I'd done, not focusing on a trivial detail?

'The money was on the mantelpiece in her flat, under a photo of the two of you. There was a sticker on it, with one word written down.' Mum reached out and grasped my hand. 'It said "sorry". It must have been meant for you. We never found any other explanation for it, and it didn't seem to matter with everything else going on ...'

It would have mattered to me. It still did matter, more than I could ever say. I had spent half my life regretting that my last words to Faye had been so cruel; that was why I had given up alcohol, so that I would never lose control and lash out that way again. I could never undo those words, but now I felt a rush of relief that at least she hadn't died hating me for them; that she had wanted to make up after our argument. I hoped with all my heart that when she wrote her 'sorry', she had realised that I would want to apologise to her too.

'You mustn't feel guilty,' Mum said. 'None of this was your

fault. You didn't put that drug in Faye's mouth. She chose to take it. The one you knocked out of her hand might have been from the same bad batch. When were any of us ever able to stop Faye when she set her mind on something? She was unlucky. We were all unlucky, losing her like that.'

I nodded. Perhaps Mum was right. I'd been through all the different scenarios, all the what-ifs, countless times, but the one element that could never change was Faye herself. We had loved her for her exuberance, her almost reckless determination to embrace every experience that life could offer. On this occasion, it had cost her life. I couldn't deny the truth; if she'd decided to take drugs that night, she would have found a way, whatever I said or did, and whether I'd given her money or not.

'Don't you think I feel guilty too?' Mum continued. 'When she phoned me that night, and said she felt ill, I didn't go to her. I thought she'd drunk too much. I'd had a few myself, and couldn't face going out. I told her to drink water and take aspirin. What if I'd gone to her then?' The tears were rolling down both our faces, and I hugged Mum as I should have done at the time, if my guilt hadn't thrown an inflatable barrier around me so I couldn't reach out to her.

'We can't go on blaming ourselves,' Mum said. She grabbed my hands. 'What have I always said? Life's too short to spend it looking over your shoulder at the past. We're the lucky ones. We're still here. Let's not waste it.'

We were a surprisingly happy group as we arrived at the bistro the next night – Luc escorting me, Mum, Caitlyn and Gran, four generations of women whose lives had all been changed by grief but who had found the strength to keep going. There had been plenty of tears after my conversation with Mum yesterday – tears for Faye, cruelly denied the chance to fulfil her potential, and tears for me too, because after years of punishing myself, I still had the opportunity to fulfil mine. It felt like a momentous point – as if life truly was beginning again.

The bistro was busy, and Tina and Graham were already sitting at a round table at the back – nearest to the ladies, at Gran's request. As we all took our seats, my stupid heart ached at the sight of the empty place where Paddy should have been. I'd sent him a text to let him know that I couldn't meet him this afternoon. Had he changed his mind about coming at all? And why was I so bothered if he had? The answer was obvious. My attempt to be neutral about him had utterly failed.

Mum ordered a bottle of champagne, and we were all clinking glasses as best we could without burning ourselves on the candles in the centre of the table, when a few whispers swept across the restaurant and the attention of most of my table refocused on something behind my back. I swivelled in my seat. Paddy was striding towards us, smiling at me with a degree of wariness, of uncertainty over his welcome, but even so his smile instinctively made my heart spin. And then he glanced at Caitlyn beside me, and my heart collapsed in a stupid, dizzy heap.

'Cutting it fine, aren't you?' Gran said, while Paddy bent and brushed such a fleeting kiss on my cheek that it was over before I could decide whether to allow it. 'We don't run on celebrity time up here, you know. You're lucky you've not missed your dinner. The champagne's all gone.'

'We'd better have another bottle,' Paddy said, and with a few nods and gestures, the waiter brought over another bottle and glass.

'Here you go,' Gran continued, pointing at the empty chair between her and Tina. 'You can be the thorn between two roses.

And you can make yourself useful and help me with this menu. Which of these foreign words means chips?'

Paddy squeezed round the table to the furthest place away from me, smiling and exchanging greetings as he went. He looked impossibly handsome; the blue shirt set off his dark hair and the sleeves were artfully rolled up, exposing firm, tanned forearms. Arms that had held me pressed to him, skin to skin, not so long ago. The champagne suddenly tasted like vinegar in my mouth, as it brought back memories of Paris: of everything that had been done and said and discovered there; of the happiness when I had thought a different future was in my sights; of the despair when I had realised that it was actually the past that had changed. I put down my glass. Why was he here? Was it to celebrate my birthday, or to see Caitlyn again? I wished I knew.

The meal was every bit as delicious as I'd hoped, and there was no denying that Paddy's presence helped the conversation and laughter flow. I'd dreamt of this, long ago: growing old with Paddy, sitting around a table, surrounded by our family and friends. But I had never imagined how small the table would be; that vital family members would have gone; that the children I had expected us to have one day wouldn't exist. And it struck me that perhaps Mum had had the right attitude all along. There was no point dwelling on the past or dreaming about the future. All we had, all we could be certain of, was now.

I reached under the table for my bag, and pulled out the box of 'Be Kind to Yourself' cards. My wrist jangled as I did; Mum had insisted on giving me some of her bangles, and I had accepted them gladly.

'Here are the final two cards,' I said, sliding them over to Caitlyn, who was sitting at my side. 'The first was for this dress, which was *very* expensive.' I laughed. 'I'll be wearing it to every occasion for at least the next twenty years to get my money's worth, so I hope you all like it.'

BE KIND TO YOURSELF
VOUCHER ELEVEN
I, Eve Roberts, have been kind to myself by buying an outrageously expensive dress!

'You could have saved a few bob and borrowed something from Mrs Pike,' Gran said. Laughing, I looked across the table at her and caught Paddy's warm gaze rising back to my face. The smile he sent me suggested that he appreciated the dress, if no one else did.

'And the final one,' I carried on quickly, 'is for this meal out, because I can't think of any greater treat than to be surrounded by the people who matter. A family isn't defined by size, or shape, or titles, or even ties of blood,' I said, smiling at Tina. 'It's about a group of people who might have nothing in common but love, but that's enough.'

BE KIND TO YOURSELF
VOUCHER TWELVE
I, Eve Roberts, have been kind to myself by having a night out with my wonderful family!

'She's getting sentimental in her old age,' Gran said, but she smiled and scrubbed at her eyes. 'Here, isn't it time you handed over your present?' She nudged Paddy. 'Distract her so she doesn't make any more soppy speeches.'

Paddy had been carrying a gift bag when he walked in, but

I hadn't liked to presume it was for me. He now retrieved it from under his chair and passed it round the table to me.

'You want me to open it now?' I asked, as everyone gazed expectantly at me. Paddy checked his watch.

'It's a birthday present. If you don't open it in the next two hours, it will have to wait until next year. Just go carefully with it, okay? It's fragile.'

I nodded, guessing that it was probably a bottle of perfume – it was an obvious present, wasn't it, for a female acquaintance? And what were we, other than acquaintances? He'd treated me no differently than Tina or Mum tonight, and apart from that one searing glance at my dress, had spent more time looking at Caitlyn than me. His gift would reflect the insignificance of our relationship, wouldn't it?

There was a box inside the gift bag, and I drew it out, lay it horizontally on the table, and lifted the lid. There was a bottle inside, but not the perfume bottle I'd anticipated. It was approximately twelve centimetres tall, with a round body and cylindrical neck, made of marbled green glass. I looked at Paddy. He smiled at me, because he knew, he must have known, what this present would mean to me.

Carefully, I removed the bottle from the protective foam it lay in and held it up. The light from the candles brought out the iridescence of the glass as I tilted it from side to side.

'Very nice, what is it?' Gran called. 'Is it a vase? It looks a bit grubby. Eh, have you been a cheapskate?' She nudged Paddy. 'Couldn't you stretch to a new one?'

'It's an unguentarium,' I said. Gran looked none the wiser. 'They were used by the Romans to hold perfumed oils and ointments.' I ran my finger over the glass. It was pitted in places but I didn't see the marks as flaws. They gave the piece character;

each one added to its history, and made it what it was. It was in remarkable condition given the likely age; the piriform shape of the bottle helped date it. 'First century?' I asked Paddy. He nodded.

'That's the most likely.'

Caitlyn was leaning against me, staring at the bottle.

'It's over two thousand years old? Wow. Did you dig this up?' she asked Paddy.

'No, I bought it.'

'But wouldn't it cost, like, millions of pounds to buy something so old?'

'Not quite millions ...'

'She'd have got more use out of a nice bottle of Chanel,' Gran said. She looked around for a waiter. 'Do you reckon they know how to make a proper cup of tea here? I'm parched.'

Mum ordered coffees and Gran's tea while I packed away Paddy's present. I could guess what he must have paid for this – not millions, but certainly hundreds – but the price wasn't the point. There was a memory wrapped up with this bottle, of Paddy taking me to the British Museum for the first time, when we had been visiting his parents who had lived outside London then. He had indulged me as I'd spent hours dawdling around the galleries, particularly the Roman artefacts. I remembered clearly how he'd stood behind me, arms holding me tight against his body as I'd studied a display of glassware, including the most amazing unguentarium made of swirls of marbled amber glass, and he had whispered in my ear that he would find one for me, one day. Had he remembered? Was there a significance in the gift that I hadn't anticipated?

Despite it being my birthday, I was driving, and when we couldn't spin out our coffees any longer, I picked up my car keys ready to take Gran back to The Chestnuts. Caitlyn and Luc decided to carry on to one of the pubs in town, and Mum, Tina and Graham were walking home.

'Won't you come back for a drink?' Paddy asked, as we left the warmth and bustle of the bistro and tumbled out into the quiet town centre. He was staying at The White Hart, an easy stagger across the square.

'I think Gran's tired ...'

'Not everyone. Just you.' Paddy lowered his voice. 'There are things we need to talk about.'

Even without his flicked glance at Caitlyn, I'd known what he meant. I'd wished all night that I'd been able to meet him this afternoon, because it had been heart-breaking to see his response to her in the bistro. He had watched her through the eyes of a parent, marvelling at even the most innocuous comment, smiling at everything she did. I knew, because I did it myself. I had recognised the pride in his expression, because I felt it myself. And now I had to take it away from him.

But as I drove back into town from The Chestnuts, one of the few cars on the road at this time, contemplating the vastness of the star-strewn sky all around, an alternative floated into my mind. Our affairs were so tiny, so immaterial in the grand scheme of things. Caitlyn had no father; Paddy had no child. Would it matter, really, if I told him I'd found evidence that she *was* his child, when the relationship would benefit them both? Could I get away with it?

Parking in the square again, I crossed over to The White Hart and looked in through the window as I tried to decide what to do. It was relatively busy with Saturday night drinkers, and happiness spilled out onto the pavement through the open windows. There were a few faces I recognised, but my eyes were drawn to the man sitting on his own at a corner table, staring into a half-drunk pint of Guinness. Even from outside, I could sense the nervous energy radiating off him like a live current. The next few minutes – what I was going to say to him – were going to shape the rest of his life. The rest of all of our lives. I pushed open the door and went inside.

Paddy looked up as soon as I walked in, and half rose, but I pointed at the bar and bought a sparkling water and another pint of Guinness before joining him at his table.

'You haven't told her yet, have you?' he said, and I shook my head, because there was no point pretending that I didn't understand. He sighed, and his hand crept across the table to hold mine. 'Please, Eve. I have to know. It's not just for me. It could make Mam happy, for whatever time she has left. It would give Dad a focus, when she's gone. I've got the kit upstairs, for the paternity test. We both need to provide cheek swabs. We could do it this weekend.'

'There's no need to do a test,' I said, and as the frown lines deepened across his forehead, and confusion clouded his eyes, any lingering doubts over what I had to do vanished. 'I went through Faye's belongings yesterday. I found evidence of who Caitlyn's father is.'

It was hard to tell if he was still breathing. He held my hand, and I could feel the tension in his fingers as they wrapped around mine. His hope was so real, so tangible, it was like a third party at the table.

'I'm sorry, Paddy. She's not yours.'

His hand slackened in mine, and he slumped back in his seat. Waves of disappointment rolled off him, and I felt terrible that I had done this to him. But when it came to it, I couldn't do anything else. I couldn't lie to the two people I loved best in the world, even if it would have been for their good; I couldn't survive a lifetime of deceit, with the constant worry of being found out. And I understood now, more than I had before, why Paddy had left us all those years ago. Not why he hadn't told me the truth in the first place – of course, he should have done that – but why, having decided against that course, he couldn't stay with us and maintain a pretence.

'Are you sure?' Paddy asked. 'There can't be any doubt?'

'No. Look.' I had the letter in my bag, and passed it to him. He withdrew his hand from mine and read it. The emotions trampled across his face: sadness, resignation, acceptance, annoyance. He tossed the note on to the table.

'Do you know who it is? This M?'

I shook my head.

'Jeez, what a ...' He cut off the word, but his expression finished the sentence for him. 'She'd have been better with me as a father, wouldn't she? I know I've not been perfect, but this ...' He shook his head. 'This jerk doesn't deserve a daughter like her. I would have done my best for her, you know?'

I nodded. I did know. I'd seen how he looked after his parents, and couldn't doubt that he would look after a child just as well. Finding out about Faye and Paddy had been a shock; the revelation that he had left Caitlyn, knowing she might be his child, had devastated me all over again; but I'd had plenty of time to think about it, without bias this time, and I truly believed that he was a different man now. Looking across the table at him, seeing the tears of disappointment in his eyes, I couldn't help wishing with all my heart that Caitlyn had been his daughter.

'Imagine if you'd found this note before – if you'd traced him after Faye died. Caitlyn could have been brought up by this tosser. She was better off with you.' He picked up his glass and drained it. 'Did you ever regret it? The decision to bring her up?'

'No.' The answer was automatic. It was the one I had always given. But as I looked across at Paddy, literally confronted by the future I might have had, I couldn't avoid digging deeper at last. What would have happened, if I'd let Caitlyn stay with Mum – or let her be adopted, another option we were offered at the time? I might have had a career in archaeology; I might have married Paddy; I might have been divorced from Paddy by now; I might have had children of my own. And yes, if I was entirely honest, perhaps there had been some moments of regret. But none of these nebulous futures could compare with the real satisfaction of the past: of having kept Caitlyn safe and happy, of having helped her to be the amazing young woman she unquestionably was.

'I don't regret it,' I said. 'Even with hindsight, I would make the same decision again.' I had never felt it with such certainty. A strange peace settled over me, seeping deep into my bones. It wasn't guilt over my part in Faye's death that had prompted me to look after Caitlyn; I was ready to see that now. It had been an act of love. I would never have done anything different; if Faye had been killed in a car crash, through no fault of mine, I would have taken Caitlyn in just the same. And in making peace with the past, I laid down a foundation for the future – whatever that might look like.

'You loved her more than me,' Paddy said.

I wasn't sure if it was a question or a statement, but I answered it anyway.

'Yes, I did.' When he'd left, I hadn't – even in the darkest moments of misery – considered giving up Caitlyn to persuade him to stay. 'It turned out for the best, though, didn't it? You were able to go on and have an amazing career. We can both look back and be proud of what we've achieved.'

I clutched my glass. Would he deny it? I'd left the door of our future relationship ajar – would he close it or force it wide open again? The birthday present he had given me tonight had stirred my hope back to life, but I needed to know what this summer had truly been about. Had it been about me, or about Caitlyn? He stared into his glass and I had no idea what he was thinking. At last he raised his head and his brown eyes looked almost black in the dim light of the bar.

'Turned out for the best,' he repeated. 'It's hard to feel that way tonight.' He sighed, and flicked at the note from Caitlyn's father that still lay on the table between us. 'So that's it, then.'

And there was the answer to my question. He was thinking about Caitlyn, not me. Hope died.

'Yes, I guess that's it.' I stood up, clutching my handbag to my chest, feeling absurdly overdressed in my expensive frock for being effectively dumped in my local pub. 'It's been good seeing you again. Take care.'

I walked out of the bar, without looking back.

Chapter 26

Mum, Caitlyn and Luc stayed for the rest of the week, and it was one of the happiest weeks I could remember us spending together; we bonded and enjoyed each other's company more than ever before, and we even persuaded Gran to squeeze into the car and join us on a day trip to Lake Windermere. The time for their flights home came round far too soon.

'Will you be seeing more of Paddy?' Mum asked out of the blue, as I helped her pack her suitcase. She didn't need my help, but I needed to give it – wanted to spend these extra few minutes with her. This was a fresh start – we had already made plans for much more frequent visits between Lancashire and the Costa Brava in future. 'He's grown up, hasn't he? More thoughtful than he was.'

I nodded, relieved she hadn't called him 'sensible'. That would have shattered his sexy image – not that I had been thinking of his sexiness. Or of him at all. It was over – whatever it had been – he had made that clear in The White Hart, and his silence since then had confirmed it. Perhaps he had felt a twinge of nostalgic passion towards me – the sex in Paris had felt real enough – but his frequent visits to Inglebridge over the last months had been in search of fatherhood, not romance.

And I was fine with that, or I would be, soon enough. I'd embraced the independent life for years, and felt no qualms about carrying on with it if I had to. This year had given me more than I could ever have anticipated: a new job in the field I loved, which would be starting in a few weeks; more cash in the bank than I had ever had before; seeing Caitlyn's blossoming independence; and a rebooted relationship with Mum. Who needed romance?

'There's no reason to see him,' I answered Mum at last, trying to squeeze her extraordinary amount of make-up back into her cosmetic bag. 'He made contact to find out about Caitlyn, that's all.'

'I always liked him,' Mum said, completely ignoring me. 'So did your dad. We could see that he made you happy. That's all we could have asked for.'

I understood that; I could see how happy Luc made Caitlyn. I wondered where this sudden show of support for Paddy had come from. It was too late anyway. What was the use of my family loving him now?

'Perhaps he lacked a bit of backbone when he was young,' Mum continued, apparently not having tired of the subject yet. 'But I believe he's found it now. He was willing to step up for Caitlyn – and just think, if that story had got into the press, it wouldn't have reflected well on him. You have to give him credit for that.'

I did – and for the way he looked after his mum. There was no doubt in my mind that Paddy was a far better person than he had been as a boy. He wouldn't bail out now, if life threw adversity his way. And I hoped I was a better person too. I'd spent a lot of time thinking about this recently, since Paris, and since my conversation with Mum about my part in Faye's death.

Paddy and I had both made impulsive mistakes in our youth, but my mistake – losing my temper with Faye, rather than supporting her – had had much more serious consequences than his. Mum had forgiven me, so how could I not try to forgive Paddy? But it didn't matter. He wasn't interested in whether I forgave him or not. At least I could look back on the years we had spent together and remember the happy times now, without bitterness.

It was another difficult parting from Caitlyn. Who knew when she would be back? Her plans for Christmas were still uncertain, and I wouldn't be surprised if she chose to spend it with Luc rather than me. He tactfully waited in the taxi with Mum, while we said our goodbyes.

'You are happy in Paris, aren't you?' I asked, although I could hardly doubt the answer.

'I'm loving it,' she said. 'But I don't think I'll stay when the year's contract is up.'

'You might come home?' I couldn't keep the hope from my voice.

'No, we're thinking we might go travelling. Have a late gap year. It's hard work looking after someone else's children, even when you're being paid for it. I could never have done what you did for me.'

'Of course you could,' I replied, but my words were muffled as she threw herself on me in a hug in which we seemed to compete for who could squeeze the most love into it.

'You know,' she said, as she extricated herself at last and dragged her case out of the house, 'you did better with the "Be Kind to Yourself" vouchers than I thought you would. But you've got to keep it up. It's your turn to have fun now – and you don't need to tell me about it, so you can do whatever you want, with whomever you choose. As long as you're happy. It was never supposed to be limited to the number of vouchers I made. It's a way of life.'

I smiled. The sun bounced off her hair, and she looked so like Faye that I could have cried; but she was good and kind, in a way that I had to accept Faye hadn't always been. I couldn't have been more proud of her.

'Who made you so wise?' I asked.

She grinned. 'You did. Love you, Mum!' she called, and after one final squeeze, she dragged her case down the drive, heading back to her new life. I watched her go, with tears rolling down my cheeks, waving until the taxi disappeared from sight.

Life rolled on. The school term started without me, and Tina regaled me with tales about the wonderful new school head, and speculated about the mysterious disappearance of Jo Blair. My new job wasn't due to start until October, but I was keeping busy by going through an archive of archaeology journals, and had joined the local archaeology group whose existence I had ignored for too long. They were about to finish excavations for the season, but I was enjoying getting involved with planning digs for next year.

Almost two weeks after my birthday meal, my phone rang, and Paddy's name unexpectedly flashed up on the screen. I hadn't expected to hear from him again, and none of my fine words about the joy of being independent could prevent my heart picking up speed at the sight of his name.

'How're you doing, Eve?' he asked, and the warmth in his voice felt like putting on a cosy jumper on a cold day. 'Short notice, I know, but I wondered if you had plans for the weekend?'

'Which day?' I asked, my heart close to racing as I wondered what this was about. 'I'm busy on Sunday afternoon.'

'Ah, visiting Phyllis. I wouldn't dare get in the way of that. I'm easy, so what about tomorrow?'

'Yes, I can manage that.'

'Great. I'll pick you up at ten. Wear your digging clothes, and bring your pack.'

'We're going on a dig?'

'You don't mind, do you? We've been analysing the finds from the test trenches up your way, and I want to go back and check something out before they're covered over for winter. My assistant has just bailed, and I thought you'd be the perfect person for the job.'

The job. My heart slowed right down to a first-gear crawl. He wanted me to stand in for his assistant, that was all. What had I expected? That he was inviting me out on a date? Thank God I hadn't let that idea slip ...

Paddy's car pulled up just before ten the next morning, and I was halfway down the drive before he'd stopped the car. This was work, I reminded myself, as I slipped into the passenger seat beside him. I was dressed for work, in my old jeans, boots and fleece, and with tinted moisturiser my only nod to personal grooming. Of course, Paddy still managed to look ready for a magazine spread even in his work clothes.

As he drove out of town, he told me more about what they had found on the bowl barrow site. It appeared that there might be a whole series of barrows, although not as well preserved as the one we had initially seen from our picnic on the hill. A few pieces of pottery and jewellery had been found, and a fragment of a bronze knife. There was enough to justify a full excavation, which would be filmed for *Travels Through Time* next year. It was great news for Inglebridge: the production itself would bring welcome business, and hopefully the publicity when the show was aired might tempt more tourists here too.

The dig site was in a field a couple of miles south of town, and three trenches, each approximately two metres long, had been dug in various parts of the field. Paddy allocated one trench to me and left me to it, with vague instructions to see what I could find, while he worked on the one furthest away. It wasn't how I'd anticipated the day would go – he was too far away for conversation – but I was soon too engrossed in the task to notice what he was up to, and it was a surprise when a shadow fell across my trench and I looked up to find Paddy standing above me, the early autumn sun making a halo around his body.

'Lunch break,' he said, and held out his hands to hoist me out of the trench. My lower legs had gone numb with kneeling on them for so long, and I wobbled as I climbed back out into the field.

'Are the old legs not what they were?' he said, putting his hands on my shoulders to steady me. 'Strange. They looked in pretty good shape in that dress the other night. You always did suit blue.'

'I thought we were here to rake through more interesting history than ours,' I said, shaking myself free; the warmth of his hands and his gaze were bringing back memories of Paris that I shouldn't still be cherishing.

'Quite right. I don't want to dwell on our past either. Did you find much?'

'A few bits of pottery and stone.' I pointed at the plastic tray beside my trench. 'Nothing of real interest. I don't think we've gone far enough down yet.'

'Try the other trench after lunch. You might have more luck there.'

He led the way back to the car, and we sat perched on the open boot, our legs dangling, while Paddy produced a proper old-fashioned wicker picnic basket.

'Only the best for your assistants?' I asked, as he lifted the lid and revealed the full set of wine glasses and china plates, along with various intriguing parcels and boxes of food.

'Only the best for you,' he said, and I sat in speechless wonder as he poured me a glass of sparkling elderflower pressé, and unwrapped a selection of healthy snacks that even in my most zealous mood I couldn't possibly object to: individual pots of tomato and carrot salad, mini spinach and cottage cheese frittatas, salmon bagels, vegetables with a hummus dip ... It was a feast, enough to feed at least a family of four.

'What are you having?' I asked. This wasn't Paddy food. 'Do you have a sausage sandwich hidden away somewhere?'

'I thought I'd give all this a try,' he said, with an unconvincing smile that made me laugh. 'And if I do, I deserve this, right?' He opened the final box to reveal two chocolate éclairs. My favourite cake. Had he remembered? Of course he had. This couldn't possibly be a coincidence. Warmth spread through me, from within, not just from the sun that was beating down on my legs. What was going on here? Was there more to this outing than I'd thought?

'Two éclairs?' I said. 'Isn't that greedy?'

'I was kinda hoping you might want to join me ...'

It was a perfectly innocent comment, but something about his smile, the twinkle in his brown eyes, brought Paris rushing straight back into my head. Not just my head. My whole body burned with the memory of it, of what Paddy had done to me, what we had done together, what he had made me feel. I turned my attention to a tortilla wrap.

'Did Caitlyn get back to Paris okay?' Paddy asked, as we finished our drinks before returning to the dig.

'Yes. She'll be there until Christmas now. Unless she chooses to stay with Luc over Christmas.' That was a thought I'd prefer not to dwell on. Paddy squeezed my arm.

'He's a good kid.' He grinned. 'Reminds me of me.'

'Exactly! As if I needed any more reason to worry ...'

'I wasn't that bad, was I?' He bumped his shoulder against mine.

'No,' I admitted. 'Not all the time.'

Only at the end, in fact – until then, I had thought he was perfect.

'We were good together, weren't we?' he asked. I jumped down from the boot and brushed the crumbs off my jeans.

'I thought we weren't talking about our past?'

'I wasn't. Not really. I was just establishing the groundwork. Like a construction worker. I need to make sure the foundations are solid before building up.'

I froze. 'Building up to what?'

'The question I want to ask you.'

'Spit it out then,' I said, sudden nerves flaring inside me. I had no idea where this was going. 'We need to get digging again before the light goes.'

'Jeez, can't a man take his time about these things?' Paddy laughed and jumped down to stand beside me. 'Spending time with you this summer has reminded me what a great team we are. I think we could be a great team again.'

My breath caught. Did he mean ...

'So, what do you say? Will you come and work for me?'

'You're offering me a job?' I hoped my voice was steadier than my pulse. After the picnic, the way he'd looked at me, all the build-up, I'd thought ... Well, never mind what I'd thought. I'd been wrong – spectacularly wrong – and I could only hope that my face wasn't displaying my feelings, because Paddy was watching me closely, waiting for his answer.

'I'm sorry,' I said, testing out a smile that felt horribly like a grimace. 'I can't. I've already accepted a job with Northern Archaeology. I start next month.'

'Fantastic! They're a great crew. Ah well, my loss.' And with that, he strode away across the field to return to his trench, while I stomped over to the new trench, trying not to fixate on how little he must have wanted me if he could move on from my rejection so easily.

My frustration may have made me less careful with my trowel than usual, because I hadn't been working for long when I heard the unmistakeable scrape of metal against metal. Brushing aside the soil with my hands, I soon uncovered a rusting black tin. I prised it out carefully, placed it on the side of the trench, climbed out and called to Paddy.

'Paddy! Come and look. I've found something.'

With infuriating slowness, he put down his tools and sauntered over. He looked down at the tin.

'You need to brush up on the Bronze Age,' he said, shaking his head. 'I don't think that's what we're looking for. It's probably not even a hundred years old.'

He started to walk away.

'Hey!' I shouted after him. 'It could be important. Has this site been excavated before?'

'Not that I know of.'

'Don't you think we should open it?'

'Sure. If you're that bothered.' He shrugged. 'But don't get your hopes up about finding another Lancaster Hoard. It doesn't look that promising ...'

I knelt down in front of the tin. It wasn't locked, but the catch was distorted and covered in rust and I needed my trowel to gently prise it open. And there, inside ...

I turned to Paddy. He was smiling at me, a smile of wary hope that melted my heart.

'What's going on?' I asked.

He knelt down beside me. 'Have a look in the tin,' he said.

The first item in the tin was an envelope with my name scrawled on it, in Paddy's handwriting. I picked it up and uncovered a square, velvet jewellery box, the sort of box that was inevitably associated with one particular thing. Ignoring that for a moment, I opened the envelope. There was a sheet of paper inside, covered with one of Paddy's sketches – one I had seen before. It was a duplicate of the drawing I had found inside the notebook in my rucksack: a Viking warrior with Paddy's face, kneeling down and offering his heart in his hands.

'I've seen this before,' I said. 'I found it in my notebook a few months ago.'

'Did you? You were meant to find it years ago. I had it all planned. The next time we went on a dig together, you were supposed to see the sketch, and then I'd drop down to my knees and give you this ...'

He took the velvet ring box out of the tin and held it out to me. His hand shook but his smile was steady. I took the box and opened it. Inside lay what I immediately recognised as a Roman ring: chunky gold decorated with a garnet in the centre. I ran my finger over the ring; it was beautiful.

'You've kept this since then?'

'I have. And now don't go thinking I'm soppy or anyth… but I took it with me on my travels, and it felt like you wer… with me. And it became a sort of lucky talisman, so I've had it with me on every dig I've been on. I could never have got rid of it, because it was yours. Even when there seemed no prospect of ever seeing you again, it was always yours.'

Paddy took my hand.

'It's yours now, if you'll have it. If you'll have me. I know you value your independence. I know you don't need me.' He rubbed his thumb over the back of my hand. 'But I'm hoping you might want me. And hoping even more that you might love me, even a fraction of how much I love you.'

He looked at me then, and it was as though I could see through his eyes and right down to his heart. I'd doubted him many times, but I couldn't doubt him now. He meant every word. As if he'd read my thoughts, he carried on.

'I screwed up before, but that was the idiot Paddy – the kid. I wouldn't do that now. And okay, maybe when I first saw you in March, I thought about Caitlyn, but it soon became more than that. Much more. I didn't find a daughter, but I found the partner I want with me for the rest of my life. It's all been about you, Eve. All my life, it was always you.'

He leant forward, eyes on mine, moving in for a kiss. I leant back.

'You set all this up? Today ... this dig ... this tin ...'

'Yeah, and I was kinda hoping for a better response than you recoiling ...'

'But what's this?' I pointed back at the tin. There was one other item inside it: an envelope, with my name on it, written in what I would have sworn was Caitlyn's writing. But how could she be involved in this?

'Open it and have a look.' Paddy grinned.

I did. There were two more 'Be Kind to Yourself' vouchers inside, but this time, they had already been completed.

BE KIND TO YOURSELF
VOUCHER THIRTEEN
I, Eve Roberts, have been kind to myself by forgiving Paddy!

I smiled, and read the next one.

BE KIND TO YOURSELF
VOUCHER FOURTEEN
I, Eve Roberts, have been kind to myself by agreeing to be Eve Friel …

My heart did a little skip. Was I really going to agree to that? There was a folded note in the envelope too, half a page of Caitlyn's looping writing.

Dear Eve

That sounds weird, but it's time, right? I know I said always mum, but I've been thinking about that a lot, and I was saying it for me, not you. You did an amazing thing for me, and you've been the best mum I could have asked for. But I think I have to let you go now – so you can be Eve, and perhaps a wife (if Paddy is persuasive enough!) and maybe, one day, someone else's mum. You're brave enough, and talented enough, and loved enough to do this – and not just by me now. You deserve it – no argument. Love you!

Your adoring niece,
Caitlyn

Paddy took me in his arms, and I sobbed on his shoulder. If I needed any more proof of a life well spent, it was there in that note. Daughter, niece – it didn't matter. It would be impossible to love Caitlyn more.

'Did you plot this with her?' I asked, when my tears subsided. I lifted my head from Paddy's shoulder, but his arms stayed round me. 'And did you speak to Mum too? I thought it was weird when she started talking about you.'

'Now I don't like the word plot ...' He smiled. 'I wanted to apologise to Caitlyn, for running out on you both. I didn't mention any of the father stuff. But if there was going to be a chance of anything between you and me, I couldn't let there be any secrets or pretence.'

'And she really forgave you?'

'Of course she did. Don't underestimate the old Irish charm,' he said, putting on his thickest Irish accent. I laughed, and he tightened his arms. His hands ran circles across my back, circles that seemed to join my memories of the past with my hopes for the future. 'And I hope you'll forgive me too.'

'It appears that I already have done. Voucher thirteen says so.' And I wasn't going to argue with it. Being here in his arms, I was as happy as I could ever wish to be. I loved him. That was all that mattered. He wasn't perfect, but neither was I. Like the unguentarium he had bought me for my birthday, our flaws made us what we were now; made us perfect for each other now. What was the point of holding on to grudges, or of dwelling on the rights and wrongs of the past, when each day might be all we had? And what kinder thing could I do for myself than let myself be happy? I wrote out another voucher in my head, one just for me.

BE KIND TO YOURSELF
VOUCHER FIFTEEN
I, Eve Roberts, have been kind to myself by choosing happiness!

'I suppose I should be glad that you didn't involve Gran in your plotting,' I said. 'But she would never have been able to keep your secret.'

'Ah, you underestimate the power of Phyllis ...' Paddy withdrew one of his hands, and pulled something from the pocket of his jeans. 'This has all been proper and above board. I asked permission from the head of the family.' He grinned. 'If she'd had her way, she'd have been sitting over there watching, ready to prod you with her stick until you gave the right answer. It took even more of the Irish charm to convince her to make do with a note.'

He handed me another envelope. This one contained a page ripped from a magazine, showing an elaborate wedding outfit in fuchsia pink, with matching wide-brimmed hat. Gran had scribbled on a Post-it Note stuck to the page.

You can have my blessing gladly, if he buys me this outfit. He's been on the telly – he can afford it. How about a Christmas wedding? We've all been waiting long enough. He's your gold. I could have told you that.

Laughing, I showed Paddy the note. He roared with laughter, and the vibrations of his body echoed deliciously through mine.

'I'll drive her to the shops myself,' he said. He pulled me to my feet, and looked down at me with so much tenderness that

I was irresistibly drawn towards him, leaning in to his che was my favourite place to be; it always had been; it always wou be. 'So it all depends on you. Will you say yes, and make Phyllis the happiest grandmother in the world?'

It was the easiest question I'd ever been asked.

'I will.'

THE END

Acknowledgements

Huge thanks to all at Avon and One More Chapter, and especially to Katie Loughnane, an amazing editor who has the miraculous ability to make a small suggestion and transform a whole book. It's been a total pleasure to work with Katie on the last two books. Thanks also to Helena Newton for vigilant copy editing!

One of the greatest pleasures in writing this book was the chance to learn more about archaeology, something I've been interested in for years. I've browsed too many websites and flicked through too many books to be able to list them all, but particularly acknowledge: futurelearn.com, romanobritain.org, *A Practical Handbook of Archaeology* by Christopher Catling and *Hidden Histories: A Spotter's Guide to the British Landscape* by Mary-Ann Ochota. I also enjoyed a fascinating tour of the dig site at Ribchester Revisited – well worth a visit if you're in Lancashire over summer. I've barely scratched the surface of the subject, and any mistakes are mine.

My writing friends have been invaluable in helping me through this book, so I'm sending lots of love and thanks to the Beta Buddies and to the Authors on the Edge; I'll never stop thinking how lucky I am to be part of these groups. Special thanks go to: Catherine Bowdler, for not letting me give up; Julie Stock, for inspiring me to write a 'second time around' story; Liz Taylorson for sharing details about tennis leg; and Marie Laval, for answering questions about school life and providing Luc's words.

A final thank you to the bloggers who have supported my books, and most importantly, to the readers who have bought and borrowed them. I hope they have given you even a fraction of the pleasure that reading books brings me. I'm always thrilled to hear from readers, so please do get in touch on Twitter @katehaswords, or through my Facebook page at KateFieldAuthor. If you've enjoyed *A Dozen Second Chances*, please consider leaving a brief review on Amazon as it helps other readers find out about the book and brightens my day more than I can say!